Family

Jewels

A Rose Gardner Investigation

Books by Denise Grover Swank

Rose Gardner Mysteries
Twenty-Eight and a Half Wishes
Twenty-Nine and a Half Reasons
Thirty and a Half Excuses
Falling to Pieces (novella)
Thirty-One and a Half Regrets
Thirty-Two and a Half Complications
Picking Up the Pieces (novella)
Thirty-Three and a Half Shenanigans
Rose and Helena Save Christmas (novella)
Ripple of Secrets (novella)
Thirty-Four and a Half Predicaments
Thirty-Four and a Half Predicaments Bonus Chapters (ebook only)
Thirty-Five and a Half Conspiracies
Thirty-Six and a Half Motives
Sins of the Father (novella)

Rose Gardner Investigations
Family Jewels
Trailer Trash: Neely Kate
(Rose Gardner Exposed Novella #1.5, April, 2017)
For the Birds (July, 2017)

Magnolia Steele Mystery
Center Stage
Act Two
Call Back (February, 2017)

The Wedding Pact Series
The Substitute
The Player
The Gambler
The Valentine (short story)

Bachelor Brotherhood Series
Only You
Until You (May 2017)
Always You (October, 2017)

Discover Denise's other books at
denisegroverswank.com

Family
Jewels

A Rose Gardner Investigation

Denise Grover Swank

Chapter One

*T*he dark clouds on the horizon were my first clue it was going to be a bad day.

June thunderstorms were a common occurrence in southern Arkansas, and truth be told, we needed the rain. But I also needed to get six azalea bushes into the ground by five p.m., or I was not only going to lose the cost of the bushes, but the labor too.

"You think we're gonna get it done?" Neely Kate, my best friend, roommate, and co-worker, asked as she cast a nervous glance to the west.

"If we don't, Mr. Henderson is gonna throw a conniption."

"Thank you, Marci," Neely Kate grumbled as she dug her shovel deeper into the dirt.

Business was booming at RBW Landscaping, enough so that my business partner, Bruce Wayne Decker, and I had been forced to hire several new employees. One of them, Neely Kate's cousin Marci, had been tasked with staying in the office to talk to the clients. Her first—and last—day had been yesterday, and the amount of damage she'd done was impressive. Without any prompting, she'd told Mr. Henderson he'd get a one hundred percent refund if we didn't have his bushes planted before five today. Apparently Marci was obsessed with *Plant or Die*, a new reality TV show in which landscapers had twenty-four hours to complete their project or be eliminated. She'd hoped to get on the show by making a series of outrageous self-imposed gardening challenges on camera. Or so she'd explained to us.

"What in tarnation are you talkin' about?" Neely Kate had asked her cousin in horror.

"I *really* need that five thousand dollars prize money," Marci had said. "I want to go to beauty school."

"Five thousand dollars?" I'd asked, suddenly wondering how we could get an audition for real.

Marci's eyes had widened as she turned to her cousin. "*Of course* I was gonna share the money with you and Rowena."

"Rose," Neely Kate said.

Shaking her head, Marci said, "No. Azalea bushes. Not roses."

Neely Kate looked like she was about to say something, then closed her mouth.

Marci took that as encouragement. "I only need thirty-five hundred dollars. You two can split the leftover three thousand."

"Fifteen hundred," Neely Kate said, looking like she wanted to strangle her cousin.

Marci's eyes squinted in concentration. "No . . . I'm pretty sure the lady said the tuition was thirty-five hundred."

"*Marci*," Neely Kate groaned. "Five thousand minus thirty-five hundred is only fifteen hundred. Not three thousand."

Marci looked confused. "Are you sure?" Then she waved her hand. "What am I askin'? You were the math genius in the family, with your D-minus in algebra and all."

Neely Kate ignored the compliment on her math skills. "And you think it's fair that you should get the majority of the money from the show? On your first day?"

Marci blinked, the expression on her face showing just how ridiculous she considered Neely Kate's question. "Well, yeah . . . I really *need* it. And besides, I'm the one who's auditioning."

"How on earth do you figure that?" Neely Kate shouted. "Where are the cameras, for Pete's sake?"

Marci pointed up at the ceiling. "Up there."

I glanced up just as Neely Kate groaned.

"*Marci*," Neely Kate forced through gritted teeth. "That's a sprinkler head."

"Oh." She laughed. "Silly me."

The very next thing Neely Kate had done was fire her.

In the end, it didn't matter why the promise to plant the azaleas had been made; all that mattered was that we were going to live up to it. Bruce Wayne had his own planting crew of two men, and they were working on a tight deadline at a commercial office site. He couldn't afford to send anyone over to help, so Neely Kate and I had put our design and estimate jobs on hold to get this project done up close and personal.

And now Mother Nature was conspiring against us.

"We can do it, Rose," Neely Kate said, with her characteristic optimism and perkiness. "Besides, what's a little rain? We won't melt."

As if to taunt us, a large bolt of lightning filled the sky and thunder shook the ground just as rain started to fall in fat drops.

Resisting the urge to groan, I moved the bushes closer to the fifty-year-old house and dragged a bag of our premixed fertilizer/potting soil in front of the containers to keep them from blowing away. Neely Kate quickly began to help. We finished arranging them just as another bolt of lightning struck, the thunderous boom following sooner this time than it had the last.

"That was too close," I said. "Let's go."

We put the shovels into the back of my RBW Landscaping truck, then climbed into the pickup, shivering in our semi-drenched clothes.

"We're not givin' up, are we?" Neely Kate asked, incredulous. But her tone also held a hint of guilt. She was the one who'd insisted on hiring Marci despite the foreboding fact that the girl couldn't fill in the address of the house where she'd lived for the last eighteen years with her parents on her job application. Not to mention the way she'd filled in the "Date of last job" blank with "last night with Bobby Hixler," mistaking "job" for something else entirely.

Being the bigger person, I'd held back my I-told-you-sos.

I was polishing those up for when I might need them later.

"Of course we're not giving up." I turned the key and the truck engine started, hitting us with a blast of cold air that made me shiver.

Neely Kate fumbled with the air conditioning knobs to turn off the air as I pulled away from the curb.

"We can come back when it blows over," Neely Kate said. She flipped down the visor and looked in the mirror as she took her long blonde hair out of the messy bun she'd put it up in before we'd started digging. She gave it a fluff, then ran a finger under her eye to wipe away a mascara smudge. While Neely Kate had learned a lot about the landscaping business since I'd hired her at the first of the year, digging in the dirt was one of the few jobs she detested and avoided at all costs. "There's a reason I moved away from Grannie's farm, Rose," she'd say, wrinkling her nose. "To get away from dirt and cow manure."

I sighed. "Let's get some coffee and look at how we can shuffle our schedule around and still get everything done."

Neely Kate snatched her pink sparkly purse from the floor board, then removed a tube of concealer and dabbed dots under her eyes. "You want to go by the office?"

"Yeah. I want to check on Muffy."

"Afterward, why don't we stop by the new coffee shop? I hear it makes a delicious white mocha."

I wasn't sure a town the size of Henryetta could accommodate two coffee shops, but so far The Daily Grind had attracted a flock of courthouse employees and city police, as well as foot traffic from the downtown shoppers and store owners. It helped that they carried pastries from Dena's Bakery, the best thing to hit Henryetta in five years. Besides, The Daily Grind's competition was on the edge of town, close to a newer neighborhood and a condo complex. Those residents tended to avoid downtown anyway.

I parked in front of our office and grabbed an umbrella from under my seat.

She held out the lip gloss. "Here. You need this."

I gave her a hard look. "Why would I put on lip gloss to get coffee?"

Neely Kate groaned. "Rose . . ." She dragged my name out like it pained her to do so. "You'll never find a man if you don't start putting more effort into your appearance."

I laughed. "You think lip gloss is going to make me look better?" I knew what I looked like—no makeup, muddy jeans, my dark hair up in a ponytail. "And besides, it's ridiculous to put on makeup when I'll just sweat it off in ten minutes."

I could see my dog Muffy in the window jumping up on the glass in her excitement. She weighed about eight pounds, but that didn't stop her from trying to break through. I hated leaving her alone out at my farm, so I brought her to work most days and even to job sites. Neely Kate and Bruce Wayne had dubbed Muffy RBW Landscaping's mascot, and lately, Neely Kate had taken to shopping for dog costumes online. Muffy was wearing one now—something that made her look like she'd been attacked by a giant white daisy. That alone could have been the reason she looked so frantic. Or maybe she was freaked out by the storm, the reason I'd left her behind.

But one look inside the window revealed the real source of her distress.

"Neely Kate, I thought you fired Marci."

"What are you talkin' about?" she asked, digging in her purse. "I did."

"Then what is she doing in our office?"

"What?" Neely Kate screeched, leaning forward to peer inside the windows. "I fired her. You heard me."

"Well, she's in there now. Let's go find out why," I said as I hopped out of the truck.

Neely Kate followed me. I opened the previously locked office door, and Neely Kate slammed into my back when I came to an abrupt halt.

Muffy stood on her back legs, and her front paws scratched frantically at my legs.

I gasped as I bent down to scoop her up. "What in the Sam Hill . . ."

Files and papers were scattered everywhere—the floors, the chairs, and the desks. Not one inch had been left uncovered. And in the middle of the chaos stood a woman with long blonde hair, cut-off jean shorts, and a lavender-colored tank top.

She spun around to face us, and a frown tugged on her lips. "You just ruined the surprise."

"That a tornado came through?" I asked in dismay.

She laughed. "Don't be silly, Rowena. I'm redoing your filing system."

"But Neely Kate *fired* you," I said.

She waved her hand and rolled her eyes. "She was always such a kidder."

"I wasn't kidding!" Neely Kate's voice rose as she stepped around me. Her foot slipped on a folder, and I grabbed her arm to keep her from falling on her booty. "What else did you do?" Neely Kate asked.

Marci put a hand on her hips and gave us an impressive pout. "I was only trying to help."

"I told you that you are not auditioning for *Plant or Die*!"

Marci lifted her chin and gave Neely Kate a defiant look. "That wasn't it. It was something else entirely."

"What was it?"

"It's something you love to do anyway," Marci said with attitude. "You've said so a million times."

Neely Kate crossed her arms. "What TV show did you think you were on this time?"

"Not me," she said. "You." Then she pointed to me. "And Rowena."

"Her name is Rose!" Neely Kate shouted. "Who doesn't get their own boss's name right?"

"Are you sure it's Rose?" Marci asked, giving me the once-over.

"Yeah," Neely Kate said. "I think I'd know since she's my best friend. Now, what did you promise?"

"That poor man needed help. He was desperate."

"What man?" Neely Kate asked.

"Radcliffe Dyer. His grandmother's jewelry is missing."

A shiver ran down my spine, but Neely Kate perked up. "Why did he come by *here*?"

"He heard that you and Rowena were good at finding things."

"Rose," I said with a sigh.

Marci shook her head. "He's not looking for roses. It was jewelry."

Tipping her head back, Neely Kate released a loud groan. "What did he say, Marci?"

"He said, 'I need to talk to the two girls who work here,' and I said, 'Well, you're lookin' at one of 'em.'"

I gave Neely Kate an exasperated look. Had we really let this girl represent our business for ten hours?

"Why did he want the two girls who worked here?" Neely Kate asked.

"He said,"—Marci's voice lowered into a deep bass—"'I need them girls to find my grandmammie's jewelry for me. My ex-wife has something to do with 'em going missing, and I want to get to the bottom of it.'"

Neely Kate put a hand on her hip again and waited. When Marci didn't continue, she asked, "What else did he say?"

"He said,"—she lowered her voice again—"'Sorry to hear about your yellow dress. When do you think they'll be back?'"

Neely Kate turned back to me. "She obviously left out what she said to him, but I'm scared to ask what it was."

"Agreed."

Neely Kate turned back to her. "What did he say when you told him when we'd be back?"

"Oh, I told him I had no idea when that would be. So he gave me his number . . ." She spun in a circle, scanning the room. "Now where did I put it . . . ?"

"Never mind," Neely Kate said. "I know where to find Raddy. Now tell me why all those files are spread everywhere."

"Oh!" Marci said, clapping her hands. "I was reorganizing your filing system."

"By spreading them out on every horizontal surface?" Neely Kate demanded.

"I just set out the files," she said defensively, then waved to Muffy. "That overgrown daisy was the one to mess 'em all up."

Muffy let out a low growl. I stroked her head to quiet her.

Neely Kate shook her head. "You were fired, Marci. *Fired.* I fired you *yesterday.* Now get your purse and get out of here. Now!"

Marci looked offended. "Does that mean I'm not getting my thirty-five hundred dollars?"

"You'll be damn lucky to get the seventy dollars we owe you for yesterday." When Marci started to protest, Neely Kate held up her hand. "And if you think we're paying you for creatin' this mess today, you're plum crazy. Now get out of here!"

Marci grabbed her purse and marched the walk of shame to the front door, nearly slipping a couple of times. When she passed us, she held up her head and kept her eyes on the door like she was Anne Boleyn marching to her beheading.

When the door closed, Neely Kate said, "Rose . . . I had no idea."

Looking at the mess made me exhausted, and we hadn't even started to clean it up yet. "We don't have time to pick this up, but we can't leave it like this either." I set Muffy down, then grabbed my phone out of my pocket and called the nursery I co-owned with my sister. Violet was in Texas, recovering from her bone marrow transplant, but we'd found the perfect person to fill in until she came back. Maeve Deveraux answered on the third ring.

"Gardner Sisters Nursery, Maeve speaking. How can I help you?"

Hearing her cheery voice helped ease some of the tension in my back. "Maeve, I was wondering if I could borrow Anna for a bit. Are you too busy to turn her loose?"

"Of course I can spare her, Rose. But she's really not dressed to be digging."

"I actually need her in the office." Then I filled her in on the details.

"Oh, dear. I'll send her over right away." Then she paused and lowered her voice. "I haven't talked to you in over a week. How are you doing?"

"I'm great. Good." And I was. Mostly. My ex-boyfriend Mason—Maeve's son—and I had broken up four months ago, and he'd moved back to Little Rock. My heart had been broken, but I'd moved on. Mostly. Even if I still refused to consider dating anyone, much to Neely Kate's dismay. "How about you?"

It was no secret Maeve had moved from Little Rock to tiny Henryetta to be closer to her only living child. She'd been lonely and eager to feel wanted and needed again. But she'd found a place for herself here, and despite Mason's decision to leave, she'd stayed. Still, I knew she missed her son something fierce. I'd kept my distance, mostly out of guilt. I couldn't help wondering if she secretly blamed me for him leaving.

"Good. I'm excited about Violet coming back." But I heard the wistful tone in her voice.

While we'd only intended for her position to be temporary, she'd been working full-time for the past four months and seemed to love every minute of it. "You know, Violet won't be back to one hundred percent," I said. "It occurs to me that we'll still need help. Would you be willing to stay on part-time?"

"Of course. I'd love to."

It warmed my heart to make her happy. Maeve had been like the mother I'd always wanted. I missed her. "Well, then that's settled. You're an official permanent employee at Gardner Sisters Nursery."

"I'll send Anna right over. And Rose . . . thank you."

"No, thank *you*. I have no idea what we would have done without you these last four months." I hung up and stuffed my phone back into my pocket. "Anna's on her way."

"Well, now that this is taken care of . . ." Neely Kate said, brushing off her hands. "Let's go talk to Raddy Dyer."

I held up my hand, blocking the exit. "Hold up. We're not going anywhere just yet."

"But Anna's coming to clean up, which means we can go."

I narrowed my eyes.

"I'm really sorry about Marci," Neely Kate said with a sigh.

"Everyone deserves a chance. I'm sorry if you're in trouble with your aunt for firing her." It was hard to hold this against my best friend. I'd met her aunt. I probably would have hired Marci too.

She waved it off. "I might get stuck with the burnt ends of Aunt Jackie's raccoon roast next Christmas, but I'll manage."

I almost blurted out, *Raccoon roast?* But I wisely kept my mouth shut. Neely Kate's family was one of a kind.

She shuffled her feet and shifted her weight before giving me a hopeful look. "I checked the weather on my phone, and it looks like the rain won't clear off until this afternoon . . . which means we have some time to talk to Raddy Dyer."

And there it was.

I sighed. "Neely Kate—"

"Now, before you say no, let me plead my case."

"Funny choice of words," I said, crossing my arms over my chest. "I'm listening."

Excitement filled her eyes. "You and I have solved cases before—"

I started to protest, but she held up her hand.

"—let me finish."

"Okay."

"I know we accidentally stumbled into some bigger things last fall and winter, but we got out of all of them, right?"

Stumbled into some bigger things was an understatement. Our last off-the-books investigation had landed us in the web of J.R. Simmons, a man of wealth and prestige who'd considered himself above the law. For a long time, he had been. He'd gotten away with murder—literally—because he'd had the connections, money, and deviousness to cover his tracks. I had banded together with James Malcolm, the king of the Fenton County underworld, to bring J.R. down, and Neely Kate hadn't hesitated to join us. J.R. was dead now—destroyed by his own evil doings rather than by us— but nothing had gone as planned. People had died; lives had been changed in an instant. After last February, I'd vowed to leave danger behind and live a quiet life.

Only Neely Kate was bound and determined to make me live boldly.

"Neely Kate . . ."

She held up her hands. "You said you'd listen." When I didn't answer, she lifted her eyebrows. "Over the last four months, we've solved some mysteries that had nothin' to do with us. Not to mention they were completely harmless."

"We found a missing garden gnome, a lost dog, and figured out a dispute between two neighbors." And I couldn't deny I'd loved every minute of it.

"So why won't you consider this?" she asked in frustration.

"This is different. From what Marci said, this man thinks his ex-wife is holding his grandmother's jewelry hostage. It's not a mystery. It's a hostage negotiation. You should tell Carter Hale," I said, referring to our defense attorney friend. "It seems more like a situation for a law shark than for two landscapers."

"We're not just two landscapers. We've solved mysteries before. You've worked with the crime lord of Fenton County, for Pete's sake. Missing jewelry should be a piece of cake."

"Neely Kate . . ."

"Let's just talk to the guy, okay?" she asked, hope filling her eyes. "We can find out what he wants."

"He wants us to get his jewelry back. His ex-wife has it. Where's the investigation? Maybe he expects us to beat the jewelry out of her with our shovels."

"Please?" She gave me a pout; then her eyes widened. "If it makes you feel better, you can have a vision. See how the meeting goes."

She had to be really desperate to ask me that.

The visions were a birthright I'd spent my life hating, but I'd come to realize they had their uses. Seeing glimpses of the future had helped me save my life—and my friends' lives—more times than I could count. Still, there were serious downsides. For one thing, I could only see other people's futures. For another, I always blurted out whatever I'd just seen, which often put me in embarrassing situations.

The visions usually happened spontaneously, but I'd learned that if I forced them regularly, I could sidestep the spontaneous ones. Of course, there were risks—sometimes I forced a vision and saw something I immediately wanted to unsee, like the time I'd witnessed Neely Kate's first foray back into dating. Although I had no idea when the date would happen, or if it already had, she was going to go all in. Blessedly, the vision had ended before I was burdened with details, and the comment that had leaked out of me afterward had been about her black bra rather than anything truly indecent.

Still, I had no desire to put myself through it again.

I groaned. "Fine." When she started to get excited, I held up my hands. "We'll talk to him. *That's all.* Then you and I will talk about it and decide where to go from there."

Her head bobbed as she nodded. "Sure. Of course."

I'd seen that look before. I suspected she'd already texted Raddy Dyer and accepted the case.

My phone began to ring, and I pulled it from my jeans pocket, surprised to see the initials SM—Skeeter Malcolm—on my screen. I shot Neely Kate a glance before I answered.

"James, I haven't heard from you in a while." A couple of weeks, to be exact.

"Lady," he said, his voice tight. "We've got a problem."

Chapter Two

*J*ames Malcolm had become head of the Fenton County criminal underworld six months ago, and ever since he'd assumed that title, people had been trying to snatch it. While I'd met him the previous summer at the pool hall he owned, we hadn't become better acquainted until November. Several peculiar twists of fate later, I found myself using my visions to help him maintain his position in exchange for his protection of my assistant district attorney boyfriend. My confident, powerful alter ego—the Lady in Black—was born to keep my true identity a secret. I may have worn sexy black dresses, heels, and a veiled black hat to disguise my appearance, but the persona had sunk roots into my soul and changed me. Some days I thought James was the only one who recognized how much.

Although I'd retired the Lady in Black in February, my friendship with James had survived. We still met up weekly at the spot where I used to meet him and his right-hand man, Jed. James would tell me about the latest issues he was struggling to resolve, and I'd offer advice and sometimes force a vision to make sure he'd survive to show up the next week.

I was sure part of him longed to give up his position in the underworld, but he worried what his successor would do to the people of the county. He had a strict code of ethics, and from the multiple attempts at his crown, he was well aware there were far more ruthless and unconscionable men waiting in the wings. So he stayed.

About a month and a half ago, he'd caught wind of a new challenger. He'd told me about a guy named Wagner who was stirring up trouble, but James had refused to discuss him the last couple of times we'd met. I'd hoped he was no longer a threat, but the fact that James had been dodging my calls for the past two weeks had me more than a little worried. It looked like my concern had been justified.

I had all kinds of questions to ask, but I didn't dare ask any of them in front of Neely Kate. "What's goin' on?"

"Can you meet me in three hours?"

I snuck a quick glance over to Neely Kate. I wasn't sure how I'd explain leaving to meet him, but then, we'd skirted where I went every Tuesday night for the past three months. This time we'd be meeting much earlier than usual, which meant she might ask more questions, but I'd figure it out. "I'll make it work."

"Good," he grunted. "I'll meet you at our usual place." Then he hung up.

Neely Kate put her hands on her hips. "What was that about?"

"Nothin'."

A scowl covered her face, but she wasn't about to let anything get in the way of our meeting with Raddy Dyer.

She sucked in a deep breath and blew it out in exasperation before she said, "Are you ready to go?"

Stuffing my phone into my pocket, I squatted down next to Muffy and pulled the white flower petal collar over her head. I tossed it onto Neely Kate's desk, then grinned. "Fine. But we're getting coffee from The Daily Grind first."

She tossed her long blonde hair over her shoulder. "I was the one who suggested we go there in the first place."

I scrawled a quick note to Anna, apologizing in half a dozen different ways, and then kissed Muffy goodbye. We closed the door to the disaster zone behind us and locked it, although any potential burglars would take one look at the mess and assume someone had beat them to the place. Anna had a key.

The rain had turned into a light drizzle, but my hair was pulled into a ponytail and I'd given up fighting the weather today. I saw no reason to worry about how the rain might affect my appearance, but judging by Neely Kate's long strides, she didn't share my sentiment.

"So where do we find Raddy Dyer?" I asked as I followed her into the crowded coffee shop. Turned out half the courthouse was in the long narrow space.

"Archer's Hardware," Neely Kate said, searching the menu board as we took our place in the back of the long line. "He runs the plumbing department."

"I'm not sure I should be goin' in there," I muttered. "You know they hate me now."

The owner of Archer's Hardware had been none too happy with Violet and me since we'd opened the nursery, although I wasn't sure why. While they used to sell plants in the spring and early summer, they'd done a poor job of taking care of them. Each year had marked a new massacre—the plants would look fresh enough at first, but on each successive visit, another half dozen would have joined the crispy half-off shelf. Truth be told, that was part of the reason I'd agreed to open the nursery in the first place. There'd been no decent places in Henryetta to buy bedding plants.

Neely Kate waved her hand dismissively as she continued to search the menu. "It's just the owner who's ticked. Remember that thank-you card and five-dollar gift certificate we got from a few of the employees, telling you how grateful they were to not have to mess with the greenhouse and all those plants? They were gonna have a Garden Witch Day in your honor."

I shook my head with a scowl. "I can't help thinking that gift card was a trick to get me to come in, because I'm pretty sure the whole witch thing wasn't a compliment, Neely Kate."

"Sure it was. It was like calling you the Good Witch of the South. Just like in *The Wizard of Oz*."

"Witch of the East."

She gave me a haughty look. "I'm not sure what you learned in geography, Rose Gardner, but we're in the *South*."

I pushed out a heavy sigh and realized it wasn't worth the effort to correct her. "So what do you know about Raddy Dyer?" I asked.

"Nothin' good," I heard a male voice say behind me.

I spun around in surprise to see my former boyfriend. "Joe."

He was wearing his tan sheriff's uniform, and I had to admit he was stunningly handsome in it. But at the moment, he also wore a frown. "Why are you asking about Raddy Dyer?"

I gave Neely Kate a look that said, *This is your idea, so you take this one.*

Instead, she smiled ear-to-ear and threw her arms around his neck. "It's my favorite brother."

He gave her an affectionate hug.

A lump swelled in my throat at the sight of them. They were both, to their shared disgust, the children of J.R. Simmons. They had only learned that they were half-siblings back in February. Joe had left town soon after and ignored Neely Kate for a couple of months. But he'd finally reached out to her when he came back to Henryetta around the first of May, and they'd started making up for nearly twenty-five years of lost time. After Neely Kate's mother's abandonment, Neely Kate needed a family member who was truly there for her.

Joe grabbed a strand of Neely Kate's hair and gently tugged. "And it's my mischievous sister. What are you two up to?"

Neely Kate stepped back, and her eyes widened in mock innocence. "We're getting coffee, of course. What are *you* doin'?"

His eyes darkened. "I just got done taking the new DA to task for caving with one of your divorce attorney's clients."

"Carter Hale?" Neely Kate asked in surprise.

He lifted an eyebrow in mock annoyance. "You have more than one divorce attorney?"

It was her turn to scowl. "I'd hire a dozen if I thought any of them could find my missing husband."

Since Neely Kate was Carter Hale's only divorce case, I presumed that Joe was referring to a criminal client.

Joe's shoulders dropped. "I've been looking, Neely Kate."

"You and everyone and his brother," she said sarcastically. "We're not meant to find him." But he'd been gone a long time, and her phrasing told me that she suspected he was dead.

Joe had returned to his chief deputy sheriff position a month ago, and one of the first things he'd done was launch an investigation into the whereabouts of Neely Kate's missing husband, Ronnie. He'd left her months ago, and Neely Kate and I had later discovered that he had some bad connections—ones that had tied him, however peripherally, to J.R. Simmons. When J.R. Simmons' empire had come tumbling down, it had taken plenty of lives with it. I knew Neely Kate believed Ronnie had been one of the casualties, and the evidence seemed to support it. It was like he'd fallen off the face of the earth, and so far, Joe and Carter's multiple private investigators hadn't turned up a single clue.

She shook her head. "You did the best you could."

He grimaced and looked over his shoulder, as if he might get lucky and find Ronnie right behind him, before turning back. "If I'd only looked sooner . . ."

"No. Joe. It's not meant to be."

Worried Neely Kate would feel down, I changed the subject. "Why were you upset with Carter Hale?"

"When am I *not* upset with him?" Joe asked. "His passion in life seems to be undermining my work. He represents sleazeballs. And he often wins."

Neely Kate lifted her chin in defiance. "Which is why I hired him."

Joe sighed. "For the umpteenth time, let me hire you an attorney from Little Rock."

She crossed her arms over her chest and shook her head. "Carter's doin' just fine. Besides, you know I can't afford a hotshot Little Rock lawyer, and I'm not letting you pay for it."

Joe looked like he wanted to dig his heels in, but he shook his head. "I like how you tried to deflect my question about Raddy Dyer."

Neely Kate cocked her eyebrow. "I think the real question is what do *you* know about him? I went to high school with Raddy, and he's never been one to stir up trouble."

Joe gave her the side-eye. "I'm pretty sure he's a good five years older than you."

"So he's a bit slow."

"How recently have you had contact with him?"

Neely Kate shrugged. "I see him from time to time."

"Well, steer clear of him. We've been called out to his property and his estranged wife's house multiple times over the last month for domestic disturbances. His wife kicked him out, but he keeps trying to get into the house. He seems to be becoming more desperate and more violent in his attempts, so I don't want you anywhere near that nonsense."

I turned to Neely Kate, my mouth gaping. The look on her face told me she already knew about Raddy's trouble with the law. Great.

"Innocent until proven guilty, Joe," she said.

His gaze held hers and the muscle on his jaw twitched. "Stay away from Radcliffe Dyer."

Huh. This was a change. Joe was usually barking the orders at *me*. I couldn't say I minded one bit that he was barking them at my best friend instead.

She lifted her hands in surrender, and a soft smile covered her face. "I hear you."

"Oh, I know you hear me," he said in exasperation. "I'm asking you to please do as I request."

She rolled her eyes. "Joe . . ."

"What can I get for you?" the girl at the counter asked. We'd been talking so long we'd made it to the front of the line. The clerk, who didn't look more than twenty, had on a bright, cheerful green apron embroidered with the name Bernadette.

Neely Kate took a deep breath, then said, "I want a medium white mocha, but I want it warm—not too hot and definitely not cold. And instead of three shots of white chocolate syrup, I'd like two. Add a shot of raspberry syrup for the third shot." Neely Kate paused. "You got that so far?"

"Got it." Bernadette's shoulder-length brown hair brushed against her shoulders as she wrote the instructions on the cup.

When she started to set the cup down next to the espresso machine, Neely Kate stopped her. "There's more."

Bernadette's face lifted in surprise. "Okay."

"What kind of soy milk do you have?"

When did she start drinking soy milk?

The owner, Vance Rankin, a man in his forties, leaned around from behind the espresso machine. "You know good and well what brand of soy milk we use," he growled. "It's the same damn stuff we used yesterday."

Neely Kate gave him a look of annoyance. "Then I want almond milk."

Bernadette still seemed unfazed. "Anything else?"

"No. That's it."

"I'll take a medium nonfat latte," I said, suddenly feeling boring compared to Neely Kate.

Joe reached over my shoulder to hand Bernadette some cash. "And I'll have a large Americano. It's all on my tab."

Neely Kate started to protest, but a harsh look from Joe stopped her.

It didn't take a genius to tell this was about more than coffee. The last thing Neely Kate wanted was to be taken for a mooch. Joe and his sister Kate came from the infamous Simmons family, which had—up until recently—meant money, power, and prestige. So when Joe abruptly left town in February, Neely Kate had worried it was because of her, that he'd thought his new little sister would want a paycheck. He'd since explained himself—he'd gone home to settle his father's estate and had only kept away from Neely Kate for so long out of his own shame. But it was going to take her a long time to get over it.

"Thanks, Joe," I said as we sidled out of line.

He shot me a worried look and whispered in my ear, low enough that Neely Kate couldn't hear, "It comes with strings."

The mere fact that he'd whispered it insinuated that it involved my best friend. No doubt he'd tell me in good time.

"Okay."

Joe took a step back, then addressed us both. "How's your new employee working out? It's your cousin, right?"

Neely Kate groaned. "Let's just say the Rivers branches of my family tree hang so low they're takin' root."

"So, not good?" he asked dryly.

"This is a story best told over a beer," I said. "Want to come over for dinner tonight?"

His eyebrows lifted in surprise, and Neely Kate shot me a questioning look. I'd mostly left him alone since his return to town. For one, he was my ex-boyfriend and we'd found a shaky truce. I didn't want to chance it, especially since he held a stake in my nursery—another long story. And two, Joe and Neely Kate had been finding their way toward a new family dynamic, and I'd tried to give them space. But if Joe was going to have a real relationship with Neely Kate, and she was living with me, I needed to make sure he felt welcome at my farmhouse.

"Sure . . ." he said with hesitation. Then he grinned. "Are you cooking or are we having deli sandwiches?"

I lightly smacked his arm. "Just for that, I'll burn your portion."

He grinned and my heart lightened at the happiness I saw on his face. It had been hard-won. "I'll bring the beer," he said. "What time?"

"How about seven?" I asked as the owner handed me a cup.

"Sounds good," Joe said. "I'll tell Maeve she can take a night off from bringing me food." The owner handed over Joe's coffee next, and Joe shot a look at Neely Kate before ushering me toward the door.

"Hey!" Neely Kate protested. "I ordered my coffee first!"

"This ain't Little Rock," Vance said with an exaggerated drawl. "We're not used to those newfangled drinks."

"You have 'em right on your board!" Neely Kate protested as she pointed to the sign. She didn't seem to notice when Joe and I slipped out the front door.

"What's up?" I asked when we were on the sidewalk outside. An awning protected us from the slight rain.

"I may have a lead on Ronnie."

I gasped. "But you just said—"

"I know. I didn't want to say anything in front of Neely Kate."

My nose scrunched as I studied him. "So why are you telling *me*?"

"I need to know why she's really trying to find him."

"Does it make a difference?"

"It might," he said carefully.

"Oh." He looked so worried that my heart went out to him. "Joe, she knows he was up to something underhanded. You don't have to worry about upsetting her."

"And I also know she thinks he's dead. But what if she finds out he's not?"

I blinked in surprise. "Where do you think he is?"

"New Orleans."

"You're kidding. What on earth would he be doing there?"

"Shacking up with a woman."

I felt lightheaded. "Oh."

"It's nothing solid, but my gut says there's something to it. Enough that I'm going to go down there to check it out myself."

"Can you do that?"

"Not officially, but I can take a couple of days off and go ask some questions."

My stomach twisted and my voice cracked. "Joe . . . you just got back to work."

"Yeah, I know," he said. "But it's Neely Kate. I owe her."

"No, Joe. You don't *owe* her anything."

A surprising fierceness filled his eyes. "I owe her this and so much more." He paused and took a deep breath. "You didn't see her, Rose. You didn't see how broken Neely Kate looked after my shitty sister got done telling her that her mother hadn't wanted her . . . that she wished she'd never been born. I swore to God I'd never let her feel unwanted like that again."

I gasped. "You two went to see Kate at the psych ward?" His sister had been hospitalized back in February, after she'd orchestrated the showdown that had ended in the death of her father, J.R. Simmons, among other casualties. Life had embittered and twisted her, and I didn't like the idea of her being anywhere near Neely Kate.

His mouth sagged. "Neely Kate didn't tell you?"

"No."

He turned to face the courthouse and scrubbed his hand over his face before turning back to me. "I thought she told you everything."

I paused. "We each have our secrets, I guess." More so than I liked. Especially since I'd sworn to myself I was done with secrets. Mostly.

He gave a hurried glance toward the coffee shop door, then said, "She asked me to take her to see Kate in Little Rock. She wanted to know how Kate had figured out that our father was her father too. Kate told us, but being Kate, she made sure to hurt Neely Kate in the process. Neely Kate held it together until we got back in the car, and then she just lost it." He swallowed. "She's been through hell, Rose. Her own mother . . . the abuse . . ."

I hid my shock. Neely Kate had told me her mother had literally dumped her as a preteen on her grandmother's doorstep, but she'd told me nothing about her life with her mother. I was surprised and a little hurt that Joe seemed to know more than I did.

"I can't let people continue to hurt her," Joe said. "So if she wants that asshole out of her life, I'm going to help her make it happen. I plan to serve Ronnie the divorce papers myself. And maybe deliver my own personal message along with them."

Tears swelled in my eyes, and I wrapped my arms around his stiff shoulders. I pulled him into a hug, holding my coffee cup out so I didn't drench his back. "I *knew* you'd be good for her. Thank you."

He leaned back and smiled. "No. Thank *you* for convincing me to pull my head out of my ass and talk to her."

"I know you're trying to make up for hurting her, Joe, but honestly, she just wants *you*."

He nodded, then glanced around before turning back to me. "Are you still in communication with Malcolm?"

His question about bowled me over. "Uh . . . maybe."

He gave me a look that told me my acting skills were subpar. "I hate to leave Fenton County right now, but my lead has suggested Ronnie's about to skip out of New Orleans. I need to catch him before he disappears again."

"What's going on here that has you concerned?" I asked, but common sense told me it had something to do with James.

"There are some rumblings in the criminal underworld. Rumor has it that someone new is making a power play for Malcolm's position." He tilted his head as he studied me, his face becoming a blank slate. "But from the look on your face, you already knew that."

"I'm not sure I should confess to anything."

Anger filled his eyes. "Are you *questioning* people for him again?"

I shook my head. "No. He won't let me near his life."

Joe looked shocked, and I couldn't decide if it was because I hadn't gotten offended by his question, that James was trying to protect me, or that I was admitting my involvement. Maybe all three. "Stay away from Skeeter Malcolm, Rose. If you're in the wrong place at the wrong time, you could end up as collateral damage."

I watched him closely. Six months ago, he would have barked this as a direct order, expecting me to blindly follow. But now, it seemed like a request—one friend pleading with the other to use her common sense. "Thanks," I said. "But you really don't have anything to worry about. I haven't seen him in weeks, and we never meet up near his business."

He nodded and started to say something, but the door to the coffee shop burst open, and Neely Kate stomped out with her coffee cup, which was encased in a pink knit coffee-cup sleeve. "I can't believe this place!"

It occurred to me she'd been in there an unnaturally long time. "What took so long?"

"They made my drink completely *wrong* the first time, so they had to make it again." She shook her head and looked up at Joe. "And here I thought we were getting a little sophistication in our town. Just goes to show you that you can't make a Coach purse out of a goat tail."

Joe opened his mouth to say something, but he must have thought better of it because he closed it the very next moment. Smart man.

"Where'd you get the cute sleeve for your cup?" I asked.

She put a hand on her hip. "Funny thing. Bernadette said she'd give it to me if I promised to just take the too-hot coffee and leave."

Joe shook his head, wearing an ear-to-ear grin. "I need to get back to work. I'll see you ladies tonight." Then he kissed Neely Kate on the cheek and headed across the street to the courthouse.

I couldn't stop thinking about his lead on Ronnie. Had Ronnie really run off with another woman? Could Neely Kate handle it if he had?

Chapter Three

*M*y stomach flip-flopped as I pulled my truck into the parking lot of the hardware store. "I'm not sure I should go in there."

"What are you talking about?" Neely Kate said as she checked her lip gloss in the sun visor mirror. A light rain hit the windshield. "I thought we agreed to put that nonsense behind us."

I pointed toward a particle board sign spray painted with something that looked like a rose with a poorly drawn face in the middle. A red circle surrounded the design, and the slash down the middle had been painted with particular gusto. "Then why is *that* there?"

"Oh, that was some of the kids they hired to take care of the greenhouse. They were just foolin' around."

"Is that supposed to be *me*?"

She returned her tube of lip gloss to her bejeweled purse. "Yeah, but it's no big deal."

"How can that be no big deal?"

"They made it back in March. It's early June. They've totally forgotten about it." She turned to look at me.

"You've been wanting to paint the kitchen—how about we pick out a color while we're here? They can't get mad if you're a paying customer."

I had half a mind to stay in the truck, but truth be told, I didn't trust her to talk to Raddy without me. I wanted to hear exactly what he wanted before we took the "case," although it felt ridiculous to call looking for some jewelry a "case." Then there was the fact that Raddy Dyer had apparently been involved in multiple domestic violence altercations. There was no way I wanted to work with him if he was a threat.

Neely Kate hopped out and popped open her umbrella. She came around to the driver's side to share it with me, but I waved off her offer as I got out. A little rain couldn't do much more damage at this point. Casting a glance around us, I asked, "Are you sure they're open? There's hardly anyone here."

"Oh, everyone's comin' later. Their big sale starts at noon, which means now is the perfect time to talk to Raddy."

We walked into the store, and Neely Kate collapsed her umbrella and shook off the water. I followed her down the lighting aisle and toward the back of the store. I kept my face down, hoping to keep a low profile, but no one seemed to notice me. In fact, I didn't see anyone at all until we walked up to a guy wearing jeans and blue vest.

"Raddy Dyer," Neely Kate said with a hint of attitude. "I heard you came by our office."

I did a double take; this was Raddy Dyer? A bright orange shock of hair stuck straight up on his head, and he looked a little lost in his own store. He definitely wasn't what I'd imagined.

"So does this mean you're gonna do it?" he asked hopefully.

She nodded. "Of course we are."

"Hold up," I said as I stepped in front of her. "Not so fast."

Neely Kate grabbed my arm and turned me back to face her. "Rose. What are you doin'?"

I pulled loose and looked Raddy square in the eyes. They were bright blue, and the contrast with his startlingly orange hair momentarily distracted me. Was it natural? I shook my head, then started my interrogation. "What *exactly* do you expect us to do?"

Raddy glanced over his shoulder, then nodded his head sideways toward the back of the store. "We can't talk here. We've gotta head out back."

We followed Raddy until he stopped beside an end-cap display of PVC joints.

"What's the big secret?" I asked, already deciding this case wasn't worth all the cloak-and-dagger intrigue.

He leaned back and glanced over his shoulder down the aisle before straightening his posture. "No secret. I just can't be seen talking to you."

"Me?" I asked in surprise.

"Yeah." He gave me a look that suggested I was naïve and then some. "My grandmother died a few years ago," he said, "and since I'm the oldest grandchild, I got some of her jewelry."

"What kind of jewelry are you talkin' about?" Neely Kate asked. She'd pulled out a small, pink, glittery spiral-bound notebook and was taking notes with a sparkly pink pen with a pink pom-pom at the tip.

"A sapphire ring. A ruby pin."

"Like a brooch?" Neely Kate asked.

He made a face and gestured to his chest. "The kind of thing you wear on your chest. It was shaped like an owl, and the eyes were rubies. There were a couple of necklaces too. One of those is missing."

"Which one?" I asked. "What's it look like?"

"Here's the thing," he said, leaning closer. "I thought the necklace was costume jewelry, so I didn't think much of it."

"So it's gaudy?" I asked.

"Yeah. Some big stones—they look like diamonds, but I thought they were crystals. Anyway, I let my lady wear them and didn't think much of it."

"But then she kicked you out?" Neely Kate asked, narrowing her gaze. "Cause you were sleeping with Hilda Ratner."

Raddy lifted his hands in defense and took a step backward. "Now, hold on a cotton-pickin' minute. I wasn't sleepin' with Hilda."

"No? Then how come you were seen coming out of a room with her at the Easy Breezy Motel?"

A sheepish grin twisted his mouth. "We weren't *sleepin'* . . ."

"No kiddin'," Neely Kate groaned, looking at her notepad. "So Rayna kicked you out and tossed your clothes in the yard and lit a big ol' bonfire."

"Well, there's no need to get into *that* . . ."

"And then you broke into the house two days later and took a chainsaw to *her* clothes."

"An eye for an eye, the Good Book says."

Neely Kate put a hand on her hip and gave him the stink eye. "And I'm pretty sure the Good Book says something about fornicatin' and adultery too."

He waved his hands. "Okay, okay. So I've made a mistake or two."

"So Rayna's holding your grandmother's jewelry hostage?" I asked.

"When Rayna kicked me out, Momma went over and demanded Rayna give her all the jewelry."

"And how'd that go?" I asked, pretty sure that accounted for domestic disturbance number three.

He grimaced. "Let's just say that Momma and Rayna have never gotten along, so there was a bit of a disagreement. But Momma walked away with the jewelry. Well . . . everything but the one necklace."

"I take it that it's not costume jewelry after all," I said.

"No. The stones in the necklace are white sapphires. It's worth some big bucks."

"Did Rayna know it was real?" I asked.

He shook his head. "No. *I* didn't find out until after Momma went to get it."

"So ask Rayna to give it back to you," I said. "Or ask for it in the divorce."

He looked surprised. "We ain't gettin' divorced."

"Rayna's fool enough to take you back?" Neely Kate asked.

"No. We were never married."

"Wait." Neely Kate blinked theatrically. "You had a big fancy church wedding five years ago."

He shrugged again. "Rayna wanted a wedding, so I gave her one."

"And she didn't care if it was real or not?" I asked.

"I forgot to mail in the wedding license."

"And Rayna didn't care?"

"Nah. She just wanted the dress and the presents." A sheepish look crossed his face. "And she didn't find out until she said she wanted a divorce." He glanced over his shoulder and then back at the two of us. "But I need that necklace pronto. The sooner the better."

"Been playin' the horses again, have ya?" Neely Kate asked.

His jaw set, but the look in his eyes gave him away. "No, ma'am." She lifted her eyebrows, looking feral enough that he corrected himself without further prompting. "I mean *miss*."

She relaxed. "Then what's the hurry?"

"That's for me to know. Now are you gonna help me or not?"

"That depends," Neely Kate said. "How much are you payin'?"

"You want money?" he asked in dismay.

"You bet your sweet patootie," she said, flipping her long blonde hair over her shoulder. "Even an accordion-playing monkey wearing a blindfold could tell you're gonna sell it, so if you want it bad enough, you're gonna pay up."

"Five hundred dollars."

Neely Kate shook her head. "A thousand."

My mouth dropped open. Was she crazy?

But to my shock, Raddy grumbled, "Fine. This is what it looks like."

He took out his phone and pulled up a photo of a gaudy necklace with translucent yellowish stones. The big oval stone in the center was surrounded by multiple smaller round stones.

Neely Kate gasped as she leaned forward for a closer look, then pulled out her phone and snapped a photo. "How much is this sucker worth?"

"Dunno. I need to get my hands on it to know for sure, but my buddy says it's probably worth twenty large."

Neely Kate's mouth dropped open. "Twenty thousand? And you had it slidin' around in your underwear drawer?"

"I didn't have it in my underwear drawer," he protested. "It was in my junk drawer."

"Even better," she muttered.

"Hey! I didn't know it was worth anything. But I need it back. So are you gonna look for it?"

Neely Kate glanced over at me, and I could tell she really wanted to find it, although only the Lord knew why. While the landscaping business wasn't rolling in money, things were looking up, and it was pretty clear she had a dim view of Radcliffe Dyer. Maybe it was just the thrill of the chase. But if Joe came back from New Orleans with news that Ronnie really was shacking up with some woman, I wanted Neely Kate to have this. So with great reluctance, I gave a slight nod.

She turned back to him and held out her hand. "Raddy Dyer, you've just hired yourself the services of Sparkle Investigations."

I started to cough, while Raddy made a look of disgust. "Sparkle? What am I gonna tell the guys?"

I found myself in the unfortunate position of agreeing with our new client.

"You're not gonna tell them anything," I said, grabbing Neely Kate's arm and giving it a slight tug. "But if we're doin' this, we're gonna need a deposit." Raddy had the look of a runner all over him.

"Fine." He reached into his wallet and pulled out a twenty-dollar bill. "Here."

Neely Kate snorted. "You think we're fresh off the turnip truck? We're gonna need more than that."

"Like four hundred and eighty dollars more," I said. "Half down. Half when we turn it over."

"But what if you don't find it?" he asked, wide-eyed.

"Then you're outta luck," I said. "We're not doin' this for our health. We're takin' time from our payin' customers at the landscaping office to look for your misplaced jewelry. So five hundred—even if we don't find it, and five hundred more if we do."

He shook his head. "No deal."

I lifted my shoulder in a nonchalant shrug. "All righty then." I tugged Neely Kate toward the exit.

"What are you doin'?" she whispered in a panicked tone.

"Trust me."

To her credit, she gave me a sideways glance and kept right on marching. Sure enough, Raddy was calling us back five seconds later.

"Okay. Okay. I'll pay it."

I gave Neely Kate a smug grin before I turned around to face him. "Can you pay all five hundred now?" I asked, sounding all businesslike.

"No."

"Bring it by the office when you get it, and *then* we'll start searching."

"That's not gonna work," he whined. "Today's Tuesday and Buck says I gotta have it to him by Friday night or no deal."

"Deal?" Neely Kate screeched. "You said you don't know what it's worth."

"I don't. But Buck says he'll pay me five grand for it. He wants to give it to his woman."

I narrowed my eyes. "Why would you take five grand for a necklace that might be worth several times that?"

"A bird in the hand, Rose Gardner," he said.

"Did someone say Rose Gardner?" a woman's voice echoed from what sounded like several aisles over.

Raddy's eyes flew open wide, and he gave me a shove. "You have to get out of here."

Neely Kate shook her head and dug her heels into the concrete floor. "Not until you give us the down payment."

"I already told you. I don't have it."

"Lucky for you there's an ATM machine up front," she said with a smug grin. "We'll wait."

He groaned and looked as frustrated as Muffy got when she saw a squirrel taunting her on the other side of the screen door.

"We're not lookin' until you pay up," she said sweetly. "Which means you might not meet your Friday deadline. Tick tock."

Raddy released a string of curses that would have made his mother blush, but Neely Kate just stood there with her feet planted wide, giving him a condescending smile. She waited until his language petered out, then said, "Now that that's out of your system, are you gonna pay up or not?"

"*Fine.*" He pointed at me. "But *she* has to wait outside."

Neely Kate gave a me a glance that read, *See you when I'm done,* but there was no way I was leaving until I got all the information I wanted.

"Nope," I said. "I have a few questions first. Then you can get the money, and we'll get out of your hair." My eyes lifted to the orange mess on top of his head.

"What do you want to know?"

"Who else besides your mother and Rayna knew about the necklace?"

"My brother Newton and my sister Leah . . . and my Aunt Tildie."

"Did Newton or Leah seem interested in it?" I asked. "Was your aunt upset that you got the jewelry instead of her?"

"Aunt Tildie never even knew I had it. My grandmammie gave it to my mother. And yeah, she was upset, but Momma's had it since Grandmammie passed away eight years ago."

"What about your friends?" Neely Kate asked. "Sounds like you told a few of them."

"I told Buck and Lionel. And Tucker."

Neely Kate snorted. "So basically half the county."

"They found out after Rayna said she didn't have it," he protested.

"Anything else to help us look?"

He gave me a look of disgust. "If I had all the answers, what would I be payin' you for?"

In all fairness, he had a point. It wasn't a lot to go on, but it was a start.

The overhead speaker crackled, and a woman said in a bored tone, "Raddy, we need you at the loading dock."

"I have to go," he said, looking worried.

Neely Kate held out her hand. "Money."

He dug out his wallet again and opened a secret compartment, from which he pulled out four crisp hundred-dollar bills. Then he handed her four more grubby looking twenties to add to the one he had in the front compartment.

I was shocked when Neely Kate took the money without commenting on his lie. She stuffed it into her purse. "We'll be in touch."

"You better find something," he grumbled. "That's my poker money."

Neely Kate's face blanched—Ronnie had kept a regular poker night—but she quickly recovered and sneered, "Maybe if you'd spent less time playin' poker and more time with your woman, you wouldn't be in this situation, Raddy Dyer." Then she spun around and stormed out of the store.

I trailed after her, wondering how much of that speech had actually been meant for her absent husband.

Chapter Four

*N*eely Kate was already out the door by the time I reached the registers. I was so caught up in my thoughts about Neely Kate, Ronnie, and that darn necklace that I physically flinched when I heard someone shout, "That's Rose Gardner!"

"What?" a second woman screeched.

I stood at the exit, watching the rain come down in sheets. Neely Kate was halfway to the truck huddled under her umbrella, and two angry-looking women were bearing down on me.

I took off running for the truck, stepping into a puddle deep enough to drench my already damp jeans. I climbed into the truck and glared at Neely Kate, who had set her purse down in the middle seat and was fluffing her hair.

"Why didn't you wait for me with the umbrella?"

Surprise filled her eyes. "I'm sorry. You didn't want to share it before."

It hadn't been raining cats and dogs before, but I let that go and moved on to my next issue. "I thought you said they weren't mad at me."

"What are you talking about?" she asked in confusion. "I was chased out of the store with a pitchfork!"

She rolled her eyes and waved a hand in dismissal. "It couldn't have been that bad."

I pointed to the door and gasped. "Look! Now they have a *literal* pitchfork!" The two employees stood at the door, glaring at my truck. A customer stood next to them with a shovel in one hand and a pitchfork in the other, presumably waiting for the rain to let up.

Neely Kate sighed. "I could have sworn they were over it. And you made it out just fine. That's what counts, right?"

I scowled as I started the truck and pulled out of the parking lot, heading back toward our office.

"Look on the bright side," she said. "We just made five hundred dollars."

"And guess where part of that five hundred dollars is gonna go?" I said in a smug tone. "We're gonna need to hire two guys from Jonah's temporary work program so we can get those bushes planted while we're traipsing around looking for a necklace."

Her smile fell. "Oh. I hadn't considered that."

I sat back in my seat, feeling like a terrible friend. Wasn't this supposed to be about cheering her up? "Hey, that's a bonus, right?" I said with a grin. "Did you want to be plantin' bushes in the mud?"

She grinned back. "No."

I pushed out a big breath. "Okay, let's look at what we know. So Raddy has this necklace that he and his pseudo wife thought was costume jewelry. Then Rayna kicks him out, he finds out it's worth something, and suddenly it's gone. We need to talk to Rayna." I turned toward her. "Do you know where we can find her?"

"She works at Walmart. We can stop by and see if she's there."

I turned at the next corner and started driving toward Walmart. "But first we need to call Jonah."

I grabbed my phone. Jonah was a semi-famous televangelist and pastor at the New Living Hope Revival Church. His non-denominational church had a band that played praise songs instead of hymns, and his uplifting sermons were the exact opposite of the fire and brimstone speeches I had listened to at the Henryetta Southern Baptist Church since before I could remember. It was no wonder he'd won over a good portion of the churchgoers in Henryetta after moving to town at the end of last summer. But he'd also started a controversial Onward and Upward program for ex-cons and teens at risk, part of which was his day laborer program for men who had trouble finding work because of their non-violent criminal records. I was counting on him having a couple of men available for the afternoon.

"Rose," he said warmly when he answered the phone. "I didn't get a chance to talk to you after church on Sunday. How are you doing?"

"Oh . . . things have been better. Say, do you have a couple of guys from your work program available this afternoon? I need them to plant a few bushes."

"Today?" he asked in surprise. "It's still raining."

"It's supposed to let up soon."

"Won't it be too muddy?"

He had a point, and part of me wondered if it would be easier to admit defeat and just give the Hendersons a refund. "Maybe, but if they could at least get them in the ground, I can go fix them when it's dryer. I can pay them each fifty dollars." I gave him the address and simple instructions, and he promised to supervise the job.

Neely Kate was surprisingly silent on the rest of the drive to Walmart, but as soon as we pulled into the parking lot, she opened her car door and popped open her umbrella. She waited for me at the end of the truck, but I waved her off again.

"I'm already drenched." The rain had let up again, but there was still a light drizzle.

We hurried for the entrance, and once Neely Kate had shaken the rain off her umbrella, we headed into the store. She grabbed a cart and tossed her umbrella inside. "We might as well get a few things while we're here. Muffy's almost out of dog food."

But she headed straight for the personal hygiene aisle. A box of tampons went into the cart, followed by some shampoo, conditioner, and toothpaste.

I gave her a look. "I thought we were here to talk to Rayna Dyer."

"We can't just march up to her and start interrogatin'," Neely Kate said, picking up a curling iron from a display and opening the clamp. "We need to make it look like we're shopping, so I might as well get these things while we're here." She glanced up at me. "Weren't you saying you needed new socks? Why don't you head over there and pick some out? I'll meet you in the dog food aisle; then we'll go find Rayna."

"What department does she even work in?"

"Housewares. But I'll meet you by the pet supplies."

Shaking my head, I headed toward the shoe department, only to realize once I got there that the socks were by the women's lingerie. I started to walk across the aisle when I heard my name.

"Rose?"

I spun around to see who it was, shocked to see Dr. Levi Romano, the new vet in town. Neely Kate and I had met him a few weeks ago. We'd gone looking for a lost dog, but we'd found another animal first. "Dr. Romano. I'm surprised you remember me."

He grinned, his blue eyes dancing. "It's hard to forget a woman who brings in a lost pig."

I self-consciously reached my hand up to my hair. "And I look even worse today than I did then." I'd been just as drenched and mud-logged the day I'd visited his practice.

Oh, mercy. What had prompted me to comment on my looks? Perhaps it was the way his gaze had swept over my face, his grin staying put. Or maybe it was because Dr. Romano was even cuter out of his doctor's coat. He was wearing well-fitting jeans and a light-blue button-down shirt that made his eyes look even bluer. His light brown hair was a little more unkempt than when I'd met him in his office. He'd been battling the rain too, only it had made him more attractive rather than less.

"You look just fine," he said.

"I look like a drowned rat."

"As someone who's been through veterinarian school and seen an assortment of animals in a wide variety of situations, I can assure you that you look nothing like a drowned rat."

I laughed. "What are you doing here on a weekday morning? I thought you'd be at your office."

He pointed behind him. "I need wading boots, but since they seem to be out of stock, I'm picking out rain boots instead."

"Are you going fishing?" I asked.

"In a manner of speaking. I'm headed out to the Baxter farm to deliver a calf, but I can't find my boots, and I really don't want to destroy another pair of shoes."

"You're delivering a calf?" I asked in awe. "That must be so amazing."

"I can't lie," he said with a grin, "it's a little messy, but it's a wonderful experience." He paused, looking like he wanted to say something but couldn't figure out how to start.

"Well, I should let you get going."

He took a step backward. "Actually, I could use your help."

"I don't know the first thing about birthing a calf," I said.

He laughed. "Well then, it's a good thing I was going to ask you to help me pick out which boots to get."

I felt my cheeks go hot. "Sure. Which ones are you lookin' at?"

He held up two pairs. "This green pair seems to fit better, but the navy pair will do a better job of hiding the mud."

I glanced up at him. "Do you really care if the boots blend in well with mud?"

"Good point."

"The green pair, obviously," I said. "If you're gonna be standing around helping deliver a cow, your feet should at least be comfortable."

He set the blue pair on the shelf. "Excellent advice. And it doesn't hurt that the green pair matches your eyes."

My face, which had felt hot anyway, was fixing to combust.

He laughed. "You're even prettier when you blush. And if you ever want to learn how to birth a calf, you let me know. I'm your man."

I couldn't think of a single blessed thing to say.

"You have a good day, Rose."

"You too, Dr. Romano."

As he brushed past me, he winked and said, "Call me Levi." Then he headed toward the front of the store.

"Oh my word," said Neely Kate. Levi had me so out of sorts I hadn't even noticed she was heading toward me. There was a pile of shopping in her cart. "Was that the new vet?"

"Uh-huh."

"What did he say?" she asked excitedly.

"He offered to teach me how to birth a calf."

"He what?"

I laughed and shook my head. "He said he was getting the green boots because they reminded him of my eyes."

Her mouth twisted as she studied me. "Sounds like he needs just as much practice at this dating thing as you do."

"*Dating?* What are you talking about?"

"Rose . . ." She shook her head. "He obviously likes you."

While I'd halfway suspected that, my first reaction was to gape at her in disbelief.

She winked and pushed her cart forward. "Let's get Muffy's food and then corner Rayna."

"You mean talk to her."

"Yeah. That."

We stopped by the pet department, and I wondered once again if I should pick a new dog food to try resolving my poor dog's flatulence issue or get the brand she liked. I grabbed the one she liked. So my dog farted a lot. That was part of her charm.

As if she were reading my mind, Neely Kate said, "You know, you could take Muffy to see Dr. Romano about her bowel issue."

"You mean her farting issue?"

"Po-tay-to, po-tah-to."

"Muffy's perfectly healthy. I see no reason to take her to the vet if there's no problem."

"I call the fact that I've considered buying one of those World War I mustard gas masks at the army surplus store a reason," Neely Kate said. "It doesn't hurt that Dr. Romano would be the one lookin' her over."

"Neely Kate." I stopped in the middle of the aisle. "I'm not ready to date yet."

"How do you know?" But something in her eyes told me this wasn't just about *my* love life.

"Are *you* ready to date?" I asked, thinking about that vision I'd had.

"I don't know," Neely Kate said quietly.

That was new. A month ago she'd said no. "Is there anyone you're interested in dating?"

"No." She said it with so much force I couldn't help wondering if she was thinking about Carter Hale. He'd made no secret of his interest in her, but I was pretty sure there were rules against him dating a client. Thank goodness. Something told me it wasn't a good idea for her to rebound with her divorce attorney.

"I know you're still married," I said. "But you're trying your best to get a divorce. You'd probably be divorced already if he hadn't taken off." I gave her a sad smile. "It's okay if you want to find someone else, Neely Kate."

"And the same goes for you," she said, sniffing and wiping the corners of her eyes. "Let's go talk to Rayna."

She left me in her wake as she started pushing the cart toward the housewares section as if they were giving away OPI nail polish to the first five customers.

By the time I caught up, Neely Kate had come to a halt. She was studying a thirty-something woman with jet-black hair that extended slightly past her shoulders. It had so many uneven layers it looked like it had been cut by Edward Scissorhands. She had on khakis, a white shirt, and a blue vest and was studying a package of bed sheets as though she wanted to light them on fire.

Neely Kate took a breath, appearing to center herself, and then her face lit up like a Christmas tree. "Rayna? Is that *you?*"

"What?" the woman asked in confusion as she hurriedly set the sheets on the shelf. "Neely Kate. Do you need help with somethin'?"

Neely Kate tilted her head and gently rested her hand on the woman's arm. "I just heard about Raddy."

The woman gave Neely Kate the same scowl she'd been giving those sheets. "Lies! He's telling lies!"

Neely Kate nodded sympathetically. "Of course they are, honey. Everyone knows about Randy Raddy's reputation."

Rayna's mouth dropped open. "What?"

Apparently everyone but Rayna.

Neely Kate leaned closer. "Rayna, you're ten times better off without him." A mischievous grin spread across her face. "I heard his clothes burned so hot in your front yard the Henryetta fire department had to send *two* trucks."

Rayna's mouth twisted into a slight grin. "He was fit to be tied when I burned his lucky bowling shirt."

"I hope you kept most of his stuff."

"Most of it was mine," Rayna said with a scowl. "Lazy-ass son of a bitch only got a job about two months ago. Probably so he could pay for those damn hotel rooms." Tears filled her eyes.

"Rayna, honey," Neely Kate cooed, rubbing her arm. "Just let him shack up with those other hussies. You're lucky to be rid of him and find you a real man."

She nodded. "Yeah. You're right."

"I don't mean to intrude," I said moving closer, "but I couldn't help overhearing. I'm Neely Kate's friend, Rose. I really hope you take him to the cleaners."

Her sad eyes lifted to mine. "We weren't even legally married. The damn fool admitted he forgot to send in the marriage license. And since Arkansas's not a common law state, I'm not entitled to nothin' of his. Not that he has anything. The house is in my name, and most of the stuff is mine. I held onto his big-screen TV for a week, but it's one of those monster things that's about five feet tall and it had funny lines through the screen. I put it out in the garage with all his fishing and bowling stuff."

"There wasn't anything else he wanted?" Neely Kate asked innocently.

"His grandmammie's jewelry, but I handed it all over to the old bat." When she saw our confused looks, she added, "His mother."

"That had to have been worth something," Neely Kate said. "You could have taken some of it and sold it, then bought yourself a brand-new big-screen TV. I bet you get an employee discount here, don't you?"

Rayna snorted. "Raddy was always bragging that the jewelry was worth thousands of dollars, but he's either deluded or he wanted *me* to be deluded. I took that stupid owl brooch to the pawn shop, and Alberto said the eyes were cut glass."

Raddy had claimed he'd only discovered the necklace's value *after* the breakup. Had he lied to us or inadvertently told Rayna the truth? I shot a look to Neely Kate, but she plowed on like she wasn't fazed one bit. "So why would Raddy think it was real?"

"His momma probably filled his head with lies. She told me that junk was real when she picked it up."

I shook my head. "Why would she say that?"

She pointed a bony finger at her temple. "To mess with my head. Now Raddy's all worked up and accusing me of hiding it or pawning it, but he can ask Alberto. I ain't been to the pawn shop since I sold his old trumpet."

I made a mental note that we should talk to this Alberto ourselves.

"Can you believe he's threatened to sue me?" she asked in disbelief. "Over some stupid costume jewelry." She shook her head and crossed her arms. "You can't get blood out of a turnip. They can turn my house upside down, and they ain't gonna find nothing."

My head tingled—a telltale sign I was about to have a vision—and I barely had time to tap Neely Kate twice with my fingertips, a system we'd created for this sort of awkward situation.

The Walmart bedding aisle faded from view, replaced by a hot tub. The woman sitting next to me in the water looked like she was in her early thirties, but life hadn't been kind. She had bleached blonde hair piled on top of her head and saggy breasts covered by the smallest bikini top I'd ever seen. There was a glass of wine in her hand, and her wide smile showed chipped yellow teeth.

"We'll get your revenge, Rayna. Just you wait and see."

I lifted my own wine glass and clinked it with hers. "Here's to gettin' rid of the garbage in our lives."

The vision faded, and suddenly Rayna was standing in front of me. I blurted out, "You're gonna get revenge."

Her eyes hardened and she threw back her shoulders. "Damn straight, I am."

Neely Kate pressed her lips together and nodded. "That's the spirit. You stand your ground, Rayna."

The woman nodded. "I need to head to the back. It was good seeing you again, Neely Kate."

"You too. Take care of yourself."

"Yeah, I'm trying," she said absently, then walked to the end of the aisle.

When she disappeared from view, I grabbed the cart and started pushing it toward the front of the store.

"You had a vision about Rayna gettin' revenge?" Neely Kate asked.

"Yes," I said, trying to focus on what I'd seen. "She's gonna cook up a plan with her blonde friend. They were in a hot tub."

"But she didn't say anything specific about her plan?" Neely Kate asked.

"Nothing other than that Rayna and this other woman wanted to get rid of the garbage in their lives."

"I can't say I blame them."

"Yeah, neither can I," I said. "Do you believe Rayna gave all the jewelry to his mother?"

"Yeah. But the non-ruby brooch doesn't fit with the necklace being real."

"We need to talk to Alberto at the pawn shop."

She nodded. "Agreed."

But first I needed to figure out an excuse to go see James in an hour.

Chapter Five

*I*t occurred to me that I had the perfect excuse for heading home early. "I should get food for tonight's dinner while we're here," I said. If I got groceries now, they'd need to be refrigerated sooner or later. It would give me an excuse to slip away without having to answer too many questions.

Neely Kate cast me a questioning look.

"It's like you said. Seein' as how we're already here, we might as well make the most of it."

"At least you won't think of some excuse to work late again tonight. I know we're busy, but you work too much."

"I'm a business owner," I said a little defensively as I steered the cart toward the food section of the store. "Besides, I like what I do."

"You like paperwork?"

She had a point, but the work needed to be done, and it kept me distracted . . . something I desperately needed.

Neely Kate must have sensed my inner turmoil and let it go. "Okay. What do you want to get?"

I pulled out my phone and opened my Pinterest app. "I found a recipe for this Tuscan chicken dish I'd like to try. How about that?"

"Sure."

We gathered the ingredients we didn't have at the farmhouse and checked out at the register. There were two pawn shops in town, and Rainy Day Pawn was the nicer of the two. Rayna wasn't high-class, but Ripper Pawn seemed a little too rough for her. As we walked toward the truck, I called Rainy Day Pawn and asked to speak to Alberto.

"He won't be in until four," the woman on the other end said. "He's getting another tattoo."

"Okay. Thanks."

I was relieved—this would give me time to meet James and then come back—but I tried not to show it as I relayed the information to Neely Kate. "So we'll need to wait until four to head over there."

"We could go talk to Mable Dyer—Raddy's momma."

I pondered it for a second. "Let's talk to Alberto first and find out if the brooch really was a fake. It would be good to have confirmation of that before we approach her."

"So what should we do in the meantime?"

I glanced at the time on my phone. "How about I drop you off at the office and you can work on those proposals? I'll grab Muffy and take her and the food to the house. Then we can head to the pawn shop together."

She gave me a look that said she knew I was up to something, but she didn't call me on it. Like I'd told Joe, Neely Kate and I both had our secrets. "Good idea, but you don't have to take Muffy."

"It looks like the rain's let up for a bit. I can let her run around the yard while I'm putting things away," I said. "And we won't have to worry about her if we want to stop by Raddy's mother's house after we talk to Alberto."

"Good idea."

While I drove to the office, Neely Kate pulled out her notebook and the pink fluff-ball pen. She cast me a defensive look. "This is how they do it on all those cop shows. They interview people and write down what they say."

"You should give some serious thought to becoming a Henryetta police officer, Neely Kate. Lord knows you've got more brains than most of those boneheads put together."

She snorted. "No way. Black is *not* my color, and those uniforms have no shape at all."

"So become a detective," I said. "Detective Taylor never wears a uniform."

She glanced up at me, and something flickered in her eyes before she grinned and said, "I like what I'm doin' just fine."

But that reminded me of what she'd told Raddy at the hardware store. "Since when do we have a name for our nonexistent investigation company?"

She grimaced slightly and kept looking down at her notebook. "We *have* to have a name if we're gonna be taken seriously."

"Sparkle? You think people are gonna take *that* seriously?" I shook my head. "If we were to have an investigation agency—and I'm not sayin' we are—it would *not* be named Sparkle."

"Have you got a better idea?"

"No. Because we don't have an investigation agency."

She didn't have a retort, but even a blind bat could see she was biding her time with this one.

Maybe this whole necklace thing was a mistake after all.

Anna was in the office when we got there, and thankfully she'd picked up all the files and arranged them into stacks. I was proud to see how many folders we'd accumulated already. Not every folder had yielded a job, of course, but a good half of them had.

Muffy jumped up on my legs when we walked in, and I scooped her into my arms. "How's it goin', Anna?"

Anna, who was sitting in the middle of the wood floor, looked up at us with her warm dark eyes. "She really did a number on these files."

Neely Kate cringed. "But it's not that bad," Anna said, smiling at her. "I've almost gotten everything back into order. I just need to return them to the cabinets."

"Thanks so much for doin' this," I said. "You're helping more than you know."

Anna pushed a skinny ringlet of her black hair behind her ear. "It's kind of nice to have an office job."

I tried not to show a reaction. Anna had been invaluable at the nursery while my sister was gone. Was she considering leaving us for an office job somewhere? "Have you and Bruce Wayne settled into your new house?" I asked.

She gave me a shy grin. She and Bruce Wayne had been seeing each other for four months and had recently rented a house together. They were a cute couple, and I was thrilled Bruce Wayne had found someone who appreciated him. "We're still unpacking."

"It takes a bit to get settled," Neely Kate said as she sat at her desk, not making eye contact. "You'll get it done."

I couldn't help but wonder if she was thinking about moving in with Ronnie last summer after her wedding. While she'd brought most of her clothes to my house, all of her furniture and other belongings were still at the house they'd shared.

"I better get goin'," I said, moving closer to the door. "I need to get these groceries to the house. I'll be back in time to head out to take care of our errand." It was probably best for us to keep our investigating to ourselves.

Neely Kate nodded, but she didn't look up from her computer screen.

Muffy was excited when I set her down on the passenger seat, even more so when I rolled down the windows partway so she could stick her head out.

I lived on a farm about twelve miles outside of Henryetta. It was part of my inheritance from my birth mother, whose existence I hadn't known about until last year. Most of the thousand acres to the west were rented to a nearby farmer, but the nearly century-old Victorian house, the big barn several hundred feet behind the house, the horse pen, and several acres of fields to the east were mine to use as I saw fit. Joe rented the house on the property that butted up to the south side of mine, which was sometimes reassuring, sometimes irritating.

When I pulled up in front of the house, I set Muffy on the ground, and she ran around like she'd been cooped up for days. I carried the groceries into the kitchen, then shepherded her back into the house. She headed straight for her dog bed. Maybe she was ready for something familiar after her morning with Marci.

I locked up and got back into the truck, my stomach twisting into knots as I headed toward the abandoned Sinclair gas station off of County Road 110. James never asked me to meet during the day. We always waited until dusk or later to lessen our chances of being seen together. I had to wonder what had made him break his own rule.

As usual, he was already parked behind the station, but he paced along the length of his sedan. Something else that was unlike him. His dark brown hair had grown out a bit, and he was wearing a dark gray T-shirt and jeans today, along with a pair of work boots. His upper body was toned, and his shoulders and arms stretched his shirt. I always felt safe around the criminals I'd questioned when I was with him. He turned to watch my pickup as I pulled in next to his car, his dark brown eyes filled with concern.

"Hey," I said, as I opened the door and climbed out. "Is everything okay?"

He moved closer. "Have you talked to Simmons lately?"

I froze. "I saw him this morning. Why?"

"Did he say anything about me?"

I narrowed my eyes. "You know I won't share his secrets, just like I won't share yours."

"Dammit, Rose. Is he preparing for something?" There was that worried look again.

I took a deep breath. "He thinks there's going to be a turf war between you and Wagner."

"So he knows that Wagner's involved?"

I hesitated before answering, but Joe hadn't said it was a secret. "He didn't mention his name, just that there's a threat. He's worried."

He nodded.

"What's goin' on?"

He ignored my question. "I need to ask a favor of you."

My eyes widened. "What do you want?"

"I need you to have a vision for me."

"Of who?"

"Me."

That was exactly how our partnership had started last November. He'd asked me to force a vision about his bid to become king of the underworld; I'd seen a vision of his death. In fact, I'd seen it again and again—he'd asked me to repeat it until we could figure out how to change the outcome. That whole mess hadn't been any more fun for him than it had been for me. He had to be really worried if he wanted to risk going through it again.

"What's Wagner up to?" I asked with a quaver in my voice.

He shook his head, his eyes hard. "The less you know, the better." Then he grabbed my hand and held it tight. "Tell me what you see me doing on Friday night."

I closed my eyes and tried to settle my nerves so I could focus on forcing a vision. They were easier to produce on command now that I had more practice, but they were a bit harder to initiate when I was on edge.

"Well?" he demanded.

I opened my eyes and shot him a look. "Give me a second. I'm scared to death, so it's taking its time."

Sighing, he opened my truck door and lifted me up onto the seat sideways so that my legs were hanging out the door. He took my hand again and gave me a soft smile. "Don't be scared. Knowledge is power. If you see something bad, I can change it, but only if I know what to expect."

I nodded, swallowing the lump in my throat, and then closed my eyes again. *James. Friday night. James. Friday night.* This time it worked.

I found myself deep in a gunfight in James' pool hall.

I was hiding behind the bar with Jed and the bartender. Leaning around the corner, I squeezed the trigger on the gun in my hand, aiming at a man behind an overturned high-top table.

"How many?" I shouted in James' voice.

"A good dozen—we've taken out four or five ourselves," Jed shouted over the gunshots and yelling. A bottle shattered against the wall over our heads, spraying glass and alcohol down on us. "Merv and a couple of men are circling around back, trying to corner a few."

"Any sign of Wagner?"

"No."

"You're not leaving here alive!" a man yelled from across the room.

I was leaning around the bar to take another shot when another bottle came flying across the room. This one had a burning rag sticking out of it. It smashed on a nearby pool table, and the felt burst into flames.

"*Shit.*"

"They're gonna smoke us out," Jed grunted, the cords on his neck standing out.

"Or burn us alive."

The vision ended and my eyes flew open. "They're gonna burn you alive."

James remained steady, still holding my hand and searching my face.

"Why don't you look more worried?" I asked.

The corners of his mouth twitched with a grin. "I told you. We'll figure out what he's planning and beat him to it. Now tell me what you saw."

I relayed all the information, and he remained silent for a moment before he said, "Okay." He nodded, then pushed my legs inside the truck. "I need you to watch your back. You still have that gun Deveraux gave you last winter?"

Mason had given me a gun and a concealed carry permit. He'd obviously obtained it by illegal means, but he'd been the county's assistant DA at the time. No one had really questioned him about it. "Yeah. At the farm."

"Good. Go get it. Keep it with you."

"Why? No one knows that you and I meet. There's nothing tying us together anymore."

"Some people have memories like an elephant. I'm ninety-nine percent sure you're safe, but I want you to be prepared for that unlikely one percent."

He tried to push the door closed, but I held it open. "Why's he doing this?"

"Control. Power. I have to be dead for him to take over."

"So you have to kill him or be killed?" I asked, my stomach churning again.

"That's the way I would have handled it a year ago," he said, looking into my eyes, "but I made you a promise. I'm gonna try to work it out with him first. At least give him a fair shake." He paused. "I'm not sure when I'll see you next."

"Because of this mess?" I asked quietly.

He gave me a brisk nod, then pushed my door closed and started toward his car.

"James!" I called through the open window.

He turned to face me, waiting.

"Be careful."

He grinned as he got into his car. Then, as usual, he waited for me to leave first.

When I pulled away from the parking lot, I headed back to the farm to get my gun. I watched him in the rearview mirror as he headed back into town, mulling over what he'd said about his promise. In the past, he would have simply eliminated the threat, but now he was waiting. I had to wonder if I'd put him in more danger.

Chapter Six

Neely Kate wasn't in the office when I got back. I'd sent her a text from the farm, letting her know I was heading back to town, but she hadn't responded to that either. Anna must have finished her task because the office was locked up tight, the lights had been dimmed, and there was a CLOSED sign on the door to alert any walk-ins.

Where was Neely Kate? James' concern for my well-being had stirred me up. If I was potentially in danger, then my best friend could be in trouble too. Pacing a little beside the truck, I tried her cell phone half a dozen times—my nerves ratcheting up each time she didn't answer. Should I call Joe? But before I could pull up his number, I caught sight of her emerging from Carter Hale's office across the street. Carter followed her to the doorway, and something about the way he watched my friend raised the hairs on the back of my neck. Was Neely Kate seeing her divorce attorney? Could he have been the man in that vision? While I honestly believed she was free to date, Carter Hale wasn't the type of man she needed in her life. He was good at what he did, certainly, and I even liked the man. But there was no denying he was conniving and self-centered. She needed a man who would try to make sure she didn't get hurt again.

She finally headed across the street toward the shop, and I stood beside the truck and waited. It was close to four, which meant we had time to go to the pawn shop, visit Raddy's mother, and still be home in time to start dinner.

Neely Kate lifted an eyebrow as she approached me. "You been waiting there long?"

"You didn't answer my text. When I didn't see you in the office, I was worried."

"What on earth for? I was talking to Carter about my options since he still can't track Ronnie down."

She walked around the truck and climbed into the cab. I got in next to her and started the engine.

"What did he have to say?" I asked.

"I can try to have Ronnie declared dead. Normally, I'd have to wait seven years, but we all know he was probably killed in that whole mess in February."

"Really?" I chewed on my bottom lip, wondering if I should tell her about Joe's lead. "How soon could he get that started?"

"He's not sure. He's going to do some digging to see if there's a precedent." She glanced at me. "He's worried because of Ronnie's life insurance money."

My jaw dropped. "You never told me he had life insurance."

She shrugged. "I hadn't really considered it. Ronnie's boss called me last week to see what I wanted to do. There's not much money, but I could afford to buy a new car. And maybe put a marker on a grave somewhere so I could take him flowers." Tears filled her eyes. "It seems wrong not to have a grave to visit."

I reached over and grabbed her hand, guilt washing through me. It seemed wrong not to say anything about Joe's trip, but what if it didn't go anywhere? The last thing I wanted to do was rewind her grieving process, especially since there was a pretty good chance Ronnie *was* dead. "I know."

She sniffed and pulled her hand free. "I'm fine. Let's go see what Alberto has to say."

I backed out of the parking space, and once I was headed in the direction of the pawn shop, I cast a curious glance in her direction. "Carter looked mighty intrigued with what you had to say outside his office."

She frowned. "Nothing's goin' on."

"I know that." Or so I hoped. "But that doesn't mean *he* doesn't want something to be goin' on."

She was silent for a moment. Finally, she said, "I could do worse than Carter Hale."

Her tone was noncommittal, but I couldn't resist saying, "You could do a lot better."

She just stared out the window, keeping quiet. I'd definitely have to corner Joe tonight and tell him about this latest development.

I pulled into the gravel parking lot of Rainy Day Pawn, then glanced around the nearly empty lot. "Doesn't look like they're very busy."

"I heard they've lost business since Ripper Pawn opened."

"Huh." Could Alberto have told Rayna the brooch was fake so he could make more money?

When we walked into the shop, I was surprised by the brightness of the fluorescent overhead lights. I had expected the place to look dark and seedy, but it seemed more like a cross between a miniature Kmart and the Goodwill store.

A woman stood behind the huge glass case at the front of the store, watching us as if worried we'd grab the cuckoo clock hanging on the wall and make a break for it.

I gave her a friendly smile. "Is Alberto here?"

She leaned backward, tilting her chin over her shoulder, and yelled, "Alberto! Someone to see you."

The curtains to the back parted, revealing a medium-height, average-weight guy with mousy brown hair and pale skin. He pushed his glasses up on the bridge of his nose as he walked toward us.

"Alberto?" I asked, trying to keep the surprise out of my voice. He definitely wasn't what I'd expected, especially after what the woman had said about his tattoo. But the black plastic taped to his forearm suggested he'd followed through.

"Yeah, that's me." He stopped and placed his hand on top of the case. I couldn't help thinking what a pain it had to be to have to clean that thick pane of glass every night. But then, judging by all the smudged glass, I suspected the glass was lucky to get cleaned once a week.

"Hi," I said, giving him my sweetest smile. "I'm Rose and this is Neely Kate. We're looking for a necklace." I glanced at Neely Kate, who needed no further prompting to pull out her phone and find the image she'd captured of Raddy's photograph.

His brow furrowed as he glanced down at it. "You're looking for that piece of junk?"

"Have you seen it before?" Neely Kate asked, shifting the phone so it was in front of the skeptical older woman next to Alberto.

He shook his head. "Nope."

"Me neither," the woman said.

Neely Kate held his gaze. "A little while back, a woman brought in an owl brooch. Her name was Rayna Dyer. The owl had ruby eyes."

He tried to look confused, but his fingers tapped out a rapid pattern on the glass. "You don't say . . ."

Neely Kate pulled out her notebook and pen, holding the pen so the tip hovered over the paper. "Are you saying you don't remember her?"

"Don't recall the name."

"Do you remember the brooch?" I asked.

"Hmm . . ."

"We ain't got any brooches in ages," the woman grunted with a look of disgust. "Nobody's buying brooches. Can't move 'em. If you're looking for jewelry, you should head over to Ripper. They have all kinds of gaudy jewelry like the necklace in that picture."

I studied Alberto. "So if you don't get many brooches, I would think you'd remember the one Rayna brought in."

He cringed, his head shrinking into his shoulders. "Well, I *might* remember something."

Neely Kate placed a hand on the glass and leaned closer. I was going to have to give her a generous amount of hand sanitizer when we left. "And what *might* you remember?"

"Some woman brought in an ugly-as-sin owl. It was gold, but it looked dirty. And it had red eyes."

"She says you told her it wasn't worth much. That the eyes were cut glass."

The woman gave him a look of disbelief. "When did you become a gemologist?"

His eyes widened with fear. She was clearly the one in charge, and the vibe between them suggested she might be his mother. "A what?"

The woman whacked him in the arm.

"I didn't tell her that!" he protested. "I told her we weren't buyin' jewelry and she should take it to Ripper."

"Did she?" Neely Kate asked.

He pouted and rubbed his upper arm. "How should I know? She just left."

Neely Kate wrote something in her notebook, then pulled out a copy of her business card. "If you remember anything else, be sure to give me a call."

He picked it up, took a long look at it, then scratched his head. "This says you're a landscaping specialist."

"So?" she asked in a challenge.

"What does that have to do with looking for a brooch?"

She tucked her notebook and pen into her purse. "We use gold owl brooches to scare off the bugs."

"Really?" he asked in surprise.

The woman whacked his arm again. "No, you stupid fool. She's shittin' you." She grimaced. "You never were quite right after I dropped you on your head when you were two."

My mouth gaped open in surprise, but Neely Kate was already backing up. "Thanks for your help."

As soon as Neely Kate and I climbed back into the truck, I turned to face her. "I don't believe him."

"Which part?"

"All of it?" I shook my head. "I don't know. Did you see him drumming his fingers? He was nervous."

"So which one was lyin'? Rayna or Alberto? You know . . . Rayna never said whether she sold him the brooch or not. Only that he said it was cut glass."

"True." I put the truck in reverse. "Maybe we should talk to Rayna again."

"I think we should pay a visit to Ripper."

I blinked in surprise. "Isn't it rough?"

Neely Kate snorted. "We've dealt with rough characters before."

"I don't have a hat and veil to hide behind this time."

While I'd gone into plenty of dangerous situations without my Lady-in-Black disguise, I was undeniably out of practice. Plus, I'd always had a bodyguard before, thanks to James, and both he and Jed had made it clear that I still had protection if I wanted or needed it.

"We've got Jed," I said. "We could call him to come with us."

"No Jed," she said in a short tone that caught me by surprise. Then she hastily added, "We need to do this on our own. We can't have Jed following us around like we can't take care of ourselves."

While she had a point, I had a feeling there was something she wasn't telling me. But now didn't seem like a good time to ask. "I have my gun in my purse in case we need it."

Her eyebrows shot up. "*What?* When did you start carrying your gun?"

I couldn't tell her about my visit with James, even if part of me wondered whether my silence was endangering her. But James wanted our visits to remain a secret, and I needed to respect his wishes. "I picked it up when I went home. I knew we were going to visit some pawn shops, so I thought it might be better to be on the safe side."

"Well, I have my gun too, so we're covered."

We were sitting in my truck, calmly talking about pulling guns on bad guys. This did not bode well for our visit.

Rainy Day Pawn was on the east side of town, but Ripper Pawn was in a small strip mall on the north side, just outside of the city limits, in a section that was known for being rough. A few new businesses had popped up over the last year. Besides the new pawn shop, there was a tattoo parlor and an adult "toy" store. A biker bar rounded out the offerings.

A neon sign that read *open till midnight* flashed in the window of Ripper Pawn.

I glanced at the digital clock on the dashboard. "At least we don't have to worry about them closing before we're done."

"I'm not sure we'd want to come here after dark," Neely Kate said, opening her bejeweled bag and looking inside. She pulled out her gun and checked the chambers. She carried her grandfather's old gun—the six-shooter revolver one of her cousins had used to teach her to shoot.

She flicked the barrel closed, then tucked the weapon into the back waistband of her jeans. "Better to be prepared." Her flowy top covered the bulge at the small of her back.

Neely Kate clearly had more experience with whipping out guns than I did, and the last thing we wanted to do was go in looking hostile, so I left mine in the bottom of my bag.

"We need a plan," Neely Kate said. "I think we should pretend to be customers. We can ask about the jewelry like we're shopping."

"Yeah, that sounds good."

We got out of the truck and headed into the shop. The difference between this pawn shop and the other one was like night and day. One entire wall was lined with guns, the center section of the shop was filled with stereo equipment, which might or might not have been legally obtained, and there was a long glass case at the back.

Neely Kate squealed and pointed. "Oh, lookie there, Beth Ann! I told you they'd have jewelry here!" She made a beeline for the back case.

"You were right, Nancy," I said in an exaggerated drawl. "It's a far cry from that *other* place."

"Other place?" a man asked from the back corner. He closed a padlock on a metal bar covering a row of guns. "You mean that sorry excuse of a pawn shop on the other side of town?"

We both spun around, coming face-to-face with a six-foot-something burly guy who was muscled up enough to be a body builder. He was wearing a T-shirt that looked two sizes too small from the way it stretched over his chest and biceps. His hair was long enough to cover his ears and his collar, and he sported a neatly trimmed beard.

Neely Kate quickly fell into her role. "I knew we shoulda come here first, but Beth Ann was sure that other place was more respectable."

Well, crappy doodles. She'd just thrown me under the bus. "No offense, Mr. . . . ?" I looked up at him with innocent eyes.

He stared at me for a long moment, as if trying to place me, but I was pretty sure we'd never crossed paths before. Not even back when I'd interrogated criminals as the Lady in Black.

"Wagner," he said, extending his hand with an amused grin. "Hugh Wagner. I'm the owner."

Wagner. I fought hard not to react. This had to be the man who was planning to attack James on Friday night. One of the few things James had told me about Wagner was that he worked in retail. I'd presumed that meant stolen merchandise, not an actual bricks-and-mortar store, but there were plenty of expensive, rare items filling Ripper Pawn. Maybe I hadn't been that far off.

He was waiting for me to respond, so I quickly got back on topic. "Well, Mr. Wagner," I said brightly. "I'm a firm believer in supportin' local businesses. Nancy wanted to head over to El Dorado, but I insisted we stay local. And since Rainy Day's been here longer, it seemed the most logical place to start, ya know?"

He grinned down at me like I was a toy poodle yapping around for treats. "So we're second choice then?"

"Not second choice," I said. "We're just movin' our way up the ladder to bigger and better."

He laughed out loud. "You're funny. I like you. What are you ladies lookin' for?"

"Jewelry," Neely Kate said in a gush. "Antique-lookin' stuff. With real gemstones."

I cringed inwardly when he looked us over. Even though Neely Kate had on her pink gauzy top, I was wearing a plain, light-pink T-shirt, and we both had on dirty jeans and shoes. Not to mention the fact that my hair had seen better days. We definitely weren't dressed for fancy jewelry shopping.

But he must have decided to look past our clothing. Smart man. You never knew who had money in southern Arkansas. A man who wore overalls and drove a thirty-year-old pickup truck just might be a multi-millionaire. "Jewelry, I have," he said, walking around us and leading the way to the case. "But most of it's newer. There's not much of a market for vintage jewelry. And what I get, I usually sell online."

Neely Kate gasped. "You sell it online?" She got an inquisitive look on her face and turned to me. "I hadn't thought of that."

I pretended to consider it. "If we can't find what we want here, we can try that next."

"Well, hold on there, little lady," Hugh said, lifting his hands in surrender. "Tell me what you're lookin' for. If I don't have it, I might be able to get it for ya. But why's a young thing like you lookin' for old jewelry?"

While he was misogynistic, he seemed genuinely friendly. Could this really be the man who wanted to eliminate James and take over the Fenton County criminal kingdom? In my vision, Jed hadn't set eyes on Wagner. What if someone else was planning the attack?

I needed to have a vision of Hugh Wagner. It was the only way I could know for sure.

"I'm just an old-fashioned kind of girl," Neely Kate said. "Some of my favorite memories are of wearing my grandmother's jewelry. I'm going to a fancy dinner, and I need a necklace to wear with my dress. Besides, older things have better stories." She gave him a once-over. "Do you know anything about the jewelry you got here?"

"Some of 'em," he said. When she didn't protest, he continued, "What are you looking for? Something light and dainty or something big and gaudy?"

Neely Kate snorted as though he was ridiculous. "The bigger, the better."

Wagner chuckled again. "You got something in mind?"

"I'm looking for something with real stones. My new man says that a real woman deserves to wear real jewels."

His eyes lit up. "You don't say. Your man sounds like a keeper."

She gave a half shrug as she examined the jewelry through the case. "I like to keep my options open, but I ain't gonna say no if he's offerin' to buy me jewels." She stopped and pointed to a necklace with a large center stone that looked like a ruby. "How much is that one?"

He turned all business. "Anything with stones that big is gonna cost ya."

"I don't care as long as it's what I'm looking for," she said as she began to peruse the cases. "But I'm wanting something with clear stones. Like diamonds."

"Something with diamonds that big would run in the thousands. Tens of thousands." He paused. "And I ain't got nothin' like that here. People in Henryetta don't wear things like that."

Neely Kate lifted her gaze to his, raising her chin enough to give him a snooty look. "I know, Mr. Wagner, and I'm tryin' to change that."

He chuckled again. "I suspect if anyone can, it's a cute thing like you."

Resisting the urge to make a face, I moved to the far end of the case.

"I guess it doesn't have to be diamonds," Neely Kate sighed out. "Aren't there other stones besides diamonds that are clear?"

"I'm much more likely to have something like that," Hugh Wagner said. He bent down and slid the back door of a case open. "What do you think of this?"

Neely Kate slid closer as he lifted out a necklace and draped it over his palm.

It wasn't the necklace we were looking for, but it sure was gaudy. There were several larger stones at the bottom, centered between ten smaller stones on either side. "What stone is this?" she asked.

"White topaz."

"It's kind of yellow."

"If you're looking for clear stones this large, they're gonna have a yellow cast. Unless you go with that cubic zirconia. I have some of that." He thumbed his free hand toward a case on the other side of the room. "But nothin' with a vintage look."

"Does it have a story?" she asked.

"It sure does. It belonged to a woman up in Columbia County. She's eighty-one years old and has hit on hard times and had to sell some of her jewelry."

"That's so sad," Neely Kate said, and I could tell that she was being genuine.

He shrugged. "Aww . . . she was happy. She said St. Peter wasn't gonna let her take it past the Pearly Gates, and I paid her good money for it."

Neely Kate took the necklace and held it up to the base of her throat. "Whaddaya think, Beth Ann?"

I pretended to give it serious thought. "I dunno. It doesn't seem quite right."

"You got a mirror?" Neely Kate asked.

"Sure," Wagner said, fumbling over himself to get to the small round mirror standing on the other end of the counter.

This was the man who was wanting to take over James' territory?

He brought the mirror back, and Neely Kate feigned giving it serious consideration as I continued to search the cases. I didn't hold out much hope for finding the necklace here. Raddy's missing necklace had more stones than the one Wagner had produced, and based on the dollar signs dancing in his eyes, he would have pulled it out if he'd had it.

Neely Kate was handing the necklace back when something in the case caught my eye.

"Can I see this?" I asked.

He returned the necklace to the case, then moved down to where I was standing. "Which one?"

I pointed. "The owl pin."

Neely Kate's head jerked up, and she moved closer to get a look. "Oh," she fawned. "That's darling."

He handed me the brooch, and even though I hadn't seen a photo of Raddy's piece, I was certain this was it. The gold pin was about an inch and a half tall, with etchings outlining the owl's wings and face. It had two one-eighth-karat-sized red stones for eyes.

"What's the story behind this one?" Neely Kate asked.

"Dunno," he said. "I got it from some guy at the other pawn shop, believe it or not."

I looked up at him. "You don't say? Do you do that very often? Swap things back and forth?"

"There weren't no swappin', little lady. I bought it from him."

"Are those garnets?" I asked.

"Nope. Those are genuine rubies. The real kind, not the lab-created ones."

"How do you know?" I asked.

He pulled a little lens out of his jeans pocket and held it up to his eye. "A lab-created ruby is pretty near perfect, but a natural one has flaws. See that line?" He handed me the lens and I cautiously held it up to my eye and looked down at the stone he was pointing to. Sure enough, there was a tiny line within it.

Neely Kate reached for the lens and spent a good twenty seconds looking over the stones. She handed the lens back to Wagner and asked, "How much?"

"Five hundred."

Neely Kate started laughing. "You gotta be kiddin' me."

"Why would I be kiddin' ya?"

Putting a hand on her hip, Neely Kate shook her head. "That brooch is worth a hundred tops."

I looked up at him. "Would you take a hundred fifty?"

Neely Kate shot me a look that told me I was crazy.

He grimaced. "Aww . . . I don't know . . . I can't—"

"Okay. Thanks anyway. Let's go, Nancy." Then I spun around and started for the door.

"Oh, dammit," he grumbled. "Come back, little lady. Maybe we can work something out."

I turned around to face him. "One twenty-five. Not a penny more."

"But you just said—" He groaned. "Fine. One twenty-five. I'll ring it up." He picked up the pin and headed to the end of the counter to write up a paper sales slip.

Neely Kate leaned her head toward mine. "What are you doin'?"

"You know this brooch is Raddy's," I whispered. "So why doesn't he want it back?"

"I don't know," she whispered. "Maybe he's focusing on the necklace because he knows it's worth more."

"But he specifically said the only thing missing was the necklace. Why wouldn't he ask for the owl? Does he even know it's gone?"

"He probably doesn't give a rat's petunia about any of it. He probably only wants the necklace because someone's willin' to pay him five thousand dollars for it."

I was about to say more, but Hugh ripped off the sheet, then walked back toward me. "At that discount, darlin', you're gonna have to pay me in cash."

Paying him with my debit card would have raised too many issues anyway—including the fact that my name wasn't Beth Ann. Besides, we still had four hundred dollars of Raddy's retainer left. I turned to Neely Kate.

"You're holding my money, remember, Nancy?" I looked her square in the eye, and even though I could see that she wasn't one hundred percent on board with this decision, she still reached into her purse. As she handed over the money, I wondered if I'd made the right decision. I suspected Raddy wasn't going to reimburse us, and brooches weren't exactly my style. Still, it was evidence, and it seemed important for us to collect any we found.

"You didn't see anything you liked?" Hugh asked Neely Kate.

She shook her head with a frown. "No, but would you give me a call if somethin' good comes in?" For a terrifying moment, I thought she was going to give him a business card, but she grabbed the pad of sales receipts and wrote down a phone number I didn't recognize along with the name Nancy. "I really have my heart set on a necklace with clear stones, and I'm willing to pay for it."

"I'll see what I can do," he said with a grin.

"Here's your pin," he said to me, holding out a tiny bag.

I realized I hadn't had a vision yet. However awkward it was going to be, I needed to make sure it happened before we left the store. Hugh Wagner—James' arch nemesis—was throwing me for a loop, and I needed to make sure James would survive to the weekend. I shot a quick glance to Neely Kate, then pretended to stumble as I took the bag from Hugh.

As soon as my hand met his arm, I struggled to force a vision of what Hugh would be doing on Friday night. I felt Neely Kate's hand on my shoulder just before the world around me fell away. I found myself looking at . . . well, myself. Vision Rose was sitting in the kitchen at my farmhouse with a serious look on her face. She was wearing dark clothes and checking her gun. Her mouth was moving, but I didn't hear my voice. Instead, I heard male voices that didn't fit with the scene in front of me.

"Why you gotta go stirrin' up trouble, Kip?" Hugh said, almost in a whine. "I like things just fine the way they are."

"And that's your damn problem, Hugh," a man snarled. "You never wanna grow or expand. This is a golden opportunity we don't want to miss."

"But we're makin' a killin' with this stuff."

"Just do *your* damn job," a man said in a gruff voice. "And let me do *mine*."

"But people are goin' to get hurt."

"That's the causalities of war, idiot."

I was slammed back into the pawn shop. "There's gonna be casualties of war," I gasped, the blood rushing from my head. I took a step backward as the room seemed to spin around me.

Hugh's eyes narrowed in confusion. "What are you talkin' about?"

Neely Kate laughed, but it sounded forced to my ears. "It's a book she's reading—*Causalities of War*. I think it's an old Civil War book. She's kind of obsessed with it." She snatched the bag with the brooch from his hand. "Call me if you get any more necklaces in."

"Yeah . . ." he stammered. "Sure."

Looping her arm through mine, Neely Kate turned me around and headed for the door. As she tugged me toward it, I caught sight of a man with short, dirty-blond hair leaning against the doorway to the back. He looked like a harder, rougher version of Hugh. His arms were crossed over his chest, and his dark eyes narrowed as he watched me.

I'd bet money *he* was Kip.

Kip Wagner.

Chapter Seven

*N*eely Kate dragged me out the door and pushed me into the passenger side, then climbed behind the wheel, which was a good thing since I still hadn't physically recovered from my vision.

"What made you force a vision?" she asked, snatching my purse from me and digging inside looking for the keys.

I didn't answer, my brain still addled.

Once she found them, she shoved them into the ignition, started the engine. "Rose. What happened? You're kind of freaking me out right now."

I moved my mouth and tried to answer, but only a croak came out. I took a breath and tried again. "I had a vision."

"I already figured that part out. What made you do it? What did you see?" She'd already driven far enough away from the shop that we were probably out of view.

I leaned over to check the mirror on the door. "Are they following us?"

"Why in the world would they be following us?"

"Did you see the guy in the doorway to the back?"

"Barely. I was too worried about you. You looked like you were about to faint."

"I saw him in my vision. Or more like I *heard* him."

"The guy in the doorway?"

I nodded, swallowing. My mouth was dry, my head was pounding, and I felt dangerously close to throwing up. My visions usually didn't affect me other than a momentary blackout, but the previous winter, I'd asked to see things that weren't going to happen, and my questions had plunged me into a gray abyss that had persisted until I'd asked to see something else. I'd ended up vomiting and having a massive headache. Right now, I felt five times worse.

"What did you see that freaked you out so much?" Her voice rose and I knew I'd scared the dickens out of her. "I'm guessing you had a vision for the sales guy?"

I leaned my head back, resting my hand on my protesting stomach. "And you."

She blinked and did a double take. "*I* was in the vision you had of him?"

"No. It was weird. I was trying to have a vision of him, but then you touched my shoulder. It was like I had visions of both of you, only they got mixed up."

"What happened?"

"My vision of you was of me in the kitchen in the farmhouse. I was dressed all in black and checking my gun."

"Were you saying anything?"

"My mouth was moving, but my voice didn't come out. I *heard* the vision I had of Hugh. I'm pretty sure he was talking to the guy in the doorway."

"But how can you be sure if you didn't see them?"

"I'm pretty sure the guy in the doorway is Hugh's brother, Kip." I paused and sat up, sending a spike of pain through my head. "Neely Kate, I think Kip is the one who's making a run for James' position in the Fenton County underground."

"What?"

I took a breath, wondering how much to tell her.

"But . . . how would you reach that conclusion?" Her shoulders stiffened, and then her voice became sharp and clipped. "Your mysterious afternoon. You saw Skeeter and he told you about that guy." She shot me a glare. "Is that why you got your gun? Because you knew we were going to see Skeeter's competition? Only, you kept it from me?"

"No! We didn't even know we were going to Ripper. Besides, I had no idea Wagner was connected to the pawn shop. James told me over a month ago that a man named Wagner is after his kingdom, but he refused to tell me anything about the threat. Once—after I pressed him more—he finally told me Wagner works in retail."

"The pawn shop."

"Yeah."

"So what made you decide to have a vision?"

"I was confused. I knew the guy after James is named Wagner, but Hugh seemed too nice to just barrel into the pool hall and start shooting."

"*What?* Why would you think he'd start shooting?"

I glanced at her. Time to come clean. "James asked me to meet him this afternoon so I could have a vision. He was worried Wagner's about to make a move. So I forced a vision of Friday night and saw him and Jed in the middle of a gunfight in the pool hall. Then one of the other guys threw a Molotov cocktail onto a pool table and started a fire."

"Oh my word. Was Jed—and Skeeter—okay?"

I gave her a startled look. "Yeah, he and James were fine in the vision. But there was a raging fire, and they were trapped. It wasn't looking good." I paused. "So when I heard that Hugh's last name was Wagner, I looked for what he would be doing on Friday night. I couldn't figure out why such a mild-mannered guy would shoot up James' pool hall."

"So in the vision, you were getting ready for battle," she said.

Well, crap. I hadn't even pondered that part of the vision yet, but it made sense. I wasn't about to spend Friday night re-watching *Gilmore Girls* episodes if I knew James and Jed were in danger. "Yeah, I was. But Hugh was trying to talk Kip out of doing whatever he had planned—without success."

"So you still didn't explain why you're *really* carrying a gun."

I sighed, my headache starting to fade. "James was worried. He figures it's unlikely anyone would associate me with him considerin' how much time has passed since last winter—we've been careful not to be seen together—but just in case, he wanted me to be prepared to defend myself."

"Well, dang."

"I know," I sighed. "We gave fake names, so I doubt Wagner will track me back to James."

"Yeah." She rubbed her temple. "Unless he saw the landscaping name on the side of the truck. Then he could figure out who you really are and connect you to James."

"Crappy doodles. Do you think he might have noticed?"

"No," she said firmly. "We didn't give him any reason to look. Sure, you looked a little weird when you had your vision, but if anything, he was probably happy to see you go."

I paused, thinking it through. "Do you really believe that one of Raddy's friends is gonna spring five grand for a vintage necklace?"

"No," she said. "It seems unlikely."

"But someone must want to pay him for it. Why else would he have hired us? He's already put down a five-hundred-dollar deposit. He can't be looking for that necklace just because it's a family heirloom. Raddy Dyer doesn't seem the sentimental type."

"No. He's not," she scowled.

"Do you think he's up to something?" I asked. "Is his momma involved? Rayna said she showed up asking for the jewelry."

She shot me a glance. "Maybe we can find out when we pay Mable Dyer a visit."

"You know where she lives?"

She groaned. "Please . . ."

It had been something of a crazy question—when it came to Fenton County, Neely Kate knew everything and then some. "Do you think we should talk to Rayna again?" I asked. "We paid one hundred and twenty-five dollars for the brooch. How much do you think she sold it to him for?"

She shrugged. "Ten? Twenty? It couldn't have been much if she was convinced it was cut glass."

I gave her a dubious look. "Could you really tell they were rubies? Or were you just goin' along?"

"I'm pretty sure they're real." She paused. "I think Mable Dyer should be our next stop."

Chapter Eight

*M*able's house was off County Road 110, not too far from the Sinclair station. The house was tucked in the woods, about a quarter mile off the county road. Based on the few pieces of stone in the path, the lane was supposed to be covered in gravel, but most had either been washed away or flung into the encroaching woods. I was glad my truck was four-wheel drive, but Neely Kate didn't seem to have any trouble navigating the bumpy drive. As soon as the ramshackle house came into view, a dog released a tirade of vicious barks.

"No sneaking up on 'em, huh?" I asked.

"Mable's husband is one of those off-the-grid kind of guys."

"What exactly does that mean?" We were known to have an off-the-grid militia hiding in the wooded hills, but as far as I knew, none of them ventured this close to town.

"He's just a wannabe. No electricity. No gas. They have a wood stove."

A woman appeared on the front porch with a shotgun pointed toward the sky.

"And ready to shoot intruders?" I asked.

"Apparently. Let me handle this," she said as she reached for the door handle.

"Be careful, Neely Kate," I said, pulling my phone out of my pocket. I drew up Joe's number, ready to call him as backup if necessary.

Neely Kate opened the door and leaned her head in the opening between the door and the truck. "Mable? It's Neely Kate Rivers, Minnie Sue Rivers' granddaughter. I'm here because of Raddy."

"What's that boy up to now?" Mable shouted, lowering her gun but still looking on guard.

"Nothing. Me and my friend Rose just want to ask you a few questions for him. Will you talk to us?"

"You're really Neely Kate?" the woman asked, squinting. "Last time I saw you, you were sportin' pigtails and overalls that made you look like you were ready to wade in high water."

I had a hard time picturing Neely Kate in overalls. I'd have to ask for photographic evidence later. Knowing her, she'd found a way to glam them up.

"I'm all grown up, Miss Mable," Neely Kate said cheerfully.

"Well, I guess you is." Mable turned sideways. "If you wanna come in, I ain't gonna stop you."

She disappeared into the house, which looked like it had once been white. Judging from the sporadic patches of paint, it might have been when lead paint was still in vogue.

"Do you think this is a good idea?" I asked.

Neely Kate made a face. "Mable Dyer's harmless." She left the keys in the ignition and got out of the truck before adding, "It's her husband Homer we need to worry about." Then she shut the door.

I looked down at Joe's name on my screen. He'd just tell us to leave, which wasn't the worst idea, but there was no talking Neely Kate out of it now. So I switched apps and quickly typed out a text to Jed.

We're at Mable Dyer's house off County Road 110 asking about a necklace. If I don't text you back within twenty minutes, I need you to come check on us.

No need to tell him who "we" was. He'd know. I climbed out and stuffed my phone into my pocket, hoping he got my message.

Neely Kate was headed toward the house, so I followed her to the porch, already having major regrets about suggesting this visit to Raddy's mother. The barking dog, tied to a tree, still lunged at us as we walked up to the house.

"Don't stand there all day," Mable called through the screen door from inside the darkened interior. "You're getting Zeus all riled up."

It took me a moment to let my eyes adjust to the light, but I soon realized the living room, dining room, and kitchen were all in one small square room that couldn't be more than twenty by twenty. Mable was standing in front of the sink, already peeling potatoes.

"Whaddaya want to know?" she asked, her eyes focused on the potatoes.

Neely Kate steeled her back. "Raddy says he's missing a necklace that belonged to his grandmother."

Mable stopped peeling for a second before resuming her task. "So? What business is it of yours?"

"Raddy hired Rose and me to help him find it," Neely Kate said.

Her head jerked up. "Why would he do a fool thing like that?"

"He wants it back, and he asked us to look for it."

Mable pointed her potato peeler at us. "You listen here—you stay away from our family business."

"We mean no disrespect," Neely Kate said. "We're only doin' what Raddy asked, and we wanted to ask you a few questions about the necklace."

"I ain't answering shit. That fool's got himself mixed up with some questionable characters."

"Raddy?" Neely Kate asked in disbelief.

The older woman pursed her lips. "He's started playing poker at the Trading Post. Everyone knows there's nothing but trouble up there."

I cast a glance over to Neely Kate. Great. Daniel Crocker had been the previous crime lord, and through a gigantic misunderstanding, I'd become involved in the police force's attempt to convict him. Crocker had been arrested and ultimately killed (by me) after he escaped. The former crime boss had been certifiably insane by the end— he'd tracked me down and attempted to murder me—but his men still held a grudge. Had Raddy really fallen in with that crowd?

Neely Kate sucked in her bottom lip, then asked, "Do you mind if I go to the bathroom real quick? I had a bunch of Grannie's sweet tea earlier, and it always makes me feel like a tropical storm's rollin' into my bladder."

What was she up to?

Mable's face seemed to soften at the mention of Neely Kate's grandmother.

"Grannie's still trying to get your apple crisp recipe, you know," Neely Kate teased. "If you don't mind, I'm gonna tell her that I tried to get it out of you while I was here. That'll earn me some brownie points over my cousin Dolly Parton, and I could definitely use 'em."

"Half the county wants that recipe," Mable said with a hint of pride.

"I think that half of the county went into mourning when you stopped bringing it to the annual church picnic at the Pickle Junction Christian Church," Neely Kate said.

The older woman bobbed her head as if to say, *I know.*

Neely Kate used to go to church? Regular church attendance was part of living in southern Arkansas, but according to Neely Kate, her grandmother hadn't brought her much when she was in her teens. Her grannie used to say that the Good Lord had deserted her after Neely Kate's grandfather and mother took off years ago, and she was deserting him too. So how had she known about the church picnics?

"So, can I use your restroom?" Neely Kate asked.

Mable studied her for a moment, then said, "Yeah, but don't flush the toilet. Homer says we can only flush twice a day." She grimaced. "The septic lines are clogged."

Neely Kate nodded like it was no big deal. "Thanks, Miss Mable."

Then she disappeared down the short hallway, leaving me alone with our less-than-welcoming host. And from the look on the older woman's face, she wasn't happy about it.

"So," I said, trying to find some inoffensive topic to break the tense silence, "is Raddy your only child?"

She snorted as she sent potato peels flying into a plastic bowl in the sink. "As if. He's the oldest though. I got five."

"All boys?"

"Three boys and two girls."

I couldn't imagine her raising five kids in this tiny house. They could have moved here after the kids were out of the house, but somehow I doubted it. But even more confusing was the fact that Raddy had only mentioned two siblings.

"And the girls didn't want your momma's jewelry?" I expected her to shut me down, but I figured it was worth a try.

Her upper lip curled. "They didn't want a box full of costume jewelry."

Costume jewelry? According to Rayna, Mable had believed the pieces were real all along. Or at least she'd claimed to. "But Raddy did?"

"He wanted to give it to that hussy Rayna Wilcox." She made a face. "Wanted to woo her with gemstones and gold." She turned to me and pointed her peeler at me. "I told that boy that any woman who was won over with baubles and shiny things ain't worth havin'." She shook her head as she tossed her potato into a pot and picked up another one. "But the fool didn't listen to *me*."

"I heard you went back to get it even though it wasn't real."

She lifted her shoulder into a slow shrug. "What's mine is mine. I wasn't about to let that hussy keep my momma's jewelry, even if it's not worth a Buffalo nickel."

"Did she give it all back?"

"I didn't even look. She shoved the box at me, and I left."

Woah. That didn't match either of their stories.

"So has Raddy been back lookin' for the necklace?"

"Nope," she said in a short tone. "He ain't been here for months."

None of this was making any sense.

"Do you still have the jewelry?" I asked. "Can we see it?"

"Nope. I gave it to Leah. She decided she wanted it after all."

"Your daughter?"

"Yep."

I made a mental note to talk to Leah.

I watched Mable toss another peeled potato into the pot, and felt the awkward silence return.

But Neely Kate emerged from the hall, wearing a big smile. "Thank you so much for letting me use your restroom."

Mable spun around. "You didn't flush it, did you?"

"No, ma'am."

The older woman relaxed. "Good. Homer would have a fit if he came home and found clean water in the toilet."

I tried not to shudder. Homer sounded like a keeper.

Mable took a breath and looked like she was about to say something, hesitated, then launched in. "I don't know what that fool Radcliffe's up to, but you two need to leave this alone. Leah's got all the jewelry now, and it sounds like Raddy's fixin' to stir up more family drama I don't wanna deal with."

"Yes, ma'am," Neely Kate said, a little too eagerly for my taste. "We sure will."

"And . . ." Mable looked nervous. "Whatever you do, don't tell Homer you were lookin' for anything. Or mention the jewelry at all."

Neely Kate's smile faded. "I won't—*we* won't. We'll get out of your hair now," she added, and I eagerly followed her out the door.

We were almost to the truck, having taken a wide arc to stay out of the angry dog's reach, when a beat-up black Jeep with a white front fender pulled in behind the truck and stopped.

"Well, crap," Neely Kate mumbled. "I didn't expect to see Homer. Last I heard, he was workin' the second shift at the aluminum plant up in Columbia County."

"So this is a bad thing?" I asked as my heart picked up speed.

"Let's just say it's not good. He's got a bit of a temper, so let me do the talkin'." Then she stepped in front of me. "Hello, Mr. Dyer. I haven't seen you since I was in middle school. It's me, Neely Kate Rivers."

The older man walked toward us with a hard expression in his eyes. He wore jeans, a T-shirt, and a pair of dirty work boots. Stubble covered his face and his salt-and-pepper hair looked in need of a trim. His dark, cold eyes were what scared me the most. He looked like he was capable of killing us both and tossing our bodies to the dog for dinner.

How long had we been here? Long enough for Jed to make his way here and save us if we needed help?

"What are you doin' here?" he asked in a low growl.

"We stopped by to see Miss Mable," Neely Kate said in a bright and cheery voice as though she was having a chat with Maeve. "My grannie's dying for her apple crisp recipe, and Grannie's birthday's comin' up, so I thought I'd make another effort to get it. But Miss Mable's got that recipe locked up tighter than the gold at Fort Knox."

Homer Dyer's expression said he didn't believe her story for a minute. He stopped in front of us, purposely blocking our path. "You're not welcome here. Mable let you in?"

Crap.

"No," I said, lying to protect her. "We kind of forced our way in."

"So you're trespassers?" he asked, making it sound like a trespasser was akin to a serial murderer.

"Not really," Neely Kate said. "It's not trespassin' if you're visiting an old friend."

Homer moved closer, practically chest-to-chest with Neely Kate, his face turning red. "You're no friend of my wife's."

"Okay," Neely Kate conceded, holding his gaze, his face only inches above hers. "More like acquaintances, but friendly enough to stop by and say hello. We've missed her at church."

His eyes darkened. "She don't go to church no more." From his tone, I had to wonder if that was his doing or hers.

But Neely Kate wasn't backing down. She glared at him. "Which is why we miss her. Because she hasn't been."

"You gettin' sassy with me, little girl?" Homer asked, grabbing Neely Kate's arm.

"Are you bein' an *asshole*, Homer Dyer?"

"Nobody talks to me with disrespect and gets away with it," he said, lifting his hand as if to hit her, when Jed's voice called out, "Is there a problem here, Dyer?"

Homer's grip tightened on Neely Kate's arm, and he glanced back at Jed, who was now standing beside my truck. "What the hell are you doin' here, Carlisle?"

Jed ignored the question as he took several steps forward, pointing a gun at Homer. "I suggest you get your grimy hand off her now, or you'll live the very short remainder of your life with a lot of regret."

Squatting for a brief second, Homer pulled a hunting knife from his boot, still holding Neely Kate's arm. "I wanna know what you're doin' here. Are you lookin' for it too?"

What did Homer think Jed was looking for? Did he know about the necklace?

"The only thing I'm lookin' for is these two girls, so I suggest you drop your hold on Neely Kate, or you're as good as dead."

Homer pushed Neely Kate away as though her skin burned his hand. "Get the hell off my land."

Keeping his gaze on Homer, Jed said in an icy cold voice, "Rose, Neely Kate, walk behind me, get in the truck, and wait for me."

Neely Kate put a good ten feet between her and Homer before she pulled her revolver from the back of her jeans and pointed it at Homer. "Not yet."

My mouth dropped open. What in the world was she doing?

Homer looked like he was liable to lunge at her. But she lowered the gun, and a shot rang out, kicking up the dirt between the man's feet.

He jumped back, shouting, "What the hell?"

"I purposely aimed between your feet, Mr. Dyer. The next bullet is goin' a lot higher, but it'll still be between your legs, if you get my drift. I'm not sure you need those family jewels anymore."

"You're crazy!" he shouted.

She tilted her head and forced a grin. "If that's the only way you can explain a woman gettin' the upper hand on you, so be it, but if you ever dare to lay a hand on me again, I won't hesitate to aim higher."

"Get the hell off my land!" he shouted.

"Gladly."

I glanced over at Jed. The veins on his neck stood out, and he looked like he was about to strangle someone, only I had a feeling it wasn't Homer Dyer.

I hurried over to the truck and got in; only, Jed climbed in after me and got behind the wheel, shoving me to the middle. He lowered Neely Kate's window before she got in.

"Don't take your eyes off of him," Jed growled as he started the truck. "Keep aiming at him."

"I'm not an *amateur*," she grumbled.

He drove forward about ten feet, then backed up the truck, angling and driving partially in the tall weeds to get around Homer's Jeep.

"You're a dead man the next time I see you, Carlisle!" Homer shouted, waving his knife. "And your girlfriends are on my list now too!"

Neely Kate continued to lean out the window, pointing her gun at him, as Jed tore off down the lane—still driving backward—bouncing all three of us around the cab since we hadn't had time to buckle up. Soon the house and Homer were out of sight. Jed backed up off the side of the road, quickly turned around, and raced for the stop sign.

"Where's your car?" I asked. He'd reached the county road, and we hadn't come across it yet.

"Down the road," he grunted as he looked behind him to see if Homer was following us before he turned east.

"What the hell were you doin' there?" Neely Kate shouted as she turned around to face the front.

"Protectin' you!" he yelled loud enough to make me flinch.

"How the hell did you even know we were there?" she demanded.

"Rose texted me. She told me to come check on y'all if she didn't get back to me in twenty minutes."

Neely Kate turned her wrath on me. "You did what?"

I shrugged. "When you said we'd be fine so long as Homer didn't show up, I got worried."

"Right before we went in?"

"Yeah."

"That was fifteen minutes ago," Neely Kate said, her ire returning. "What hell were you doin' there five minutes early, Jed?"

"I already told you!" he shouted, the veins on his neck now throbbing. "I was there to protect you!"

"We don't need your protection! I'm pretty dang sure I just proved that!" Neely Kate shouted as Jed pulled over on the side of the road. His car was parked ahead of us, pulled into a short drive that led to a field.

He threw the gearshift into park and turned to look at her, his face red. "He had a knife, Neely Kate. You could be lying on the ground back there bleeding to death, and your damn twenty minutes still wouldn't be up yet!"

"In case you didn't notice, I have a gun, Jed Carlisle!"

"Then where the hell was it when I walked up, Neely Kate? He had his hands on you. He could have pulled his knife out and stabbed you at any moment!"

"I was about to pull it out when you showed up and played the hero!"

Jed wasn't backing down. "If you pulled out that gun while he was holding you, he would have wrestled it out of your hand and likely shot you in the process!"

I sat between the two of them, my back pressed against the seat in an impossible attempt to get out of the way.

"And then," he continued, still shouting, "I had the damn situation under control, and you pulled out your gun and shot at him. *What the hell was that?*"

"*I don't answer to you, Jed Carlisle!*"

Jed took a breath and ran his hand over his head. "What in God's name were you two doing talking to Homer Dyer?"

"We weren't there to talk to him," Neely Kate said. "We wanted to see Mable. I thought Homer would be working his shift at the aluminum factory."

"Dyer lost his job two months ago after he took a swing at his boss." He seemed to have calmed down a bit now that the danger was behind us. "He was an angry guy before, but now he's a ticking time bomb. There's a very real chance he would have hurt you, Neely Kate."

"How the hell was I supposed to know?" she demanded.

Jed took several seconds before he said, "You still didn't tell me what you were doing there."

"I had no idea we were supposed to run everything we do past *you*," she said in a snotty tone.

What in the world was going on? Neely Kate was usually happy to have Jed as backup. He'd saved my life on more than one occasion, and I was sure he'd saved hers too.

I let out a long sigh and leaned between them. "Okay, enough of this nonsense. I'm not sure why you two are at each other's throats, but it's not helping anything." I glanced at Neely Kate. "I asked Jed to come, and I'm glad he did. Jed's right. That man was dangerous."

"I could have handled it, Rose," Neely Kate protested. "We'll never be taken seriously if we keep calling Jed for backup."

Jed released a loud groan. "I *still* don't know what you were doing there."

"We were asking Mable questions," I said, turning to face Jed. "Raddy Dyer asked us to find a necklace he'd given to his wife—I mean his fake wife. She says she turned all the family jewelry he gave her over to his mother, but according to him, one of the necklaces was missing. Raddy claims it's made with white sapphires, but Rayna thinks all the jewelry's fake, and his momma just told me the same thing."

"So he's been hoodwinked?" Jed asked.

"I don't think so," I said. "She had an owl brooch with red stones for the eyes. Rayna took it to the pawn shop. The clerk told her it was fake, but—"

His eyes widened. "*Which* pawn shop?"

Oh crap. I didn't want James to know I'd been anywhere near Kip Wagner. "Rainy Day Pawn."

Some of the tension left his shoulders.

"But we also—" Neely Kate started to protest, and I elbowed her in the ribs.

"We found the pin, and it has real rubies for the eyes."

Jed looked skeptical. "Who told you that? The same clerk who told her they were fake?"

"No," Neely Kate said in a huff. "I know a thing or two about gemstones."

"So you think that means the necklace is real too."

"I don't know what to think," I said. "Mable says the jewelry's worthless. According to her, she didn't even notice the necklace was missing before she gave the whole stash to her daughter."

"She lied," Neely Kate said. "I saw several pieces Raddy told us about in Mable's bedroom."

"What?" I asked, twisting at the waist to face her.

"I don't think they were all there," Neely Kate said. "But a good portion of them were in a box in the top drawer of Mable's dresser." She pulled out her phone and showed me a photo after she tapped on the screen. "Look."

I took the phone and scrolled through the half-dozen photos of jewelry in an underwear drawer.

"Did she sell the missing necklace?" I asked. "We didn't see it at the pawn shop."

"I don't know," Neely Kate said. "None of their stories are matching up."

Jed put his hand on the steering wheel. "Why would you agree to look for a necklace for Raddy Dyer?" Then he sighed and shook his head. "He's paying you. You're playing private eye."

Our silence gave him all the answer he needed.

"Raddy's up to something," Jed continued. "And it's bound to bite you both in the ass in the end."

I suspected he was right. Especially if he was mixed up with some of Crocker's guys.

I sat back in the seat and rubbed my forehead. "We need to rethink everything, but first I need to go home and make Tuscan Chicken."

"Rose," Neely Kate protested.

"No," I said. "We weren't gonna do anymore tonight anyway, so let's let it sit until tomorrow and make a decision then."

Neely Kate grumbled but didn't offer any further protest.

Jed's voice lowered. "You two need to stay away from Homer Dyer."

"Oh, for goodness' sake," Neely Kate exploded. "We have no reason to talk to Homer Dyer again. We're not goin' anywhere near there."

Jed opened the door and climbed out without a word. It occurred to me that I'd never seen him talk so much in one sitting. What in Sam Hill was going on?

I slid out after him and shut the door behind me. "Jed."

He was already almost to his car door, but he turned around to face me.

"Are you okay?"

"Why wouldn't I be okay?" he asked. His face had returned to its usual unreadable mask.

"You and Neely Kate . . ."

He sucked in a breath and looked away, then glanced at the front end of the truck before finally returning his gaze to me. "She was in more danger than she's willing to admit, and I'd hold myself responsible if something happened to her—to either of you—when I could have prevented it. Next time you go someplace like that, would you please give me more notice?"

"We can't expect you to keep playin' babysitter for us, Jed."

His face softened and he took a step closer. "You know I'll always be here for you, Rose."

When James had assigned Jed the task of watching over me last winter, he'd taken the job both more seriously and more personally than I'd expected. "I know, but just because I know you'll be there when I need you doesn't mean I want to abuse the privilege."

A soft grin spread across his face. "And *that's* why I'm more than willing to help you—because you *don't* expect or demand it." He looked down into my face. "If you're going to continue to look into this, I want to be more directly involved."

"I think we're gonna let this one go," I said. "But thanks for the offer."

"In any case, keep an eye out for Homer Dyer. He's usually a lot of talk, but it's not a bad idea to watch your back."

"Thanks."

He nodded and then got into his car and drove off, leaving me to wonder why he was really so upset with Neely Kate.

I didn't believe his story for a second.

"What was that about?" Neely Kate asked when I got back into the truck.

"I was thanking Jed for helping us."

"I can't believe you called him," she said, messing with the glove compartment latch to avoid looking at me. "I could have handled it."

I just shook my head as I pulled back onto the road. She was sulking. "I don't want to talk about it right now, especially since Joe's coming over in an hour. He'd flip his lid if he knew about any of this."

"I know that, Rose," she grumbled. "I'm not gonna say anything."

We were silent for a few moments before I said, "What was going on between you and Jed back there?"

"What are you talking about?"

"That argument. The way you both jumped all over each other. Has he done something I don't know about?" Although I couldn't see how. I'd been with her every time she'd seen him, and they'd always been good-humored with each other.

But she just crossed her arms and looked out the window, making it clear she wasn't ready to volunteer more information.

Chapter Nine

A couple hours later, Joe, Neely Kate, and I sat at the dining room table in my farmhouse while Muffy lay at Joe's feet.

He pushed his empty plate toward the center of the table. "Between you and Maeve, I'm going to have to increase my workouts."

"It wasn't that good," I said with a laugh. I wasn't being modest. I'd been distracted from the recipe by thoughts of Homer Dyer, how Neely Kate would react once she found out Ronnie might still be alive, and that danged necklace. Plus, Jonah had called while I was mixing the bread crumb topping for the chicken to tell me that Mr. Henderson had chewed out both him and the two guys planting the bushes for making a muddy mess. By the time I hung up, I couldn't remember if I'd added both teaspoons of basil. It tasted like I'd missed a few other spices too.

Joe shot me a grin. "It was better than what I'd make myself."

I gave him a pointed look. That was an outright lie. Joe was a better cook than me, and all three of us knew it. I'd seen plenty of firsthand evidence of that back when we were dating.

Neely Kate was being quieter than usual, and judging from the worried glances he kept shooting me, Joe had picked up on it. I was desperate to pull him aside so we could talk about Ronnie, but I wasn't sure how to do it without setting her off.

"I made dessert," I said. "Strawberry cake. Would you like some?"

Joe laughed. "When did you ever know me to turn down dessert?"

I stood. "I'll clean off some of these dirty dishes and bring it out with me."

Joe rose, his chair scooting across the wood floor. "I'll help. Moving around might help me make room for *two* pieces."

When Neely Kate started to get up, I said, "Neely Kate, do you think you could let Muffy out? But stay out with her if you don't mind. She tried to chase a raccoon into the fields last night." When she hesitated, I said with a grin, "Or you can clean off the table, and I'll take her out."

She snorted. "Like that's a choice. Come on, Muff. Let's go outside."

Muffy was already giving us her full attention, watching us pick up plates from the table in the hopes we'd drop something, but she jumped to her feet at the sound of her name and ran toward the door when she heard the word "outside."

Joe and I headed through the swinging door to the kitchen, balancing our load of plates, silverware, and serving bowls. When the door closed, I lowered my voice. "When are you going to New Orleans?"

"First thing in the morning, but I still think it's best not to say anything to Neely Kate until I get back."

I turned on the faucet in hopes of drowning out our voices. I wouldn't put it past Neely Kate to try spying on us. "I think you should tell her."

A stubborn look filled his eyes. "No. I don't want to tell her until I know it's true."

I leaned closer. "Joe, you don't understand. She's trying to get Carter Hale to declare Ronnie dead so she can collect his insurance money. The policy's about to run out, but Ronnie's old boss has agreed to pay the premium another month."

His eyes widened. "How much is the policy for?"

"I honestly have no idea, but she wants to use the money to buy herself a decent car as well as put a headstone somewhere. So she can pay her respects."

"Dammit." He glanced down as he rinsed a plate in the sink and set it on the counter.

"You have to tell her."

"No." He turned his face close to mine and lowered his voice. "This will only take a day or two, tops. I have to be back by Friday afternoon for my evening shift, and that will be enough time to know if my source was accurate or not. If he's alive, I'll have the divorce papers signed; if not, she'll be none the wiser."

I pursed my lips together as I weighed my options. Did I tell her anyway? "Where'd you get a copy of her divorce papers?"

He gave me a look that told me I'd asked the most ridiculous question in the world.

"How's she been acting with you?" he asked. "Because with me, she hasn't been herself for the last week or so."

"I know," I said grudgingly. "She's been that way with me too." I wasn't about to tell him that she'd laid into Jed right after she'd whipped out her gun and shot the ground between Homer Dyer's feet. Besides, that wasn't the only thing that had felt off. She usually talked a mile a minute, but she'd been quieter lately. More withdrawn.

"She's already upset about going through the motions to declare her husband dead. I refuse to tell her he might still be alive until I have hard proof." He paused. "I won't hurt her for no reason."

"She's going to be angry with you," I said. "When she finds out that you kept this from her, she's going to be furious."

"Maybe when she first finds out, but not when she takes a good look at the situation. She'll understand I'm only trying to protect her."

"I think you're delusional," I said, shaking my head. "But I'll keep it to myself for now."

Relief filled his eyes. Maybe because we'd been on the precipice of an argument and we hadn't tumbled over. "What did Skeeter Malcolm say when you talked to him?" he asked, focusing on rinsing off another plate.

"Who said I talked to James?" I asked as I pulled three dessert plates from the cabinet.

He gave me a dubious look.

"Who I talk to is no longer your concern, Joe Simmons."

He pulled back his shoulders, seeming to grow a few inches taller before my eyes. "I never said it was. I just wanted to know—" His words cut off when his cell phone started to ring. He groaned and pulled it out of his jeans pocket.

Whatever he saw on the screen made him frown. "Simmons," he barked into the receiver.

I set the plates on the counter and studied him. From his expression, it was obvious whatever the person on the other end was telling him was serious.

Joe rubbed his forehead and said, "I'll be there in twenty minutes."

"What happened?" I asked as he stuffed his phone back into his pocket.

"Rayna Dyer is dead."

I gasped and took a step back, my butt hitting the counter. "*What?*"

"You knew her?" he asked. Then his eyes narrowed. "You were asking about her husband this morning. Did you go see her?"

I saw no reason to lie. Not if it could help Joe figure out what had happened to her. "Yeah," I said, feeling a little lightheaded. "We talked to Rayna just this morning."

"What'd you talk to her about?"

"Raddy had some jewelry that belonged to his grandmother. Rayna hung onto it after she kicked him out, but then she gave most of it back to Raddy's mother. There was a necklace missing, and Raddy wanted it back. He asked Neely Kate and me to help him."

Neely Kate moved through the kitchen doorway. "Raddy thought I could talk to Rayna and get it back for him."

Joe's expression darkened as he turned his attention to his sister. "After I told you to stay away from Radcliffe Dyer?"

Neely Kate put a hand on her hip. "Talking to Rayna Dyer isn't the same as talking to Raddy."

"Well, you're done talking to anyone that has anything to do with either Dyer right now, because Rayna Dyer was just found dead in her hot tub."

"What?" Neely Kate asked breathlessly. "Somebody killed her?"

Joe shot her a grim look. "We don't know what happened yet, other than that Rayna's friend showed up at her house and found her dead in her hot tub. I'm heading over there now to meet the county coroner."

Rayna had been in her hot tub in my vision. I put my hand on my chest in an effort to calm my racing heart.

He pointed his finger toward Neely Kate and then swung it toward me. "But you two need to stay as far from this as possible. Got it?"

"Yeah," we both said in unison.

He pushed out a breath and dropped his hand to his side. Now that he had our assurances, his tone was softer. "Is there anything else I should know?"

Neely Kate started telling him all the conflicting information we'd collected about Raddy's family jewels.

Joe's phone rang again, and he held up his hand. "Stop right there." He answered it in his cop voice. "Simmons." He rubbed his temple, then sighed. "Just hold him off. I'll be right there." He hung up and shook his head. "Unbelievable. The press has already shown up."

"Henryetta has press?" I asked in surprise. I wouldn't exactly call *The Henryetta Gazette* a press. They published a paper once a week, but their biggest news was usually the Friday night bowling league scores—or it would be if the scores weren't a week old by the time the paper went to press on Friday mornings.

Joe's forehead wrinkled with irritation. "Some kid's started an online news channel on YouTube. He tries to stir up trouble where there's none to be found, but somehow Barry figured out there's a real situation unfolding. He's camping out on Rayna Dyer's front yard. I need to head over there to make sure his camera is nowhere near that hot tub." He headed for the front door, but his hand lingered on the doorknob for a moment. "Neely Kate, before I forget, I wanted to let you know that I have to leave town tomorrow, but I should be back by late afternoon Friday. If you need me for anything, you can still call me."

Her eyes widened. "You're leaving town?"

"Yeah," he said. "Some business with my father's accounts."

"Can you still go now that Rayna's been murdered?" she asked.

"Now, we don't know what happened to Rayna, so there's no reason to start throwing out the word murder. Deputy Miller said she was floating in the water along with an empty bottle of wine. For all we know, she got drunk enough to pass out and drowned." He pointed his finger at us again. "But that's official information, and I don't want it gettin' out. Especially to that pain in the ass, Barry Whitlow. Got it?"

"Yeah," we said in unison again.

"Besides, I don't need to be around for every violent crime investigation. There were a few suspicious deaths while I was gone this spring, and they were handled just fine. I'll make sure things are taken care of before I leave."

"Is your trip about Kate?" Neely Kate asked, her eyes full of worry.

Joe gave her a soft smile. "No. Nothing to do with Kate. Just some legal paperwork is all. Nothing to worry about, okay?"

She nodded.

He walked over to her and kissed her cheek. "This means I'll have to take a raincheck on the cake. You two stay out of trouble." Then he was out the door.

"Do you believe him?" Neely Kate asked as she stood in the front doorway and watched him drive away.

"About his trip?" I asked, trying hard not to act guilty. "Why wouldn't I?"

She turned to look at me. "Because I've been getting letters from Kate."

"*What?*" I asked in shock. "What does Joe say about that?"

A frown tugged at her lips. "I haven't told him. But I wonder if he's been getting them too."

She hadn't told *me* about the letters, and I wasn't sure what to think of that either. "How many have you gotten? When did they start? What has she said?"

"Only a few, and they started a couple of weeks ago," she said, shutting the front door and locking it. "They're mostly to taunt me about my mother."

"Why didn't you tell me?" I asked. Given the way Kate Simmons liked to mess with people's heads, I was sure she was currently toying with my best friend.

She shrugged and went into the kitchen. When I followed her, she gave me an exasperated look. "Maybe this is why—because I knew you'd make a big deal about it."

"It *is* a big deal, Neely Kate. Your half-sister's in a mental institution for messing with people's lives. How is she even sending these things?" I asked, getting more and more riled up. "I would think they'd do a better job of monitoring her outgoing mail." I pushed out a breath of frustration. "We need to contact the hospital and put a stop to this."

"No!" she said in a panic. "We can't."

"Why on earth not?" I asked in dismay as I stepped closer.

"Because," she said with tears in her eyes, "what if she's about to tell me something important and I prevent her from doin' just that?"

I wrapped my arms around her and pulled her close. "Oh, Neely Kate. Surely you can see that she's messing with you. It's what she does. Remember the way she confirmed that you're her and Joe's half-sister? She'd *never* give you information without taking a pound of flesh."

Neely Kate leaned her forehead on my shoulder and began to cry while I rubbed soothing circles on her back.

"When Joe comes back on Friday, you need to tell him," I said.

"I can't."

I leaned back and held her teary gaze. "You can and you *will*."

"She says if I tell him about the letters, she'll *never* tell me what else Momma said to her," she hiccupped.

What a mess. Kate Simmons was a manipulative bitch who got off on hurting other people. There was little chance she'd tell Neely Kate anything, but Kate knew she had my best friend on her line with the hook sunk deep.

I leaned back and soothed Neely Kate's hair from her damp cheeks. "Okay, we'll do it your way for now, but how about I read the letters first from now on? And if there's nothing helpful, I'll won't show them to you."

Panic filled her eyes. "No."

"Neely Kate. Has she given you *anything* yet? Anything new to prove she's going to tell you what you want to know?"

"No, but . . ."

"Then let me screen them for you."

"*No.*"

"Why not?" When I could see she wasn't going to budge, I decided to compromise. "Okay. I understand, but you don't have to do this alone. Show me the letters, and I'll help you figure out what she's really up to."

She shook her head. "No. There's nothing in there you need to know about."

The way she said it made me realize she was hiding something. "She's put in something in there you don't want me to see."

"Things I'm ashamed of. Things from my past."

I studied her face, trying to decide whether to press the issue. Neely Kate had told me that she'd left town for two years sometime after her high school graduation. She'd alluded to having some regrets about those years, but I had no earthly idea what she'd done, and it was pretty obvious she wasn't going to tell me now. "Okay." I smoothed her hair again. "But you know there's nothing in those letters that is going to make me change my mind about you, right?"

The fear in her eyes suggested she was unconvinced.

I gave her a warm smile. "How about you go up and take a nice warm bath in my claw-foot tub? I'll clean up the kitchen."

She looked torn. "I can't leave you down here with this mess."

"Of course you can. I've left you with more than a few messes on those Tuesday nights I spent away from home."

"I can't believe Rayna's dead," she said, wiping her eyes with the back of her hand. "Who do you think killed her?"

"We don't know that she *was* murdered."

"Do you believe she wasn't?" Neely Kate asked.

"No." I searched her eyes. "Do you think Raddy did it?"

"No. He's not the murdering kind."

"Are you sure?" I asked, moving over to the sink. "From what his momma said, he might be mixed up with Crocker's guys . . ." My voice trailed off when I saw the disappointment in her eyes. She knew if Crocker's men were involved, I would call the investigation off. "We'll talk about this tomorrow when we have more details. You go take your bath before I change my mind and make you help scrub that skillet."

"I told you to use the nonstick spray," she said in a slightly sassy tone.

"Yeah, well, if you keep saying I told you so, I'll make you clean it all by yourself."

She lifted her hands in surrender and grinned as she took a step toward the door. "You win."

I beamed in my momentary triumph.

Placing her hand on the door frame, she turned serious. "I don't know what I'd do without you, Rose." That fear was back in her eyes, and it broke my heart.

"If you think you can get rid of me, you've got another think comin'," I said.

"Other people said they'd stay too," she said. Tears flooded her eyes.

I swallowed the lump in my throat. We'd both had more than our fair share of people leave us. "Well, it's a good thing we're not like other people then." I turned back to the sink and turned on the hot water. "Now go, or I really *will* make you wash these dishes."

"I love you, Rose."

I took a breath and turned to face her, but she was already gone.

I opened another beer—my second of the night—and spent the next ten minutes washing dishes and wishing I'd used that five hundred dollars from Raddy Dyer to buy a dishwasher. My farmhouse hadn't been lived in for nearly twenty-five years by the time I moved in, although my Uncle Earl had kept it up with yearly cleanings and occasional servicing for the appliances. The house and land had been in the family since at least the turn of the twentieth century. I wasn't sure who exactly had owned it before my birth mother and her grandparents. But one thing was certain: no one had bothered to install a dishwasher.

Muffy danced around my feet, and I glanced down at her as I put the last serving bowl in the cabinet. "You want to go outside again, girl? I guess Neely Kate didn't give you enough time out there." I grabbed the dishtowel and dried off my hands, then tossed it onto the counter. "Okay, let's go."

I opened the back door, and she took off like a lightning bolt toward the barn. My gut clenched. She didn't usually head in that direction.

My purse was sitting on the kitchen table, and I pulled out the gun and turned off the safety. I was sure I was being ridiculous—I suspected there was a poor raccoon hiding out in the barn, just like the story I'd told Neely Kate. Part of me wondered if I should call Joe, but he was busy with poor Rayna Dyer, and what was I going to say? That Muffy had run off to the barn? It wasn't exactly 911 material, but my gut told me something wasn't right. I wasn't about to let Muffy run into danger without trying to protect her. She'd protected me more times than I could count.

I considered asking Neely Kate to come, but the sound of the water in the pipes overhead came on, which meant her bathwater had gotten cold and she was warming it up.

Muffy was already in the barn when I walked out the back door. Part of me wanted to call out her name, but if there was someone in my barn, I didn't want them to know I was on my way in. I needed all the help I could get—and that meant preserving the element of surprise.

Still, I didn't waste any time making my way to the barn. After a rainy spring, a piece of rotten wood had broken off at the bottom of the double door in the front, which was how Muffy had gotten in. She was small enough to wedge herself through the hole, which was about a foot in diameter. I was creeping around the side of the barn, making my way to the back door, when I heard the low sounds of two men's voices.

My heart leapt into my throat, and I reached into my pocket to pull out my phone and call the sheriff's office. Only, I hadn't brought my phone. I must have left it in the kitchen.

I stood next to the barn, my heart racing as I struggled over what to do. Then Muffy released a low growl, and one of men barked, "Be quiet." There was a male grunt, and my little dog let out a squeal and began to whimper.

There was no question now. I was going in.

Chapter Ten

I edged around the back corner of the barn and noticed that the back door was standing open. Muffy let out a yelp, and then I heard several loud grunts. Part of me wanted to just run in there and save my dog, but I needed to try to be safe about this. Before last February, I would have gone in without giving it a second thought, but I'd become more cautious. I'd seen people murdered in front of me. I'd lost Mason. The night of J.R. Simmons' death had changed me, but standing there now, I wasn't sure it had been for the better. I felt more like the woman I'd been a year ago instead of the fierce woman I'd become last winter.

Pushing those thoughts out of my mind, I placed my back against the wall. I kept my elbows pinned to my sides as I held the gun with both hands and pointed it toward the sky. I was still working out a strategy, but Muffy's crying sent a spike of anger through my body, burning off any residual fear.

I leaned around the open doorway, pointing my gun into the space that was only slightly illuminated by a kerosene lantern. Two men were in a heap, or rather one man was in a heap, and the other was delivering a sharp blow to the man's side with his boot. The man who was standing had his back to me. I cast a quick glance toward the corner and saw Muffy hunkered down on the floor, whimpering.

"Both of you stop right there and lift your hands into the air before I shoot you," I called out in a loud voice, holding my gun on them.

The man who was standing slowly lifted his hands and started to turn as the other guy continued to cover his head with his hands and release pained whimpers.

"Rose," the standing man said as he turned toward me. I recognized his voice, his shape, *him* before he showed his face. "Don't shoot."

"James?" I gasped, lowering the gun to point at the man on the ground. "What are you doing out here?"

Anger flashed in his eyes. "Taking care of this trash."

The man on the ground dropped his hands and started to push himself up to sitting. "Don't shoot! Rose, it's me! Raddy!"

"*Raddy?*"

"Can you put the gun away?" he begged.

"Not until you tell me what you're doin' here."

"Lookin' for you. I'm in trouble, and I need your help. Yours and Neely Kate's."

I shook my head in confusion, my gun still trained on Raddy. "James, what's goin' on?"

"I found this piece of shit in your barn."

"I told you!" Raddy said to James. "I was waiting until the coast was clear to go talk to them. The deputy sheriff was here, and I had to wait until he left."

"You were hiding in my barn?" I asked Raddy in disbelief.

"No." He shook his head frantically. "Well . . . I guess so, yes. But I didn't plan on hurtin' you like Malcolm thinks. I only wanted to talk to you."

I was still shocked that James was here. As far as I knew, he'd only been to my farm once—and that was months ago, after we'd teamed up to bring down J.R. Simmons. I kept trying to get him to come over to my house for one of our Tuesday night meetings, but he always refused, saying he didn't want anyone knowing we were friends. Yet now he was standing in my barn and beating the sense out of Raddy Dyer. That couldn't be a coincidence. None of it could be.

"You were beating him up?" I asked.

James met my dark look with a scowl of his own. "Before you start judgin'," he said in a tight voice, "I never laid a hand on him."

I lifted an eyebrow in challenge.

He lifted his hands from his sides. "I didn't say I didn't hurt him. But I only kicked him after he kicked your dog."

"*You did what?*" I demanded, still holding the gun on Raddy.

"She was gonna bite me!"

"Bullshit," James growled. "You owe her dog an apology."

"*What?*" Raddy shouted in disbelief.

"Did I stutter?" James snarled. "Tell her dog you're sorry for hurting her."

"I ain't apologizing to no damn dog."

That ticked me off even more. "Her *name* is Muffy."

Muffy heard her name and crawled toward me. Fear shot through me; Muffy never crawled. I squatted down next to her and gently placed my hand on her back, then slid it down to her side. She let out a soft whimper when I pressed my finger on her back hip.

Now I was good and pissed.

"Why are you here, Raddy Dyer?" I demanded as I stood, pointing my gun at him again. "What was so important that you had to sneak around in my barn?"

"It's Rayna," he said, climbing to his feet. "She's dead."

That was like a bucket of cold water on my anger. I lowered my gun and turned on the safety. I didn't trust Raddy, but I knew James wouldn't let him get away with anything. Still, I wasn't about to put the gun away. "I know. Joe got called in to help with the investigation. That's why he left."

"They're gonna pin this on me," he said, pressing his hand to his side where James had kicked him. "They're gonna say I did it."

"Did you?" I asked in a firm voice.

His eyes flew wide. "No! Why would I kill her? I'd already left. We were through."

"Maybe she had your necklace," I said. "Maybe you thought you could make her tell you where it was."

"No!" he insisted, sounding desperate. "That's not what happened."

James stiffened. "Then why don't you tell us what *did* happen, Dyer." His tone left no doubt that it was a demand and not a request.

"My momma called and told me that you and Neely Kate stopped by to see her," Raddy said to me. "Homer was fit to be tied."

"Wait," I said. "You call your father by his first name?"

"He ain't no father of mine," he said in disgust. "He's my stepdaddy, but my momma saddled me with his name. If I was gonna kill anyone, I woulda killed that mean bastard years ago."

I'd barely spoken to the man, but I couldn't disagree with Raddy's sentiment.

"Why'd you have to go by there?" Raddy asked in a whine. "I didn't know you were gonna talk to my momma. I thought you'd butter up Rayna and get the damned thing back from her."

Raddy had paid us a five-hundred-dollar down payment just to talk to his ex? That didn't make sense at all. Especially if he'd planned on paying us the rest of the money, though I suspected the worst.

"We talked to your momma because you gave us next to nothing to go on," I said, my anger heating up again. "And I suspect just about everything you told us was a lie. So we had no choice but to ask her questions."

He shot me a glare. Something clicked.

"You went to see Rayna again after you talked to your momma, didn't you?" I asked. "What happened when you got there?"

He licked his lower lip and cast a nervous glance at James. "I knew she was home because her car was in the driveway and a light was on in the window. But she wasn't answering the door. Then I heard a Marvin Gay record through the open window. She only played Marvin when she was wanting to fool around." He scratched his head. "I wanted to find out who she was entertaining."

My eyebrows shot up. "Rayna had a boyfriend? Why do you care? You're the one who dumped her."

He pointed a finger at me and protested, "Now that's not true! She kicked me out."

"After you cheated on her," I said, shaking my head. But it was a moot point, and I knew it. "So you realized she had a man with her and then what?"

"I beat on the door, insisting she open up. When she still didn't answer, I thought about busting it down, but I suspected it wasn't as easy as they show on TV. Besides, the lock on the back door doesn't work, so I figured I'd go through the back door and sneak up on her."

"Again," I said, "why did you care? You were done with her."

"I don't know," he said, tears filling his eyes as he rubbed the heel of his hand on his chest. "I guess I didn't realize I wanted her until I thought someone else did."

I squelched a few of the disparaging insults that popped up in my head. "So what happened next?" I asked, although I was pretty sure I already knew.

"I went around the corner, and I saw her in the hot tub. She was lying back with her head on the corner, but her body was floating all weird." He looked at me, and I nodded for him to go on. "So I called out her name . . ." He sucked in a breath. "But she didn't answer, so I walked over to her. It was then I realized her eyes were open, and she wasn't moving." His voice broke. "I knew she was dead."

"Did you kill her?" I asked again in a cold voice.

"No!" he shouted. "I heard a noise in the house, and when I went inside to check it out, a guy ran out the front door. He took off around the corner, and I heard a car drive away."

"Do you know who it was?"

He shook his head emphatically. "No. But he was in the bedroom. The drawers were ripped out, and they'd all been overturned. I think he was looking for the necklace. You have to help me, Rose."

I put my free hand on my hip, still holding the gun at my side. "And why on earth would I do that after you hurt my dog?"

"I didn't mean to."

"I'm calling bullcrap, Raddy Dyer."

"Okay! Okay! I was scared. Malcolm was towering over me, and she was growling, and I felt trapped. I was trying to run out of the barn, but she was in the way."

I wasn't so sure I believed that, but James wasn't volunteering any information. I shot a look at him, surprised he hadn't jumped into the interrogation, but he wore a perfect poker face. I had absolutely no idea what he was thinking.

"Raddy, listen to me," I said. "You have to tell me who knows about the necklace."

"I already told you. My friend Buck was the one who wanted to buy it."

"And how do you know Buck?" I asked. "From your poker game?"

He squirmed. "Yeah."

"What did you do? Bring it with you to a game?"

"No, but I told him about it. He believed me when I told him it was real."

Suddenly, his ridiculous story about some guy offering to pay him five thousand dollars for the necklace, sight unseen, made sense. Raddy had hired us because he was desperate. "You bet this necklace in a poker game, sight unseen, am I right?"

He swallowed and nodded. "Yeah."

"And you lost . . . to Buck."

He didn't answer.

"And Buck gave you until Friday night to pay up . . . or else." When he didn't respond, I asked, "Is the necklace even real? Your momma claims it's fake."

"I don't know."

I almost told him what we'd discovered about the owl pin but decided to keep it to myself for the moment. "So if Buck was still waiting for the necklace, why would someone else swoop in and try to get it?"

James shifted his weight. "Because Dyer shot off his big mouth, and everyone at the game thinks the necklace is real. They want it for themselves."

Raddy looked up at me with pleading eyes. "You gotta help me, Rose. The police are gonna think I killed Rayna, but I didn't do it. And if they don't arrest me, Buck's gonna kill me too."

I released a groan of exasperation. "I have no idea what you expect me to do, Raddy."

"Help me hide. Find the necklace."

I shook my head. "Your momma collected all the jewelry and said you haven't been by her house in months. How'd you even know it was missing?"

"I snuck into her house to look for it. After she got all the family jewelry from Rayna, she wouldn't give it back to me. She said she was gonna give it to my sister." His eyes filled with desperation. "You have to help me, Rose!"

"I don't have to do a cotton-pickin' thing for you."

His eyes turned cold as his back stiffened. "I paid you five hundred dollars. If you're not gonna find the necklace, I want the money back."

"And we told you that the money was nonrefundable."

"But the agreement was that you would *look*. You talked to my momma—did you talk to my Aunt Tildie?"

"No, but—"

"Then you owe me!" he shouted. "You're supposed to be lookin'!"

Dammit, he had a point, but this seemed like a matter for the sheriff's department now. "Lookin' for the necklace aside, I'm not hiding you. You bein' wanted for Rayna's murder is your problem, not mine."

"But—"

"No," I said firmly. "As for the necklace, I have to talk to Neely Kate. I'll let you know tomorrow what we decide to do. I'm sure Neely Kate has your number."

"I don't know if you should call it," Raddy said. "What if the police are usin' it to track me?"

"Then get a dammed burner," James barked. "She's not makin' a decision tonight, and if you keep badgering her, she's going to tell you no. Got it?"

Raddy jumped. "Yeah," he mumbled, sounding none too happy about it.

"Now get your ass out of here before I call the dammed sheriff myself," James said, pointing toward the open back door.

Raddy's only answer was to try and make a beeline for the door. But James grabbed him by the back of the collar and pulled him to a halt. "I think you're forgetting something, Dyer."

"What?" Raddy's voice shook.

"You owe a couple of apologies. One to Muffy and the other to Rose for ruining her evening."

Raddy looked like he was ready to protest, but James' hold on his collar tightened, and then he gave him a good shake.

"Okay!" Raddy shouted, then lowered his voice. "Muffy, I'm sorry I kicked you." Then his gaze lifted to mine. "Rose, I'm sorry to disturb your evening, but I hope you'll keep look—"

"Since I obviously didn't make myself clear enough," James said in a tone that would have scared the pee out of me if I were Raddy, "she's not deciding tonight, and the time for pleadin' your case is over."

James planted the sole of his boot on Raddy's backside, giving him a push as he released his collar. Raddy stumbled out the door.

James stopped in the doorway and glanced back at me. "I'm going to make sure this piece of trash really leaves your property. Then I'll be back to help you make sure Muffy's okay. Don't move her."

My jaw dropped, but not because of what he'd said about making sure Raddy left. What did James know about animals?

But I dropped to my knees beside her, worried that she was still flat on her belly. "Are you okay, Muff? Did that mean man hurt you?"

She looked up at me with sad eyes, then licked my hand.

I set my gun down on the dirt floor and felt down her sides with both hands this time. The only time she flinched was when I pressed on her back hip. She climbed slowly to her feet and stood in front of me.

"She's standing," James said from behind me. "That's bound to be a good thing. She's stopped whimpering, too."

He squatted to the ground in front of me, Muffy between us.

"How do you know about dogs?" I asked.

He shot me a wry grin. "I was raised on land, so I learned a thing or two, although I confess it's been quite a few years."

"Where's your car?" I asked. "I didn't see it out front, and I definitely didn't see one for Raddy."

A smirk crossed his face. "You think I'm stupid enough to park my car next to Chief Deputy Simmons in front of your house? And as for Dyer, he apparently has more sense than I would have given him credit for." He glanced up. "I parked on the other end of your farm by the fields . . . next to Dyer."

He slowly put his hands on Muffy and started palpating her sides. "Dyer got a couple of kicks in, but only one really connected."

"She flinched when I pressed on her right back hip."

James pressed on her hip, and she yelped and snapped at him.

"Muffy!" I admonished, but James looked up at me.

"She's fine." Then he moved to her belly, taking his time feeling around. When he was done, he gave me a soft smile. "I don't think she has any internal injuries, but watch her back leg. If she doesn't put weight on it tomorrow, you might want to take her to the vet."

"Thanks," I said in amazement. Never in a million years would I have expected Skeeter Malcolm—the king of the Fenton County underworld—to squat down next to my dog and give her an examination.

He gave a half shrug and got to his feet, reaching a hand down to help me up. I wrapped my fingers around his.

He pulled me up, bringing my chest close to his, but he didn't let go once I was standing.

"Do you need money?" he asked quietly, searching my face. He was a different man than the one who'd been raging against Raddy Dyer mere minutes ago. I knew this was a rare gift. Few people saw him this way. Hardly anyone knew James Malcolm could be a gentle man.

"No," I said, staring into his soft brown eyes.

"Then why are you working for Radcliffe Dyer?"

"It's a long story."

"I've got time."

There was a slight edge to his voice this time. Something twisted in my stomach, catching me off guard. He was still holding my hand, and I knew I should break free, but part of me didn't want to. Why?

"I'm doin' it for Neely Kate," I said, still watching his face as I forced myself to pull my hand free and take a step backward.

He watched me with an intensity that sent a jolt through my gut, and I took another step back.

"Why would Neely Kate be workin' for Dyer?" he asked.

"She's got it in her head that we should be private investigators. So I indulge her from time to time. Remember when we looked for that missing garden gnome?"

He closed the distance between us, and I backed up again.

"Looking for a garden gnome and working for Radcliffe Dyer are two totally different ballgames."

"Too bad I didn't know that this morning," I said as I took another step back, feeling warm even though it had cooled off outside.

James continued his pursuit. "Why were you talkin' to *Homer* Dyer?" he asked in a low voice.

"Is that why you're here?" I asked, hating that I sounded breathless. Why was I so nervous? "I told Jed we weren't there to see Homer. We wanted to talk to Mable. I had no idea he was trouble." Another step and now my back was against the barn wall.

"But Neely Kate knew." He stopped in front of me, his chest mere inches from mine. My legs felt rubbery, and I struggled to catch my breath as anticipation raced through my blood. What was wrong with me? Then it hit me.

Oh, no.

He planted a hand on the wall next to my shoulder. "You're supposed to call Jed when you think you're going to be in danger."

"I already told you that I had no idea we were heading into trouble. As soon as I felt uncomfortable with the situation, I sent him a text." I felt claustrophobic with him so close. I warred with the opposite urges to push him away and pull him even closer. But I had to use my head and pretend this was no big deal.

"Do you have any idea what Homer Dyer is capable of?" he said, his low, husky voice sending a shiver down my spine.

"No," I pushed out, dropping my gaze and starting to panic at my reaction to him. When had this happened?

Placing his hand on the wall on my other side, he leaned down so his mouth was next to my ear. "We've been watching him for two months now, ever since he lost his job. He's a stupid man with a hot head, a dangerous combination. He's angry at the world, Rose, and he's lashing out at anyone he thinks is out to get him."

"I didn't know," I whispered, a new shiver washing over me as his warm breath tickled my neck.

"I know. And that's what scares the shit out of me." He suddenly grabbed my arms and pulled me hard to his chest. "Now try to get away from me."

I looked up at him and blinked, thinking I must have heard him wrong. "What?"

"Get away from me."

I still stared at him in confusion.

"If you're going to throw yourself into these dangerous situations, I'm going to make damned sure you know how to get out of them. Now break out of my hold."

I dropped my gaze in horror. Here I was, fighting lustful feelings for James Malcolm, and all he was trying to do was teach me to protect myself. "I don't want to hurt you," I finally said, still looking down.

"You're not going to hurt me," he chuckled, and his chest vibrated against mine, sending another wave of lust through me.

I had to get away from him before I did something stupid. "Last warning," I said.

"Give it your best shot."

My first instinct was to knee him in the groin, but I couldn't bring myself to hurt him like that, so I jerked backward and swung my arms wide and then down, loosening his hold enough that I managed to pull loose and run for the door. He was on me again in seconds, wrapping an arm around my waist and hauling my back to his chest.

"Where do you think you're going?" he asked, his voice low in my ear.

"I'm escaping. Isn't that the purpose of your exercise?" I asked, proud of myself for not betraying my wounded pride but eager to get away from him before I made a fool of myself.

"That was good, but not good enough," he said, his breath blowing my hair against my neck.

My breath came in short pants. Why was this happening? I couldn't start something with him. Our friendship was important to me, and changing it to something else would risk ruining it. Not to mention he was on the wrong side of the law. Could I really date a criminal? Because no matter how ethical he seemed to be, James Malcolm *was* a criminal. Besides, even if I ignored that not-so-minor fact, Skeeter Malcolm didn't have girlfriends . . .

But did *James* Malcolm?

His hold on me tightened, but it felt different this time. His free hand rested on my hip and slowly slid up my waist. "You're supposed to break free," he said in a voice gruffer than before.

I closed my eyes, warring with myself. How had this happened? *When* had this happened? I knew I should slip away, try to escape, but I couldn't bring myself to do it.

His grip around my waist loosened, and his hand slid up over my T-shirt, stopping underneath my breast. I tensed but didn't stop him.

"What are you doing, Lady?" he asked in a husky tone. "Why aren't you fighting me?"

Lady. The name fit me more than I cared to admit. The Lady in Black had been both civilized and wild, rule-abiding and lawless. I'd never felt more myself than when I was the Lady. And that scared me. What scared me even more was that James Malcolm was the only one who'd ever understood that.

His breath hit the sensitive part of my neck, and I sucked in a breath of surprise, my body igniting. I became boneless, melting into him as his arms held me up.

"When you charged into this barn with your gun trained on me, you scared me shitless."

"I was careful," I said in short pants. "I never would have shot you."

"I know," he grunted, then spun me around to face him, his hand snaking around the small of my back to hold me in place. "I was proud because you knew how to handle yourself. But I was scared of what might happen if you tried that with someone more dangerous than me."

"Is there *anyone* more dangerous than you, James Malcolm?" I half-teased.

His eyes were filled with lust, and I waited for his lips to cover mine. But then something shifted in his eyes. His hold around my back tightened, and he grabbed a handful of my hair, tilting my head back until our eyes met. "You're supposed to be getting away."

I couldn't answer.

He slowly shook his head, an evil grin spreading across his face. "You had it right when you said I was dangerous. You have *no* idea."

"I don't believe you."

His face lowered over mine. I was sure he was going to kiss me, but then he abruptly dropped his hold and took two steps back. "You failed."

I gaped at him in shock. "What?"

His back straightened. "It was a lesson in defending yourself, and you failed."

"Have you lost your mind?" I demanded.

"No, but *you* clearly have." He walked over to where Muffy still lay beside my gun. She got to her feet, but he ignored her and grabbed the gun. Standing, he held it out to me, butt first. "When you broke free the first time, you should have given me a blow to slow me down. A head butt to my nose or your knee to my groin."

Shame and embarrassment washed over me, more effective than any cold shower could have been. I took the gun and checked the safety before shoving it down the back of my jeans.

"What about what just happened?" I asked. "You're telling me that groping me was part of the exercise?"

"It was a lesson on not becoming distracted."

I clenched my hands into fists at my sides. "You think some random man is going to grope me, and I'm *just going to let him?*" I asked in furious disbelief.

The determination in his eyes wavered.

"You think you're so big and bad, Skeeter Malcolm!" I shouted. "But you're just as scared as I am!" As I started out of the barn, Muffy jumped to her feet and raced ahead of me.

Thank goodness.

"Rose!" James called after me, following me around the corner of the barn.

I ignored him, but he quickly caught up and grabbed my left wrist. A vision burst into my head. I was ripping a woman's shirt over her head, then fumbling with the button on her jeans, but everything was fuzzy, and I lacked the coordination to get it undone.

The girl giggled. "Let me get it for you, Skeeter." I felt her hand on my thigh, sliding higher. "You're drunk."

I jerked myself out of the vision. "You're gonna go sleep with someone else."

"What?" he asked in confusion; then his eyes filled with understanding. "You just had a vision."

Pain and humiliation sucked my breath away. He'd turned me away, and now he was going to run off and sleep with someone.

Without hesitation, I repeated my arm swing move, breaking free of his grip as I simultaneously pulled my gun out with my right hand. I took a step backward, aiming my gun at his chest.

His eyes darkened. "If you're gonna pull a gun on someone, you better be damned well prepared to use it."

"*Bang*," I said, tilting the gun forward a fraction of an inch, then raising it level again. "I just shot you in your heart. Oh, I forgot. You don't have one." Then I spun around and stomped toward the house.

"I'm not running after you!" he shouted. "I don't run after women!"

"Good!" I shouted back, not turning around to face him. "Because I might have to turn off the damn safety next time!"

I heard him let out a string of curses, his voice getting farther away with each long stride I took.

Muffy was waiting for me at the door. I let us both inside, but not before I looked back at the barn. I was furious with myself for being disappointed when I didn't see him.

Then I groaned—I'd forgotten the lantern.

Before I could stalk out there to grab it, I heard a buzzing sound. My phone was vibrating on the kitchen counter.

Anger burned through my veins as I read the text from SM.

I blew out your lantern so your barn doesn't burn down.

That was it. No I'm sorry. No admonishment to be careful. Just that he'd snuffed out my freaking lantern.

Tears stung my eyes. How could I be so stupid?

Had I just ruined everything?

I turned off the kitchen and living room lights and headed upstairs, picking up Muffy when I realized she was limping.

When I reached the top of the stairs, Neely Kate was standing in the doorway of her bedroom in a bathrobe and wet hair.

"Did I hear shouting just now?" she asked. At least her sadness seemed to have given way to genuine curiosity.

"You missed an eventful evening," I said. "I found Raddy Dyer in our barn."

"*What?*"

I gave her a quick run through of what had transpired, leaving out James' *lesson* at the end.

She looked down at my arms. "Is Muffy okay?"

"James thinks so."

"What was Skeeter doing here?" she asked, sounding suspicious.

"I think he wanted to check on us because Jed told him about our run-in with Homer Dyer. James says he's dangerous."

"Jed already told us that." Putting her hands on her hips, she gave me a skeptical look. "I bet Skeeter's after the necklace too."

That caught me by surprise. "What? Why would James want that necklace? For all we know, it's fake."

She shrugged. "Just the fact that some people think it's real makes it a big deal."

Her theory about James wanting the necklace didn't hold weight, yet part of me had to wonder if there was some truth to it. James hadn't just come over—he'd been in my *barn*. *Why?* He'd mentioned parking next to Raddy's car. Had he followed Raddy in there? Or had he gone in on his own?

I shook my head. "I don't know what to think anymore. We should wash our hands of the whole mess."

"But—" Neely Kate started to protest.

"I'm too tired to make any decisions right now. I just want to go to bed."

Something in my voice must have told her I'd reached my limit because her expression softened. "Okay. We'll talk after we've both had a good night's sleep."

I nodded, then went to my room and shut the door. While I stood in my bathroom mirror getting ready for bed, I gave my body and my face a long, hard appraisal. I wasn't skinny, but I wasn't overweight, and all the landscaping work I'd been doing lately had toned my muscles. My long, wavy brown hair was capable of looking good when I wore it down—although I wore it in a ponytail most of the time. I knew I could look pretty, but I'd rarely worn makeup since Mason had left. There were many women who were prettier than me, and I couldn't help but wonder if the woman James was going to sleep with fell into that category. I hadn't seen her face; typical man that he was, his gaze had gone straight to her chest. There was no doubt her breasts were plenty bigger than mine.

Tears stung my eyes, and I splashed my face with warm water. *Enough.* I wasn't going to cry over that man. He'd told me exactly who he was. He'd never made any secret of it. Why had I thought I'd be different? Did I really think I could change him?

Some part of me knew my parting accusation held merit. He was *scared*—hell, I was scared too—but at least I'd been brave enough to take a chance.

James Malcolm was an unworthy coward.

So why did his rejection hurt so much?

Chapter Eleven

*T*he sun woke me up the next morning. I rolled over in bed to face the side where Mason used to sleep. After he first left, I used to wake up every morning, put my hand on his empty space, and cry. But after a few weeks, I would just put my hand there and let the melancholy wash over me. Then I'd get out of bed and move on with my day. But I hadn't thought of him in the morning for several weeks. Did that mean I was over him?

Then the memory of how I'd acted with James the night before returned, flooding me with humiliation. What would Mason think of me throwing myself at Skeeter Malcolm? But a new irritation took root—Mason no longer had any say in what I did. Maybe I was looking at last night through the wrong lens. Up until now, I hadn't felt tempted by any men since the breakup. Regardless of how it had turned out, I was going to consider it hard-earned progress.

Of course, that didn't make me any better equipped for the dilemma of how to handle things with James. I didn't want to lose his friendship—something I'd thought of and then promptly forgotten right before I made a fool of myself. Maybe I could claim temporary insanity. Or I could claim I was drunk even though I hadn't even had two full beers.

Muffy was still curled up at the foot of the bed when I got up to get ready for the day. I didn't have any manual labor jobs today, so after I took my shower, I decided to spend more time on my hair and put on a little makeup. The forecast claimed it would be sunny and in the eighties, so I decided to take a gamble on a cute summer dress. I'd bring a sweater in case it got chilly in the office.

But as I swiped on a coat of mascara, it occurred to me that I'd let the night's upset distract me from what had happened to Rayna. I probably knew some facts about her death that might be useful to the sheriff's department. Raddy could have lied about what he'd seen, but what if it was all true?

I grabbed my phone and texted Joe, asking him if he'd left town yet. He called me back within seconds.

"I'm heading to El Dorado to talk to our family attorney before I head down to New Orleans. Is everything okay?" he asked.

If I told him that Raddy Dyer had been hiding out in my barn, I knew he'd turn back. And while I suspected Homer was dangerous, I was quite certain Neely Kate and I could handle his stepson. "Of course," I said. "I was just calling to ask what you've found out about poor Rayna Dyer."

"Do you want the public story or the inside scoop?"

"You'd really tell me the inside scoop?" I asked in disbelief.

"No," he said with a laugh. "I wanted to see if you'd ask."

"Well, what *can* you tell me?"

"Rayna Dyer was found dead in her hot tub."

"Come on, Joe. Really? That's it?"

"That's the official story. The cause of death is unknown."

"I know she was murdered. Do you think Raddy Dyer did it?"

"How . . ." His sudden silence was nerve-racking. "You've talked to Radcliffe Dyer."

"He reached out to *me*, Joe, and I encouraged him to go to the police with his story. But I doubt he will, so it occurred to me that I might know a few things that could help with the investigation."

"What did he tell you?"

If I told him what I really knew, he'd change his mind about finding Ronnie. "Not much. But the fact that he came to see me—"

"*He came to see you?*" he barked in my ear. "I thought he'd made a call!"

"Joe, calm down. I sent him away." When he didn't say anything, I continued, "I thought it might be helpful for me to talk to the person who's investigatin' the case, is all."

He hesitated. "Maybe I should come back."

"*No*. If Ronnie's living in New Orleans, then you need to find him and get those papers signed. Just tell me who's in charge of the investigation."

He was silent for a moment.

"Joe," I said. "I promise. If I thought we were in danger, I'd tell you. I'm only trying to help out if I can. So will you tell me?"

He pushed out a breath. "I have a feeling I'll regret not coming back. Do you promise Raddy didn't threaten you?"

"I promise. He asked for our help, but I sent him packing."

He was silent for several seconds. "Deputy Miller's helping with the investigation. Go to him with what you know. He'll be more understanding of your involvement."

"Thanks," I said, not hiding my relief.

Deputy Randy Miller was one of the few deputies I trusted. He'd helped me on several occasions, and we'd become friends. But I'd been staying out of trouble for the last few months, and I'd only seen him in passing since February. Knowing that I'd be dealing with Deputy Miller made me feel a whole lot better.

"You're not planning on doing something crazy like tryin' to investigate this murder yourself, are you?" Joe asked.

"My murder investigation days are over," I said. Then a wave of guilt hit me, making me dangerously close to tears. "I talked to Rayna yesterday morning, Joe. She was alive and now she's not. I . . . I need to help if I can."

Joe was quiet for a moment. "Okay, but call me straightaway if Dyer threatens you."

"I will," I said. "I hope you find Ronnie."

"Me too."

I hung up and realized Muffy was still lying on the bed. Gently rubbing her head, I asked, "What's going on, girl? Decided to sleep in today?"

She looked up at me with sad eyes, and I slid my hand down her back and under her belly. No reaction until I pressed on her back hip, which made her yelp.

"I'm sorry, Muff," I said, picking her up and setting her on the floor to see what she would do. She made tentative steps toward the door before picking up the pace, but I noticed she barely put weight on her back leg.

When she reached the top of the staircase, she stopped and looked back at me, so I picked her up and carried her downstairs. She made her way to the kitchen, still limping, and stopped again at the back door.

"You look pretty today," Neely Kate said from in front of the open refrigerator door. "What's the occasion?"

"Nothing," I said, feeling my face start to flush. "I just decided to look nice for a change."

"Huh."

Muffy just looked up at me when I opened the door, so I picked her up again and carried her to the lawn. I crossed my arms as I watched her limp around. When she tried to balance to go to the bathroom, she fell on her butt. I rushed over to help her back on her feet.

"Is she okay?" Neely Kate asked, joining me in the doorway. "She's limping."

"I don't know. James said she seemed okay, but he's not a vet. Besides, he told me I still might need to take her to one."

Neely Kate nodded. "I'm going to make the appointment right now."

I let Muffy wander around for another minute, then carried her inside and set her down in front of her water bowl and food dish. While she drank, she ignored her food.

Neely Kate walked into the kitchen from the living room, stuffing her phone into her front pocket. "It's a good thing you're ready because they have an opening in twenty minutes."

I looked up at her in surprise. "That means I have to leave right *now.*"

She picked up my purse and handed it to me. "I'll drive my car into town. You just take Muffy and go."

I took my bag from her, then gasped. She seemed strangely eager, and that could only mean . . . "Oh no. Who did you make the appointment with?"

"The *vet.*" She gave me a push toward the door. "Now go."

"Dr. Romano?"

She gave me a wry grin. "Well, he *did* replace Dr. Ritchie."

"I have to go upstairs and change!"

"What? *Why?*"

"I dressed up today," I said, waving a hand down my front. "I fixed my hair and even put on makeup."

"So . . . ?" Then she squealed. "Oh! You *do* like him!"

"No! But . . ."

"He likes *you*," she finished for me.

I flushed. "It's not that. I've looked terrible the only two times I've seen him. He's going to think I dressed up for him."

"So what?" she said, her eyes sparkling. "It's not a crime. In fact, I'm sure he'd appreciate it."

"But I'm not . . . ready."

Her gaze held mine. "Are you sure you're not just scared?"

"I don't know." I hadn't been scared last night when I'd tried to get James to take our relationship to the next level, but it would be pretty loose of me to try to catch the eye of another man twelve hours later.

But that hadn't stopped James from going off to sleep with someone else.

Besides, it didn't matter how I felt about James. Starting something with him was a terrible, *terrible* idea. He might have developed a conscience, but he still condoned and ordered illegal activities.

Dr. Levi Romano was cute and interested, and didn't seem like the type of guy to have ties to criminal dealings—a definite plus. But was I interested in *him*?

Neely Kate moved a few steps closer, still holding my gaze. "I'm not saying you have to go out with him. Just don't say no because you're scared, okay?"

I sucked in a deep breath. "Yeah. Okay." Then headed for the front door.

I was on the front porch when Neely Kate laughed and called out, "Uh, Rose . . . I think you're forgetting something."

When I turned back, she was holding Muffy and wearing an ear-to-ear grin. "I'm half tempted to go with you. This should be good."

I felt my cheeks pinken as I lifted Muffy out of her arms. "I hope I don't make a fool of myself."

Neely Kate's grin softened. "Just be yourself."

I gave her a pointed look. "That's what I'm afraid of."

I stewed for a good ten minutes of the drive before I looked down at Muffy, who was lying on the seat with her head in my lap. The sight was enough to make me realize my priorities were totally screwed up. I was going to Henryetta Animal Clinic because Muffy was hurt, not because I was looking for a date.

By the time I'd pulled into the parking lot, I'd convinced myself that I was about to see Dr. Romano in a professional setting. Nothing more would happen.

When I walked into the office with Muffy in my arms, the receptionist looked up from her desk and heaved an exasperated sigh. Her light brunette hair looked just as crazy as it had on my last visit—when Neely Kate and I had come in after finding that stray baby pig.

"Honey," she said with an exaggerated sigh. "I hope your dog's really hurt, because I'm tired of fitting in all these emergency appointments. This ain't a matchmaking service."

The last thing I wanted to do was react, but I felt my cheeks burning again. "Why would I make an appointment if Muffy wasn't hurt?"

She rolled her eyes. "You're single, aren't you? Shoot, some of the women in town are buying pets just to have an excuse to see Dr. Romano. Besides, you were covered in mud the last time you were here, and now you're all spiffed up."

I gasped in outrage. "Are you suggesting that I made an appointment—"

"Mary," Dr. Romano said behind me in a good-natured tone. "Leave Rose alone."

Mary looked ticked. "Dr. Romano—"

But he ignored her and motioned to the hall behind him. "Rose, why don't you bring your dog on back."

I walked into the exam room he was pointing to—the first door on the left—and he followed me inside and shut the door.

"Who do we have here?" he asked, letting Muffy sniff the top of his hand.

"This is my dog, Muffy," I said, then shook my head, feeling like an idiot. "But then I guess you can tell she's a dog."

He grinned and his blue eyes twinkled. It was easy to see why so many women had suddenly become pet owners. "And I didn't even need those four years of veterinary school to figure it out."

Heat bloomed in my cheeks.

"So what seems to be the trouble with Muffy?"

"Her back hip hurts, and she's not putting much weight on it."

"Has she had this problem before?"

"No," I said. For a moment, I struggled with what I should tell him, but if he was going to help Muffy, he needed to know the truth. "Someone kicked her last night. Twice."

His lightheartedness instantly vanished. "Someone kicked your dog?"

"I didn't condone it," I said with more defensiveness than I'd intended. "And the man who kicked her was dealt with."

"Put her on the floor and let me watch her walk."

I did as he instructed, feeling unsettled at his change in attitude. I set Muffy down, but she huddled next to my leg and refused to move.

Dr. Romano stuck his hand into his pocket and pulled something out before he squatted down in front of her. She sniffed the small treat in his hand and then gingerly took it from him.

"Is she usually shy around strangers?" he asked, still watching her as he scooted back several feet and held out another treat.

"No, but she seems to sense when someone's a threat."

He grinned up at me. "So she sees me as a threat?"

"No. She'd be growling if she did."

He nodded. "Does she usually take treats?"

"Yes, she eats anything and everything." I paused. "But she also . . . passes gas. A lot of it."

The corners of his mouth twitched with the hint of a grin. "Well, let's deal with first things first. Has she eaten since she was kicked?"

I cringed. "No, but it happened late in the evening. She seemed okay—she even ran off to the house—so I took her to bed."

"She sleeps with you?"

I nodded.

"Did she cry in the middle of the night or make any sounds of distress? Was she restless?"

"She didn't make a peep, but she was still sleeping on my bed after I got up and showered. When I set her down on the floor, she didn't put much weight on her leg. And she refused to go down the stairs. Once we realized she was in pain, Neely Kate made this appointment for me."

"And she didn't eat this morning?"

"No, there wasn't time," I said, sounding guilty.

That earned another warm smile. "I'm not judging your pet ownership. I'm just trying to determine when she last ate."

"Last night. About seven, I think."

He put the treat on the floor, and Muffy stood motionless.

"I'd really like to see her walk," he said as he stood. "Let's try something else." He walked over to the door and opened it. "Go out into the hall and see if she'll walk to you."

I did as he instructed, then squatted down and held my hands out to her. "Come here, Muff."

She made a beeline toward me with a skip-hop. When she reached me, she tried to put her front paws on my knees, but her back leg wouldn't support her. Her whimpers made my eyes sting.

"Don't worry," Dr. Romano said as he reached down and picked her up. "We'll get her fixed up."

"What do you think's wrong with her?"

"I suspect she's bruised," he said, cradling Muffy to his chest, "but let me palpate the area. Then I'd like to take an x-ray just to make sure nothing's broken."

I nodded. "Okay."

"Rose."

I stared up into his warm eyes.

"Don't look so worried. She's going to be fine."

"I should have called last night."

"If she wasn't in obvious distress last night, I would have told you to wait until the morning." He set her down on the exam table. "Can you hold her up while I examine her?"

I nodded and slipped my hand under her chest by her front legs. He spent several minutes feeling every part of her front legs, her back, her tummy, and her back hips, leaving the right side for last. She flinched and looked back at him with a low growl.

"I'm so sorry," I said, horrified. "She usually never growls unless there's danger."

"It's normal," he said, rubbing behind her ear. "She's in pain. I suspect that's why she wasn't overly interested in the treats. It could be because she's *here*—many dogs get nervous in our office—but if she's a good eater, it's probably because of her pain."

"Can you give her something for it?"

"Let me take her x-rays; then I'll make a diagnosis and we'll figure out how to treat her."

"Okay."

"Hopefully we'll be back in a few minutes." He picked her up and carried her through a door at the back of the room, leaving me alone in the small exam room.

I had just sat down on a metal chair when my phone rang. I pulled it out of my purse and checked the caller ID.

It wasn't a number I recognized, but I answered anyway. "Hello?"

"Rose, this is Deputy Randy Miller. Joe said you were going to call me with some information about Rayna Dyer."

Of course he had.

"I'm free now," he continued, "so I wondered if I could come by your office to talk to you."

"You could if I were there. I'm at the vet with Muffy."

"Is she okay?" he asked with a worried tone. He was one of the few people who appreciated my little dog almost as much as I did.

"Dr. Romano thinks she'll be okay. He's taking x-rays now."

"What happened?"

Seeing no point in keeping it to myself, I said, "Raddy Dyer kicked her last night."

"*What?* Does Chief Deputy Simmons know Dyer was at your place?"

"He knows Raddy showed up, but not the part about him kicking Muffy. And I don't plan on telling him, or he might come back early from his trip."

"Why didn't you call the sheriff's department last night?"

"Because he left, and I doubt he'll be coming back. Not after the send-off I gave him." No need to bring James' name into it. "But he told me a few things I think you should know."

"You mean that a man ran out of Rayna's house and drove away?"

"Yeah," I answered in surprise. "How'd you find out? Did you arrest Raddy?"

"No. He called it in. Said he saw a man running out after ransacking her room, but none of the neighbors remember seeing another car *or* a man, while several of them sure remembered Raddy and the ruckus he made."

"So Raddy's a suspect?"

"Who said it was murder?"

"Come on, Randy. If she got drunk and drowned in her hot tub, why would you be so interested in her husband's whereabouts?"

"Someone ripped her room apart, Rose. A crime was still committed. Do you know anything *else* that might help?"

"Raddy told me she was dead when he got there. And yeah, he claimed there was someone in the house. He thinks the guy was looking for one of Raddy's grandma's necklaces. Rayna had a bunch of his family jewelry when they broke up, and while she swears she gave everything back to Raddy's mother, Raddy claims one necklace is missing. Yesterday morning he asked Neely Kate and me to find it because he'd used it as a bet in a poker game."

"How much is the necklace worth?"

"That's the thing—I don't know for sure. Raddy told us it's real, but his mother and Rayna both claimed otherwise. But Rayna pawned one of the pieces, and it *was* real. Honestly, I don't know. But the guy Raddy made the bet with believes it's real, and he expects Raddy to pay up. It sounded like the other guys in the poker group think it's real too."

"Thanks, Rose," he said. "This *is* helpful."

"So what are you gonna do?" I asked.

"Re-question the neighbors. And try to find Raddy. He's not in the clear, but if he's not the killer, we'll be interested in what he knows."

"So she *was* murdered. How?"

"Dammit." He groaned. "She was strangled."

I was glad I was sitting down because I suddenly felt lightheaded. Strongly suspecting that she'd been murdered and hearing how it had happened were two different things. I couldn't stop thinking about the fact that Neely Kate and I had talked to her less than twenty-four hours ago. "I hope you find whoever did this," I said.

"We've been trying, Rose, and now we have a credible reason to widen our search. But if Radcliffe Dyer contacts you, you need to encourage him to cooperate so we can find the real perpetrator." He paused. "You know, even if we don't arrest him for murder, we can arrest him for animal cruelty."

"I think he got the ever-loving crap scared out of him last night. I doubt he'll be kicking another dog for a long while." Then, before he could ask questions, I continued, "I hope you find the *real* murderer."

"Let me know if you think of anything else."

"Okay." I looked up and saw Dr. Romano standing in the open doorway with Muffy in his arms. The distressed look in his eyes told me he'd overheard part of our conversation. "I have to go." I hung up and dropped my phone into my purse.

"*Murderer?*"

I lifted my shoulders in a lazy shrug, then stood. "Just talking about a TV show. How's Muffy?"

He gave me a look that suggested he didn't believe me but thankfully didn't ask more questions. "Just as I suspected, no broken bones. There's quite a bit of swelling, which fits with deep tissue damage. I'll send you home with a non-steroid anti-inflammatory, and you'll need to keep her in a crate for a few days to force her to let it rest. I suspect her romp last night after she was injured made matters worse. Do you have a crate?"

I couldn't hide my surprise. "No. I've never needed one before."

"I have one you can borrow."

"I'm sure I can get one."

He gave me that big grin again, the one that made his eyes twinkle. "It will give me an opportunity to see you again."

I wasn't sure how to answer that—or even how I wanted to answer. Obviously I sucked at this whole flirting thing.

"Do you have someone to watch Muffy?" he asked as he handed her to me.

I stared at him in confusion. "I usually bring Muffy to the office with me."

"What about tonight? Can Neely Kate watch her?"

"Yeah, but I don't have plans for tonight."

He shifted his weight. "I know this is unprofessional, and I'm sorry if it's awkward—I'll understand if you turn me down—but I can't seem to help myself." He grimaced, then plunged on. "Would you go out to dinner with me tonight? I'm about to go on call for five days, which means we'd have to wait until next week otherwise, and I find myself uncharacteristically impatient."

"Dinner?"

He grinned. "Some people call it supper."

"I . . . uh . . ."

"I can pick you up at your office," he said. "You're already beautiful, so there's no need for you to go home and get ready."

I blushed again. I was about to turn him down, but then I remembered my humiliation with James. Maybe James' rejection was a good thing. He and I would be a disaster, but it was the catalyst I needed to entertain the idea of being with someone else. Someone more dateable. "Uh . . . sure. Okay."

His mouth gaped. "*Really?*"

"You expected me to say no?"

"Honestly, I expected it to take a few more tries."

I laughed. "I can take back my yes."

A grin spread across his face. "No, I'm good. Does six work? I heard your office is open until six."

The fact that he knew when my office closed was a little disconcerting, but for all I knew, he was interested in having some landscaping done. "Okay. Six."

My stomach dropped to the floor with nerves. I was going on a date. I felt more nervous than excited. Was that normal? "Do you need directions to my office?"

"Nope. I know where it is."

"You do?"

He laughed. "At the risk of sounding like an episode of *Law and Order: SVU*, when two beautiful women blow into your office like a hurricane, bringing a wayward baby pig to boot, you tend to ask questions."

"So you asked about us."

"I didn't have to ask many people to find out."

I wasn't sure whether that was a good thing or not. But I didn't have time to think about it because my head started to tingle and I was plunged into a vision. I was in an exam room with a woman who looked like she was close to fifty, but a toned and tucked kind of fifty. She was wearing a red dress with a plunging neckline and had a cat nestled beneath her generous breasts.

"Dr. Romano, I know I dropped in without an appointment," she said. "But my Tiffany needs your expert help," she said, tugging down the neckline of her button-up dress to better showcase her cleavage.

"I . . . uh . . ." I said in Dr. Romano's voice, then took a step backward. "What's wrong with Tiffany?"

The woman set her cat down on the exam table. "She's lonely. Sooo lonely." Then she quickly unfastened several buttons to reveal a black bra covered in tiny crystals. "Can you help me?"

"*Mary!*" I called out in panic.

The door burst open, and Mary was inside the exam room in an instant, grabbing the woman's arm and dragging her out of the room.

"My cat!" the woman shouted.

Mary gave her a look of disgust. "I have it on good authority that you adopted that cat from the shelter this morning. I'll find that poor creature an *actual* home."

The vision faded, and I found myself staring into Dr. Romano's face. "A woman's gonna show you her crystal-covered bra."

"What?"

How was I going to explain *that*? "I have to go." I spun around and reached for the doorknob.

"Wait. You can't go yet. I need to get Muffy's medication."

Oh crap. Of course he did.

Thankfully, the door opened and Mary's stern face appeared in the frame. "Dr. Romano, your next appointment is waiting."

"All right," he said. "Becky's in the back, getting Muffy's anti-inflammatory. Can you make sure Rose gets the medication and a crate before she leaves?" When she hesitated, he added, "Her dog has a real injury, so please make sure she's treated well."

The woman scowled, but her boss's assurance seemed to relax her. "I'd say your next appointment is fifty-fifty."

Dr. Romano sighed. "Little did I know Henryetta, Arkansas, would turn out to be so dangerous."

He had *no* idea.

Chapter Twelve

*B*y the time I got back to the office, I had worked myself up nearly to the point of a panic attack. Bruce Wayne was sitting at his desk—a rare occurrence these days—talking on the phone while he studied a yellow invoice in his hand. But Neely Kate's face lit up as soon as we walked through the door.

"Well?" she asked in excitement. "How'd it go?"

Bruce Wayne hung up his phone and swiveled his chair to face me, taking in the crate I was carrying in my free hand while I cradled Muffy with the other. "What's that for?"

I knew Neely Kate was eager to hear about the romantic part of my visit, but I wasn't eager to talk about it. Better to focus on Bruce Wayne's question. "Muffy got hurt, so I took her to see the vet. Dr. Romano said Muffy doesn't have any broken bones, so that's good. But she has deep tissue damage, so she needs to rest and move as little as possible."

"You're not gonna actually put her in that cage, are you?" he asked, sounding slightly outraged.

"Only when we leave her alone somewhere. She's not moving around much, so I'm hoping she'll just lie on her dog bed." I set the crate down, and Neely Kate scooted the small dog bed out from under my desk. Moments later, Muffy was curled up on it.

"So she's going to be okay?" Neely Kate asked, perching on the edge of my desk.

"She has to take an anti-inflammatory, but other than that, he says she just needs some rest."

"Okay," she said, her face lighting up again. "Now get to the good stuff."

Bruce Wayne looked confused, but she waved him off and gave me her full attention.

I sat in my chair, then spun to face her. "Did you know that women have been buying and adopting pets for the sole purpose of meeting Dr. Romano?"

Bruce Wayne's jaw dropped, and he studied me with renewed interest, ignoring his now-ringing phone for a few beats before he answered it.

"And why does this surprise you?" Neely Kate asked. "Think of all the women who brought Mason baked goods back when he was in the running for most eligible bachelor." Her eyes filled with horror as soon as she realized what she'd said. We had an unspoken rule between us— both of us tried to avoid saying the name of the other's ex. "Oh, Rose. I'm sorry."

Shaking my head, I gave her a soft smile. "It's okay. It happened. It's true."

She cast a glance to Bruce Wayne to make sure he was engrossed in his call before she lowered her voice. "Do you still miss him?"

"Mason?" I paused, trying to come up with the right words. "I think I still love him, but I'm used to him being gone." I tilted my head. "Does that make any sense?"

"I think it makes perfect sense."

I wondered if she felt the same way about Ronnie, but on the rare occasions when she did talk about him, she insisted that while she'd loved Ronnie, she hadn't been in love with him. Maybe it was different for her.

"Now tell me what happened," she said. "That pink dress does wonderful things for your complexion, and he was sure to notice."

"You didn't tell me that before I left," I said with a frown.

"That's because I knew you'd change. What happened?"

My face flushed. "He flirted with me."

"Of course he did. He's not blind. What else happened?"

I decided to make her wait for it. "I had a vision."

"Of what?"

"One of Dr. Romano's patients. Actually, the patient's owner. She only adopted a cat so she'd have an excuse to come see him. Then she started unbuttoning her dress in the exam room."

"What?" Neely Kate said, her brows shooting up. "What did you blurt out?"

"That a woman was going to show him her crystal-covered bra."

I realized Bruce Wayne had ended his call, and judging from his red-tipped ears, he'd heard my last words loud and clear.

She put a hand on her chest. "Oh, no."

"Then the receptionist walked in and told him his next appointment had arrived."

"So that was it?" she asked, sounding disappointed.

"No," I said, reaching over to switch on my computer. "He asked me out to dinner tonight."

"Please tell me you accepted," she begged.

I looked up at her. "He's picking me up here at six."

Neely Kate let out an ear-piercing squeal.

"Neely Kate!"

Bruce Wayne stood and made a beeline for the front door. "You still planning on helping me on the job site tomorrow?"

"Why wouldn't I?" I asked in confusion.

He muttered something under his breath and then pushed his way out the door so forcefully that the bell attached to it chimed for several seconds.

"Don't mind him," Neely Kate said. "You know he hates any touchy-feely stuff. But let me just say how proud I am of you."

"I didn't do anything to be proud of," I said, slightly annoyed. "I agreed to go out to dinner with him."

"But it was scary, and you said yes."

I couldn't help wondering if I'd only agreed to the date because I was trying to prove something to James. Or maybe myself. "But I don't even know him, Neely Kate," I said, spinning in my chair to face her. "How can I tell if I'm even interested in him?"

"That's the whole point of datin', Rose. You go out, ask each other about your pasts, your jobs and interests, and then you decide if you want to keep goin' out."

"I still don't think I should go," I said. "Muffy needs me."

"Muffy will be fine. I'll make sure she doesn't move around much. We'll have a girls' night in."

"Maybe *I* want a girls' night in."

"We've had four months of girls' nights. It's time for one of us to escape, and you're it. You're goin'. End of story."

I was about to get to work but decided to broach the touchy subject of our case. "Neely Kate, you know we need to back off from looking for Raddy's necklace. It's part of a murder investigation now. We might mess something up, not to mention it could be dangerous."

She turned to face her computer and refused to look me in the eye. "Yeah, I know."

The rest of our day got busy. I had a few jobs to bid on, and I'd arranged to meet a couple at the nursery at three to look at plants for their design. I got back to the office by five forty, and my stomach tied into knots when I realized Levi Romano would be here in twenty minutes to pick me up.

"I've changed my mind," I said as I sat down in my chair and leaned over to rub Muffy's head.

"Changed your mind about what?" Neely Kate asked.

"My date. I really think I need to stay home with Muffy."

"Muffy's gonna be just fine. We've covered this multiple times already. You're gonna go out to dinner, eat a nice meal, and then let him bring you back here. You're not marrying the man. It's a date."

"That's just it. I've hardly dated anyone. I already knew Joe and Mason when I started dating them. Other than that, I only had one blind date with a guy who ditched me."

"All the more reason to go out. Now why don't you go to the bathroom and freshen up before he gets here?"

I opened my mouth to protest, but the door opened, and Homer Dyer crossed the threshold.

Neely Kate must have seen the look of surprise on my face because she turned toward the door. "What are you doin' here, Homer Dyer?" she asked in a short tone.

"We have some unfinished business," he snarled, moving to the middle of the room.

He looked madder than a wet hen. I reached for my phone, about to call Jed, but then I remembered how adamant Neely Kate had been last night. She'd wanted to handle Homer by herself then; should I trust her to do so now? I hid my phone in my lap . . . just in case.

I expected her to whip out her gun—all the more reason to consider calling Jed for backup—but she stayed in her seat, looking up at him like he was just an annoying bug. "I can't think of a single thing that needs to be said, *so get out.*"

"Not until I get some answers." He took several steps toward her desk. "I wanna know two things: one, where's my boy, and two, where's that damned necklace?"

Neely Kate gave him a fierce look. "We don't know the answer to either one of those questions, so like I said, *get on out of here.*"

"You thought you were mighty big pulling a gun on me yesterday," he said, reaching behind him and hauling out a hunting knife. "But I don't see no gun now."

Time to text Jed. I hid my phone under my desk and speed-typed a text that sounded like a Clue guess: *Homer Dyer in our office with a knife.*

"Have you officially lost your mind, Homer Dyer? Or are you just plain drunk?" Neely Kate asked in disbelief, pointing her finger toward the door. "The police headquarters is just down the street."

I slowly reached into my purse and pulled out my Taser, keeping it out of sight.

Homer moved in front of her desk. "Where's my boy?"

She got to her feet, rising to her full five-foot-four inches. He towered over her, and she had to tilt back her head to glare up at him. "How in the world would I know?"

"You've been talking to him. Where is he? He's not answering his phone."

Was Homer worried about his stepson? He didn't strike me as the worrying sort.

"I don't know," Neely Kate said. "Haven't seen him since yesterday."

My phone vibrated in my lap with a response from Jed.

Hang tight.

Homer was still staring Neely Kate down with the knife in his hand. "That's not what I heard," he snarled. "I heard he was hiding out in your barn."

"Never saw him."

Homer's face reddened and he looked ready to pounce.

Hiding the Taser behind my back, I stood upright and said, "*I* was the one who saw Raddy last night."

Homer turned his beady eyes on me. "Is that right? Did he have the necklace?"

"What do you think?" I asked, walking to the side of my desk.

"Don't get smart with me," he snapped.

"He hired us to find the necklace," I countered. "We didn't make any secret of that when we were talkin' to Miss

Mable. If we didn't have it when we left your house, when would we have found it to give to Raddy?"

"How the hell would I know?" he asked, moving closer.

"Stop right there or I'll shoot," Neely Kate shouted, now pointing her gun at him.

Homer turned to face Neely Kate, giving her the scariest grin I'd ever seen. "I think I'll take my chances."

"I've got this covered, Neely Kate." I hoped she believed me. Tasing a guy would be a whole lot easier to explain than shooting one, and while I wasn't convinced he didn't deserve it, I didn't want his blood on our hands. Or the floor.

"Raddy said he saw someone running out of his wife's house after he found her dead," I said. "Know anything about that?"

"How would I know about that?" Homer asked, but he didn't come across as one hundred percent convincing.

"Because you knew Rayna was the last person to have seen that necklace."

"I didn't have nothing to do with killing her."

I tilted my head. "No one said anything about her being murdered."

He lunged for me with the knife, and I pulled my hand out from behind my back, aimed the Taser at his chest, and pressed the button.

Homer was on the floor within seconds, and the smell of urine filled my nose.

"Oh, my stars and garters," Neely Kate groaned as she walked over to him. "Did he just pee himself?" She glanced up at me with a dark look. "I'm not cleaning up that mess."

"It'll be easier to clean up than blood."

The front door burst open, and we both glanced up at the newcomer—a young man I didn't recognize.

Neely Kate turned to face him, still holding the gun at her side. "If you're here for the necklace, you can get on out of here. We don't know where it is."

"Jed sent me."

"Jed?" Neely Kate blinked. "Jed *Carlisle*? Whatever for?"

"To take care of him." He pointed to the man lying on the floor.

"Jed sent someone else?" I asked, trying to hide my disappointment.

The man looked at me, although *man* might have been a generous word for him. He looked to be in his late teens. "He was a half hour south of town, so he asked me to help."

"Who the heck are you?" Neely Kate asked. "You got any ID?"

I narrowed my eyes at her. "What good is an ID gonna be? He's not with the police. He's not gonna have some badge he can whip out."

"I'm Brett Hollander, ma'am," he said and nodded toward her.

"*Ma'am?*" Neely Kate screeched.

I released a loud groan. "Take him to task for callin' you ma'am later, Neely Kate. Right now we have to deal with the unconscious, pee-soaked man on our office floor before a customer walks in." I was glancing up at the clock to see how soon we could lock the doors when I realized my date was going to show up sooner than I'd like. "Look what time it is!" I said in a panic. "Dr. Romano's going to be here in five minutes."

"What?" she asked in confusion; then her eyes flew open wide. "Oh, no!" She turned to Brett. "What do you propose we do with him?"

Brett looked more than a little lost, but a half second later his jaw locked with determination. "We'll move him to the alley."

"Good idea," Neely Kate said, moving for Homer's feet. "You get the top half, and I'll take the bottom."

She started reaching for his boots, then waved a hand in front of her face and gagged. "Oh my word. I think he's been walking in cow poo."

Brett walked around to Homer's feet and bent down to look at the soles of his boots. "I reckon you're right."

Neely Kate put her hands on her hips and steeled her back. "I am *not* holding that end."

"I'm not gonna do it," Brett said.

"Somebody has to do it," I groaned, sending a panicked look toward the door. "Dr. Romano's gonna be here any minute."

Neely Kate gave me a resigned look, then turned toward Brett. "Go look out back. See if the coast is clear for us to haul him outside."

Brett headed out the back door just as the front door opened. My stomach dropped to the floor when I saw Dr. Romano walk in.

"Oh, my stars and garters," Neely Kate mumbled as she spun around and tried to stand in front of Homer. "Hello, Dr. Romano!" she said a little too enthusiastically.

He frowned and leaned slightly to the side. "Why is that man lying on the floor?"

"He was tired," Neely Kate said, then gave my arm a shove. "You better get goin', Rose."

"Is he okay?" Dr. Romano asked, moving closer. "And what's that smell?"

"We were cleanin'," Neely Kate said, then hastily added as she blocked his path, "With ammonia."

"Does that man need medical assistance?" he asked, sounding concerned.

"Nope," Neely Kate said. "He's just a homeless man we let hang out here from time to time. He likes to nap on our floor."

"Wow," Dr. Romano said. "That's very generous of you."

Neely Kate shook her head in mock sympathy. "We keep trying to get him to go to the New Living Hope Revival Church, but he always turns us down. Still, we keep hoping."

Brett came in from the back door. "The alley's clear, so we can move him out back." He stopped short when he saw Dr. Romano. "Oh. Hey."

"The alley?" Dr. Romano asked.

"Well," Neely Kate drawled, "We're getting ready to lock up. Sometimes we set him up with a little place out back so he can keep comfortable."

"I had no idea Henryetta had such a homeless problem," Dr. Romano said.

Neely Kate shrugged. "I guess no place is perfect. Now you two need to get goin'."

Dr. Romano looked at me and lifted his eyebrows. "Are you ready?"

I wasn't, but I couldn't let him stay here a moment longer than necessary. Still, I hated to leave Homer with Neely Kate. What if he woke up and hurt her?

But she must have read my mind. "Brett and I have everything under control. We'll make sure Homer gets taken care of. Once we do, I'll take Muffy home and we'll see you there later."

Homer was going to wake up at some point, and when he did, he was going to be good and ticked. It couldn't be that hard for him to figure out where we lived. Sure, we had guns and an alarm system I mostly forgot to set, but I didn't like the thought of living on guard.

I squatted in front of the crate, opened the door, and rubbed Muffy's head. "I'll be home in a little bit. You be a good girl." Then I stood and grabbed my purse. "Neely Kate, you call me if you need . . . to chat."

She gave me a forced grin. "If I need to chat, I have Brett here."

I quickly hurried out the front door, so fast that Dr. Romano didn't have a chance to open it for me. He gestured to a pickup truck, and I walked to the passenger door. He grinned as he opened it for me. "I had no idea our date would start out with a foot race."

I grimaced. "Sorry."

He shut the door behind me, then got behind the wheel and started the engine. "I made reservations at Jaspers."

"Oh," I said, trying not to sound worried. I'd had several bad dates there, but that didn't mean *our* date wouldn't go well. Still, I couldn't help thinking the odds weren't in my favor.

As he drove to the restaurant, he told me several incidents from his day, which involved a parrot, a cat, and a dog who'd swallowed a plastic hot dog. It felt nice to listen to stories that had nothing to do with the whole mess involving the necklace, the Wagner brothers, and the Dyer family. Even so, I couldn't help thinking that I should be back at the office, helping Neely Kate with the Homer situation.

Jarring me out of my thoughts, Dr. Romano asked, "How did you know about the woman with the crystal-covered bra?"

"Lucky guess," I said, thankful he was pulling into the parking lot at the restaurant.

He let it drop, and I climbed out when he turned off the engine. He met me at the back of the truck and snagged my hand in his. "You look beautiful tonight, Rose."

"Thank you, Dr. Romano," I said, resisting the urge to pull my hand free.

He chuckled. "I told you to call me Levi. Do you know how awkward it will be when we're married and have kids and you're still calling me Dr. Romano?"

I gaped at him. Married? Kids?

He burst into laughter. "I'm kidding. But I *do* want you to call me Levi."

"Okay," I said, giving in to the urge to pull my hand out of his. "Levi," I said, testing it out.

He grinned and put his hand on the small of my back, steering me toward the entrance to the restaurant.

Maybe I wasn't ready for this after all.

But Dr. Romano—no, Levi—was nice, and he was cute, and he was interested in me. And he had absolutely nothing to do with either criminals or law enforcement. Neely Kate was right. I should at least get to know him.

He'd made reservations, so the hostess led us right to our table, which, ironically enough, was the same one I'd sat at for that failed blind date almost a year ago.

My date with Levi was already off to a better start. He hadn't been coerced by my brother-in-law, didn't look scared that I was about to bean him in the head with a rolling pin, and he was charming.

Our waiter came by with menus and took our drinks order. After he left, I cleared my throat. "So, Dr. Romano— I mean, Levi—how did you end up in Henryetta?"

"My grandparents live here, in the Forest Ridge neighborhood. I always loved coming to visit when I was a kid, and when it came time for me to start looking for a practice, my grandmother told me Dr. Ritchie was retiring. It was kismet."

"You're not from Arkansas, are you?" I asked.

He laughed. "Does my non-accent give me away?"

I grinned. "That and the fact you don't say yes, ma'am and yes, sir."

A grimace crossed his face. "I guess I should work on that."

"No," I said. "You just be you. But you still haven't told me where you're from."

"Missouri. I grew up in the Kansas City area."

The waitress came back with our drinks and took our orders. When she left, Levi's eyes lit up. "So, Rose Gardner, what about you? Are you originally from Henryetta?"

"Born and raised," I said. "Never left except the semester and a half I went to Southern Arkansas University."

"What brought you back?" he asked.

"My father died."

His smile fell. "I'm sorry."

I shook my head and picked up my glass of wine. "I came home to take care of my invalid mother. It was seven years ago, and she's since died, but everything worked out in the end."

"And now you own a landscaping business." That reminded me of what he'd said earlier, how he'd asked around about me.

"Indeed, I do. If there's one thing you need to know about Henryetta, it's that there's no such thing as a secret here. Or at least it's much harder to keep one." I put my glass down. "So what else did you hear about me?"

"Not much."

"Come on," I said. "If you asked around about me, I know you heard things, which are probably either untrue or only partially true. Tell me what you heard, and I'll let you know if you can believe it."

He grinned as he picked up his glass. "I think I like this game. I heard you dated both the sheriff and the district attorney."

"That's only partially true."

"Which part?"

"I dated the *chief deputy* sheriff, but he was with the state police when we were together, and Mason was the *assistant* district attorney."

"So am I already out of the running because I'm not in some type of law enforcement career?"

"No," I said. The wine had already dulled my inhibitions, and I was surprised when I added, "I think it's time for me to branch out." But then I flushed and looked down at the table. "So what else?"

"Your sister is in Texas . . ."

"Dying?" I asked, looking back up to him as I shook my head. "She has cancer, but she had a bone marrow transplant. She's doing really well and should be coming home soon. Anything else?"

"You've been the target of a few dangerous criminals."

"Which is how I became involved with men in law enforcement," I said. "But my time with criminals is done. I'm a simple landscaper now."

He gave me a wicked grin. "Who helps homeless men."

I paused and studied him, trying to decide if he was being sarcastic. Had he figured it out? He was obviously intelligent, and it wouldn't take many brain cells to figure out that most people didn't let urine-soaked men lie in the middle of their office.

But the waitress saved me by returning with our dinners. She gave me an odd look, then said, "The manager says to tell you that your meal's on us tonight. After what happened the last time you were here."

Levi's eyes narrowed as he looked up at her. "What happened last time she was here?"

The waitress gave me an apologetic look—so much for helping me avoid an awkward conversation—and ran off.

He turned to me this time. "What happened the last time you were here?"

There was no way I was going to tell him I'd been kidnapped from the restroom ten minutes after my then-boyfriend had proposed. I hadn't been to Jaspers since, partially because my whole life had tipped on its head that night and partially because I'd holed up at the farm, licking my wounds. "Let's just say some things are better discussed on a second or fifth date."

A grin spread across his face. "So things are going well enough that we can plan a second date?"

Well, crap. I hadn't meant to say that. I finished off the last of my wine. "This chicken looks really good."

Levi turned his attention to his sirloin steak, but thankfully the waitress's announcement hadn't made the silence tense. After about a minute, he asked, "How did you end up in the landscaping business?"

I gave him a teasing smile. "With a name like Rose Gardner, it seemed like destiny." I stabbed a piece of broccoli on my plate. "The short version is that my sister wanted to open a nursery, and she needed my help to do it. We opened last September, and one of our very first orders was to re-landscape the New Living Hope Revival Church, but part of the deal was that we had to install the plants. It all kind of evolved from there. My partner Bruce Wayne and I split the landscaping business from the nursery in December."

"Wow," he said as he grabbed his glass of water. "That's all fairly recent."

"Most new businesses take two years to make a profit, but we just had our first month in the black." I was proud of what we'd accomplished, especially since Bruce Wayne and I had wondered if we were destined to fail in a fiery ball of flames only a few short months ago.

He gave me a dubious look. "Did you say your business partner's name is Bruce Wayne?"

I laughed. "His father is Clark Kent."

I was about to tell him more about the business, but the woman who walked through the doorway caught my attention. Something about her looked familiar, and then it hit me.

She was the woman in Rayna's vision.

I set my fork down, my gaze still on the woman as she disappeared into the bar. "Excuse me for a moment, Dr. Romano."

"Levi," he said, but it was an automatic reply. He was looking at me with about a dozen questions in his eyes. He watched as I stood and headed for the bar, but to his credit, he didn't ask.

After seeing the woman's hot tub attire in my vision, I wasn't surprised to find her wearing a gold sequined tube top, a pair of low-rise, skin-tight jeans, and four-inch fake leather above-the-knee boots. Her blonde hair was teased tall enough to look like an inviting home for a family of mice, and she wore enough dark eyeshadow to warrant a part as an extra in a vampire movie. I had no idea what her name was, but I had a sneaking suspicion what her profession might be.

"Is this seat taken?" I asked as I slid into a bar stool in front of her, thankful we were out of Levi's line of sight.

"Actually, I'm waiting on somebody," she said, looking around me. Presumably that somebody was a man.

"How about I buy you a drink and keep you company while you wait?" I asked.

She licked her lips. "I guess that would be all right." She waved a hand to the bartender. "He's cute."

She had a point, although the guy walking around the end of the bar looked a good ten to fifteen years younger than her. He glanced at the woman and then back at me, doing a double take. I was sure my innocent-looking pink sundress was a strange contrast to her attire.

"I'm gonna have a Long Island iced tea," she said. "Luke . . ." she added, squinting at his name tag. Then she tilted her head and looked at me.

"I'll take a glass of wine," I said. "Pinot grigio."

Luke nodded, then headed back to his station without a word.

The woman watched his butt as he walked around the corner, then turned to me and narrowed her eyes. "Whaddaya want?"

"Who says I want something?" I asked.

"It's the only reason a stranger buys a drink for someone. So whaddaya want? But I gotta warn ya, I don't swing that way." She gestured her fingers back and forth between us.

Ignoring her statement, I took a breath and decided to approach this as honestly as possible without giving away what I'd seen in the vision. "We had a mutual friend, and I thought it might be nice if we talked about her."

Her eyes narrowed. "Who?"

"Rayna," I said softly. "Rayna Dyer."

Her mouth dropped open, and then she closed it and swallowed. "How did you know Rayna? You don't look like her kind of friend."

"I hadn't known her long." It felt better to tell the truth, even if it was misleading. "I think that's part of the reason I was so shocked."

The woman didn't look convinced. "How did you know her?"

"From Walmart."

Her guard dropped slightly.

I glanced around before leaning forward and lowering my voice. "I know she was wanting to make Raddy pay for humiliating her like he did, and I know you two were coming up with a plan."

The woman's lips pressed together, and she reached into her purse and pulled out a cigarette.

"You can't smoke that in here," Luke said as he placed our drinks in front of us.

"I know," she said in a snotty tone, putting the cigarette between her lips anyway. "I'm just holding it." Then she added, "Is that a crime in this damn town?" The cigarette bobbed up and down in her mouth with each word.

The bartender scowled and stalked back to the bar.

The woman took the cigarette out of her mouth and held it between her fingers as she drained half of her cocktail.

I tried not to show my surprise when she finally set the glass on the table with a clunk. "You don't know shit," she said, repositioning her cigarette.

Well, crap. "I know you were supposed to go over to her house last night to help her plan her revenge on Raddy."

Surprise flickered in her eyes. And something else. Fear. What was she afraid of? I decided to try to trick her into telling me something. With any luck, most of the information about Rayna's death was still being kept from the public.

"Rayna told me Raddy was coming over to see her, but she kept it from you because you'd think she was weak for wanting to take him back."

Disgust washed over her face, and I felt guilty for besmirching Rayna's character—or at least her common sense. But I suspected this woman knew something, and I needed to find out what it was.

"That damn fool," she muttered, then took another long swig. "I told her to stay strong."

"I heard you were the one to find her and call the police." It was a gamble, but I'd decided to go with my gut.

Her eyes filled with shock, and her hand trembled a little as she put the cigarette back into her mouth.

"I heard she was murdered," I said quietly.

She nodded again. "I called it in anonymously. I told 'em I saw him strangling her, but last I heard they hadn't arrested Raddy yet. What are they waiting for?"

I blinked. Deputy Miller hadn't told me that. Had she really seen Raddy strangle his wife? "I think he's on the run. But I heard he's only one of the suspects."

Her hand began to shake again, and she grabbed her glass. "There's more than one? Who?"

"I heard they're keeping it under wraps, but it has something to do with that necklace."

"What necklace?" a man said from behind me.

I couldn't help but startle a little as a man I didn't recognize slid into the seat between me and the woman.

"Who's your friend, Trixie?" he asked, eyeing me up and down like I was dessert.

"She was just leavin'."

I held out my hand to him. "Hi, I'm Beth Ann," I said, giving him the name I'd used with Hugh Wagner in the pawn shop. "Trixie and I had a mutual friend."

He looked me up and down again like he couldn't bring himself to believe it. "Who?"

"Rayna Dyer."

His eyes shuttered closed. What did he know?

"I didn't catch your name," I said.

"Buck Reynolds."

Oh my word. Trixie was friends with Buck. The same Buck who wanted the necklace.

I had to have a vision.

I didn't have anyone to help cover for me, which meant I had to be careful. "Thanks so much for talkin' to me, Trixie. I just wanted to talk to someone who knew Rayna. This whole thing's been so hard." I slid out of my seat and walked around behind Buck's seat, resting my hand on his shoulder and focusing on whether Buck was going to talk to Trixie about Rayna.

The vision came quickly. I was sitting next to Trixie in a car, her face gripped tightly in my hand. "What did you tell her?"

Fear widened her eyes and her nostrils flared. "Nothin', Buck! I swear!"

"If you told her, I swear to God, I'll—"

"I didn't tell her nothin'!"

The vision ended, and I found myself back in the bar, staring into Trixie's pissed off face. "You're gonna hurt her for talkin' to me."

Trixie looked startled, and Buck's shoulder stiffened under my hand. "What did you say?"

I was in deep trouble.

Chapter Thirteen

*F*lashing a weak smile, I put my hand to my head. "I think that wine went straight to my head."

"You didn't even drink it," Trixie said.

"I know, right?" I said. "So weird . . . I think I'd better go."

I started to walk away before realizing I hadn't paid for the drinks. With a groan, I walked to the end of the bar and flagged Luke. Leaning in, I said in an undertone, "I'm paying for that woman's Long Island iced tea and my wine, but my purse is over at my table in the restaurant. Can you send the bill over to me?"

"Since I only work a few nights a week, I'm not sure about all the rules," he said. "But I think it's probably okay."

This probably bordered on stupid, but I leaned a little closer. "Can you do me a favor? I think that woman might be in trouble. Could you give her a note from me without letting him see it?"

The bartender's smile wavered.

"Just try."

"Okay." He handed me a napkin and a pen, and I quickly scribbled: *Trixie, call me if you need help. 501-555-2638*

I folded it over and handed it to him. "Thanks."

"No guarantees," he said.

When I turned around, Trixie and Buck were both watching me with open suspicion. There was no way I was going to drag Levi into this, so I headed for the bathroom, leaned against the counter, and waited.

What was I doing? Why hadn't I called Randy Miller and told him about Trixie? But Randy didn't know about my visions. I could tell Neely Kate, of course, and I would, but I wanted someone else to know what was going on. Someone who could help. I could only think of one person, but I wasn't ready to talk to him yet. So I called the next best thing.

"Is everything okay?" Jed said when he answered the phone.

"Yes, well . . . maybe."

"Do you need me to come get you out of trouble?"

"No," I said. "I don't think so." I took a breath. "What do you know about Buck Reynolds?"

"Why are you asking about him?"

"Do you think he's capable of murder?"

"I'm damn sure of it." He paused, his voice harder. "Why are you asking about Buck Reynolds?"

"I'm at Jaspers and I ran into Buck and his . . . uh . . . girlfriend, Trixie."

"What are you and Neely Kate doin' at Jaspers?"

"I'm not with Neely Kate. I'm on a date."

He was quiet for so long, I thought we might have gotten disconnected. "Who are you on a date *with*?" he finally asked.

"That's neither here nor there. He's a perfect gentleman, so there's no need for you to worry."

He didn't respond.

"Look, Jed. I think Buck Reynolds may have gone to Rayna Dyer's house last night to look for the missing necklace and killed Rayna in the process. From the way Trixie was acting, I think she was either part of it or knows what happened, especially since she's the one who supposedly found Rayna and called the sheriff."

"Aren't you calling the wrong side of the law about this?"

"I can't call Deputy Miller," I said. "I found out that Trixie was Rayna's friend through a vision, which is the same way I learned Buck is pissed at Trixie for talking to me. Deputy Miller doesn't know anything about my visions. He'll have no reason to believe me."

"Rose, it doesn't sound like you have information he can do anything with anyway."

"But *you* can," I said.

"What exactly do you want me to do?" he asked in disbelief. "Perform a citizen's arrest?"

"I don't know, Jed," I said, getting exasperated. "But I think Buck Reynolds is a murderer."

"Which means you need to stay away from him, Rose."

"I will. I am. That's why I'm calling you from the women's restroom."

"You're hiding out? Where's your date?"

"He has no idea what's goin' on. In fact, I need to get back out there."

"For God's sake," Jed groaned. "Get your pepper spray out before you leave the restroom. Let's not have a repeat of last February."

While free dinners at Jaspers were a nice perk, he had a point. One kidnapping had been enough.

Thankfully, no one was waiting for me when I walked into the hall with the pepper spray in hand.

Buck and Trixie weren't at their table when I passed the bar, so I made a beeline to Levi's table. He was bent over his phone, but he looked up and gave me a curious stare. "Is everything okay?"

"Of course. Fine," I said, sliding into my empty seat and hastily slipping the pepper spray into my purse. Had he seen it clenched in my fist?

Levi's plate was mostly empty, and when I took a bite of my chicken, I wasn't surprised that it had become cold. I set my fork down and picked up my water glass. I needed to turn the focus from my lengthy absence, if that was even possible. "Levi, what's been your most interesting case as a vet?"

He stared at me for a moment, as though shocked by the sudden request, but then he launched into a funny story about a cat and its unlikely tormentor—a hamster. While I listened, I marveled over his reaction to my ten-minute disappearance. He hadn't asked any questions, nor did he seem particularly upset. I couldn't help wondering why.

The waitress returned with a dessert menu, and although I was desperate to go home and tell Neely Kate about my encounter with Burt and Trixie, I decided an extra twenty minutes wasn't going to change anything. Jed was right. They'd left me with plenty of questions, but neither of them had given me any evidence I could use to press for an arrest.

If Levi noticed my anxiety, he didn't let on. He carried the conversation easily, telling me stories about his four years in veterinary school at the University of Missouri and asking questions about the daily routine of running a landscaping business.

When the waitress walked over with a black bill folder, I had a moment of panic since I'd told the bartender to send me the bill for the drinks, but she winked at me as she set the bill down in front of Levi. "*Everything* was covered tonight."

"Thanks for bringing the bill, even if you didn't charge us, Alisha," Levi said, pulling out his wallet. "I wanted to tip you accordingly."

"Thank you, Dr. Romano," she said. "I really appreciate that." She smiled at both of us. "You two make a cute couple." Then she turned on her heel and walked over to another table.

"Why do I have a feeling half the town will know about our date tomorrow?" he asked with a laugh and placed a twenty-dollar bill on top of the receipt in the open folder.

"Because you're a smart man," I said as I scanned what I could of the upside down receipt.

Sure enough, there was a Long Island iced tea and an additional glass of wine at the bottom.

I glanced back up at Levi. "Regretting this impromptu date?"

A slow smile spread across his face. "While I may have asked you to dinner on short notice, I can assure you it was far from impromptu. And as far as regret . . . there's absolutely none. Ready to go?"

I nodded and he stood, reaching a hand toward me to help me up. I wondered why he hadn't said anything about the additional drinks at the bottom. Maybe he hadn't seen them, or maybe he'd thought they were on there by mistake.

The sun had begun to set by the time we walked out to the parking lot, and the sky was particularly spectacular tonight—reds and pinks and oranges blending together and mixing with the deep indigo on the horizon. My fingers itched to text James and tell him to take a look at it—we'd begun planning our Tuesday night meetings at sunset after he'd admitted he'd never sat and watched one. Ever since, I'd texted him whenever I saw one that was particularly dazzling. But I couldn't do that now. What in the world was wrong with me? I was out on a date with another man.

Levi and I walked to his truck. He didn't hold my hand this time, and even though I was a little relieved, I couldn't help wondering if he'd decided to cut his losses.

The drive to the town square was silent, setting my nerves on edge.

"Do you like Henryetta?" I asked to fill the silence. "I know you loved it as a kid, but does it meet your expectations?"

He stopped at a stop sign and turned to me with a soft smile. "It got off with a bumpy start, but things seem to be settling in."

I had a feeling "the bumpy start" comment might have more to do with our date than his move. Was he still interested? Did I even want him to be? The rest of the short drive was silent until he pulled into the parking space next to my truck.

"Thanks for coming to dinner with me, Rose," he said. "And thank you for an entertaining evening."

Entertaining. I suspected that wasn't a good adjective for a romantic dinner. "Thank you," I said, feeling awkward. I'd completed my first *real* first date—the kind you go on with a near stranger—and while I was proud of my accomplishment, I was suddenly anxious about what he expected of me now. A goodnight kiss? I wasn't ready for that, and I wasn't going to be coerced into it. Rose Gardner was taking charge of her own life now. "Good night, Levi. Thank you for a nice dinner."

Had I really said *nice* dinner? I stopped myself from rolling my eyes, then opened the door and scrambled out before he could ask me for another date—as though he'd ask for one now.

"Good night, Rose," he called after me, but I cut him off when I shut the door.

Great.

Like the gentleman he appeared to be, he waited until I got into my truck and started the engine. I lifted a hand and gave him a small wave. His warm smile assured me that my abrupt departure hadn't upset him, but I was still grateful when he drove off in the opposite direction. The last thing I wanted to do was to keep exchanging awkward glances with him all the way home. I wondered if he was living with his grandparents or if he'd found his own place. The latter was more likely. Why hadn't I asked him? Had I asked enough questions? Had I been too awkward?

But more importantly, did I like him? I'd backed out of his truck like my dress had caught fire, but maybe that was just nerves . . . I didn't have an answer. These seemed like questions for Neely Kate's expertise.

I was halfway home on the nearly deserted stretch of county highway my farm sat off of when I heard a low male voice behind me.

"I thought you were smarter than this."

Startled, I turned to look over my shoulder and nearly drove off the road in the process. My anger exploded when

I found myself staring into James' expressionless face. I pulled over to the shoulder and slammed the truck into park.

"*What in Sam Hill are you doin', James Malcolm?*"

"Checking up on you," he said in a low growl.

"By scaring the bejiggers out of me?"

"You'd be more than scared right now if I were Buck Reynolds."

That blew the indignation right out of me.

He rested his hands on the top of the front seat. "What the hell are *you* doin', Rose? Why are you looking into Rayna Dyer's death?"

He'd just asked two very good questions, and I didn't have an answer for either one. "I didn't set out to look into it."

"Then why the hell are you doing it?"

I released a groan as I turned to face the road. "I don't know. I had a vision of Rayna yesterday morning. There was a woman in the hot tub with her, and she was helping Rayna plot her revenge. When I saw her in the bar at Jaspers, I had to talk to her. I had to find out who she was and what she'd seen."

"Why?"

"Because Rayna died in her hot tub, so I wondered if Trixie had gone over the last night after all. If she'd seen anything. The sheriff's department probably wouldn't know about her intended visit, so they wouldn't know to ask her anything."

"But *you* did. Why not just tell the sheriff's department and let them handle it?"

"Because I didn't know her name until Buck showed up. I didn't even know Buck and Trixie were connected." I turned to look over my shoulder at him. "Buck's the man Raddy lost the bet to."

"I'm well aware of that fact," he said in an even voice, his impassive eyes holding mine.

"I couldn't go to Deputy Miller. There's no evidence, but my gut says Buck's involved and Trixie knows what he's doin'."

"Rose, why do you care?" he asked in exasperation. "Rayna Dyer's murder has nothing to do with you."

"Because it's the right thing to do."

His gaze held mine for a good two seconds before I remembered I was pissed at him—not just for hiding in my backseat, but it was a good place to start. "I can't believe you! Did you have to hide in my truck and scare me? I almost ran off the road!"

"You should check your backseat before you even get in a vehicle," he grunted, his face a mask again. "You're smarter than that, Lady. Your head was addled by your date with that vet."

I gritted my teeth. I hadn't told Jed who I was out with, but James must have seen him in the truck. "My head wasn't addled." Not quite true considering how much of a hurry I'd been in to get away from him, but it wasn't a total lie either.

"If you're gonna keep messing around with bad guys, you need to start doing a better job of protecting yourself."

I thought about his *lesson* in my barn the night before. "You should have warned me about that last November," I snapped.

His jaw tensed and his eyes narrowed. "Seems to me I warned you plenty."

Headlights appeared in my rearview mirror, and a vehicle pulled up behind us. A jolt of fear hit me until I realized it was Jed's sedan.

"Pay more attention to your surroundings, or you're going to get yourself killed." James opened the back door but hesitated before getting out. "If you're going to keep picking at this sort of thing, you need more training. Jed'll call you tomorrow."

"What's your hurry? One of your bimbos waiting to get you naked?" I asked in a snotty tone, then instantly regretted it.

Surprise washed over his face, but it vanished in an instant, and he looked furious by the time he climbed into Jed's car. I twisted in my seat, and pulled back onto the highway, trying to figure out why I was so angry.

But that was the easiest thing in this whole mess to figure out.

Chapter Fourteen

Neely Kate was watching TV on the sofa with Muffy, but she grabbed the remote and turned it off the moment I walked through the door. Jerking upright, she said, "Well? How'd it go?"

"First tell me what happened with Homer Dyer."

She rolled her eyes. "Brett and I dragged him out into the alley."

I cocked my head to the side. "Who held his cow-pie-covered boots?"

Her mouth twitched with a sly grin. "We rock-paper-scissored for it. I won."

Of course she had. "Did he wake up before you left?"

"Yeah, he was as angry as a three-legged cat on a tightrope, but Brett told him that if he bothered you or me again, Skeeter Malcolm intended to deal with him personally."

"And what did Homer say to that?"

"He cursed like my cousin Alan Jackson when he got stung on the behind by a hornet at the last Rivers family reunion, but I'm pretty sure he'll obey."

"What makes you think that?"

Neely Kate held my gaze. "The fear in his eyes. No one inspires fear like Skeeter Malcolm."

I swallowed. Just one more reminder of the true nature of the man I'd thrown myself at the night before. The man who'd inspired more of a response in me in less than five minutes than Levi had all evening.

"Are you satisfied now?" she demanded. "Because I need details. How was your date?"

I sat down on the opposite end of the sofa. "Good, I guess."

Some of the excitement left her eyes. "*Good* isn't good when it comes to a date, Rose. What happened?"

"Well, he's nice and easy to talk to. He also didn't say a word when I disappeared for ten minutes to talk to Trixie and Buck in the bar."

She shook her head. "Who are Trixie and Buck?"

"Trixie is the woman from my vision of Rayna. Turns out she found Rayna's body after Raddy took off. She's the one who called it in."

Neely Kate's eyes widened.

"And I'm pretty sure Buck is the guy Raddy lost that necklace to in the poker game."

She gasped. "Do you think Rayna's friend was spying on her for Buck?"

"I hate to accuse her of something so devious, but it seems possible. She looked like she knew something, especially after I had my vision."

"You forced a vision?"

I nodded. "I had to. If there was even the slightest possibility it could help solve Rayna's murder."

"What did you see?"

After I told her, she narrowed her eyes and asked, "And Levi really didn't say anything?"

"No. But I doubt there will be a second date." I let out a sigh. No need for her to know I'd practically jumped out of his truck to avoid the possibility he'd ask. "Why did I go talk to Trixie? Who leaves their date long enough for their food to get cold?"

Compassion filled her eyes. "You're a good person, Rose Gardner. Of course you'd try to help Rayna, even if she's dead."

I flopped back and sank into the back cushions. "James was none too happy with me."

"James *Malcolm*? How did *he* find out?"

"Because I left Buck and Trixie in the bar and then hid in the bathroom and called Jed."

"Why?"

"I was hoping he could do something about it." And because Buck Reynolds had scared me, but I didn't want to tell her that part.

"Rose, Jed operates on the other side of the legal system. What did you think he was gonna do?"

"I don't know, Neely Kate. I think I just wanted to tell someone who could help me if things took a turn. Buck Reynolds gave me the creeps."

"Didn't you have your gun in your purse?"

"No! I was on a date! I hid it under my front seat." But it was definitely in my purse now.

She pursed her lips and gave me a look of disapproval. "Raddy Dyer was skulking in your barn last night, his wife was murdered for a necklace he hired us to find, and Homer Dyer showed up at our office fit to be tied—you should have had your gun."

"And what would Levi have said if I'd whipped out a gun during dessert?"

"He would have said, 'Thank you for saving my life, Rose.'"

"Very funny," I grumbled.

She shrugged, wearing a goofy grin. When she saw I wasn't laughing, she turned serious and grabbed my hand, clasping it between both of her own. "Maybe it was too soon after all."

We were silent for a few moments before she asked, "So what are we going to do with what you found out with Trixie and Buck?"

"I guess there's nothin' to do. I can't exactly call Deputy Miller and tell him I had a vision, and besides, I didn't even see anything useful. Suspicious, yes. Useful to the sheriff's department? No." I sighed, thinking about James' questions. "Why do I even care? It's not like Radcliffe Dyer is a model citizen."

"True, but neither was Bruce Wayne when you got him out of his murder charges last year. He had a record."

"That was different. It was plain as the nose on my face he wasn't a murderer. I'll never forget how scared he looked in that courtroom. I couldn't let the rest of that jury convict him, and Mason was well on his way to having them on his side."

"Whoever murdered Rayna wanted that necklace," Neely Kate said. "So I say we keep lookin' for the necklace. That's how we help find the real murderer."

"I don't know . . ."

"Let's just sleep on it. We can't do anything tonight anyway."

"Okay." She was right. I wasn't ready to make a decision one way or the other.

***

The next morning, Neely Kate and I planned to drive separately to the office. I was helping Bruce Wayne today, but first I needed to go by the Hendersons' to replant the bushes Jonah's guys had attempted to plant.

Muffy seemed to feel better when she woke up, but she was still drugged. I didn't want to leave her alone at the office since Neely Kate had a few outside-the-office appointments of her own, but I also wasn't sure taking her with me to the job sites was a good idea.

I called Maeve to ask if Muffy could hang out at the nursery. "I can bring her by when you open."

"You know that Muffy is always welcome," Maeve said. "I'll see you both soon."

When I headed downstairs, Neely Kate was already sitting at the table. She looked up as if I'd startled her and gave me a wobbly smile. I realized she'd been staring at her phone.

"Everything okay?" I asked as I carried Muffy to the back door.

"Of course." But her answer was a little too quick to suit me.

When I came back inside, she had gotten up and was buttering a piece of toast.

"Have you heard from Joe?" I asked, worried he'd found something. If he had, I couldn't believe he'd tell her on the phone.

"He texted last night to make sure we were okay. Rayna's murder makes him nervous."

Rayna's murder made *me* nervous. "I suspect we might hear from Jed today."

She whipped her head to face me. "Why?"

"Last night James said if we plan to mess with bad guys, we need to learn how to handle ourselves."

"I can handle myself just fine," she snapped.

I considered telling her that I wasn't so confident, but let it go for now. "I'm dropping Muffy off with Maeve at the nursery this morning, so I should probably leave soon." I hesitated. "Are you sure you're okay?"

She gave me a weak smile. "I just have a lot on my mind—Ronnie, Kate . . . and things."

I wasn't sure what *and things* entailed, but I had my suspicions. She'd made tremendous progress the last month, but Ronnie wasn't the only thing she'd lost in the last few months. Before they split up, she'd lost her pregnancy . . . and then found out there wasn't likely to be another one. Ever. It stood to reason she'd have setbacks. "You know you can talk to me about anything, right?" I asked. "No judgment. Just a sympathetic ear."

"I know. Thanks."

I was stewing over Neely Kate on the drive into town when Bruce Wayne called.

"One of my guys is off sick today," he said when I answered. "How soon do you think you'll finish the Henderson job and head over to mine?"

"Did you call Jonah?" I asked. "He's usually got a few men standing by."

"Jonah said they were all hired to work on some construction site. Any chance you can shuffle things around and help me knock this job out? Then I can come help with yours. It'll go quicker that way."

I glanced down at Muffy. "We'll have time to get to the Hendersons'?"

"I don't see why not." He paused. "But if you'd rather stick to the original plan . . ."

"No. Your idea is a good one. I'll see you in a bit."

The nursery was quiet when I pulled in. Anna was standing outside, watering the rows of potted plants arranged on the tables. She gave me a warm smile as I carried Muffy inside.

Maeve was dusting off a display shelf and had her back to me, but I heard her say, "You need more sleep. You spend far too much time at the office."

I sucked in a breath. She was talking to Mason.

"Rose is coming by with Muffy," Maeve said in a quiet voice.

I knew I should say something, but I couldn't move. I hadn't spoken to Mason since he'd moved to Little Rock in February. Maeve never told me anything specific about him, only that he was doing well and keeping busy with his job.

"She's good. The landscaping business is booming, so it keeps her busy. Just like your job is keeping you occupied. Have you ever wondered why you two are so busy?" She turned slightly, and her eyes filled with worry when she saw me. "I have to go, Mason. I love you."

She hung up and took several steps toward me.

"Mason . . ." I said. "He's good?"

"Yeah. He just works too much, even more than before. He's . . ." Her voice trailed off. "That was the first time I've gone into that much detail about you. He asks about you every time we talk, and I always tell you're doing well." She paused. "I hope you don't think I'm giving him reports."

I shrugged slightly. "It's okay. I trust you, Maeve."

"That means more to me than you know." She closed the distance between us, placing her hands on my upper arms and searching my face. "I've missed you too, you know."

I'd kept my distance over the past months, mostly because it hurt too much to see her. She was a reminder of what I'd lost. I'd been hurting, but she'd been hurting too.

"Maeve, I'm so sorry. I've been so self-centered."

"You stop that," she chided.

"No. It's true. I haven't given much thought to how you were handling all of this, and I'm truly sorry."

She studied me for a moment and then smiled. "Why don't you come over for dinner tonight? You and Neely Kate. Are you free?"

My chest warmed. "I'd like that. Thank you."

"And there's no reason for you to make a special trip back here for Muffy if you have a busy day. You can bring her home after dinner."

"Okay. Thanks." I handed Muffy to her, along with her medication and her crate.

When I started for the door, Maeve called after me, "It's okay to live your life, Rose. Mason doesn't expect you to wallow."

No, but he'd left because he knew I still needed to figure out who I was and what I wanted—something I'd never be able to do with him around. Had he sacrificed his own happiness? Had he sacrificed his relationship with his mother?

More guilt for me to mull over while digging in the dirt.

Chapter Fifteen

I wiped sweat from my forehead with the back of my hand. Our cool spell was definitely over.

"You still miss diggin' in the dirt?" Bruce Wayne asked with a chuckle.

I rested my foot on my shovel and leaned my shoulder into the handle. "Would you believe it if I said yes?"

He grinned. "Ain't that how we got started in the first place?"

"True enough." I glanced over at the other man on Bruce Wayne's crew. "Sean's a hard worker."

"He is, but his buddy? Not so much. This is the third time he's called in sick in three weeks, and he's been slackin' when he's here. I think I'm gonna have to let him go."

I nodded. "It's your crew, Bruce Wayne. I trust your judgment. I'll fill in to help you as much as I can until you find someone else."

"Thanks."

My phone began to vibrate in my pocket. I tugged off my glove and pulled my phone out. I didn't recognize the number, but I regularly gave my number out to clients.

I swiped to answer. "Hello?"

"I need to talk to you," a woman said. She sounded scared.

I recognized her voice. Thank goodness. The bartender had given her the note after all. "Trixie?"

"I need to tell you about Rayna. Will you meet me?"

I scanned the work site. We'd been working hard for several hours. Bruce Wayne and Sean could easily finish on their own. "Okay. When and where?"

"One Eyed Joes. In thirty minutes." Then she hung up.

Crap. That wouldn't give me time to clean up.

"Bruce Wayne, I have to—"

"Go," he said. "We can finish up just fine." He hesitated. "Before I forget, Anna wants you and Neely Kate to come over for dinner next week. To celebrate our new house together."

I grinned. "Domestication suits you, Bruce Wayne."

A blush tinged his face.

When I got into the truck, I called Neely Kate. "I need you to meet me at One Eyed Joes in twenty-five minutes."

"What happened on the job site that's pushed you into day drinking?" she asked.

Actually, it was our other "job" that had done that. "Trixie called me and asked me to meet her there."

"You're kidding."

"She said she needs to tell me something about Rayna."

"Okay," she said. "See you there."

I hung up and tried to think of where I could go to clean up a little before heading to the bar. Then it hit me. Violet's house—the house I'd lived in for twenty-four years until I'd moved into the farm last November.

The house was dark and cool when I let myself in. I'd been checking on it a couple of times a week since she'd left for Houston, but I never stayed long. Violet and I had a complicated relationship; this house and I, even more so. My momma, or at least the woman I'd thought was my momma, had tormented me. Now I knew it wasn't just my visions that had made her hate me—she'd likely seen me as a reflection of my birth momma, the woman her husband had briefly left her for.

I went into the bathroom, stripped off my shirt, and washed off with a washcloth. Since Violet and I were the same size, I grabbed a shirt out of her closet and put it on. At least I wouldn't stink now.

As I locked up the house, I heard an old woman shout, "I'm gonna call the police!"

Cringing, I turned around to face my old across-the-street neighbor. "Miss Mildred. This used to be my house, and you darn well know it."

She hobbled to the end of the driveway. "It's Violet's house now."

"And you know I have permission to check on her house, so why would you call the police?"

She pointed at me with a single gnarled finger. "For thievery. That's Violet's shirt."

"Maybe you should just ask her if she wants to press charges when she comes home in a couple of weeks."

Some of the bitterness left her eyes. "Violet's comin' home?"

"If all goes well, yeah, she'll be home soon." Then it occurred to me that I was talking to one the busiest busybodies in Henryetta. Perhaps her eighty-three years of gossip and elephant-like memory might come in handy.

"Say, Miss Mildred, I suspect you knew Mable Dyer's mother."

She lifted her chin. "What makes you think that?"

I lifted my shoulder into a slight shrug. "Well . . . I know that you know everyone who's been in the garden club for the past sixty years. Shoot, you know James Malcolm's grandmother, Roberta, and she was one of the founders."

Her eyes narrowed. "James Malcolm? Are you talkin' about Miriam's son?"

I realized my mistake and sucked in my breath. "I don't know his mother's name. But most people call him Skeeter." I wasn't sure why it surprised me. We'd been hanging out for months, and there was so little I knew about him.

Her lips pursed. "That's him. How do you know James Malcolm? He's a hoodlum." Then she shook her head. "But then, why am I surprised?"

Crappy doodles. I'd really screwed this up. There was a good chance she wouldn't tell me anything now. "You're pretty observant," I said. "There's no way you missed my name in the news last February in connection with the arrest of J.R. Simmons. And James' name was in there too. He helped bring that madman down."

The severe lines on her forehead eased.

"Neely Kate and I have been helping Raddy Dyer look for his grandmother's missing necklace. He thinks someone stole it, and he wants it back. But we keep hearing conflicting reports as to whether it's worth anything. Do you know if Mable's mother had expensive jewelry?"

Miss Mildred laughed, but not in a kind way. "That woman didn't have a pot to piss in. Oleander was known for wearing big gaudy jewelry, but it was all from Woolworths up in Magnolia."

I heaved out a sigh. What in the world was going on? What had Rayna been killed for then? And where in tarnation had that owl pin come from?

"If Radcliffe Dyer is telling you that his grandmother's necklace is worth money, he's selling you a piece of swampland." Chuckling, she turned and started to hobble toward her house. "You always were a gullible girl."

Frowning, I called after her. "Thanks for the information."

I got in my truck and drove to One Eyed Joes, a bar on the east side of town that was frequented by truckers and some of the older farmers. I'd never been there. While its reputation was milder than the Trading Post, it was known to host a rough crowd from time to time, but surely things wouldn't be too out of hand just after lunchtime.

Neely Kate's car was in the parking lot along with a dozen other cars. I'd had no idea a country bar would be so popular on a Thursday afternoon. She was talking on the phone in her car. From the look on her face, she was in the middle of an argument with someone. When she saw me, she abruptly ended the call and got out of the car.

"Everything all right?" I asked.

She gave a little shimmy as she centered her purse strap on her shoulder. "Fine. Let's find Trixie."

I was bursting with curiosity, especially after finding Neely Kate at the kitchen table with her phone that morning, but I decided to let it go. For now.

She gave me a quick once-over. "You changed. And that's not your shirt."

"It's Violet's. Since I spent the morning working with Bruce Wayne on a job site, I wasn't exactly fit for a social visit. I didn't have time to go home, so . . ."

"Good idea."

"But when I left, I saw Miss Mildred."

"That was bound to be trouble," she said as she started walking toward the entrance.

"Well, she *did* threaten to call the police over me stealing Violet's shirt."

She stopped in her tracks. "What?"

I waved it off. "That's not important. What you need to know is that Miss Mildred knew Raddy's grandmother."

"Oh my word," she said, lightly smacking her palm against her forehead. "Why didn't I think of that?"

"Miss Mildred said his grandmother wore gaudy Woolworths costume jewelry. From the way she told it, there's no way that necklace is real."

She put a hand on her hip. "But the owl pin was."

"I know. None of it makes sense."

Shaking her head, she continued toward the entrance. "Let's talk to Trixie and see what she has to say."

I was nervous about meeting her, more so than I would have been before that night in February, but the array of self-defense weapons in my purse made me feel a lot better about the situation.

We stopped a few feet inside the bar that reeked of stale beer and sweat. The walls were covered in cheap pine paneling and rodeo photos. The tables were all thick pine, but the patrons seemed to favor the bar.

"Do you see her?" Neely Kate asked.

"No."

"It's barely one. Maybe she's running late."

"Maybe." But I didn't have a good feeling about this. "What if she set us up?"

"How would she set us up? It's not like we have anything she wants. Shoot, we don't even know where the necklace is."

"I don't know," I murmured and started to walk toward a table for four. "I just have a bad feeling."

"Do you want to have a vision?" she whispered.

"That's not a bad idea." We both got settled at the table. I reached for her hand, but a waitress walked over to us before I could start.

"What can I get you girls?"

I was starving, so I figured I might as well kill two birds with one stone. "I'll take an iced tea, and if you have hamburgers, I'll take one with fries."

The waitress turned to Neely Kate, who ordered a salad and water. As the waitress walked away, Neely Kate's mouth dropped open.

"What?" I asked, turning to see three women walk in, silhouetted by the bright sunlight from the open door.

"It's Leah Dyer."

"What's she doing here?" I asked, more to myself.

Neely Kate's mouth pressed into a tight line.

Dread crept into my stomach. "Why do I think there's history between you two?"

"Never you mind about that. Didn't you say Miss Mable said she gave the jewelry to Leah?"

"Yeah. But you found the jewelry in her drawer."

"Maybe we should have a chat with Leah anyway."

The mischief in her voice had me worried. "I think we should wait for Trixie. We might not get the chance to talk to her at all if your conversation with Leah goes the way I think it will."

When she frowned and lifted her shoulder into a noncommittal shrug, I let out a sigh of relief. But the glances she continued to shoot toward Leah made me nervous. I needed to distract her. "When I walked into the nursery this morning, Maeve was on the phone with Mason."

That got her attention.

"Could you hear what she was saying?" she asked.

"I didn't mean to eavesdrop, but once I realized she was talking to him, I couldn't help myself. She told him he was working too hard and needed more sleep. I suspect he's not eating well either."

Sadness filled her eyes. "He doesn't have you to bring him lunch and take care of him anymore. That man loved you, there was no doubt about it. He's probably trying to fill the gap with work." She lifted an eyebrow. "Like someone else I know."

I shot her an annoyed look. "She told him I was coming in with Muffy. But then she saw me and hung up. She said she never tells him anything specific about me, but he always asks if I'm doing okay."

"He still cares," she said quietly. "But what about you? How are you feelin'?"

"I still love him. I think a part of me will always love him, but he's gone." I tried to keep my voice from cracking with emotion. "And I don't think about him nearly as much as I used to." If part of me still loved Mason, how did I categorize my new feelings for James? Not that I was even sure what they were . . . "Do you think it's possible for part of me to still love Mason yet have feelings for someone else?"

"If you're asking if I think it's possible to love two men at the same time, then yeah, I think that's possible. But one of them is here and the other left you. I think that makes your choice clear."

I held my breath. Had she figured out the sudden shift in my feelings for James?

"If Dr. Romano doesn't call you by tomorrow, maybe you should call and ask a question about Muffy."

We were talking about two different men. I looked down at my fork. "Then I'd be like every other woman in the county—usin' her pet to gain access to him."

"Don't give up on him," she said insistently. "There's a few tricks you can use to get his attention. But even if he doesn't want to see you again, there are plenty of other men in this county."

"Neely Kate, you know I'm not the kind of woman to use tricks to get someone's attention."

She studied me for a moment. "No. I suppose you're right." She sighed. "Not to worry. We'll get you dating again. There are plenty of fish in the sea."

I considered telling her I wasn't particularly interested in fishing but decided to change the subject. "Maeve invited us to dinner tonight."

Her eyes lit up. "Oh. I've missed Maeve's cooking, even if my hips have not."

I laughed.

The waitress brought our food. I glanced at the clock and then did a double take. It was a horse wearing a saddle, raised up on its back legs, most likely to fit in with the rodeo theme, but the hands of the clock were actually his male parts—his longer one was the minute and the two small, circular ones were lined up for the hour. I shook my head and shifted my focus to the time. Trixie had said she'd be here in half an hour, but a good hour had come and gone since her call. It seemed unlikely she was going to show up. "Do you think Buck found out what she was up to?" I asked.

"I don't know," Neely Kate said. "She called you, right? Maybe you should try to give her a call."

"Good idea."

I pulled out my phone and called her back, but there was no answer and no voice mail. "She didn't answer."

"Maybe she changed her mind. Or got scared."

"Or both," I said, frowning.

A grin spread across Neely Kate's face.

"Don't tell me you're going to go stir up trouble with Leah."

She released a short laugh. "Nope. She caught me lookin' at her, and she's savin' me from gettin' up."

I turned to see the brunette strutting toward us. She had on dark, tight jeans and a white tank top that left little to the imagination. Her face was heavily made up, and she looked liable to use her stiletto boots as lethal weapons.

Leah put her hands on her hips and popped her hip to the side. "Well, well. Fancy seein' you here, Neely Kate. Slummin', are you?"

Neely Kate was all innocence when she looked up at her. "I'm not sure what you're talkin' about, Leah. I'm enjoying a working lunch with my friend." She cast a glance at Leah's friends, who were watching with rapt attention from their table across the room. "But from the looks of your friends, you're up to the same. Y'all lookin' for work after that strip club south of town closed?"

Leah scowled, wrinkling her forehead with deep creases.

"Be careful," Neely Kate said. "If you leave your face like that, you might get wrinkles. You don't want your tips to go down."

Leah's face turned red. "What are you doin' here, Neely Kate?"

"I already told you."

"I know you're spyin' on me."

Neely Kate did a double take. "What are you talkin' about?"

"I know you and your friend"—she gave me a look of disgust—"are working for my brother, looking for my grandmammie's necklace. I don't have nothin' to do with it."

Neely Kate lifted her chin with attitude. "I never suggested you did. Why would I think such a thing?"

Leah was clearly struggling to form a response, so I decided to give it a go. Neely Kate was being way too antagonistic to get anything out of her. "Leah," I said, "we're only trying to help your brother. I'd like to offer my condolences on your sister-in-law's death."

She released a bitter laugh. "Rayna? The world's a better place without that bitch."

I gasped.

"Don't look all shocked, Miss Goodie Two-Shoes," she sneered. "You're not so perfect." She nodded toward me. "Oh yeah, I know all about your *helpin'* Skeeter Malcolm last winter." She gave me an exaggerated wink.

I tried to hide my surprise. "I helped apprehend a man charged with murder. Skeeter Malcolm cooperated with the police to set up the sting operation. There's nothin' more to it."

"Were you sleepin' with him? Because Skeeter Malcolm wouldn't be caught dead cooperating with the police. Unless he was doin' it for a piece of ass," she said with a leer. "I heard Skeeter really knows how to please a woman. Is it true?"

The blood left my head. A waitress at Merilee's, a restaurant I used to frequent downtown, had asked me the same thing a month ago, albeit in a less tawdry way. I hadn't taken to it any more kindly then.

"Rose sleepin' with *Skeeter Malcolm*?" Neely Kate laughed like it was the most ridiculous thing she'd ever heard. My cheeks flushed. Did she really think the idea of me sleeping with James was so preposterous? But she paid me no mind and pushed on. "Your delusions are getting worse, Leah. Maybe it's time to up your antipsychotics."

Leah's face turned even redder.

"You're barking up the wrong tree," Neely Kate said with plenty of attitude. "And you're so obviously trying to throw us off that I have to wonder what it is you're hiding. Could it be that you really *do* know something about Raddy's missing necklace?"

"It's not *his* necklace!" she shouted. "It should be mine. But he gave it to the stupid bitch he pretended to marry. It's mine, and I want it back!"

I stared at her in amazement, but Neely Kate's previous amusement had taken a more pensive turn. "Maybe we can help you out."

Leah looked suspicious. "What do you mean by that?"

I had to wonder myself.

"Do you know why Raddy really wants it?" Neely Kate asked.

"No," Leah said hesitantly. "Why?"

I gave Neely Kate an exasperated glare. "We're not allowed to tell you," I said. "Client ethics."

Leah barked a laugh. "Ethics? Neely Kate wouldn't know ethics if the authors of the damn dictionary showed up and read her the definition."

Neely Kate stood. I jumped to my own feet, reaching for my wallet—this was going south fast—but in my haste, my pepper spray fell out of my purse and onto the table.

"You're gonna mace me?" Leah screeched, taking several steps back. Her friends were instantly on their feet and across the room.

"No," I said, shaking my head frantically as I stuffed it back inside my purse and grabbed my wallet. "I'm just leavin' money to pay our bill. Then we're out of here." I tossed more than enough money to cover the tab and grabbed Neely Kate's arm. "Come on. Let's go."

"That's right, Neely Kate," Leah said, planting both hands on her hips. "Run away."

Neely Kate shot arrows of hate from her eyes but let me drag her toward the door.

"Coward!"

Neely Kate stopped and looked me in the eye.

I shook my head. "Don't do it."

"You were always so big and bad when you had your cousin Witt with you," Leah said. "But did you ever wonder why he stopped havin' your back?"

Neely Kate whipped around to face her. "That was high school, Leah Dyer. You need to grow up and let it go."

"Have *you* let it go?" Leah asked, taking a step closer. "Your cousin sold you out for a blow job."

Neely Kate stood deathly still. For one split second, I thought she was going to call Leah a liar, but then she marched over to a table, grabbed a pitcher of tea, and dumped it over Leah's head. "Maybe the sugar will do you some good."

Leah released a scream loud enough to scare the occupants of the cemetery a quarter mile down the road, then started swinging at my friend.

Without hesitation, I called the one person I knew who could try to salvage this situation.

Chapter Sixteen

*J*ed, we need your help," I said in desperation.

I scrambled out of the way as the two women moved in my direction. Leah had wrapped her arms around Neely Kate, and it looked like she was trying to pull her T-shirt over her head. They had garnered the full attention of the men at the bar.

One of them shouted, "Take 'em off! Show us your tits!"

A waitress rounded the bar holding a pitcher of what looked to be beer. She put her free hand on her hip and groaned, "Not *again*."

Another man slapped some money on the bar. "I've got five bucks on the blondie."

"No way," his friend said. "That tall girl's gonna kick her ass."

"What the hell's goin' on?" Jed demanded over the phone.

"Neely Kate's gettin' attacked by Raddy Dyer's sister."

"Is she hurt?" he asked, his voice surprisingly tense.

"They seem to be in a tug-of-war with their clothes at the moment, but both of them are good and ticked."

"Sit tight," he said and hung up.

I hadn't told him where we were.

But the door burst open seconds later. Jed marched over to the two of them without a word. He slipped an arm around Neely Kate's waist and pulled her back, but Leah followed, grabbing a handful of her hair.

Now *I* was ticked. "Let her go, Leah!"

"That bitch is gonna pay! She ripped out one of my extensions!" Sure enough, a long strip of dark hair lay on the floor.

Jed tried to twist Neely Kate out of Leah's grasp, but she wouldn't let go of Neely Kate's hair.

Neely Kate kept screeching, "I'm going to kill you, Leah Dyer!"

I rushed over to the waitress and gave her a sheepish look. "Sorry."

"Hey!" she shouted as I snatched the pitcher from her. It made me feel a little better that I'd left enough money to cover the beer and a generous apology.

Leah and Neely Kate were so close together that there was no way I could only toss the beer on one of them. With a silent *I'm sorry* to Neely Kate, I tossed the liquid in Leah's direction.

The effect was as immediate as pouring water on the Wicked Witch of the West. Leah screamed and dropped her hold on my friend.

"Rose! Let's go!" Jed shouted, already dragging Neely Kate toward the door.

"Let me go, Jed Carlisle!" Neely Kate shouted, trying to pry his hand off her waist. "You have no reason to be here!"

I made a beeline to my truck, not even looking back to see if Leah or her friends were following. Jed had dragged Neely Kate over to his car, holding her off the ground as easily as if she were a rag doll.

He glanced over at me as he opened the back door of his car and unceremoniously dumped Neely Kate inside. "Go!" he said, exasperation on his face.

I wasn't sure which one of us had earned his exasperation, but I suspected it might be both. I hadn't told him where we were, so I also suspected he'd followed us. Had he been tailing me all day? I hadn't noticed him, which told me I was majorly failing this PI gig. Maybe I could convince Neely Kate to pursue a different hobby. Like crocheting. Or sudoku.

My phone vibrated with a call, and I pulled it out of my pocket and answered without looking.

"Hey, Rose," Joe said. "I'm just checking up on you and Neely Kate."

Oh crap. "Hey Joe," I said, trying to sound nonchalant as I put him on speaker.

"I tried calling Neely Kate twice. She didn't answer, so I got worried and called you."

"We're just fine," I said in a cheerful voice as I watched Jed's car speed away from town. I wondered if he expected me to follow him or leave him and Neely Kate to their own devices, but given the way they'd been at each other's throats lately, I wasn't so sure that was a good idea.

I pressed the gas pedal down to catch up.

"Why isn't she answering her phone?"

"Um . . . she's in the bathroom."

A car stopped at an intersection honked its horn as I passed, and I cringed.

"Is that a car horn?" Joe asked.

"Yeah. Somebody's driving past the office and laying on their horn."

"Uh-huh." He didn't sound convinced.

"Was there something you wanted, Joe? Or were you just calling to check on us?"

"Just calling to check. Is Neely Kate out of the bathroom yet?"

"Um . . . no. She had some tacos for lunch, and they're not sitting well."

"Is she okay?" He sounded concerned.

"She's fine, just sitting on her porcelain throne."

"Have her call me when she gets out."

Jed hit the brakes and turned a corner onto a county road.

"Sure," I said, turning the corner to follow Jed, but the phone slipped off my lap and fell to the passenger-side floor.

"What was that noise?" Joe asked, his voice muffled from under the seat.

"Bad connection," I said. "Bye." I could only hope he'd hung up since I couldn't see the phone.

Jed turned off on another county road that went between two trees. He came to a stop in front of an oversized outbuilding that had two double garage doors on one end.

I parked the truck and leaned over the seat to find the phone on the floor, thankful Joe had actually hung up.

As I got out, Jed opened up the back door of the truck, and Neely Kate bolted out. With her long blonde hair flying everywhere and her hands clenched at her sides, she looked wild and ruthless and beautiful. Her white T-shirt was wet and plastered to her lacy black bra.

"What the Sam Hill do you think you're doin', Jed Carlisle?" she demanded. "This is kidnapping!"

"Me?" he shouted back. "You're the one stirrin' up shit in bars! What were you thinking?"

"How'd you even find out we were there?" she asked.

He just glared at her.

If I didn't intervene, they would go at it all day. "Why did you bring us here, Jed?"

He turned his attention to me. "Skeeter thinks you two need to learn how to take care of yourselves. After walkin' into that bar fight, I have to agree with him."

"You think I can't take care of myself?" Neely Kate asked with her hands on her hips.

"I dragged you away from a catfight!"

"I was holding my own!"

Rolling my eyes, I wedged myself between them. "I want to learn what he has to show us." I paused. "But I don't have much time. I've got to get back to work."

Neely Kate shot me a glare that suggested she thought I was a traitor. I could only hope she'd see reason once she calmed down.

Jed had taken a step toward the building, but he stopped and seemed to take in Neely Kate's appearance for the first time. The stupor on his face clued me in on the potential source of their bickering—Jed was attracted to my best friend.

Did she like him too?

That stare only lasted for a moment before Jed turned back to his car and opened the trunk. Moments later, he tossed a T-shirt in Neely Kate's direction while trying not to look at her. "Put this on."

She snatched it in midair, then looked down at her chest. A rare blush tinted her cheeks. For a moment, I was sure she'd refuse on principle, but she pulled her own shirt over her head, tossed it into the back of my truck, and changed into Jed's shirt. All without saying a word.

Jed's shirt hung down to her mid-thighs, but Neely Kate could wear a gunnysack and make it work.

Refusing to look at us, Jed led us into the building and flipped a switch by the door. Fluorescent lights flipped on overhead, and I was surprised to see a gym on one side and what looked like a shooting range on the opposite end. He led us to the shooting range first.

"Get out your gun," he said, moving toward a cabinet and opening a door. "And put it on the table."

He set a box of ammunition on the table. I almost asked him how he knew what to get, but then I remembered he was the one who'd given me my first gun. The exact model of the one I had now.

He gestured for me to sit down. "When I gave you the gun, I never had time to show you how to use it."

"We've had target practice behind the house on Rose's farm," Neely Kate said defensively. "I showed her how to shoot."

"You can never practice too much," Jed said. "Rose needs to become so familiar with her gun that she can use it blindfolded."

He spent the next ten minutes showing me about the gun, and then he had us both use the shooting range. Of course, Neely Kate made all her shots—in the head, in the heart, and then quite a few in the groin. My own shots were all over the place—but by the time we finished, I hit the target more often than I missed.

All that shooting must have bled some of the anger from Neely Kate because she was a lot calmer by the time we finished.

Jed walked us to my truck. "Next time we'll work on some self-defense moves."

"Next time?" Neely Kate asked.

He turned to her. "Skeeter wants her to be able to defend herself."

Neely Kate started to protest, but I stopped her. "No, Neely Kate. They're right. I've been in too many situations I didn't know how to get myself out of."

"Don't sell yourself short," Jed countered. "You've gotten yourself out of plenty of dangerous situations, but you can learn more." Then he shot Neely Kate a smart-assed grin. "And maybe someday you'll be as badass as NK." Then he got into his car and left.

"What was that about?" I asked.

Neely Kate watched his car disappear. "Nothing."

It was definitely something.

Chapter Seventeen

I took Neely Kate back to One Eyed Joes to get her car. I half-expected Leah to run out and chase us down, but I didn't see any sign of her or her friends. Bruce Wayne, bless his heart, had texted to say he was already at the Hendersons' and could replant the bushes on his own. Plenty of potential clients had contacted us for consultations, so I called a couple of them and set up appointments for the rest of the afternoon.

By six, I'd just finished the last client and was about to text Neely Kate when my phone rang. Henryetta Animal Clinic popped up on my screen, and my stomach twisted into knots. Should I answer?

I pressed accept before I chickened out.

"Rose, it's Levi," he said in a cheerful voice. "I'm calling partially to check on Muffy. How's she doing?"

I felt like an idiot for worrying it would be a personal call. He was just a good vet, checking on his patient. "She seems to be the same. I haven't seen her much today because I've been working on job sites, but I left her with a friend. However, last night and this morning she was pretty out of it."

"That's to be expected. Is she limping as much when you let her down?"

"No, she didn't seem to favor it as much this morning."

"Good. Why don't you cut back on the dosage? Try a half pill twice a day instead of a whole one. But if she gets too frisky, we might have to move it back up to three-quarters."

"Okay."

"And how about you bring her in on Monday and let me reexamine her? If the swelling's gone down, we can cut it back even more."

"Thanks, Dr. Romano."

"Levi." He paused. "Remember how I said Muffy was partially why I was calling? I'm moving on to the next part now."

My mouth went dry. "Okay."

"I know we talked about your former boyfriends, but we didn't go into details." He paused. "I know you went through a bad breakup last winter."

"Oh."

"Like you said, the gossips love to wag their tongues in this town."

Great. Had he also heard the rumor that I'd hooked up with the notorious outlaw Skeeter Malcolm?

His voice lowered. "But even if I hadn't gotten the warning, I could tell you were being cautious. I respect that." He hesitated. "I had a good time with you last night, and I'd like to go out with you again, but I also want to let you know that I'm willing to take this as slow as you want.

No pressure. Okay?" For the first time, he sounded unsure of himself.

I leaned back in my truck seat. "Thank you."

"So maybe when you come in on Monday, we can discuss the possibility of a second date. Say, a movie up in Magnolia. Or bowling."

I laughed. "I've never been bowling."

"What? How is that possible?" he asked with a laugh. "Then we'll *have* to go bowling."

"Levi, you're a really great guy—"

"Stop right there," he said. "Don't give me the dreaded but. Just take the weekend to think about it. We'll talk on Monday, okay?"

I smiled. What could it hurt? He was easy company, and I could use fewer complications in my life. I wasn't ready to commit to another date, but I also wasn't ready to turn one down. "Yeah. Okay."

"Good. In the meantime, I'm on call this weekend, so feel free to call me if Muffy needs any medical attention or if you have any questions at all—even if they're personal in nature."

I laughed. "It's no wonder all the women are flocking to your office."

"The offer only stands for you," he said, then hung up.

My guts were all twisted up, so I sat in my truck for a moment, staring out the windshield as I tried to decipher my feelings. What was holding me back? My feelings for Mason? But that hadn't stopped me from wanting to kiss James the other night . . .

There was no doubt about it. If I wanted to de-complicate my life, starting something with James Malcolm was the absolute worst decision I could ever make. A relationship with James would be like being in a category five hurricane while going through an earthquake.

So why didn't that scare me like it should?

My phone vibrated with a text from Neely Kate asking me how much longer I'd be. I sent her a text telling her I was on my way to Maeve's.

My last client's house was less than five minutes from Maeve's, so I wasn't surprised when I arrived before Neely Kate. I considered waiting until she arrived to go in, but then I realized I was being silly. No need to act any weirder with Maeve than I already had.

But sadness washed over me as I walked up to Maeve's front door. Maeve was the only loving mother figure I'd ever had, and I'd practically cut her out of my life.

She opened the door with a warm smile, but she took one look at me and worry filled her eyes. "Rose, is everything okay?"

I laughed and wiped tears from the corners of my eyes. "I've just missed you is all. I've been so stupid."

She pulled me over the threshold and into her warm embrace. "You've been dealing with your pain in your own way. I just waited until you decided you were ready to come back."

"How did you know I'd come?" I asked, leaning back and searching her face.

"I didn't, but I prayed you would."

I gave her a tight hug, then took a breath and smiled. "Enough nonsense. What can I do to help you with dinner?"

Neely Kate arrived soon after, and we helped Maeve finish preparing dinner. Then the three of us sat around the table and talked for several hours, making up for lost time.

But Maeve didn't mention Mason at all. In some ways, it was a relief, but it didn't seem fair for her to have to hold back on my account.

"Maeve, you can talk about Mason if you'd like," I said, then lifted my hand when she started to speak. "No. Just listen." I took a breath. "We both agreed that going our separate ways was the best option, and I'll confess part of the reason I've stayed away from you is because any reminder of him was painful. I'm in a better place now, and I want you in my life. I've missed you. But Mason is your son—your only remaining family member—and I don't want you to censor yourself around me. You can talk about him as much or as little as you want. I just want you to know that I'm a big girl, and I can handle it."

She leaned over the table and covered my hand with her own. "Rose, you would be perfectly within your rights if you didn't want to talk about him."

"I know. And I appreciate you considering my feelings, but I still care about him too. Maybe it will help to know how he's doing. If he's really okay."

She looked into my face. "You really want to know?"

I nodded, my eyes blurring with tears. "Yeah."

Sitting back in her seat, she studied me. "He's thrown himself into his new position with the state's attorney general. They have him working on a special case, and he's loving every minute. But I can tell he's lonely, if nothing else than from the fact that he's working so much. Even more than when he was an assistant DA in Little Rock and here in Fenton County."

"Has he moved on?" I asked, my tongue feeling heavy. "Has he dated anyone else?"

She held my gaze. "The truth?"

He had. My stomach plummeted to my toes. I regretted asking the question, but for some reason I *needed* to know. I nodded. "Yeah."

"He's been on a couple of dates that I know of."

I stared at her in shocked silence. The knowledge hurt worse than I'd expected.

Neely Kate gave me a sympathetic glance. "Are you okay?"

Maeve looked worried. "I shouldn't have told you."

I shook my head, wiping away a tear falling down my cheek. "No. I needed to know. I think I've been waiting in limbo for him to change his mind and come back. Now . . . now I know it's okay to move on."

"Rose, I'm so sorry," she said as her own eyes filled with tears.

"Well," I said, forcing a smile, "I'm not. I've spent a lot of time thinking about it, and the truth is that I wouldn't change a thing. I saved Mason's life. I stopped J.R. Simmons. That has to be enough."

Maeve didn't look entirely convinced, but she flashed me a smile. "After this discussion, I think we all need cheesecake."

"Not me," Neely Kate said, pushing back her chair. "I'm going to head home, but Rose, you should stay."

I gave her a worried glance. "Are you sure?"

She grinned. "There are a lot of perks to gaining an older brother, but there are a few drawbacks as well. Like the fact he makes me check in with him every six hours or so while he's out of town." She winked at me. "Thanks for the save about being in the bathroom this afternoon."

My eyes widened as I realized I'd forgotten to tell her about Joe's call.

She laughed. "It's good. But now he's calling me Princess Porcelain." But the light in her eyes told me that she liked having a big brother to tease and annoy her.

Maeve beamed. "I'm so happy Joe finally came to his senses and realized what a gift it was to find a half-sister he never knew about." She turned to me. "And I know you might have had a thing or two to do with that."

Shaking my head, I laughed. "Someone had to shake some sense into him."

Neely Kate gave Maeve a hug goodbye, then scooped up a drowsy Muffy and took her home.

Maeve and I had a slice of cheesecake, and after I helped her clean up the kitchen, she walked me to the door. We stood there for a moment, and then she took my hands and looked into my eyes.

"I love you like a daughter, Rose Anne Gardner, and you were the best thing to happen to Mason in ages. But I understand if you change your mind and decide it's too painful to see me."

I shook my head. "Sorry, Maeve, you're stuck with me." My voice stuck in my throat. "I need you more than you know."

"I need you too." She pulled me into a warm hug.

"Thank you for being truthful with me," I said.

"I think we've had too many secrets for too long."

While I agreed with her in principle, I seemed to be jumping back into more of them.

***

I was less than a mile away from home when my phone rang. The number was the one Trixie had called me from earlier.

"Trixie?"

"Yeah," she said in a soft voice.

"What happened this afternoon?"

"I couldn't make it."

"I was worried."

She released a short laugh and then began to cough. When she caught her breath, she said, "That's funny."

"I was. I know Buck's not nice to you. I was worried he'd found out about our meeting."

"What do you know about Buck?"

"Honestly, not much, but it doesn't take a fool to realize he's trouble with a capital T."

She hesitated. "Let's just say I got tied up."

I hoped she didn't mean literally. "How can I help you, Trixie?"

"Who says I want help?"

"Because you hardly know me, yet you've called me twice. I'll try to help, but I need to know what you need."

"I can't talk about this on the phone. Meet me at One Eyed Joes. I'm headed there now."

I cringed. I wasn't sure that was a good idea given what had happened at lunch. But it was too late to ask her to meet me somewhere else. She'd already hung up.

I drove for ten more seconds, trying to make a decision, but who was I kidding. Of course I was going. The only question was whether or not to include Neely Kate, but after her earlier performance, I made the executive decision for her to sit this one out. I considered texting her to let her know, but she'd be ticked. Better to ask for forgiveness than permission had been my philosophy for the last year. No point in switching things up now.

Chapter Eighteen

One Eyed Joes was hopping when I walked through the door. If it was this busy on a Thursday night, what was it like on the weekends?

I spotted Trixie right away. She sat at the bar, smoking a cigarette with one hand and holding a tumbler in the other. She was dressed more sedately than the last time I'd seen her, but that wasn't saying much. While she wasn't wearing a sequined tube top, she had on a halter shirt with a deep V, a short skirt, and four-inch spike heels. I wondered again about her profession.

The stool next to her was occupied by a middle-aged man covered in tattoos, and when Trixie saw me approach, she gave him a rough shove. "Beat it."

He growled at her, and for a moment I thought he might hit her, but he wandered over to a group of men at the other end of the bar. One look at her made me realize that somebody else *had* hit her. She was good with makeup, but I could see the hint of a bruise under her eye. I took his seat, inwardly cringing that it was warm.

"Is that from Buck?" I asked, lifting a finger to point in the general direction of her face.

"He found out I called you earlier." She pinched her lips together and shifted her gaze to the four couples who were doing a line dance on the dance floor. "I need a drink."

I gave her a hard stare. "Looks like you have one."

She gulped down the quarter inch of amber liquid in her tumbler, then slammed the glass onto the counter with enough force I was surprised she didn't break it. "And now I don't."

And now I was good and irritated. "If you're insinuating that I'm gonna buy you another drink, you've got another think comin'."

The bartender caught my eye and moseyed on over to me. "What can I get you?"

I glanced around the room. This didn't seem like a wine kind of place. In fact, I had to wonder if they stocked any wine at all. "I'll take a bottle of beer."

"And I want a whiskey," Trixie said with a slur. Great, she was already drunk. Was she even going to tell me why she'd called?

"She's on her own tab," I told the bartender.

"That's okay," he said with a wink. "Yours is taken care of."

"By who?" I asked.

The bartended tilted his head sideways, and when I turned my attention to the opposite end of the bar, I found myself staring into the amused face of Buck Reynolds.

"You set me up," I said to Trixie, trying to decide if I should be ticked or scared. Probably both.

She gave me an apologetic look. "After he found out I called you earlier . . . he made me."

Before or after he'd given her that black eye?

"Did Buck kill Rayna?"

Tears filled her eyes. "Rayna was my best friend."

That didn't answer my question. I lowered my voice. "Do you need help?"

She cast an anxious glance at Buck before turning back to me, her eyes now hard. "Buck's waitin' for ya, and he doesn't like to be kept waitin'."

The bartender handed me an open bottle, and I hopped off the stool and headed over to Buck's side of the bar. If I'd learned one thing last winter, it was this: if you find yourself in a dangerous situation, one you can't leave, take charge of it. Buck may have called this meeting, but I could still gain the upper hand.

I walked over to him with a confident strut, reminding myself that I had a full arsenal. My loaded gun was in my purse, along with my Taser—loaded with a new cartridge and my full can of pepper spray. I could handle this. But now I was cursing myself for not contacting Jed.

No one knew I was here.

I stopped next to Buck. He'd turned in his stool and leaned his forearm on the bar. "Well, aren't you like a cold glass of water on a hot day?"

I shot him a glare. "What do you want, Mr. Reynolds?"

He laughed. "Mr. Reynolds? Do I look like an old fart to you?"

I could play this two ways—nice or sassy—and right now I was feeling pretty cranky. I decided I could take the nice approach with the next Fenton County lowlife I encountered.

If there *was* a next time . . .

Who the heck was I kidding?

I put my hand on my hip. His features were strong, but there was a bit of droopiness under his eyes, plus some crow's-feet in the corners. I'd guess him to be in his early forties, but I decided to goad him. "As a matter of fact, you do. So what do you want, gramps?"

His jaw tensed, but the surprise in his eyes was quickly replaced by amusement. "You're a funny one . . . Rose Gardner."

I tried not to show my shock. I'd definitely given them my fake name at Jaspers. "Aren't you the clever one," I said, slipping into my Lady persona without even thinking about it. Something else I'd learned while masquerading as the Lady in Black was that attitude mattered, particularly with dangerous men like this one. "You obviously went to a lot of trouble to bring me here—beating up your girlfriend and all—so why don't you just cut to the chase?"

"I want that necklace."

"You and everyone's brother."

His eyes narrowed to dark slits. "It's mine."

"Well, congratulations," I said with a hint of sass. "I'm not sure what you want *me* to do about it."

"I know Raddy hired you and your friend to look for it. And I know you two have been known to get results. So when you find it, you're gonna skip the middleman and bring it straight to me. Got it?"

"So you're gonna pay us the five hundred dollars Raddy promised us upon delivery?"

He laughed, but it wasn't a pleasant sound. "Yeah. Sure."

We were far more likely to win the bucking bronco event at the Fenton County Rodeo than we were to get our money from Buck. But that was beside the point.

"I'm gonna need that necklace by tomorrow night," he said.

"I'm very well aware of the deadline."

"How'd you get mixed up with Skeeter Malcolm?"

I should have expected that question. That's probably why I was here. It occurred to me that I hadn't just used my pseudonym with Buck; I'd given it to Hugh Wagner too. Were the Wagners mixed up in this? "Coincidence. Same place. Same time."

"To take down J.R. Simmons."

"That's right. It was all in the news."

"Funny how Malcolm got involved."

I gave a noncommittal shrug.

"Rumor has it you were the Lady in Black."

I laughed and then took a swig of my beer. "I heard she was a sophisticated business woman from Louisiana."

Rather than answer, he picked up his drink and took a sip. "You're an interesting woman, Rose Gardner."

I set my bottle on the bar. "I think I'll be going now. I would say it was a pleasure, Mr. Reynolds, but that would be a lie."

I turned around and headed toward the door.

"We're not finished here," he called after me, his voice carrying over the noise.

"I say we are." I kept walking toward the door, my heart beating wildly in my chest. I expected him to have someone stop me, but I reached the door and walked out. Moments later, I got into my truck, turned it on, and instantly locked the doors. No one had stopped me. No one else had even called out my name. What in the world was Buck Reynolds up to? Why had he arranged for me to come meet him? Had I given him what he wanted to know? What had he gained by seeing me in person rather than talking to me on the phone?

Against my better judgment, I called James. If Buck was asking around about him, I had a feeling he should know.

"Rose," he said when he answered, his tone hard to read.

"Something happened I think you should know about."

"Are you okay?"

"I'm fine. But someone was asking about me working with you last winter."

"Who?"

"Buck Reynolds."

He was silent for several seconds. "He asked you when you saw him last night?"

"No. Tonight. Just now."

"What were you doing hanging out with Buck Reynolds?"

I released a long sigh. "Trixie called me. She said she needed my help and asked me to meet her at One Eyed Joes."

"You went back there after what happened this afternoon?"

Of course Jed had told him, but it didn't sit right that James was now getting half his information about me secondhand. "I didn't bring Neely Kate this time."

He paused, and when he responded, his voice was hard. "Jed's sittin' across from me, so who the hell was your backup?"

I understood his concern, but I wasn't interested in a lecture. "Do you want to hear what happened or not?"

"Did he hurt you?"

"What? No."

"Did he threaten you?"

"No. Not directly. Now shut up and let me tell you what happened." When he didn't interrupt, I continued. "When I saw Trixie with Buck last night, I could tell she was scared of him, so I asked the bartender to slip her a note."

"And what did this note say?"

"I told her to call me if she needed help. I left my number, but she didn't have my real name. I used the fake name that I used when Neely Kate and I went to the pawn shop."

"So Trixie called you and asked you to meet her at the bar."

"She called me around lunchtime and asked me to meet her at One Eyed Joes—that's why Neely Kate and I were there, but Trixie never showed. She said Buck found out." I told him about her black eye, the way Buck had announced his presence, and how he'd known my real name and that Neely Kate and I were looking for the necklace. "He told me to bring the necklace to him when we found it, and then he wanted to know how I knew you."

"He said my name."

"Yes."

He waited a beat, then asked, "So what did you tell him?"

"That we only worked together because we both had our own reasons for taking down J.R. He asked if I was Lady, but I laughed it off as ridiculous and then left."

"He let you?"

"He said we weren't finished, but I walked out anyway, and he didn't stop me."

"Where are you now?"

"On my way home."

"Is anyone following you?"

"No. I've been lookin'." I'd learned my lesson with Jed earlier in the day. "Was Jed followin' me all day or just to One Eyed Joes?"

"Neither. He saw you pull into the lot. Figured if you were hanging out in a trucker bar, you might need backup. And he was right. So let's talk about why you chose to go there alone tonight."

"After what happened this afternoon, I didn't want to bring Neely Kate."

"Good call. So why didn't you call Jed?"

"Come on, James. Isn't he tired of playing babysitter?"

"It doesn't matter if he is or not. His job is to do what I tell him to do."

"You don't have to send anyone at all. I did just fine on my own tonight."

"You got lucky, and you damned well know it."

I saw no reason to agree. "I'm not your responsibility, James. Not anymore. When I was Lady, you had a vested interest. That's over."

"Don't make me go there, Rose."

I rested my elbow on the door and rubbed my temple to stave off the headache I could feel coming on. "I'm not. But I'm pointing out that you're putting your most valuable guy on what is now a very low-priority job. It doesn't make business sense."

"Fine. Call me next time."

I released a laugh. "*You're* gonna come runnin'?"

"I'm gonna assess the situation and determine what resources to allocate."

"James, why do it at all?"

"Because we're friends. If the situation were reversed, would you come help me?"

"Of course, but you're not calling me all the time to do it."

"Not true. I used your resources last winter, often with little notice and at great personal burden to you. Hell, I called you just a couple of days ago."

I couldn't help but grin. "You said we're friends. You told me once that you don't do friends."

"I was an idiot. Now are you safe?"

I checked the rearview mirror again. "Yeah."

"If you hear so much as a tree branch scrape your window, you call me straightaway. Got it?"

"Got it."

"Rose. Be safe."

I was going to try my best, but trouble seemed to find me, even when I wasn't looking.

How long until Buck Reynolds showed up on my doorstep?

Chapter Nineteen

Neely Kate was already in her room with the door closed when I got home. She'd sent a text earlier saying she was going to bed early and she was taking Muffy with her.

I was having an uneasy, nonsensical dream about James, Raddy Dyer, and Buck Reynolds when I awoke with a start and realized my phone was ringing. I didn't recognize the number on the screen. Who was calling me at 2:39 in the morning?

"Rose, I need your help," a man pleaded after I answered.

"Raddy?" I asked, bolting upright in my bed.

"If you don't help me, he's gonna kill me."

My breath caught in my throat. "Who's gonna kill you?"

"I can't tell you on the phone. You have to come to me."

"No," I said. "Call the police. Call a friend. I'm not coming."

"He's gonna get Malcolm."

That got my attention. "*Who's* gonna get Skeeter Malcolm?" Oh my word. Was he talking about Buck?

"Meet me at the fertilizer plant in thirty minutes, and I'll tell you then. Come alone. If I see anyone with you, I'm leaving."

"No," I said in a harsh tone. "You're not gonna coerce me into meetin' you with some vague threat. Someone's always out to get Skeeter Malcolm. What makes you think I care about him anyway?"

He released a harsh laugh. "I'm not sure how much you care about him, but I saw how he was with you in the barn—he's got it bad for you. Right now it's my secret. But if you don't come, you have no idea who I'll tell."

I was already scrambling out of bed. This was James' nightmare come true. "I'm coming."

"That's what I thought." He sounded happy with himself. "But if he or one of his guys comes even close to the place, I'm gonna tell everyone I know." Then he hung up.

I grabbed a pair of jeans out of the closet and pulled a T-shirt out of my drawer. My heart hammered in my chest as I pulled on the clothes. Should I call James? After our conversation several hours earlier, I wasn't sure he'd condone this outing since it was specifically about him. Still, he'd been right. I couldn't meet Raddy without letting someone know what I was up to, and there was no way Neely Kate would let me go alone.

Grabbing my phone, I crept down the hallway and then the stairs, avoiding a few of the wood boards I knew to squeak. My keys were in my purse in the kitchen, so I grabbed it off the table and slipped out the back door.

The night was cool for early June, and I wished I'd grabbed a jacket, but I couldn't risk going back inside for one. Raddy had said I had to be there within thirty minutes. I didn't plan on being late.

The fertilizer plant was on the southwest end of town, but the quickest way to get there from my farm was to go through town. At least I wouldn't need to worry about traffic at this time of night.

When I was less than five minutes from the plant, I figured it was as good a time as any to give James a heads-up. I drew up his number and hit the call button, then put it on speaker and rested the phone on my lap.

He answered on the second ring, his voice tense. "Rose."

"I'm okay," I said. "But I'm about to do something that I might need help with."

"Anything at three a.m. is bound to be trouble."

"You're right . . ." I hesitated, trying to figure out the best way to say this without embarrassing either one of us. "I'm meeting Radcliffe Dyer."

"*What the hell for?*"

"He says he needs my help."

"Then tell him to go fu—"

"*James.* He's going to tell people that you . . ." I forced myself to continue. "He says he knows you care about me because of how you acted in the barn." And just then it occurred to me that I'd never tried to dispute it. I could attribute my stupidity to the fact that I'd been roused from a deep sleep, but that one slip of judgment might cost both of us more than we were willing to pay.

"When and where are you supposed to meet him?" His voice was calm and cold, but a slight hitch told me he was furious.

"He told me I had thirty minutes, which means I have ten. I'll have about five minutes to spare."

"You turn around and go home. Just tell me where you're meeting him, and I'll take care of it."

"No," I said, my voice rising. "What are you gonna do?"

"I'm gonna take care of it."

I knew exactly what that meant. "*No. I'll* take care of it."

"By talking to him?" he asked, sounding incredulous. "By having a vision?"

That pissed me off. "You sure as hell appreciated my visions and my negotiatin' skills last winter."

"That was different!" he barked in my ear.

"How the hell was it different?"

"If Dyer spreads this around, you'll have a bull's-eye painted on your back. You'll be my Achilles' heel. When you were working as Lady last winter, no one knew who the hell you were."

"James—"

"This is deadly serious, Rose. If this gets out, I'll have to claim you to protect you."

"You claimed me before," I huffed. "When I first started working for you. You said you claimed me to protect me then."

"That was different. I claimed your business. This time I'd have to claim *you*."

"And would that be so bad, James?"

"It would be a goddamned disaster."

Tears stung my eyes. I was about to give him a stinging retort, but I saw flashing red lights in my rearview mirror. "I'm getting pulled over. I have to go."

"By Simmons?" I was surprised he sounded hopeful.

"No, I'm still inside the city limits." Although barely. I'd already skirted around downtown and was on the road leading to the plant. I was probably less than a mile away. "I wasn't speeding. I don't know why I'm getting pulled over." I slowed down and turned on my blinker.

"That damned Henryetta Police Department is full of a bunch of idiots. Now where the hell is your meeting? We can't let that fool Dyer spread the word."

"James, I have to go."

"Keep the damn phone on. Don't hang up."

Setting the phone on the seat next to me, I came to a stop on the shoulder of the two-lane road. I watched in my rearview mirror as a lanky officer climbed out of his patrol car, hitched up his pants, and started to meander toward me.

"It's Officer Ernie." Lord only knew why he'd seen fit to pull me over, but I hadn't been on his radar for months. Maybe he'd missed me.

I rolled down the window as he approached.

"Rose Gardner," he drawled in a confrontational tone. "Why am I not surprised?"

"Officer Ernie, what seems to be the problem?"

"What are you doing driving around in the middle of the night?"

"I don't see that it's any of your business, but if you *must* know, I couldn't sleep, so I decided to take a drive."

He started whirling his hand around in circles. "Just drivin' around at three in the morning."

"Like I said, I wish I could be sleepin'," I said. "But it begs the question, what are *you* doin' up? I thought you worked days."

"There's trouble afoot, Rose Gardner, and where there's trouble, you're usually not far behind."

"Trouble?" I asked innocently. "What kind of trouble?"

"Don't you go sassin' me, little missy."

I took a deep breath. "Officer Ernie. I'm not up to any trouble. Like I said, I couldn't sleep. I'm driving around trying to sort out a problem."

"What kind of problem?"

I resisted the urge to tell him again that it was none of his business. "I'm worried about my sister."

"Violet?"

The genuine concern in his voice sent a pang of guilt through me. "She's supposed to come home in a few weeks, but she might be coming down with a cold. It could turn into something serious because she's immunosuppressed."

"I'm sorry. Violet's a sweet woman. She's been in my prayers."

My mouth dropped open in shock.

He took a step back and gave me a curt nod. "You go on with your drive, but be careful. There was some trouble up at the Trading Post earlier tonight, a big fight with some gunshots fired. We haven't figured out who's behind it yet."

I gasped, truly in shock. The Trading Post? The coincidence wasn't lost on me. "Oh my word. Thanks for the warning."

"You headin' back to your farm now?"

"No," I said, still reeling from the news about the shooting. "But I'll head back soon."

I rolled up the window as he walked back to his car. He was clearly waiting until I pulled back onto the highway, so I started driving and hoped he didn't follow me. How would I explain pulling into the abandoned fertilizer plant? But he did a U-turn and headed back into town.

I pushed out a loud sigh of relief, then realized I'd forgotten that James was still on the phone. "James, what do you know about the shootings at the Trading Post?"

"I wasn't part of it, if that's what you're asking."

"That's where Crocker's men hang out. It's also where Raddy met the guys he plays poker with. I bet the shooting has something to do with Raddy and that stupid necklace. That's why he's so desperate for help."

"Which makes him dangerous. *So where the hell are you going?*"

"I can't tell you. If you or anyone else shows up, he says he's going to blab."

"If you let me go, I'll make sure that never happens."

"No. No violence."

"Rose, he's threatening you. He's threatening *your life*. He's already brought violence into it."

"He just wants my help. He asked me to come and help him, and I told him no. Then he pulled out his threat to get me to come. Alone."

"He didn't want Neely Kate to come too?"

"No. He asked me to come alone."

"Something's not right here. He's up to something—and it's nothing good."

"I can't *not* go." The fertilizer plant came into view, and my heart thudded wildly against my chest. "I'm about to turn into the place. I need to hang up."

"*No. Do not hang up.*"

His voice was so commanding I jumped in my seat. "James, I'm not telling you where I'm meeting him."

"Just keep me on the line and let me hear what's going on. Then if you feel like you need me, I'll step in, but I have to know where you are so I can be ready. Otherwise, I might not get there in time."

"You won't come in unless I tell you to?"

"You're calling the shots, Lady."

Did I believe him? He'd trusted my judgment when I was the Lady in Black, and he hadn't lied to me yet. "I don't know how carefully he's watching, so you can't get too close. There's a gas station across the street where you can park."

"Fine. Agreed." I heard the ding of his car as he opened the door. "Now tell me where."

"I'm meeting him at the fertilizer plant, but I'm not sure where yet."

"You got your gun?"

I glanced over at my purse. "Yeah." I turned the corner onto the cracked asphalt and headed toward the small complex of buildings. Raddy hadn't told me where to meet him, but I wasn't surprised to see an old car parked out in front of a smaller office building. "It looks like he's hanging out in the old office."

"It makes sense. If he's paranoid, he's gonna want a more controlled environment so he can see who's coming and going. But he didn't take into account the fact that he's basically trapped."

"You're not gonna come storming in, are you?" I asked.

"Not unless you ask me to, but try to get him to meet you outside. If you go in, you could become a hostage. Or worse."

As I pulled up behind the old car and parked, I didn't want to let my mind wander to *or worse*. But I was sure as shooting going to take my gun. I checked the clip, then said, "I'm about to go in. I'm going to put the phone in my jeans pocket so you won't be able to talk to me."

"We need a code word," James said. "For when you want me to jump in."

I thought for a second. "Blue cheese," I said. "I'd never say that otherwise."

"Blue cheese it is." I heard a grin in his voice. "Jed usually picks something like ace of hearts, or 1957 T-bird."

"I'll remember that for next time," I said as I stuffed the gun into the back of my jeans, hoping there wouldn't be a next time. I'd worn a fitted T-shirt, and the bulge at the small of my back was noticeable. I only hoped it was dark enough that Raddy wouldn't see it. "I'm getting out now," I said. "So you need to stop talking."

"Rose," he said, his voice insistent. "Be careful."

"I will."

Chapter Twenty

I grabbed my phone and stuffed it into my front pocket. Heading toward the entrance, I glanced around to see if anyone was lurking in the darkness. "Raddy!" I called out. "I'm here and alone, and I got here before your deadline."

The only response was silence.

"Raddy Dyer, I'm tired and cranky, and I really want to go back to bed, so get your booty out here and tell me what you want."

"Did you bring him with you?" Raddy called out from the shadows.

"Bring who?" I turned toward the direction his voice had come from—the front door of the small office building.

"Malcolm. Your bodyguard."

"You told me to come alone, so I came alone. Now what do you want?"

"Come inside and I'll tell you," he said.

"No way. I have no idea who's in there, and I'm not stupid. I don't owe you a thing other than to help you find your stupid necklace. So if you want to talk to me, you'll have to do it with me standin' out here."

"I ain't comin' out there," he said in a belligerent tone. "I'm not stupid either."

I groaned. "I came alone, Raddy, just like you asked. Now tell me what in the Sam Hill you want from me, or I'm goin' home." I pointed my finger toward the door. "And you won't tell a soul a blessed thing about Skeeter Malcolm. You said you'd talk if I didn't come. Well, I'm here, so you better keep your trap shut unless you want me to hunt you down myself—if Skeeter doesn't get to you first."

He stepped into the doorway, his face beaming. "So I was right? You and Malcolm are a thing."

"No. We are *not* a thing."

"Then what's going on between you two?"

"That's none of your cotton-pickin' business. My personal life is none of your concern, Radcliffe Dyer. You have no right to be snoopin' and pryin'."

"And I want to keep my personal life private too, but people are snoopin' and pryin' like crazy. All my skeletons are fallin' out of the closet."

"Then you shouldn't have shoved so many in there," I snapped back, getting good and ticked. "Now what do you want?"

"Malcolm really does have feelings for you. I'm right, huh?" He seemed pretty pleased with himself. "That's why you showed up."

Something about the way he kept hounding on this topic felt off. "What happened tonight at the Trading Post?"

"How would I know?" His hasty response didn't fool me one bit, but I could circle back to that question. First I needed to understand his fascination with my relationship with James. It wasn't idle curiosity. I suspected he planned to use it as a bargaining tool. "Why ask just *me* to come out? And why couldn't I bring Neely Kate?"

"Because you're the one with the ties to Malcolm. Better to leave Neely Kate out of it."

I had to agree with him on that. "All right. You got me here, so tell me what you want. We keep beatin' around this bush, so just *tell me*."

He paused. "I want you to put in a good word for me. Tell Malcolm that last night was a misunderstandin'."

"Why?"

"Because I need him. He's the man who rules this county. I want an in with his men. I want his protection."

"Sorry to bring you bad news, but Skeeter Malcolm doesn't respond well to blackmail."

"He doesn't have to know about the threatening part. Just get him to help me."

"You're plum crazy if you think Skeeter Malcolm is gonna help you just because I asked him to. I'm nothin' to him."

"He didn't act like you were nothin' last night. Men only act possessive like that when someone's threatening their woman. You're his."

"You are so far away from the truth you might as well be in Antarctica. We've worked together as *business* partners. If you want to work out a deal with Skeeter Malcolm, you'll have to negotiate it yourself." I took a step backward. "Because you're wasting my time and yours. I'm goin' home and goin' back to bed."

He stepped out of the shadows, pointing a rifle at me. "I don't think so."

I told myself that Raddy was scared, that he was only using the gun as a prop to get me to do what he wanted. But my heart sped up anyway. The fact that he was scared made him reckless. "Put that damn shotgun away, Radcliffe Dyer, before someone gets hurt. If you really want to get a deal with Skeeter, do you think shootin' me is the way to go about it?"

He didn't budge.

Oh crap. James was listening and probably on his way now. I couldn't let this escalate. "*Put it down, Raddy!*"

He hesitated, then lowered the tip.

"Thank you for putting the gun away," I said, even though it wasn't totally gone. But hopefully it would be enough to hold James back. I took a breath and gave myself a second to gather my wits. "Now stop all this nonsense and let's get to the heart of the matter. You want me to approach Skeeter and tell him what exactly?"

"Tell him to protect me."

I shook my head. "Protect you from what?" I tilted my head. "You *were* part of that shooting tonight, weren't you?" A new worry hit me. "Did you shoot anyone?"

"No, but I was there."

"What happened?"

"I went to talk to Buck, to try to reason with him and ask him to help me leave town. But he was good and pissed. He reminded me that I have until 8:00 on Friday night to hand over the necklace. If I don't, I'm as good as dead."

"So go to the sheriff."

"No!" He ran a hand over his head in frustration. "That's where those skeletons come in. I've done some bad things, and Buck Reynolds knows what they are. If I have him arrested, he'll blab all my secrets to the sheriff."

"So let me get this straight. You can't find the necklace, and Buck has threatened to kill you if you don't hand it over by tomorrow night?"

He nodded.

"And you want Skeeter to offer you protection. You know you have to give him something in return, right?"

"Yeah, I'm gonna promise to not tell anyone about you."

I shook my head. "No. That's never gonna work. He could just make sure you never talk to anyone again and be done with it."

His eyes went as wide as pool balls.

"You have to give him something valuable."

The tip of his gun rose again. "Yeah. And I'm lookin' at it."

"*Dammit, Raddy!*" I shouted. "Will you just stop and use the twenty brain cells God gave you? That's not gonna work!"

My insult didn't seem to faze him, but it didn't sway him either.

I pushed out a tension-filled breath. "You have to give him something he can use."

"You think he wants the rest of the jewelry?"

I shook my head and groaned. "Not the jewelry. *Information.* You've been playin' poker with Crocker's old cronies, right?"

His eyes narrowed. "What of it?"

"Are you part of their group?"

"I play poker with them on Tuesday nights, but that's it."

"Surely they talk about business while you're there."

"Sometimes . . ."

"Do they ever talk about Kip Wagner?"

His eyes widened. "Why?"

Bingo. That's what I was looking for. "Because that might be something you can use to bargain for protection. What do you know?"

He shook his head. "Nuh-uh. I'm not telling you nothing. I'm only telling Malcolm."

"You think if I approach Skeeter Malcolm and ask him to protect you in exchange for information, he's just gonna do it? He'll want to know what you have to offer."

"I think Skeeter Malcolm would rob the Piggly Wiggly in broad daylight without a mask on if you asked him to."

I gave him a look of contempt. "Well, *someone's* sadly deluded. And even if Skeeter Malcolm would entertain a meetin' with you, I'd never set it up unless I knew for a fact you actually had something to offer. So start talkin'. What do you have to offer?"

"Some of Crocker's men are aligning with Wagner."

"What else?"

"*What?* Ain't that enough?"

"Shoot," I said in disgust. "I found that out while pumping gas at the Short Stop last week. I bet my kindergartner niece knows that. Give me something else."

"This could get me killed, you know," he whined.

"And I can guarantee you that pointing a shotgun at me like you're doing now is far more likely to make that come true."

He lowered the gun but didn't look too happy about it. "Wagner's planning something for next week."

My irritated expression didn't slip one bit, but I secretly rejoiced that Wagner didn't have a big gun battle planned for Friday night. Maybe we'd somehow altered the timeline of my vision. "What's he plannin'?"

"I don't know."

"Think harder."

"I'm not in the inner circle," he said. "I don't know much. Just bits and pieces. Names and things they're doin' to spy on Malcolm."

I slowly reached my hand toward the phone in my pocket. "I'm getting my phone out to call Skeeter, so don't go shootin' me unless you want to meet Skeeter Malcolm's bullets before you ever see his face."

He nodded and I carefully pulled out my phone and pretended to call him. "Raddy Dyer wants a face-to-face to share information about Kip Wagner in exchange for protection."

"Did he really hold a shotgun on you?"

"Mr. Malcolm," I said. "I know this is the middle of the night, but Raddy seems insistent."

"Tell him we'll come to him there."

I glanced at Raddy. "He says he'll come here."

He looked worried. "Is he gonna kill me?"

"I give you my word he won't kill you."

James grunted in my ear. "What the hell are you doing, Lady? Don't go promising him that."

"How can I believe you?" Raddy asked.

"You do or you don't," I said to Raddy, trying to sound nonchalant. "You're the one who's desperate to talk to him. He seems unconvinced that you actually have something to share."

"Fine," Raddy groaned. "But only Malcolm—like the other night. None of his men." He lifted his gun. "And you stay to make sure he doesn't try anything."

I suspected my role would be as a hostage and not a diplomatic peacekeeper. "Fine. I'll stay."

James grunted in my ear. "Like hell you're staying."

I knew he wanted me as far away from this mess as possible, but I was part of it, whether either one of us liked it or not.

"We're at the old abandoned fertilizer plant," I said. "By the office."

Raddy's eyes darkened and his gun was trained on me again. "I didn't say you could tell him."

"If you want to meet with him, he has to know where to come," I said, trying not to freak out about the large gun this angry, frightened man was aiming at my gut. "And I can promise you that when he arrives, your negotiations will go south pretty quickly if you're pointing a gun at me."

"He's a dead man," James growled.

Raddy pointed the business end of his gun toward my phone. "Hang it up. He can hear what's goin' on."

Little did he know.

When I didn't move, he stepped closer, sounding more insistent. "End the damn call and toss the phone to the ground."

James' car was already speeding around the corner, but I did as Raddy requested. He was skittish enough. I wasn't about to give him any reason to pull that trigger.

Fear filled Raddy's eyes. "Move closer to me."

"Raddy, listen to me," I said, lifting my hands. "You can work this out with Skeeter, but you can't look like you're threatening me."

"Move closer!"

I took several steps toward him, but apparently not fast enough. He grabbed my wrist and dragged me to him, positioning me so the tip of his gun dug into my upper back.

That's when I knew things were about to get ugly.

Chapter Twenty-One

*J*ames' car screeched to a stop, and he leaped out in an instant, his car still running, his gun pointed in our direction. "Let her go, Dyer."

"No. I need your word that you won't hurt me."

"My word doesn't mean shit," he said as he stalked around the front end of his car.

"Don't come any closer or I'll shoot her!" Raddy shouted.

I pushed out a breath, trying to stay calm. Panicking wouldn't help. I had to de-escalate this situation and fast. "Everybody just take a moment to calm down. Let's think about this logically. Raddy, if you shoot me, you're as good as dead."

James' eyes darkened. "You'll *wish* you were dead by the time I get done with you."

The look on his face told me he meant it. "James."

"I knew it!" Raddy shouted, starting to sound panicked. "She *is* your woman!"

"I'm not his—"

James took a step closer. "She's mine, and I guaran-*damn*-tee you that I'll cut off your balls and shove them down your throat if you harm one hair on her head, so I suggest you send her over to me now." He shot a quick glance at me, flicking his eyes down and then back up. "Rose, you ready?"

He wanted me to duck so he could shoot Raddy, but we needed him alive. "No," I protested. "Just give me a minute."

"I've given you about ten. The negotiating is done."

"He knew you were meeting me?" Raddy asked in disbelief, jabbing the tip of the gun into my flesh. "*You told him?*"

"I'm giving you one last warning, Dyer," James said in a deadly tone. "Let her go by the time I get to three. One."

Raddy's grip tightened. Would I be able to drop to the ground in time like James wanted me to?

"*James! Stop!*" I pleaded, trying to hold his gaze, but he was keeping his focus on the man behind me. "Raddy's not really going to shoot me, so just take a few steps back and give us a second," I said. How could I get them to calm down?

James' jaw clenched. "No."

"*James.*" I glanced over my shoulder at Raddy, not surprised by the wild look in his eyes. "Raddy, you've screwed this up, but it's not hopeless. You can still get out of this. Let me help you."

His gaze flicked over to James before returning to me. "He's gonna kill me."

"James," I said in a firm voice, still holding Raddy's gaze. "Assure Raddy that you aren't going to hurt him."

He was silent for so long, I was certain he wasn't going to agree. "Fine, I'll let him leave, but I have a few conditions of my own."

Wariness washed over Raddy's face, but I held his gaze, trying to exude calming energy despite the fact that my heart was beating in my throat. "Okay, what are they?" he finally asked.

"First, you drop your hold on her and lower your gun. Second, you tell me what you know. Three, you leave and keep this entire incident to yourself."

Raddy started to speak, but James cut him off. "I'm not done."

"What?"

"Four, you will never contact Rose Gardner again. If I so much as find out you were two people behind her in line at Walmart, I'll hunt your ass down and kill you. And it won't be one of my men—it will be *me*."

Raddy gave me a questioning look.

I lifted my eyebrows. "Given the fact that you're holding me at gunpoint, it's a generous offer. I suggest you take it."

"Fine," Raddy said, swallowing then glancing over at James. "But she stays between us."

"No."

"*Yes*," I said. "Now let me go, Raddy."

He slowly loosened his hold, and I took a cautious step to the side, turning so I could see them both, which was when I realized they were both still holding their guns on each other.

"Raddy, drop it," I said.

"Not until Malcolm does."

James looked at me, his face hard, and I gave a slight nod. I knew he'd seen the lump at the small of my back. He knew I had my gun. Raddy must have been too focused on the situation to notice.

James tossed his gun onto the gravel parking lot, then narrowed his eyes at the man to my right.

Raddy looked like he was about to burst into tears, but he relented.

"What do you know?" James demanded.

"Only bits and pieces. Buck Reynolds has been creeping into some of your pot markets, undercutting your prices."

"He's got to be losing money with that strategy."

"He was going to slowly cut you off, but he's gotten impatient. He and Wagner are planning a full takeover next week."

It was worse than I'd thought. Two of them were plotting against James.

"They're gonna attack my pool hall?" James asked.

Raddy's head bobbed up and down.

"What about the sheriff? They're not afraid of getting caught?"

"Buck's planned a distraction, but I don't know what it is."

"Where's the necklace?" James asked.

I shot a surprised glance at him, but his expression was unreadable.

"The shootout tonight was over that damn necklace," James said. "Why's it so important? Was it really your grandmother's?"

Raddy looked like he was about to swallow a basketball. "No. And I didn't bet it in no poker game either. I stole it from Buck after a poker game last month. I hid it with my grandmother's jewelry, but then Rayna kicked me out and changed the locks. I stirred up shit with my momma, hoping she'd be able to get it back without letting Rayna know it was worth anything. But when I snuck into Momma's house to steal it, the necklace wasn't there."

"Reynolds didn't miss it?" James asked in disbelief.

"He kept it in a safe. He was showing it off to me and a couple of other guys, but someone walked in. I snatched it out while Buck was distracted. He shut the safe door and was none the wiser. I snatched a couple of smaller pieces too, but he's most interested in the necklace."

"Smaller pieces," I said. "Like an owl pin?"

His eyes widened in surprise as he nodded.

"But when Buck realized it was missing, he had to know it was one of the three of you. How'd he pin it on you?"

"The other two guys ratted me out. He realized it was gone on Monday and gave me until Friday night to find it. That's why I hired you and Neely Kate. I figured Rayna had it and you could convince her to give it back."

"You hired them to find a necklace you stole? And put them in danger?" James asked, his voice as cold as ice.

"Rose and Neely Kate were never in any danger!" Raddy protested. "Buck never knew they were lookin'!"

"Until you told him," I said. "He knows now."

James looked like he was about to shoot Raddy and be done with it. "Why not break into your own house and get the damn thing yourself?"

"I tried that, but I couldn't find it anywhere."

I turned to Raddy. "Why did Buck kill Rayna if he was giving you until Friday to turn it over?"

"Because Trixie found out about it. She was gonna try to convince Rayna to split whatever they hawked it for. Buck must have caught wind of it and decided to step in sooner."

I gave Raddy a scrutinizing look. "When I saw Rayna at Walmart, she didn't look like a woman who thought she was sitting on thousands of dollars' worth of jewelry."

"She'd heard so many stories, she wasn't sure what to believe," Raddy said with tears in his eyes. "I know I cheated on her, but I loved her. I never wanted her dead."

"Are you sure Buck killed her?" I asked.

"I thought so. I saw a guy running out. But when I confronted him tonight, he swore he didn't do it."

"Then who did?" I asked.

"I don't know." His voice broke. "No one else had a reason to."

"Do you believe him?" I asked.

He looked torn. "He had no reason to lie to me. He's admitted to killin' people before. He threatened to kill me if I don't deliver the necklace, but he said he wouldn't waste his time killing Rayna."

I shot a glance to James, but he was wearing his crime king face—expressionless and scary at the same time.

"Why didn't you hawk the necklace right away?" I asked. "Why sit on it?"

James answered this one. "Because Buck would have put feelers out in every pawn shop within two hundred miles. If Dyer tried to sell it, Buck would know. He had to let it cool off."

Raddy nodded. "I never thought he'd connect it to me. I didn't mean no harm. What does Buck need with a white sapphire necklace? I planned to pay off my gambling debts, then take Rayna on the dream vacation to Six Flags like she wanted. She has a thing for Looney Tunes."

She must have if she'd spent over five years with Radcliffe Dyer.

"How did Reynolds become associated with Wagner?" James asked.

"They're banding up together. Partners," Raddy said to James. "Buck said you'd put a chokehold on a lot of money-making ventures since February. They plan to take over and change things back to the way they were before."

James was silent for a moment, and I studied him. He'd told me he'd been making some changes in the underworld, but I had no idea what form that had taken.

"How many men are involved?" James asked.

"I dunno. Maybe fifteen. Some of Crocker's old guys won't commit. They're too scared of you."

"Has Wagner planted any spies?" James asked.

"I've heard he has, but I never heard any names."

James hand clenched at his side. "I want the names of the ones who are loyal to Wagner and Reynolds."

Raddy's mouth twisted. "If I tell you, I'm a dead man."

"Without the necklace, you'll be a dead man without my protection, so you better start talking."

"But if Rose and Neely Kate find it—"

James looked like he wanted to throttle Raddy with his bare hands. "Rose and Neely Kate aren't looking for shit for you. You got it? Now start naming names or I'll shoot you and be done with it."

Raddy nodded, then listed off a string of names, none of which I recognized other than Buck Reynolds and Kip Wagner.

"What about Hugh Wagner? Is he involved?" I asked. James gave me an odd look. I wasn't supposed to know much about the Wagners, let alone *know* them.

"No." Raddy shook his head. "Hugh stays out of it. He doesn't want to be involved."

For some reason, that made me feel relieved.

"Anything else you can think to tell me?" James asked Raddy.

"No."

"James." I hoped he understood the meaning of the message I was about to give him, because there was no way I was going to come right out and say I wanted to have a vision. "I've ensured the negotiations," I said when he shifted his gaze to me. "Now I want to do the other."

James gave me a long hard look before he gave his head a small shake and turned to Raddy. "Do you still want protection?"

Raddy started to cry. "Yes."

James reached for his phone and then held it to his ear. "I'm sending you a package. Put him in a safe house for a few days. I'll send him to the usual spot. Meet him in half an hour." He stuffed his phone into his pocket and gave Raddy a hard stare. "One of my men will meet you at the Atchison parking lot. The code word is Atlanta. Get anything you want to take and meet him there in thirty minutes."

"Thank you, Skeeter," he said between sobs. "You saved me."

"Don't thank me," James said in a gruff voice. "You should be thanking Rose. If it was up to me, you wouldn't be walkin' away in one piece. You held a gun on her and threatened her multiple times. But she's set on following through with the original agreement, so make no mistake about it—I'm doing this for her. Not you."

Raddy's head bobbed up and down as he reached for his gun.

"You're gonna leave that right where it is," James said. "You're lucky enough to be leaving of your own accord. Don't push it."

Raddy didn't answer, instead scrambling to get into his car. The moment the engine sputtered to life, he made a tight U-turn and drove toward the road.

James stood in place, wearing his poker face. I couldn't tell if he was angry with me or if he was pissed at Raddy. Most likely both.

"James," I said softly. "Thank you."

He looked like he wanted to cuss me out, but then he stooped and picked up his gun and Raddy's. Stalked over to his still-running car and opened the door. "Let's go."

"What are you talkin' about? My truck's right over there." I thrust my hand in that direction.

"I just let Dyer drive away. Rose, that fool has the ability to spread the word to half of Henryetta that you have me on speed dial. I'm not letting you out of my sight until I know it's safe."

"You just offered him protection. Surely he knows that will negate your offer."

"I'm not taking any chances. For all I know, he's running off to Wagner and seeing if he can get a better deal. Until I can figure out the fallout, you're staying with me."

"At a safe house?" I cringed. I'd stayed in several, and their accommodations were lucky to rate two stars.

"No, my place. Now get in."

"*Your* place?" I asked in disbelief.

"You say that like I just announced I was bringin' you to the county dump."

"I'm just surprised." In the entire time I'd known him, I'd never been to his house. I didn't even know where he lived. My stomach fluttered with excitement at the thought of seeing his personal space. Whenever I thought about Skeeter's home, I envisioned the pool hall, although I knew that didn't make much sense. Still, I had to wonder what I'd find.

Had he left a woman in his bed?

"You know," I said, my stomach churning. "On second thought, I think I'll just go home and sleep in my own bed."

His jaw tensed. "That's not an option."

I blinked and glared at him. "*Excuse me?*"

"I let you have your way with Dyer. I followed your rules, and now you're going to follow mine."

It wasn't that I disagreed with his request—given the circumstances, it wasn't a bad idea to stay with someone who could protect me. But staying with James . . . at his house? I suddenly appreciated his reluctance to come to my own home. It was just so personal, so intimate. After everything that had happened between us these last few days, I wasn't sure I could handle it.

"Maybe I could just stay with Jed."

His eyes narrowed. "Jed's busy doing something else."

"At three in the morning?"

"He's digging into what happened at the Trading Post."

"Merv?" While Jed was James' right-hand man, Merv was a close second. But Jed actually liked me. At best, Merv tolerated me, and he liked me even less after he'd gotten shot helping me back in February.

James' face hardened and he pointed to the open door. "Get in the damn car."

Part of me rebelled at the command, but he was right. He'd played by my rules with Raddy; it was time for me to bend to his. "I have to get my purse out of the truck."

Looking leery of my sudden agreeableness, he said, "Get in. I'll get it."

I squatted and picked up my cell phone, then pulled the gun out of the back of my jeans and got in the car. James was back in a matter of moments, handing me the purse as he climbed behind the wheel.

"I hid your keys. I'll have one of my guys pick up your truck tomorrow." He shifted into drive, pulled a U-turn, and headed toward the road.

"Just how long do you expect me to stay with you?" I asked with a bit of attitude as I stuffed my gun in my purse and set it on the floor in front of me.

"As long as it takes, Lady," was his terse reply.

"I have jobs I need to work on tomorrow."

He shot me a glare. "Then I'll send someone to watch over you."

"Jed?"

He hesitated. "No. I'll send Miguel. Brett handled the Homer Dyer situation well enough, but he's still too green. I don't trust him with this."

"Why not Jed?"

James slowed down when we got to the road, then turned right and headed south of town. "The truth?"

"Of course."

"Earlier today, he asked to be pulled off as your backup."

I sucked in a breath. It hurt that Jed didn't want to be my guardian anymore—we'd been through so much together, and he was as much a friend as he was a protector—but I had a sneaking suspicion his request didn't have anything to do with me.

"What's going on with Jed and Neely Kate?" I asked.

He shot me a sharp look. "What the hell are you talking about?"

"When Jed saved us from Homer Dyer the other day, he and Neely Kate were at each other's throats, not to mention the repeat this afternoon. What's goin' on?" But I had a feeling I knew.

"How would I know? You're with them a hell of a lot more than I am."

Was Jed's attraction to Neely Kate new? Before this mess with the necklace, Neely Kate and I had last seen Jed in April, the week before my trip to Houston to donate my bone marrow to Violet. I'd seen him a few times since my return, but never with Neely Kate. Had they seen each other when I wasn't around?

I wanted to solve the mystery of Jed and Neely Kate, but I also wanted my friend and protector back. Jed was someone I trusted, literally, with my life. The look James was giving me told me that he understood. "Is this going to be a problem?"

"You trust Miguel?" I asked.

His eyes narrowed.

"Okay," I conceded. "Stupid question."

"But you might not be going out in public at all tomorrow. I need to assess the situation."

"So you expect me to hide out indefinitely?"

"You're the one who decided to give Dyer the proof he needed that . . ."

His voice trailed off, and I wondered what he'd intended to say. That I meant something to him? It was the reason he refused to be seen with me in public now that I'd retired my Lady in Black veil. "He would never have tied us together if you hadn't found him in my barn. What were you doing there, anyway? You never come to my farm."

"It's like I said. I was checking up on you. Jed told me about your run-in with Homer."

The pieces fell into place. "Jed didn't want to come, and you were afraid that it would scare the bejesus out of me if you sent someone I didn't know."

He was quiet for a moment. "No. I wanted to check on you myself."

I had to wonder if it was partially because he'd missed me. Sure, we'd seen each other on Tuesday, but there'd been no chance for us to talk like we usually did. But the last thing I wanted to do was chat about my behavior that night in the barn. "Why wouldn't you let me have a vision?"

"There was no reason to take the risk."

"What risk? How many visions did you ask me to have last winter when I worked for you? Dozens."

"That was different."

"How was it different?"

"You know why it's different. You wore a damn disguise back then. You could spout off about whatever you'd seen, and it wouldn't matter—*they didn't know who you really were.* But Raddy knows you plain as day. If you'd said anything to spook him, our agreement would never have worked."

"Jed and I explained away tons of visions. Neely Kate too. And you said knowledge is power. It might have given us information we *need*."

"*No.*" He shot me a quick glance, his jaw tight. "Do you know how I got in this position as the king?"

"You're forgetting I was there at the auction where you won your position, Skeeter Malcolm, watching you bid," I said, pissed at his condescending tone. "I was the one who kept you alive. Because of my visions. I saw you die every which way before we got it right."

"Yes, you kept me alive, but you didn't get me a seat at the table." He shook his head in frustration. "It took a lot of planning. A lot of biding my time. Knowing when to pursue something and when to let it go. Even when it goes against everything you want." He paused. "You do it for the greater good."

Was he talking about me? On second thought, it was pretty narcissistic to think so. He'd lived in the criminal world for over fifteen years. Despite the trials and tribulations he'd faced in his new role, he'd prospered. Then I reminded myself that he'd prospered as a *criminal*. It wouldn't do to forget that. James Malcolm had killed men. But had he done it in self-defense or cold blood?

Everything I'd seen of James told me it was the former. But did it really matter? Dead was dead.

"The fact is that one more group of men is gunnin' to take you down," I said. "They want to kill you, James. You said it yourself: you make more money with your legal ventures than your illegal ones. So stop the illegal ones and become a regular law-abiding citizen."

He ignored my statement and asked, "How do you know Kip and Hugh Wagner?"

I almost played dumb, but it would be a waste of time. "When we were looking for the necklace, we went to both pawn shops after we found out that Rainy Day doesn't sell jewelry. We met Hugh at Ripper."

"And Kip?"

"I never met him, per se. But a man was watching me from the doorway after I forced a vision of Hugh. My gut tells me it was him."

He held his tongue for a moment. "You forced that vision because of me."

"Well, yeah. I was confused. You'd hinted that Wagner works in retail, which would fit with a pawn shop, particularly one with a rough reputation. But Hugh hardly seems ruthless. So after I bought the brooch—"

"What brooch?"

"The owl I asked him about. It's gold with red rubies for eyes. It fit Raddy's description of one of the pieces that he said belonged to his grandmother. When Hugh handed it to me, I grabbed his arm and forced a vision of what he was doing Friday night. I heard Hugh talking to someone named Kip. They didn't say anything you could use, but it confirmed that Kip was ambitious—and he acknowledged people were gonna get hurt."

"And what did you say when it was over?"

"That there would be casualties of war, a phrase he used. But Neely Kate smoothed it over by saying I was talkin' about a Civil War book I was reading."

"You said you *heard* Hugh and Kip talking," he said. "Why didn't you see him?"

I wasn't so sure he'd be happy to hear I'd been preparing for battle with Neely Kate, so I'd hoped that part would slip past him. I should have known better. "When I started to force the vision, Neely Kate put her hand on my shoulder too. So I had two visions at once—I *saw* hers; I only *heard* Hugh's. It was the first time that's ever happened, and I felt like crap afterward."

"But you blurted out something related to your vision of Hugh." From the way he muttered it, he was talking more to himself than me.

"Yeah. Although I'm not sure what I would have said about Neely Kate's vision. We were standing in my kitchen."

He was silent as he drove. It took me awhile to realize we were going around in circles, though it was obvious why—he didn't want to draw anyone to his home. It only made it more surprising he was bringing me there willingly. He finally turned off the county road onto a drive that I could barely make out in the dark and thick vegetation. I considered offering him a free landscaping consultation, but he probably kept it that way purposefully. After we drove for a couple of minutes, a two-story house came into view, with a single light glowing in a downstairs window. It was fairly new—much newer than my farmhouse—with river rock siding, wood accents, and a small front porch made of raw timber. A large four-car garage sat to the side, but he parked on the circular drive in front of the house. The large lawn was neatly trimmed, but I noticed that other than the grass and the woods surrounding the house, there was absolutely no landscaping.

This was definitely not what I'd expected. While I'd known better than to assume he actually lived in one of his rat-trap safe houses, I hadn't expected something so *civilized*.

"This is your house?"

He turned the car off and opened the door. "Yep."

I opened the car door and followed him to the front door. Two Adirondack chairs sat facing the gravel driveway. He punched a code into a keypad on his seven-foot-tall wooden front door, then swung it open and waited for me to walk in first.

My mouth dropped open. The living room was two stories tall. A river rock fireplace stood on the opposite wall, flanked by two sets of double French doors. Comfortable leather furniture was arranged around it, but I didn't see a TV.

"Are you hungry?" he asked as he set his alarm system.

I hadn't been until he asked, but my stomach broadcast a loud growl at the reminder of food.

The grin he gave me wasn't his bad-boy grin; this was more real. "I'll make us sandwiches."

I followed him into the fanciest kitchen I'd ever seen, full of natural wood cabinets with a shiny gloss, dark granite counters, and stainless steel appliances.

Definitely not what I'd expected. This kitchen looked like it belonged to a chef.

He opened up the right side of the double-door refrigerator and pulled out packages of turkey, cheese, and a loaf of bread, all of which he arranged on the island.

"You shouldn't keep bread in the fridge," I said as I opened cabinets and found two plates.

He laughed. "Is that right?"

"It gets stale faster."

I grabbed the bag and opened it, then pulled out four slices and put two on each plate.

"I can do it," he said.

"We always work better as partners, don't you think?"

"Yeah," he said, his voice rough. "We do."

I looked up at him, but his face was devoid of expression. While I could see how his poker face would serve him well in his life as a criminal, I found it extremely frustrating. "How long did it take you to learn that?"

His brow wrinkled. "Learn what?"

"To hide what you're feeling?"

His mouth quirked to one side. "I learned that skill long before I started my apprenticeship with J.R. Simmons."

"From your father?"

He nodded.

James told me once that his father had been a cruel man who'd abused him, his younger brother, and their mother. His daddy was the one who'd given him the nickname Skeeter—an insult he'd worn as a symbol of his guilt. James thought he deserved it. He'd been forced to watch his father's abuse, but had been too young to stop it. Ever since I'd learned the truth, I'd called him only by his given name.

"Where's your mother now?"

"Dead."

"And your father?"

"He got what he deserved." He looked away, making it clear he had no intention of explaining the how of it. I suspected he might have had a hand in meting out that punishment.

"Does Scooter live with you?"

"No. He lives in town."

I glanced around and wondered how many women he'd made sandwiches for in this kitchen. The thought made me queasy.

He arranged the plates in front of two stools on one side of the island, then grabbed two bottles of water from the fridge.

I slid onto one of the bar stools, and he sat down next to me. I took a bite, surprised by how hungry I actually was. Apparently negotiating with criminals worked up an appetite. I took in the fancy stainless steel appliances and asked him, "Do you cook much?"

He laughed. "No. I can feed myself the basics, but every Monday and Thursday Sandra leaves me something to heat in the oven, when she comes to clean."

"Sandra?"

He glanced up. "The waitress at the diner in town."

"She knew you when you were growing up," I said. He'd brought me to that diner back in February, when we were planning how to take down J.R. Simmons. Sandra's warmth for James had helped me see a new side of him. "Considerin' how much she adores you, I'm sure she loves cleaning your house."

"She doesn't know it's mine," he said, then took the last bite of his sandwich.

I stopped, my own half-eaten sandwich in midair. "How could she not know it's yours?"

"I had a service arrange it. I never talk to her directly and always pay cash. I got her a smart phone as a Christmas bonus a couple of years ago—she was wantin' to video chat with her son and grandkids in Louisiana—and I text her when I want something specific done."

"Why?"

"Why ask her to do specific things?"

"No, why the secrecy?"

"This is my refuge. I only come here a few days a week, but I can't afford for the wrong people to know about it. And I'd never put Sandra in the position of keeping it a secret."

"So how many people know you own this place?"

"Two. Jed and now you."

I let that sink in. So this wasn't where he brought women after all. "Why did you bring *me* here?"

He took a breath and started to say something. Then he closed his mouth like a steel trap and slid off his stool. Grabbing his plate, he set it in the sink and looked out the window into the darkness. "There are two bedrooms upstairs. The one on the left is mine, but the one on the right is the guest room. It has a private bathroom and towels."

"Why do you need a guest room if no one ever comes here?"

He turned and gave me a look that suggested it wouldn't be wise to push it.

Too bad I wasn't good with orders. I stood next to the island. "Why didn't you take me to a safe house?"

"Would you rather be in one of those dumps?"

I took a step toward him. "You didn't answer my question."

"Because most of them aren't fit for dogs. You know that. Plus, no one's going to be looking for you here."

I stopped in front of him, my heart beating furiously against my ribcage. My head told me to let it go, but something wouldn't let me. "Why did you *really* bring me here?"

The look he gave me was so conflicted, I almost backed down. Almost. "Don't go there, Rose. You don't know what you're doing."

"Do *you*?"

"No. Not with you." He started to walk past me, but then he wrapped an arm around me and hauled me to him so quickly I had to lift my hands to his chest to brace myself. His mouth lowered to mine and then he kissed me with a hunger that might have shocked me if I hadn't shared it.

I slid my hands up his chest and looped them around the back of his head, clinging to him. There was nothing gentle about James Malcolm, and his kiss was possessive and demanding.

His hand slid under my shirt and found my breast. When his thumb brushed over my thin bra, I released a frustrated moan that tightened his hold around my back. But then he dragged his mouth from my lips and buried his face in the hair at the base of my neck. His chest heaved against mine. I waited for him to speak as confusion set in.

"Rose." The regret in his voice was like a stab to my heart.

His hold on me tightened, but then he lifted his head again, dropped his arms, and backed away. My humiliation returned, even more intense than it had been that night in the barn.

He refused to look at me. "I'm never gonna be that man, Rose," he finally said, scrubbing a hand through his hair.

I shook my head in frustration. "What man?"

"The respectable, law-abiding citizen you need. Even if I left this world behind me, I've lived in it too long to be free of the stench of it. But truth be told, I'm not the kind of guy to work a nine-to-five job. Or to have a wife with two-point-five kids."

"And a dog," I said, trying keep my emotion out of my voice. "You're forgetting the dog."

He turned back to me, and his gaze held mine. The sadness in his eyes wrenched my heart. "And the dog," he said ruefully. "I'd rather take a bullet to the head than live that life. It will never be me."

Anger mushroomed in my chest even though I knew he was right, maybe because of it. "You don't get to decide what I want! I never asked you for anything more than you are, James Malcolm," I said, my voice hard. "I never asked you for *anything*."

"You did. Tonight. Radcliffe Dyer is a huge risk to your life. And to mine. I should have eliminated that threat. But I didn't. For you."

I sucked in an angry breath. "You're chiding me for reminding you to have a conscience? For placing value on human life?"

"There's no room for that in this world. You heard what he said. It's why Wagner and Reynolds are coming after me."

"You're full of crap. I *know* you value human life. You valued your mother's life and your brother's. You value mine."

Anger filled his eyes. "To my detriment. Emotion makes me weak. Caring about someone makes me vulnerable. I had to get out of bed at goddamned three o'clock in the morning to deal with a mess created by my own sloppiness." He took several steps away from me and started pacing.

"Are you saying that you don't want me in your life?"

He still refused to look at me. "No. And that's exactly what makes me weak. I'm giving Wagner and Reynolds a weapon to use against me." He turned back to face me. "The most damned effective weapon they could ever have. I'd do anything to save you."

"James," I choked out. "I'd do the same for you."

"I know. And that scares the shit out of me." His face was drawn and he looked like he wanted to throw up. "This can never happen again. *Never.*"

"You can't make that decision on your own. This is between the two of us."

"It's not up for discussion."

"We could work this out. You're not the first man who is a . . . works on the other side of the law to have a relationship."

His eyes hardened. "Criminal. Say it, Rose."

My mouth parted as I watched him.

"I'm a *criminal.* The sheriff could file a dozen charges on me, and I'd probably be guilty of them all. But I'd pay Carter a hefty sum to defend me. Then he'd offer a nice cash gift to multiple people to get me off the charges, and I'd walk free because of my own corruption." He shook his head. "You can't live with that. Even when you worked for me as the Lady in Black, you only did it to save Mason Deveraux's life. You had a higher purpose. My purpose is to make money and gain power."

"I did it to save your life as well."

"But not my business."

I couldn't argue with that. He was right. Tears filled my eyes. "But that's not you. Not the real you."

"Rose," he said so softly I could barely hear him. "It's the most real part of me." He ripped his shirt off over his head, and I gasped. His chest was solid, and his abs rippled down into his jeans. He moved toward me with a purpose in his eyes, and I held my breath, thinking—hoping—he'd changed his mind. Instead, he grabbed my hand and put it on a scar on his side. Electricity zipped through my blood. "See this? This was from a knife fight in my pool hall. It was over a gambling debt."

I gasped and tried to pull away, but he held tight and moved my hand to his left shoulder. "This is from a gunshot wound when I worked for J.R. Simmons."

I looked up into his face.

"I've been on death's door nearly half a dozen times, but it didn't matter because no one gave a shit. I can't afford to worry about someone giving a shit."

"Too damn late, James Malcolm," I said, trying not to cry, trying not to think of all of those horrible things happening to him. "I started caring about you months and months ago. Even before *this*." I motioned between us. "We were friends first, and you damn well know it. Whether we do *this* or not, I care about you."

He shook his head. "No."

"You're full of talk about how bad and brave you are. But it's all talk, because you're a *coward*," I said, my temper heating again. "You want to choose your life of crime over the chance to have a real life, then go ahead. But you're living in denial if you think something could happen to you and no one would care." I poked my finger into his chest. "I know the real reason you're doing this—because you believe you don't deserve to have someone love you. Because your father convinced you that was your truth, yet I'm here to tell you that's a lie." I took two steps up the stairs, then turned around to look into his stunned face. "But guess what? You and I are a whole lot more alike than you give us credit for. You're just too stubborn to see it."

He gave me a long hard look, then walked to the front door.

Chapter Twenty-Two

I hadn't slept well, which wasn't all that surprising. After I'd gone into the guest room, I'd stripped off my T-shirt and jeans and tossed them on a chair in the corner. As soon as I climbed into the smooth sheets, I knew that James had paid a fortune for linens he'd never intended for someone to use. Why?

Our argument kept running over and over in my head, and with each replay, the realization that there was truth in James' proclamation grew heavier and heavier until it felt like it was dragging me to the bottom of the Fenton County Lake.

The time James and I spent together was such a small sliver of his life—a peaceful oasis he'd carved out of the chaos. James had once confessed that his legal businesses were much more profitable and less of an aggravation than his illegal ones, but it seemed unlikely that he'd ever just walk away. The truth of the matter was that he was up to his elbows in dozens of messes that could land him in handcuffs at any moment.

While I liked the man I had grown to know—the one buried deep beneath the intimidation and harshness—that man did not live in this world. But that wasn't entirely true. Glimpses of him had begun seeping out, like the way he'd offered Raddy protection despite himself. Still, I was worried James was right, that the men in his world would consider him weak. And the weak became prey.

The bottom line was that I could never live with a man whose life was in constant danger, not when it was because he was thwarting the law rather than upholding it like Mason did.

Still, the hardest pill to swallow was that he hadn't even given me a choice. He'd made the decision for both of us. I didn't know what I would have chosen if given the option, but I knew one thing for sure: whatever I felt for him was genuine.

I'd spent so much time mulling it over, tossing and turning, that I slept until eight—much later than intended. When I saw the time, I realized that Neely Kate was probably worried sick.

Scrambling out of bed, I dug my phone out of my jeans pocket. There was one missed call from Neely Kate.

Only one?

I called her back, and she answered right away.

"Do you think you'll be at the office today?"

"What?" I blinked and shook my head even though she couldn't see me. "Aren't you gonna ask where I am?"

"No, Jed already told me. He said Skeeter put you into hiding because he's worried about your safety, but he refused to tell me why. This has something to do with Raddy Dyer, doesn't it?"

Did Jed know I was at James' house? And had he conveyed the news to Neely Kate in person? I wanted to ask, but I had a feeling she wouldn't tell me anything. "Raddy called me in the middle of the night and asked me to meet him. He said he was in trouble and needed help."

"Why didn't Raddy call *me*?"

"He told me to come alone. He specifically told me not to bring you."

"Why would he do that?" she asked, sounding good and ticked. "And why would you listen to him? We were supposed to be workin' on this together. Why would you go without me?"

I paused, ignoring the last question in favor of the first. "Because he was exploiting my friendship with James. He threatened to tell the other side about me and James if I didn't show."

"What did he want?"

"Raddy got scared after he pissed off Buck Reynolds last night at the Trading Post. So in exchange for James' protection, Raddy told James what he knew about the guys who are making a bid for James' position."

"But Skeeter went and killed him anyway?"

"What? No! He sent Raddy to meet a guy who was going to take him to a safe house."

Neely Kate paused. "Rose, Raddy Dyer is dead."

The room swayed, and I sank down on the bed. "*What?*"

"They found him shot in the head in the Atchison parking lot."

I felt like I was going to throw up. "No."

"Why are you so surprised?" she asked flatly. "Skeeter Malcolm wouldn't let someone threaten him and then walk away. He's already got enough turmoil in the county. It would set a precedent that would make regaining control next to impossible."

I put a hand on my stomach, hoping to settle my nausea. "James said he let Raddy go. Because of me." But he'd also stormed out of his own house, pissed that he'd caved to me.

"Rose, Raddy Dyer's dead. There's no disputing that."

"It could have been Buck. Turns out Raddy stole that necklace from Buck. It was never his grandmother's. He just put it with the family jewelry in Rayna's drawer to try and hide it." But I said the words in a kind of daze. I couldn't stop thinking about how Raddy had been found dead at the very place he was supposed to meet James' man. And why would Buck kill Raddy when he still hadn't turned over the necklace?

"So the necklace is still missing?" Neely Kate asked.

"Yeah. Although I'm not sure what it matters anymore. Raddy's dead and it belonged to Buck Reynolds all along." Then I thought about my conversation with Buck at One Eyed Joes. Would he still expect me to find it?

"When's Skeeter gonna spring you loose?" she asked.

She was being so short with me, I sucked in a breath. "What bee's crawled up in *your* bonnet?"

"Because I think it's one giant coincidence that Skeeter Malcolm was out in your barn talkin' to Raddy Dyer right after Rayna was murdered. Other than that one time we were working with him to bring down J.R. Simmons, when has Skeeter ever been in your barn?"

"As far as I know, only that once."

"And Raddy Dyer happened to be out there the only other time he made an appearance?"

Irritation prickled the hairs on the back of my neck. "What are you suggestin', Neely Kate?"

"It's nothing I haven't already told you. I think Skeeter knows all about that necklace, and he wants it for himself."

"And you think he's usin' me to get it?" I asked in disbelief.

"It's a twofer for him. He makes sure you're safe, and he gets to keep the prize. He knows you never wanted it for you. We were gonna hand it over to Raddy."

"You're forgettin' something," I said in a curt tone. "Raddy called *me*. He threatened *me*, Neely Kate. The only reason James met us was to protect me, and he let Raddy go because he knew I wanted him to."

"Are you sure that was his plan? Maybe he just let Raddy—and you—think they'd worked out a deal. You have to know that Skeeter Malcolm is not widely known for negotiating tactics. How do you think he got where he is now? Besides, some people think he's gone soft. With all those guys makin' a run at him, he might have been trying to set an example."

Could she be right? Was that the reason he'd refused to let me force a vision? Because I'd see that Raddy was dead? Did James have Raddy killed?

Her voice was softer when she continued. "You said Skeeter was tryin' to keep Raddy from tellin' people you two are friends. Is that all you two are?"

"What does that mean?"

"Mason's gone, so there's nothing holding you back from starting something with him. You disappear every Tuesday night. We both know who you've been meetin'."

I didn't say anything, but my silence was statement enough.

"I'm not judgin' you, Rose. You deserve a fling. Just make sure it's not something more." She paused. "But I know you. You don't do flings. You're a relationship kind of girl, and Skeeter Malcolm doesn't do long term. He's not a safe bet. At all. You're gonna get hurt, and I'm worried it's gonna be more than just your heart."

What could I say to that? She wasn't saying anything I didn't already know. "I'll let you know when I'll be in," I said with resignation.

I hung up and quickly got dressed, then headed downstairs. My stomach twisted with nerves. Doubts over Raddy were floating around in my head, but I felt guilty for even entertaining them. James would never lie to me. Our entire relationship was founded on truth, which was ironic considering his position. But one thing I could count on was the fact that I could be entirely honest with him without worrying about judgment or recrimination, and I counted on him being one hundred percent honest with me. Sure, he still held lots of secrets, but he told me what I needed to know.

Even as I assured myself, I knew that wasn't entirely true. We were both lying about our feelings for one another. But that was different, wasn't it?

As I landed at the bottom of the staircase, memories of his kiss the night before filled my head, making my stomach flutter. How was I going to face him?

After James' speech about running from domesticity, I wasn't sure what I'd find waiting for me at the bottom of the stairs. It sure wasn't big, bad James Malcolm sitting in a chair on his deck with his feet propped up on an ottoman. He was drinking a cup of coffee, and his laptop was resting on his thighs.

I stopped and stared at him through the set of the French doors that opened to the deck. As I watched him, I realized I had two choices—I could cut him out of my life completely, or I could try to go back to the way things had been before. The choice was obvious. I'd lost too many people lately. I didn't want to lose James too.

Taking a breath to steady my nerves, I said, "I'm surprised to see you here."

"You thought I'd just leave you here alone?" he asked, setting the coffee on a table beside him.

"No. I might go snoopin' into your secrets if you did that."

"Other than the house itself, there's not a single secret here." He shot me a quick glance before turning back to his screen. "I can't risk Sandra finding out who I am."

"So there's nothing personal here?"

"This whole house is personal. It's my refuge. But there's not a single thing to tie it to my *name*. Not even the title."

He'd told me once that no one knew he owned several properties, including the recycling business, around town. A dummy corporation in Texarkana owned it. But I wasn't up to discussing his properties at the moment. "Did you have Raddy Dyer killed?"

He slowly closed his laptop and looked up at me, his face a blank slate. "Do *you* think I killed Raddy Dyer?"

"So you're not surprised to hear he's dead?"

His eyes darkened. "Are you insinuating that I know he's dead because I ordered it?"

Criminal or not, my gut told me to trust him, and my instincts had served me well in plenty of dangerous situations. Sometimes it was all I had to go on. "No. You know what's goin' on in this county, and if you knew there was a fight at a bar last night, you'd sure as heck know about the murder of a man you were talkin' to at three a.m."

His shoulders relaxed—not much, but enough for me to notice.

"So this means I'm safe," I said. "I can go about my business."

"It doesn't mean shit. My man found him dead, lying face down on the hood of his car with a bullet to the back of the head. Who knows what they got out of him before he was shot?"

"They were lookin' for the necklace." But even as I said it, I wasn't so certain.

"What if he offered them information in exchange for his life? Just like he did with me?"

I pushed his legs to the side of the wicker ottoman, and he swung them to the floor as I sat in front of him. "Let's think this through," I said.

"What the hell do you think I've been doin'?"

I shook my head. "Stop blowing your stack and listen." When I was sure I had his attention, I said, "Look, it wasn't any secret that you and I were working together last winter. Shoot, I woke up in the hospital and found you sitting in a chair next to my bed. Not a single person has bothered us about that. Why is this any different?"

He leaned forward, his elbows resting on his thighs, his face a foot from mine. I tried—and failed—to ignore the butterflies in my stomach.

He shook his head. "No one knew I was in your hospital room. I paid a nurse handsomely to keep her mouth shut. And as far as working together, it was business, and we made sure to spread the word that you'd played your part and were done."

"And the criminals in this county believed that?"

"The fact that you and I were never seen together confirmed it. So did the disappearance of the Lady in Black. We let it be known that you were working as a free agent to bring down J.R. Simmons and help your boyfriend. As far as everyone in this town was concerned, you meant nothing to me. You were a means to an end. I had no further purpose for you, so to take you and use you as a bargaining chip would be an exercise in futility."

My eyes widened as the truth hit me. "Oh my word. The very act of showing up yourself last night . . ."

"Proved you meant far more to me than anyone would have suspected."

"So why come yourself? Why didn't you send Jed like you usually do? He might have asked you to shift him to a different duty, but you know he would have come. You could have pulled him off the bar fight for a half hour."

"Because I didn't trust anyone else."

That was new. I'd spent far more time with Jed last winter than I had with James.

"What are we gonna do?" I asked quietly.

"My men are trying to find out what Wagner and Reynolds know."

"Your men know about me and you?"

"*No.* I have them snooping into what Dyer said before he was snuffed."

"So I'm hiding out here?"

"No. I need you to go about your life as though nothing's happened. If you disappear, it will confirm that I'm protecting you. If you go about your business, it will give them a moment of pause, because if you were mine, I'd never risk letting you gallivant in public at a time like this."

The air stuck in my lungs. Was he trying to convince me that I meant nothing to him? But there was no way he'd let me loose unless he was practically guaranteed I was safe. "So who's watchin' over me?"

A small grin tipped the corners of his mouth. "Jed."

"But Neely Kate—"

The grin was gone. "I don't give a damn if those two were goin' at it with bayonets. I don't know what's goin' on with Wagner and Reynolds, and there's no one else I trust to protect you like Jed will." He studied my face, and his expression softened. "You good with that?"

He'd done this for me. He knew I felt safer with Jed than I would with someone else. The knowledge sent a shiver down my back. I tried to convince myself that it meant nothing. Last winter he'd made sure to put his most trusted man in charge of protecting me, but at the time he'd been protecting his business asset. What was he protecting now? "Other than you, there's no one else I trust more with my life."

His eyes changed, and I saw a longing that hadn't been there before. My nerves tingled. He was going to close the distance between us and kiss me; I was sure of it. But that poker face of his slid into place again. He gave me a small nod, then stood and moved to the doorway. "You'll need to drive your truck to your office, but it's been moved. Now that you're up and ready, I'll tell Jed to come get you in fifteen minutes. Once he takes you to your truck, you'll need to head to your office. You're usually there around nine, and if you're out at your farm changing clothes, people will notice you're straying from your normal schedule."

I stood too. "Can I take a quick shower?"

"You don't need one," he said, his voice low. "You smell—" But he cut himself off and stalked into the house.

"James."

He turned around to face me. "Take fifteen minutes, but then we have to go. Your life depends on it."

I shook my head. I'd spent months living in jeans and a T-shirt, with ponytails and no makeup. Why worry about what I looked like now? The forecast for today was hot and sunny, so if I was working outside, I'd be sweating long before noon. "No. Just tell Jed to come get me."

Because the only person I wanted to impress was walking away from me.

Boy, was I stupid or what?

Chapter Twenty-Three

Neely Kate looked up in surprise when she saw me walk through the office door. "Hey."

Muffy was curled up on her dog bed next to Neely Kate's desk. I made a beeline for her, then knelt beside her and rubbed behind her ears. "Hey, girl. Did you miss me?"

She was wagging her tail so hard I worried she'd dislocate something.

"I gave Muffy half her medicine," Neely Kate said. "She seems more alert today."

She did look a little perkier. "Thank goodness."

"I'm surprised to see you here."

I ran a hand down Muffy's back. "We decided it would be safest for me to go about my business."

"So Skeeter *did* kill Raddy."

I shot her a glare. "No. He swore he didn't. And what would that have to do with anything?"

"If he was protecting you because of what Raddy knew, and one of his guys took care of the problem, then he eliminated any threat. You don't need to be under twenty-four watch. Besides," she continued, "if that man cares about you half as much as I suspect he does, then he wouldn't let you out of his sight if he thought you were in danger." She searched my face. "Did you ask him if he killed Raddy?"

"Yeah, and I already told you that he told me no. His guy found Raddy facedown on his car, shot in the head."

"So how is it that you're here now? He wouldn't leave you alone." By sheer coincidence, that was the exact moment three raps landed on the back door. Her brow furrowed. "*No.*"

"Now, Neely Kate . . ." I said as I moved to the back.

"That better not be who I think it is."

This was about to get ugly.

I stood in front of the steel back door and looked out the peephole at Jed's distorted face. I let him in and then closed and bolted the door behind him.

Jed pushed past me, all business as he stood in the short hallway and scanned the office space. "I'm going up to the roof to make sure nothing's amiss up there."

"Okay." I set to work on the padlock on the door to the spiral staircase. The original lock had opened with a key, but I'd switched it to a combination lock for easier access. Working with the seedy underbelly of the Fenton County criminal world had taught me to always have an accessible escape route—more than one if possible. Once I had the door open, Jed slipped through the opening, but I grabbed his arm. "If you're going out onto the actual roof, there's a padlock up there bolting the door closed." I rattled off the combination, and he gave me a curt nod before slipping into the dark stairwell.

"We don't need him here," Neely Kate said as soon as he disappeared. "We did just fine yesterday when Homer showed up."

I headed toward my desk. "We *do* need him, and you know it."

"Why him? Why can't Skeeter send Merv or the guy he sent yesterday?"

I sat down on the edge of her desk and studied her. "What happened between you and Jed?"

Her face turned a soft shade of pink, and she turned back to her computer. "Nothing."

"That's a bunch of malarkey if I ever heard it. Try again."

She looked up at me, and her mouth opened and closed a few times like a fish trying to breathe on dry land before she started to say, "A month ago—"

"The roof's all clear," Jed said in a no-nonsense voice I wasn't used to hearing from him. He'd set aside the formality early in our time together.

"Why are you *inside* our office, Jed?" Neely Kate demanded. "Why can't you wait in your car and watch the front like you usually do?"

"Two reasons. One, I feel like I'll have you two covered better inside; and two, I have work of my own to do." He lifted the bag hanging from his shoulder to demonstrate.

"Work?" Neely Kate scowled. "What kind of work could you have in that bag?"

His gaze held hers. "I could tell you, but then I'd have to kill you."

She held her hands out from her sides. "Then let's go, Mr. Big Talk. I can take you."

I slid off the desk. "No one's havin' a go at anyone." I pointed to the table we kept in the back corner for the few customer consultations we held in the office. "Jed, you can sit back there if you want. We have a folding screen we can set up to block view of you from the street."

A nod was his only response. I started to walk toward the back to grab the screen, but Jed was already headed back there.

"What's your schedule for the day?" he asked as he set up his work space.

"I need to work on some designs and estimates, and then we have to go to a few houses and draw up some plans. Our first appointment is at 10:30, so we need to leave in forty-five minutes."

"Is Neely Kate planning to go?" he asked.

"No, she's staying—"

His mouth pressed into a tight line. "She's going now."

"You don't get to boss me around, Jed Carlisle!" she shouted over her shoulder.

The look Jed gave me insinuated he'd throw her over his shoulder if need be.

Pushing out a long sigh, I sat down at my desk and turned on my computer.

This was going to be a long day.

Neely Kate must have thought so too because she hopped to her feet after all of five minutes. "I'm going to get coffee from The Daily Grind. Do you want something, Rose?"

I hadn't had any coffee at James' house, and my head was beginning to protest the lack of caffeine. "Yeah, my usual." When she started for the door, I called after her. "Aren't you goin' to get anything for Jed?"

She stopped with her hand on the knob. For a moment, I wondered if she was going to ignore me, but she turned and called out in a saccharine-sweet voice, "Would you like something, Jed?"

His response was short. "No."

Without a word, she stomped out, slamming the door behind her.

There was no way I could deal with this all day. I walked back to Jed's makeshift work space and put my hands on my hips. "What on earth is going on with you two?"

He continued to study the laptop he'd set up on the table. "Nothing."

I slammed the lid and shot him a glare. "Don't you *nothing* me. She started to tell me before you came back down from the roof, so I know there's *something*. Now tell me."

He leaned back in his chair, crossing his own arms and giving me a hard look. "It's not my story to tell."

"Then whose is it?"

"Neely Kate's."

What on earth? I dropped my arms and put a hand on my hip. "Did you two have an argument?"

Silence.

"When did you see each other to *have* an argument?"

More silence.

"Did she do something to upset you?"

Something like guilt flashed in his eyes before it was completely replaced by impassiveness. I wondered if he and James had practiced their poker faces together growing up.

What could have possibly happened? I dropped my hands to my sides. "Well, you two need to make up before you drive me crazy!"

I stomped back to my desk and started to text James that this was never going to work. But I stopped before hitting the send button. I was a grown woman—too old to be tattling and complaining. Besides, Jed had played babysitter for Neely Kate and me often enough. I could suck it up for one day.

I'd just sat down when my phone rang. Given what had happened the previous night, I wasn't all that surprised to see Joe's name on the screen. I steeled my back and answered, "Hey, Joe. How's your search goin'?"

"What do you know about Raddy Dyer's death?"

"Well, good morning to you too."

"That didn't answer my question."

"If you're asking if I had anything to do with it, you're barking up the wrong tree. I had no idea he'd been murdered until I woke up this morning."

"Why am I having a hard time believing that?"

Probably because I'd been evasive with him a half-million times before. "I don't know who did it, but I suspect it's because of the necklace."

"No shit," was his terse reply.

"Do you want me to tell you what I know or not?"

I could practically hear his teeth grind before he said, "Go on."

Obviously I couldn't tell him the full story, but I could condense it. "Raddy called me in the middle of the night and told me he'd had a run-in with Buck Reynolds." Basically true.

"Buck Reynolds? What do you know about Buck Reynolds?"

"Honestly, not much. Only what Raddy told me."

"You never had a run-in with him last winter?"

This was the first time Joe had ever asked me for any specifics about my time working for James as the Lady in Black. I'd admitted the truth to him about a month ago, but I'd refused to give details. Until now, he hadn't pressed. "No. Was he one of Mick Gentry's guys?"

"You'd be in a better position to know than me." I was surprised there was no antagonism in his voice.

"I only met the top guys. I never saw the lower ones unless they were standin' guard, in which case I wasn't introduced. They were just there."

"Do you know what Reynolds is up to now?"

I hesitated, then said, "I'm Switzerland, Joe. All information that comes from either side stays with me. I don't tell James what I learn from you and vice versa."

I expected him to argue, but instead he said, "What *can* you tell me?"

"Raddy admitted that the necklace he was looking for was stolen. He'd stowed it with his grandmother's jewelry, which he'd given to Rayna. His plan was to let it sit and cool off before he tried to sell it."

"Let me guess. He stole it from Buck Reynolds."

"Yeah."

"So why did he call you last night?"

I couldn't very well tell him that part. "Obviously he was desperate. Maybe he'd gone through his Rolodex of friends and was down to the slim pickin's at the bottom of the barrel."

"Huh." He didn't sound like he believed me. "Do I need to come home early?"

My heart sank. "I take it you haven't found Ronnie yet?"

"No, but I have one more place to check."

"We're fine," I said. "Keep looking."

"You wouldn't admit if you needed help, would you?"

"Would it make you feel better if I told you we're bein' protected?"

He paused. "Malcolm."

"I'm fine. We're fine. Find Ronnie."

He hung up and I cast a glance down at the screen, realizing Jed had heard my side of the conversation. Well, I'd done nothing wrong, and I had nothing to hide.

Neely Kate popped back into the office a few minutes later and handed me a to-go cup. "Did I miss anything?" she asked in a chipper tone. I almost did a double take. Maybe she was pretending Jed wasn't sitting in the back.

"Joe called."

"Uh-oh."

"He'd heard about Raddy, of course, and asked if he needed to come home early. I told him we were fine."

"And he bought it?"

"Enough that he's not gonna come rushing home."

She nodded, then went back to work. The three of us worked in silence for the next half hour, although I could hear Jed talking in a low voice on his phone from time to time in the back. When it was about time for us to leave for our appointment, Jed got up and moved to the edge of the screen. He cast a glance toward Muffy, who was still curled up on her bed.

"Is she okay?" he asked, pointing toward her.

I leaned over and stroked the top of her head. "She will be."

"What do you plan to do with her when we leave? Are you sure you want to leave her here alone?"

"I'll stay with her," Neely Kate said, still looking at her computer.

"Not an option," Jed said dryly.

I cast a glance at Neely Kate. "I'll see if she can spend the night with Maeve. Since we don't know what's going to happen with our deadline."

"Good idea."

I handed Jed a list of the places we planned to go in case we got separated for some reason.

Jed slipped out the back door, then texted when he was in his car and ready to follow us.

"This is ridiculous," Neely Kate mumbled on the sidewalk as she locked the front door. "No one's gonna bother with me."

When she turned around, I looked her square in the eye. "You matter, Neely Kate."

She blinked in surprise. "What does that mean?"

"It means you're important—to me and to Joe. And to Maeve and Bruce Wayne and Jed, for that matter."

Anger washed over her face. "I don't mean a hill of beans to Jed Carlisle."

I shook my head. "I have no idea what's going on with you two, but the fact that he's insisting that you come despite being frustrated with you is proof that he cares."

She pressed her lips together and headed toward the truck, obviously done talking about it.

After we dropped Muffy off with Maeve, who was more than happy to watch her, we spent a half hour at the first house, talking to the owner and making suggestions.

We were on our way to our next client when I got a call from Jonah.

"Hey, Jonah."

"Rose," he said, sounding uncomfortable. "I hate to ask, but is there any way you could bring by the money you owe the two guys who worked at the Hendersons'? They usually get paid the day they do the work."

"Oh my word," I said in horror. I'd forgotten all about it. "I'm so sorry! Of course! I have an appointment and then an hour-long break. How about I bring it then?"

"That will work. I hate to bring it up . . ."

"No! I'm sorry I haven't paid them already. I'll be by in an hour or so."

When I parked in front of the next client's house, I sent Jed a text telling him about the change in plans.

"We won't have much time to get lunch," Neely Kate said. "Maybe we should move our one o'clock appointment back by half an hour?"

"Then we'll have to move the two o'clock. How about we go through the drive-through at the Chuck and Cluck?"

"You hate that place."

"Hate is a strong word."

"Jed hates that place." A grin lit up her eyes. "Sounds great."

She started to open her door.

"Neely Kate," I said, grabbing her wrist. "What's goin' on with you two? You started to tell me earlier, but tell me now."

She looked over her shoulder. "Mrs. Benson is peering out her picture window at us."

"Then let her look. Talk to me."

Inhaling deeply, she sat back in her seat and looked out the windshield. "When you were in Houston, I went out one night."

"Went out? You mean out to dinner?"

"No, to One Eyed Joes."

"*Oh.*" That shocked me. "By yourself?"

"Yeah." She shrugged. "You were gone, Joe hadn't come back yet, and . . . I was in a weird mood. So I went to the bar, and several guys started hitting on me. It felt good to be wanted, you know?" She looked over at me with pleading eyes.

"Oh, honey. I *do* know." I knew all too well, and I feared how this story would end.

Her mouth twisted as she looked away. "In any case, I drank way too many beers—too many to even *think* about drivin'. I'd been hanging out with one guy, and he offered to take me home." She cast a worried glance at me. "To his home."

"*Oh.*"

She looked down at her lap. "When we got there, we were makin' out, and he was givin' me the hard sell to sleep with him. I mean, I went home with him, right?" she asked in a self-deprecating tone. "Of course he expected it."

I grabbed her hand and squeezed, worried over what she was about to tell me. "No means no, Neely Kate. You didn't owe him a thing. Even if he drove you to Little Rock and back."

She didn't look me in the eye. "I couldn't go through with it, and he got so pissed I thought he was gonna hit me.

So I grabbed my phone and locked myself in the bathroom and called Jed."

"Then what happened?"

"Jed made me stay on the line while he drove to get me. The guy kept beatin' on the door and callin' me names, and Jed heard everything. Then he hung up. The next thing I knew, there was a lot of banging and shouting, and within less than a minute, Jed knocked on the bathroom door to tell me it was okay to come out." Her voice broke. "I was only wearing my panties, and the guy was such a pig he didn't even have towels in his bathroom. Only a couple of hand towels and washcloths. I opened the door, trying to cover myself with my hand, but Jed slipped off the jacket he was wearing and helped me into it, all while avertin' his gaze. Then he put his arm around me and led me out to his car. But I saw the guy's apartment as we left." She turned to me with tears in her eyes. "Jed had busted down the door and beaten the crap out of that guy."

"Was he angry with you? Is that why you two are fighting?"

She shook her head. "No. He asked if the guy had hurt me and looked me over. When he saw the red mark on my arm, he told me to stay in the car and he went back inside for a few minutes. When he came out, he had my clothes. Then he got in the car and took me home."

"Then what happened?" I prodded again after she was silent for several seconds.

"He walked me into the house and insisted on spending the night on the sofa. I told him the guy didn't know who I was. I didn't give him my real name. But Jed said while he doubted the guy would dare to come near me, he was gonna make sure he was there if he did."

"So he stayed all night?"

She nodded. "He was asleep on the sofa the next morning when I went let Muffy out, but he woke up when the stairs creaked."

I shook my head. "I still don't understand why you two are angry with each other."

"I was terrible to him. I started yelling at him, telling him that he shouldn't have beaten the crap out of that guy for me. That all I'd wanted was a ride home. Then I asked him why he had done it."

"What did he say?"

She swiped at her cheeks. "He didn't say. He tried to pull me into a hug, but I pushed him away and kept saying awful, hurtful things. He just stood there, until I finally pushed him too far and he stomped out. Now he won't even look at me."

I wanted to remind her that he'd gotten an eyeful of her yesterday, but it didn't seem like the right time.

"Neely Kate," I said quietly. "Why did you call Jed? Why not Witt?"

She just shook her head. "Why did he even come? Why did he spend the night on our sofa?"

"Because he obviously cares about you."

She shook her head, and a tear spilled down her cheek. "*Why?*"

I wanted to find her mother and shake the snot out of her for destroying her daughter so much she didn't believe anyone could love her. I pulled her into a hug. "I really wish you could see yourself as we do." I leaned back and cupped her wet cheeks. "You're fun and witty and so, so smart. You have a good heart, and you're the most loyal friend a person could have. Even when you're going through hell, you're like sunshine on a cloudy day. You've made the past year bearable, even when things were so bad I felt like I was drowning in sorrow. And if Jed or any other man sees even a fraction of what I see when I look at you, he'd trip over himself to help you."

Her lips twitched into a tiny smile. Then she got out of the truck and walked toward our waiting client.

As I watched her, I couldn't help thinking that if we were really going to start investigating cases, maybe I needed to add tracking down Jenny Lynn Rivers to my own personal list.

Chapter Twenty-Four

We pulled into the parking lot of the New Living Hope Revival Church a little after noon, and I was surprised to see six or seven cars in the parking lot.

"Is something goin' on I don't know about?" I asked Neely Kate.

She studied the front of the church. "No. I don't think so, but it's probably guys from Jonah's work program. I think some of them ride together to jobs."

Like the one I hadn't paid them for. I hope they didn't tar and feather me when we walked inside.

My phone rang, and despite the fact that I could see his car, I wasn't surprised to see it was Jed.

"There's a lot of cars here," he said, parking a couple of rows in front us. "This doesn't follow your typical daily schedule, so I doubt anyone would know you're coming unless the reverend spouted it off, but he does run an ex-con program. It might not be a bad idea for me to go in ahead to scope it out."

While he had a good point, we really didn't have time for that. "Give it to me in percentages. What are the chances someone who's intent on hurting me is gonna be in there?"

"Twenty-eighty."

"Then I'm runnin' with those odds." I hung up and told Neely Kate about our exchange, not surprised she agreed with me. She'd been itching to use her pink, bejeweled Taser, especially after watching me zap Homer a couple of days before.

When we walked through the front doors, we didn't see anyone until we reached the church offices. The door opened to an office for the church secretary, and a door to the left led to Jonah's office. His door was closed, but Jessica, who was both his girlfriend and secretary, greeted us with a warm smile.

"If it isn't two-thirds of the RBW Landscaping company," she said. "Jonah's with someone right now if you want to wait."

"Actually," I said, "I need to leave Jonah some money. He's expecting it, so he'll know what it's for. But it's in cash."

"Not a problem."

I turned to Neely Kate, who had the remaining cash from our exchange with Raddy, and watched as she counted out the hundred in twenties.

"I hear your landscaping business is flourishing," Jessica said. "Bruce Wayne calls a couple of times a week asking for help."

Jonah's office door opened, revealing a man who looked vaguely familiar. "Thanks, Reverend."

Jonah appeared behind him, smiling wide enough to show his sparkling white teeth. His hair was as coiffed as always, and it looked like his streaks had been recently highlighted, although I hadn't worked up the nerve to ask him who he'd found in Henryetta to do them. I hadn't heard word of him showing up in Beulah's Nip and Clip on the square. I couldn't fault Jonah Pruitt for being more put-together than me—shoot, three-quarters of the county looked better than me lately—especially given that Jonah was a semi-famous national TV evangelist. Perfection was expected of him.

"Newton, my door is open any time," Jonah said in his warm baritone voice. "Whether you're a parishioner or not. The Good Lord doesn't care where his children go to church. He has enough love for everyone." Jonah put a hand on his shoulder. "And please, call me Jonah."

"Thank you, Reverend Jonah. I know my brother wasn't a good person, but I still loved him."

My ears perked up.

"Of course you did, and the fact that he was suspected of murdering his wife will make your grief more complicated. But I'm here to talk if you need it." I almost gasped. Newton was Radcliffe Dyer's brother.

Jonah glanced up at me and smiled before he returned his attention to Newton. "I've counseled quite a few of Henryetta's citizens since I came to town last year, and I offer my services free of charge."

"Newton," Neely Kate said as she walked over to him. "I heard about your brother. I'm so sorry."

"Thank you," he said, swiping at the corners of his eyes.

"We're about to go to lunch," Neely Kate said. "Would you like to go with us?"

He shook his head. "I gotta get back to the plant."

"Can we walk you to your car?"

"Sure."

"You two go on ahead," I told Neely Kate. "I'll catch up in a minute." I knew she would try to get information out of him, and he was far more likely to talk to her if I wasn't around.

I turned to Jonah as they walked into the hall. "I'm sorry that I forgot about the money."

"Rose, you have a lot going on right now. I wasn't worried. I just thought you might need a reminder."

"Do you have a moment to chat?"

"Of course!" He gestured into his office, and I took a seat in the chair in front of his desk.

He took the chair next to me and studied my face. "Is everything okay?"

In the past, I'd had multiple informal counseling sessions with Jonah. I'd always trusted his advice, and I could definitely use some wisdom now. I considered going through some pleasantries but decided to cut to the chase. "I had dinner with Maeve last night. While we were there, I asked her about Mason."

"Oh."

"She says he likes his new job and that he's working even more than he did here." I paused. "But she also said he'd been on at least two dates that she knows of."

"How did you feel when you heard that?"

"It hurt. A lot. But I feel like I'm ready to move on. I don't think about him as much. I can go days. I still love him. I think part of me will *always* love him, but I'm confused. I have feelings for someone else too."

He was quiet for a moment. "Do you remember when you realized that you had feelings for Mason? You were getting over your breakup with Joe. Part of you still loved him, but you were ready to move on. You decided you didn't want to be with Joe anymore." He folded his hands on his leg. "If Mason walked through the door right now and asked you to take him back, would you do it?"

My mouth parted as I gaped at him. I'd never considered that. Would I?

"Rose, I don't know who you have feelings for, but if you really care about him, you'll make sure that he's not second choice. Otherwise, it's not fair to him."

Considering James' reluctance to *talk* about us having a relationship, let alone to give it a try, it was probably a moot point. But he was right. I gave him a grin. "How'd you get so smart?"

"After that two-day-old ham on rye I had for an early lunch today, I'm not so sure about my intelligence, but I do know people, and I know their hearts." He smiled at me. "You have a good heart, Rose. You're going to be okay."

I stood. "Thanks, Jonah. You always know the right thing to say."

When I reached the parking lot, Neely Kate was standing next to a beat-up old car with Newton. Jed was still in his car on the other side of the parking lot, talking on his phone. He shot me a glance that told me he wasn't happy.

I considered joining Neely Kate, but I needed a few moments to think about what Jonah had asked me. If Mason drove back to town, knocked on my door, and told me that he wanted to be with me again, would I go back to him? It surprised me that I couldn't immediately say yes. But I couldn't say no either.

Neely Kate gave Newton a hug, and he got in his car while Neely Kate walked toward my truck. When she got in, she gave me a wicked grin. "Well, that was interesting."

"Why do you look so happy? That poor man's brother died."

"Because I found out all kinds of information about Raddy's family."

"What are you talking about?"

"Leah was ticked as all get out that Rayna still had their grandmother's jewelry after she kicked Raddy out. When she found out her mother had taken it from Rayna, she demanded that Mable give it to her."

"So did she?"

Neely Kate gave a look that suggested I'd lost my marbles. "Remember? I saw it all in her drawer. Leah went home last week right after Mable picked it up."

I shook my head. "But that necklace wasn't part of their grandmother's collection in the first place." I gasped. "Raddy told me that he stole the necklace and hid it with the jewelry he gave Rayna. When she wouldn't return it to him, he nagged Mable until she agreed to get it back. But then Mable wouldn't hand it over, so he broke in to steal it. But it wasn't there."

"So what if Leah did the same thing?" Neely Kate asked. "She's the type who wouldn't let a simple *no* deter her. I can see her going and getting what she thinks is hers."

"Why didn't she take the other jewelry?" Then it hit me. "What if she knew that one necklace was real?"

"How would she know?"

"Maybe Raddy let it slip. Or maybe she was familiar with her grandmother's showpieces and realized it wasn't one of them. She might have taken it to see how much it was worth."

My phone rang with an unknown number. Neely Kate and I exchanged a look, and she nodded. I answered, putting it on speakerphone.

"Hello?"

"I found out some interesting things from Raddy before he died." I recognized the man's voice.

My eyes flew open. I looked at Neely Kate and mouthed, "Buck Reynolds."

Her mouth turned into a surprised 'o'.

"So you're the one who killed him?" I asked. "He turned over the necklace?"

"No necklace, but he had some things to say about *you*."

So James had been right. Raddy had tried to see if Buck would give him a sweeter offer, and he'd died for it. Neely Kate and I exchanged a dark look.

"What you want, Mr. Reynolds?" I asked.

"I want my necklace back."

"Sorry. Our client was Raddy Dyer, and he's no longer around. We're done."

"You're *not* done. You will bring me that necklace to the Trading Post by eight p.m., or you'll be meetin' Raddy sooner than you'd like."

I hesitated. Buck hadn't straight out told me what Raddy had revealed to him. I didn't want to tip him off, but I also needed to know what he knew. "If you believe what Raddy told you, then I would think that would be a very bad decision."

"Oh, that's the beauty of it. Malcolm's outrage and vindictiveness will be his downfall."

Neely Kate's eyes looked as large as quarters. Maybe it was petty, but a part of me wanted to say I told you so. The rest of me was confused by why Buck didn't just kill me and set James off now. If a turf war was what he wanted, it would be a sure way to get it. Maybe I was stupid, but I decided to call him on it. "How do I know you're not gonna kill me and be done with it?"

"Where's the fun in that? Besides, before my ultimatum, I thought you were my best shot at recovering that necklace. With the added threat to you and your boyfriend, I'm sure of it. And make no mistake, Rose Gardner, I want that necklace."

"He's not my boyfriend."

He laughed. "Yeah, and I'm the king of France. See you at eight."

We were in big trouble.

"How did Buck Reynolds have your number? What aren't you telling me?" Neely Kate asked.

Well, crap. I still hadn't told her about going back to One Eyed Joes. "When I was on my way home last night, I got another call from Trixie. She asked me to meet her at One Eyed Joes. She wanted to see me right away, and I didn't think there was time for you to come."

The fire in her eyes told me that she wasn't buying it.

"When I got there, Trixie had a black eye and Buck was sittin' at the end of the bar. I'm still not sure why she called the earlier meeting, but apparently Buck found out and forced her to call me last night so we could have a chat. It was a setup." I paused to gauge her reaction.

"Go on."

"He said to skip the middleman and bring the necklace to him. That it was his. Then he asked how I was tied to

James. I told him it was a coincidence, but I wasn't sure he bought it. After James gave Raddy that deal to protect him, Raddy must have called Buck and offered to give him information about me and James, presumably in exchange for an extension on turning in the necklace."

She looked ticked. "You had quite the night."

"Neely Kate."

My phone rang. Jed. I could see him in his car, the phone lifted to his ear, but of course he couldn't come out and confront us in person. I put him on speaker.

"What the hell are you two doing?" he practically shouted. "I thought you had to be across town in thirty minutes."

"We're chatting."

"Uh-huh," he mumbled. "Why did you split up and Neely Kate came out on her own?"

"Because I had to talk to Jonah in private."

"About what?"

Neely Kate leaned closer to the phone. "Apparently you don't know the definition of private."

I needed to tell James about my phone call with Buck, but I wasn't sure how much to tell him. I was pretty sure he wouldn't approve of me turning over the necklace to Buck, but at this point, I didn't have anything to give the man. But what if I *did* manage to deliver it? Could I use it as leverage to at least delay Buck and Kip's attempted coup?

First things first.

"Jed, you don't have to follow us anymore," I said.

"Why not?"

"Part of the reason we've been sitting here is because Buck Reynolds just called me."

"*What?*"

"He wants us to finish our job of finding the necklace, and he won't hurt us if we're helpin' him."

He responded in a gravelly voice. "You should have led with, 'I got a call from Buck Reynolds.'"

I glanced over at him in his car across the lot and lifted my shoulders in an apologetic shrug. "I was working my way up to it."

"If you think I'm going to leave just because—"

"Jed," I said quietly. "Buck knows. Raddy must have contacted him after he left me and James."

He cut himself off and listened in silence.

"His phone call was a threat. He admitted to being responsible for Raddy's murder. He said if I don't deliver the necklace, he's coming for me, and he's counting on James to lose it."

"So he can pull off his takeover. We need to get you and Neely Kate into a safe house."

"No," I said with more force than intended. "Wait." I took a deep breath to steady my nerves. "What if we can avoid a war altogether?"

"Whether you find the necklace or not, Reynolds and Wagner are determined to have a war. There's no way in hell Skeeter or I will let you and Neely Kate get swept up into the middle of it."

"What if I can negotiate a peace treaty?"

"What in the hell makes you think you can do that?"

"I don't know," I said, brushing stray hairs from my face. "Everybody wants something. Buck Reynolds wants his missing necklace. What does Kip Wagner want?"

"He wants Skeeter's throne."

"Maybe. But he didn't make a bid in the auction last November. Raddy said they're upset because their income is

Denise Grover Swank

down. That James has put a stranglehold on some of their business ventures. What if we can find a way for them to regain their income?"

"Their income is none of our damn concern, Rose."

"But it is," I said, grabbing the steering wheel. "If they're making money, they're happy."

"What do you plan to do?" he asked sarcastically. "Give them small business loans?"

"No. But there has to be a way. What is Kip Wagner's illegal business?"

"He sells stolen goods through his pawn shop."

"And how has James cut his income?"

"That's just it, Rose, he hasn't. What he's done is curtailed it. Wagner wants to branch out into the sex industry."

"He wants prostitutes?"

"Skeeter hasn't been tolerant of the idea because most pimps treat their women like shit. He's all for a woman making the call on what she does with her body, but in a lot of cases, once they start working for someone, they're treated like dogs. Skeeter's trying to put a stop to that."

He'd told me that he had rules for women and children. Here was the evidence.

"What if he can find a new venture?" I paused. "Or maybe we can figure out something else he wants."

"Rose, the man is a ruthless, greedy bastard. Men in this world don't negotiate."

"Isn't it worth a try?"

"Skeeter will never approve."

"Give me until tonight. Neely Kate and I will keep searching for the necklace—because if we don't find it, I suspect this war's goin' down sooner rather than later. But if we can deliver it, maybe we'll have the opportunity to negotiate."

"There's no way in hell he'll let you go."

"Jed," I said in frustration. "Aren't you both tired of the turmoil? Sure, James can squash them, but if they survive, he's gained more enemies. If we can find a solution that appeals to their mercenary sensibilities, he'll gain allies instead, even if they're shaky. Can I at least give this a shot?"

"You're putting your lives at risk, Rose."

"Then you can come as backup when I meet Buck. Bring Merv and Miguel." I paused. "I had a vision of James earlier in the week. It was a vision of tonight. I saw you both in the pool hall under heavy gunfire, and then the place caught on fire. You and James were trapped behind the bar with the bartender. I can't let that happen, Jed. You can try to lock me up somewhere, but I'll figure a way out."

When he didn't protest, I knew I had him.

"Fine," he said after a long pause. "But I'll have to run this by Skeeter, and there's no way in hell you two are going off on your own."

"Jed—"

"No. If you're gonna keep looking for the necklace, I'm gonna keep followin' you. We'll talk to Skeeter about the other. It's the best you're gonna get."

It wasn't close to good enough. We could get so much more done if we lost our tail, and I was confident that Buck wouldn't hurt us. He had too much riding on the possibility that we might succeed. Besides, Jed might not approve of the place I wanted to go next.

"Fine," I said. Neely Kate's mouth dropped open in protest. "But first Neely Kate and I have to go inside to talk to Jonah about hiring a few of his guys for a job next week."

"Fine, but don't be gone too long."

He hung up, and Neely Kate gave me a dubious look. "We're not really goin' with Jed, are we?"

"No, we're going to borrow Jessica's car. I know she parks it at the back of the building. That way, we can escape sight unseen and keep investigating. We'll save time if Jed isn't trailing us. Besides, it'll give us more freedom to question people."

"This is crazy."

"You can stay behind if you want," I told her. "You can walk away right now."

"As if," she scoffed. "I'm in this just as much as you are."

"Then let's do this."

We both got out and walked into the church. Jessica was still at her desk, and she greeted us with a huge smile.

"I really hate to ask this," I said, "but is there any way I can borrow your car?"

Her mouth parted in surprise, and she looked back and forth between the two of us. "My car's in the shop."

My heart sank. We hadn't come up with a plan B.

"But," she said, "the church just got Jonah a car and he hasn't sold his old one yet. You can borrow it."

"Where's it parked?" Neely Kate asked.

Jessica's forehead wrinkled. "In the back."

Perfect. "Thank you," I said.

"Are you having trouble with your truck? Do you need me to call a garage or a tow truck?"

"No, I think it will be fine tomorrow."

She handed over the keys, and Neely Kate and I quickly snuck out the back door and drove through the neighborhood behind the church. We'd been gone ten minutes before Jed called.

"Is everything okay in there?"

"We're fine."

"Then where the hell are you?"

"Sorry, Jed. We have to find that necklace on our own."

"Rose!"

"I'll be in touch." I hung up and glanced at Neely Kate. "Jed's ticked."

She laughed. "I'd like to see his face right now."

Maybe she was happy about it, but I felt bad about duping him—although I didn't have time to feel too bad. My phone rang again, and sure enough, the initials SM glowed on the screen.

"Lady, what the hell are you doing?" James growled when I answered.

"I'm doing what needs to be done."

"Like hell."

"Buck wants the necklace by eight. I'm gonna try my best to deliver."

"Why the hell would you want to help that man?"

"To avoid a war, James Malcolm. To save your skin."

"That's not your concern, Lady."

"Sorry. You don't get to decide that. I'll let you know what I find out." Then I hung up.

Neely Kate turned to me. "So we're doing this?"

"Yeah." I'd been full of a lot of talk on the phone, but now I found the whole thing intimidating. Still, I couldn't stand back and do nothing. But a second piece to this plan counted on James being on board, or at least Jed. Sure, I wanted to meet with Buck, but I really needed backup.

However, it would all be for nothing without the necklace. "Where do we start?" I had an idea of my own but was curious if Neely Kate had thought of something.

"Maybe we were onto something earlier. Leah could have it," she said.

"If Miss Mable had it in the first place," I said. "We have to find out if Rayna gave it to her or not."

She gave me a solemn look. "Then we have to go back to Mable Dyer's."

This day just got better and better.

Chapter Twenty-Five

Part of me was already regretting the way we'd ditched Jed.

"Okay," I said, trying to steady my nerves. "We need a plan so that, one, Miss Mable will talk to us, and two, Homer Dyer doesn't kill us."

"Maybe we could lure her away," Neely Kate said. "You know, like when the police tell crooks they won a Sony PlayStation and they get arrested when they go to pick it up."

"What on earth would Miss Mable leave for? And even if we found something, she'd be ticked off enough she wouldn't tell us a thing." I shook my head. "Seems to me that we're lurin' away the wrong person. We're afraid of Homer, not Mable."

"I ain't afraid of Homer."

I shot her a frown. "Well, *I* am. What would that man run after?"

"Money," Neely Kate said. Then she grinned and shook her head. "No. The necklace. He was lookin' for it at our office."

"We don't have it."

"But he doesn't know that," she said, getting excited. "We'll call and tell him we have it and Raddy wanted us to give it to him. Then we'll set up a meetin' to hand it over and go see Mable while he's gone."

"He's gonna be so pissed when we don't show, Neely Kate."

"Do you want to try to stop this war or not? We'll deal with him later."

"Okay," I conceded. "Let's do it. Do you have his number?"

She glanced at me, then rolled her eyes. Pulling out her phone, she searched through her contacts list and then placed the call.

"You really have Homer Dyer on your contact list?" I asked.

She grinned. "Shoot, no. But I looked up their landline in the white pages the other day. Homer Dyer might pretend to live off the grid, but he's too cheap to pay for a private number."

She had a point.

I worried that no one was going to answer—which might not have been a bad thing—but then Neely Kate stiffened slightly and said, "Homer, this is Neely Kate Rivers. We have your necklace."

Leave it to Neely Kate to deliver news like that without preamble.

"If you want it, meet us at the burned down Atchison plant in an hour." Then she hung up, presumably before he had a chance to respond. "I'm starving, and you promised me Chuck and Cluck. Now we've got time."

Grabbing lunch on the go wasn't a bad idea, but the thought of eating all that grease made me queasy. Still, I *had* promised.

"Okay," I said. "But then we head straight for the Dyer property."

"But it only takes fifteen minutes to get there."

"And it takes ten minutes to get to the plant from their house. When he gets there and we don't show, he's gonna come home angrier than a crocodile with dentures, so we need to be gone before he gets there."

"Good point," Neely Kate said with a frown. "I should've picked somewhere farther away. It was the first thing that popped into my head."

"I'm not surprised since it was where our big showdown with J.R. Simmons and Kate happened." I turned to her. "Any more letters from Kate?"

"No."

"Well, we don't need more than twenty minutes, so don't worry about it. It's not like we're gonna search their land for the thing. We only need to figure out if Mable had it."

We rolled through the drive-through so Neely Kate could get her Chuck and Cluck three-piece chicken dinner, and I ordered a questionable wrap and a water. As we drove out to the Dyer property, Neely Kate began to devour her food.

"Are you gonna eat yours?" she asked.

"I'll wait until we're hiding out and watching for Homer to leave. I want to examine what's in this thing first."

She gave me a look that said suit yourself and finished off the thigh she'd been working on.

When I pulled onto County Road 110, I drove past the road to turn onto their property and drove another mile to the old Sinclair station.

"Are you meeting Skeeter?" she asked in an odd voice.

"No. But we can hide out of sight here and still see the traffic."

After I backed Jonah's car behind the building, I turned off the engine and rolled down the windows. "We need to cancel our afternoon appointments."

She was quiet for a moment. "This is hurtin' the business."

"We can reschedule." But one of the clients had been insistent that we see her this afternoon. "Okay, this should take a half hour or less. We can still meet with the second client. We'll just reschedule the first. And she was flexible, so it shouldn't be a problem."

"Okay."

I turned to face her. "Neely Kate, I'm not sorry we're doin' this. I'll admit that I wasn't all that excited in the beginning, but I'm all in now."

"Because of Skeeter Malcolm," she said, giving me a look.

"Is that so bad?"

"I know *you* trust him, but I'm not so sure. I still say he wants that necklace for himself. We still don't know why he was with Raddy in the barn."

I shook my head. "Why would Skeeter want that necklace?"

"Because it's worth a fortune. And more importantly, he knows how much Buck Reynolds wants it." She watched me for a moment. "You need to set aside what *you* know about Skeeter Malcolm and take a moment to think about what everyone else knows. Can't you see that it's a possibility?"

My traitorous mind found something, and it must have shown on my face.

"What?" she asked. "What is it?"

I fought the panic rising in my chest. "James wouldn't let me force a vision of Raddy. When I asked him why afterward, he said it would have been too dangerous. That since Raddy knew me, I couldn't risk blurtin' out some secret he didn't want known. But I didn't quite believe it. I wondered what he didn't want me to see." I was more relieved than I cared to admit that Buck had basically admitted to killing Raddy, but what was James hiding? Could Neely Kate be right?

"Rose."

A black and white streak on the highway caught my eye, and I realized it was Homer's Jeep heading west. I'd almost missed it. "That's Homer."

Neely Kate's gaze moved to the road. "He's early. Are you sure that was him?"

"Yep, I recognized the white front fender. Let's go."

I started the car and pulled out onto the highway.

It was time to start getting real answers.

Chapter Twenty-Six

I was nervous as we drove down the Dyer driveway. Were we crazy to expect Mable to tell us anything? I cast a glance at Neely Kate and wasn't sure whether to be relieved or worried that she looked just about as nervous as I felt.

The barking dog greeted us as we pulled up, and I wasn't surprised to find Mable was standing in the doorway.

"You know," I said, "There's one possible problem to our plan."

"What's that?"

"What if Homer told Mable he was going to meet us at the factory?"

"Well, crap . . ."

"Yeah."

She shook her head. "No. We're safe. Homer firmly believes his business is his own. If he stumbled upon the necklace and sold it, there's not a chance in Hades he'd share the money with his wife. He wouldn't tell her he was goin' to get it."

"I hope you're right. This is a long shot as it is."

"Just let me take this one. I know her, so she might be more inclined to tell *me*."

"I'm good with that." Although it didn't seem like a good time to remind her it hadn't mattered much last time.

We climbed out of the car, and at the last minute, Neely Kate grabbed the box of her half-eaten Chuck and Cluck lunch.

What in the world?

Mable walked out onto the porch. I saw it as a step in the right direction that she was holding a broom instead of a shotgun this time.

"What are you girls doin' back here?" the older woman asked, shouting over the frantic barks of the dog. "You still tryin' to get that recipe?"

Neely Kate gave her a sad grin as we sidestepped the dog and approached the bottom of the steps. "Well, you can't blame a girl for tryin', but we're here for a different reason." She paused, lifting the chicken box in front of her. "We're here to pay our condolences." She mounted the bottom step and handed the woman the box.

"Oh." The woman's hard exterior seemed to crumble a bit as she took the box.

"Raddy was so full of life," Neely Kate said, shifting her weight. "I just can't believe he's gone."

"Radcliffe Mussleman Dyer was a fool. It's a wonder he didn't get himself killed sooner," the older woman grumbled, and while her words were shocking, the tears gathering in her eyes softened them.

"As you know, he'd hired us to find his grandmother's necklace, and we've vowed to complete the mission in honor of his memory. Of course we'll bring it to you straightaway," Neely Kate said. "I'm sure he would have wanted his momma to have it."

She nodded and wiped her eyes.

"But we're tryin' to track down the last person to have seen it before it disappeared. We think it might have been you."

Mable didn't answer.

"We know you got all the jewelry from Rayna, but we think there was a necklace in there that didn't come from your momma. Do you remember seeing it? It had big, yellowish-clear stones."

The woman pursed her lips. "No. I don't rightly recall. I just grabbed the jewelry and brought it home."

"And you gave it to Leah?" I asked even though I knew that wasn't true.

The older woman pressed her lips together.

The frenzied dog made a forceful lunge, and Neely Kate flinched and jumped a foot to the right. "Has Leah been out to see you since you brought the jewelry home?" Would she admit to the truth?

"Yeah. She and Newton came over a couple of days later."

"Newton was with her?"

"Yeah. She said her car was broke down, and he gave her a ride."

"Did you see Leah the entire time, or did she slip away?"

"She said she was goin' to the bathroom, but I caught her comin' out of my room," Mable said. "When I called her on it, she said she was lookin' for the picture albums."

"What do you think happened to the necklace?" I asked.

Her eyes turned hard. "I think that hussy Rayna hid it somewhere good where no one's ever gonna find it. You're on a fool's errand. You need to give it up." She opened the box, and confusion flickered in her eyes as she lifted the mostly eaten chicken thigh.

"That's for Zeus," Neely Kate said, reaching for it. She snatched it from the older woman, and then before I could stop her, she tossed it sideways toward the tree where the animal was chained up.

The dog pounced on it like a hammer in a whack-a-mole game, making scary gnawing sounds.

"Miss Mable," I said hesitantly. "You mentioned you had five children. I know about Raddy, Newton, and Leah, but what about the other two?"

"They've moved off." She waved the chicken box in a sideways motion. "My boy's not comin' home for Raddy's funeral." Tears filled her red-rimmed eyes, and I felt terrible for asking.

Neely Kate pulled a card out of her back pocket. "If you think of anything else to help us find the necklace, I'd appreciate it if you'd call." She handed Mable her business card.

"Yeah." Mable fingered the edges of the card, then looked up at us with tears in her eyes. "Do you think that's why my boy was killed? Because of that daggum necklace?"

"I don't know, Miss Mable," Neely Kate said softly. "Maybe."

Her jaw quivered and she put her hand on her stomach as she watched the dog. She gave a brisk nod, then turned and started to go into the house. Zeus began to make gagging noises, and Mable whipped around to face him. "He's chokin' on that chicken bone!"

"Oh crap," Neely Kate mumbled.

"Don't just stand there," Mable shouted, pointing her broom toward him with one hand while still holding the box of chicken. "Go give him the Heimlich."

Neely Kate's mouth dropped open. "You can't be serious."

"My boy died this morning. You gonna let my dog die too?"

Neely Kate gave me a look of panic. I stared back at her in shock. Then, for the second time within minutes, she lunged toward the dog.

Well, crappy doodles. This would not end well.

I snatched the broom from Miss Mable and followed Neely Kate, hoping the dog would just cough it up already. But he was leaning down on his front legs with his butt in the air, coughing and hacking like a twenty-year, three-pack-a-day chain smoker.

"You're not really gonna do this, are you?" I asked.

"I have to," she grumbled in exasperation as she stepped behind the dog and slowly reached for his sides.

I lifted the broom, ready to put it between my best friend and the dog's sharp teeth. I wasn't sure it would work, but it was my best option at the moment.

Neely Kate reached under his belly with both hands, then delivered a sharp push to his gut.

He released a growl and started to reach his head around. I stuffed the broom in front of his face, and he coughed again, which quickly turned to wheezing. A giant stench filled the air.

"You made it worse!" Miss Mable shouted at us.

Neely Kate started gagging into her arm.

"I'll say," I said, frantically waving a hand in front of my face. "You squeezed a fart out of him, and it smells worse than Muffy's."

"I'm doing the best I can!" Neely Kate shouted as she squatted down, pressing her chest to the dog's back. She gave a couple of hard thrusts, and noises came out of both ends of the dog. My eyes burned and Neely Kate looked like she was holding her breath while Zeus made a gagging noise that didn't sound so good.

"Look in his mouth!" Neely Kate said.

"I'm not looking in his mouth! Are you crazy?" I pulled my phone out of my pocket and pulled up my recent calls.

"You're making a phone call *right now*?" Neely Kate demanded.

I ignored her and prayed the person on the other end picked up quickly.

"Henryetta Animal Clinic," the receptionist said in an annoyed tone.

"Mary, this is Rose Gardner and I have a medical emergency. I need to speak to Levi right away."

"Sure you do . . ."

"Mary!" I said in a panic as Zeus collapsed onto his belly, his feet sticking out on his sides. "A dog is dying!"

I must have sounded halfway convincing because she called out, "Dr. Romano. I think this is a real emergency."

Seconds later, Levi picked up the phone. Sounding like a consummate professional, he said, "This is Dr. Romano. What's the problem?"

I put the phone on speaker. "Levi, this is Rose Gardner. I'm at Mable Dyer's home, and her dog Zeus was choking on a chicken bone. Neely Kate tried to give him the

Heimlich. It sounded like it almost cleared, but now he's layin' on the ground making weird wheezing noises."

"How far are you from here?"

"I don't know. Maybe fifteen minutes."

"Too far to get here in time. Has she tried the Heimlich since it got worse?"

"Yeah, it sounds like it's stuck."

"Okay, try lookin' in his mouth."

"We can't look into his mouth," I said, glancing over at Neely Kate. "He's vicious."

"He's not right now," Neely Kate said as she pulled her hands free.

Levi continued, "You could try hitting his back with the palm of your hand."

Neely Kate maneuvered in front of Zeus, whose eyes looked unfocused, and pried his mouth open.

"Be careful, Neely Kate," I said.

"What's she doing?" Levi asked.

"Zeus is practically passed out, so she's checkin' in his open mouth."

"Tell her if he starts to revive to back up and put something between her and the dog," Levi said.

I held up the broom, ready to act.

Neely Kate tipped his jaw up and looked in his open mouth. "I see something."

"Can you put your hand in his mouth and pull it out?" Levi asked.

"I'll try." She jammed her hand into his mouth. "Oh, my lord." She cringed and turned her head to the side. "I think I've got it, but it seems kind of stuck."

"Give it a good yank," Levi told her.

She got a look of concentration on her face and pulled hard, then fell backward and landed on her butt with her hand full of something that didn't look like a chicken bone.

"What in the world is that?" I asked.

She held it closer and her face turned a pale green. She made a gagging sound as she tossed it to the ground in disgust. "It's a slimy tube sock."

"Where's the cotton pickin' chicken bone?" I asked.

Neely Kate's eyes grew wide, and she started crab-walking backward. Now that the sock wasn't blocking his airway, Zeus was coming to.

I stuffed my phone in my pocket, wielding the broom with one hand as I reached for Neely Kate's arm, pulling her back as the dog started to get to his feet.

He shook his head, sending his spit flying all over us, and released a warning growl.

"Neely Kate!" I shouted. "Move!"

She scrambled faster, but Zeus was on a good fifteen feet of chain and we'd started out at ground zero. I stepped between her and the dog, holding the broom out in front of me. He lashed out and grabbed the broom bristles in his mouth. I held tight as he started to tug, looking over my shoulder to make sure Neely Kate had backed up far enough. Then I released the broom and took off running, Zeus hot on my heels. I'd just reached the area outside of his reach when he made one last leap toward me. I let out a yelp as he took a chunk out of the bottom of my jeans.

Neely Kate pulled me to the side of the car, and we leaned against it as we caught our breath.

"Your dog was choking on a sock, Miss Mable," Neely Kate shouted at the older woman. "How'd he get a sock?"

"That's his damn toy," the old woman grumbled. "And you ruined my damn broom." Then she disappeared into the house without another word.

"You're welcome!" Neely Kate called after her.

I heard someone calling my name—although it was muffled—and then I realized I'd put my phone in my pocket.

"Sorry," I told Levi as I pulled it out. "I had to act fast."

"So the dog was choking on a sock?" he asked.

"Yeah, it wasn't our fault after all."

He was silent for a second, then said, "I take it there's never a dull moment with you."

I could deny it, but what would be the point? "I have a knack for finding trouble. Sorry to bother you."

"I helped you and Neely Kate save a life. I think that makes us superheroes. We should get ourselves some capes."

Neely Kate laughed, although it was shaky.

"Feel free to call me anytime, Rose Gardner. My life could use a little excitement."

I was beginning to think I could use a whole lot less.

Chapter Twenty-Seven

We pulled out of the Dyer driveway and were headed back to town when I saw Homer's Jeep in my rearview mirror. I was worried he'd realize it was us, but he turned onto his drive.

At least one thing was going our way.

We made it to our three o'clock consult, but it took longer than I'd expected. We were quickly running out of time and were no closer to finding the necklace.

"What are we gonna do?" Neely Kate asked, sounding worried.

"I don't know. Maybe we should confront Leah."

"She's not gonna admit to havin' it. Maybe we should just tell Buck she's got it. Then he can worry about the recovery."

"But what if she *doesn't* have it?" I asked. "He could hurt her. Or worse. We can't do that. Rayna might have kept it, and if she did, I don't think anyone knew. Trixie sure didn't, and I think she was Rayna's closest friend."

"Should we break into Leah's house?"

I turned toward her. "Do you know where she lives?"

"She was livin' with her boyfriend, but I think she moved out over the weekend. She's stayin' in a house with her cousin and two of her friends."

"So there's probably someone there," I groaned. "It's gonna be a little weird if we show up and start searching her room."

"Then what are we gonna do?"

I thought about it for several seconds. "I think we should talk to Hugh Wagner."

"What on earth for?"

"I don't know. Maybe we can convince him to help us. In my vision, he was upset with his brother for stirrin' up trouble. Or maybe we can find out something about Kip we can use to negotiate. We have to do *something*."

"I know." She patted my hand. "It actually might not be a bad idea. But you're not plannin' on *goin'* there, are you?"

I ignored her question while I dug out my phone from my jeans pocket. I still hadn't figured out the answer myself. "I should give Jed an update," I said as I pulled up my speed dial numbers. "But we'll never be able to negotiate without that necklace."

"Finding that necklace was a long shot," she said sadly. "How are we gonna stop them now?"

"Let's pray Hugh gives us something," I said as I sent Jed a text telling him we'd come up with a big fat nothing. "I think goin' to his shop to see him is too risky. Let's call him."

We were still parked in front of our potential client's house, and she was watching out of her front door and giving us strange looks. I decided to head toward the office until we figured out where else to go.

Jed sent back a reply as I pulled away from the curb.

You tried. Now tell me where you are. We need to get you out of the line of fire.

Jed and James were preparing for battle. I had to put a stop to this.

Neely Kate took my phone and read the message. She glanced up at me and said, "Like Hades we will."

Relief washed over me. *We* had to put a stop to this. This whole scheme could crash and burn, but at least she and I were united.

"I'm gonna look up the number for Ripper Pawn," she said, huddling over my phone. When she found the number, I pulled over in the parking lot of a strip mall. Then she placed the call and put it on speaker.

"Ripper Pawn."

It was Hugh's voice. I pushed out a sigh of relief and nodded to Neely Kate.

"Hugh?" Neely Kate asked in the higher-pitched voice she'd used when we'd visited the store while undercover. "This is Nancy, and I've got Beth Ann with me."

As she uttered those words, my stomach sunk. I should have warned her.

Buck knew about my alias. And so did Kip.

"Hey!" he said in a strained voice. "If it isn't my two favorite customers of the week, Nancy and Beth Ann. Only, I know your names are Neely Kate Colson and Rose Gardner."

Neely Kate's eyes widened with shock, but I was too distracted by a sudden worry to comfort her. We'd asked Hugh about his business when we were at Ripper Pawn. What if he thought James had sent us? "We weren't there

341

spyin' on you, if that's what you're thinkin', Hugh. We were only tryin' to find the necklace for Raddy."

"You two work for Malcolm." While he sounded less friendly, he didn't spit out James' name the way an enemy would.

"No. *We don't*," Neely Kate said. "We're PIs. We run Sparkle Investigations."

I shot her a glare, but now didn't seem like a good time to protest.

"You haven't happened to come across the necklace we were looking for, have you?" I asked. It was a long shot, but it was worth asking. For all we knew, Kip kept him in the dark.

His humorless laugh proved me wrong. "If I did, don't you think I'd have given it to Buck already? He'd rip me a new one if I found that damn thing and didn't return it to him." Then he hastily added, "Excuse my language."

We needed to assume he knew everything.

Neely Kate lifted her eyebrows. I wondered if she was thinking what I was thinking: Hugh sounded scared of Buck and more than a little bitter.

"Hugh," I said, my voice sounding more resolved than I felt. "We need your help."

"What do you need help with?"

I took a breath. "You know that Raddy's dead—Buck told me this afternoon that he was the one who killed him—but Buck still expects Neely Kate and me to find the necklace for him. If we don't turn it over by eight tonight, we're in big trouble."

"I haven't seen it. I swear."

"We believe you. But we have no idea what to do. Do you have any suggestions?"

"Me?" he screeched. "How would I know?"

"You don't have any idea who might have it?" I asked.

"If I did, I'd have already given the info to Kip and Buck. They're countin' on the money to . . ." His voice trailed off. "You say you don't work for Malcolm, but I know you're helpin' him. You're finding the necklace for him."

I leaned my head back and stifled a groan. "Believe it or not, Hugh, all I want to do is give it back to Buck. This county can't handle another war."

Hugh was silent long enough that I looked down at my phone in Neely Kate's hand to see if he'd ended the call. But maybe his silence confirmed what I'd sensed in my vision. "Hugh, I think you can help stop this."

"*Me?*"

"Do you know Buck Reynolds at all? Is he a fair man? Will he listen to reason?"

"Buck Reynolds is nothing but trouble," he said in a sneer. "Kip has always skirted the line, but he was never this ambitious before he became friends with Buck this past winter."

"So are Buck and Kip equals?"

"They say they are, but I think Buck's planning to take charge. Right now Kip's providing the funds for their takeover, but once Buck gets that necklace, he'll have more capital . . . and more say."

Potential power grab within a power grab. That was good to know.

Neely Kate leaned closer to the phone. "Maybe Kip has the necklace. Surely he's not gonna just sit back and let Buck take over."

"Buck's got him hoodwinked good. When I tried to warn Kip, he told me I was too stupid to understand syndicate politics." Hugh's voice was tight. "The damn fool thinks Buck's loyal and they're equals. But he's wrong. There's something in Buck's eyes. He's gonna pull a fast one on my brother. All he needs is the necklace to do it."

"Are *you* hiding the necklace?" Neely Kate asked softly.

He paused. "I swear on my momma's grave that I've never laid eyes on it." He paused again. "But I sure wouldn't give it to you either. If Malcolm gets that necklace . . ."

I ignored his intimation that James wanted the necklace. "So the whole takeover is hinged on getting that necklace back?"

"Hell, no," he said in disgust. "They're goin' through with it no matter what. They'll do away with Malcolm and his top men. Then Kip and Buck will have their own takeover war between themselves. Things are only gonna get uglier."

I suspected he was right. "Do you know what they're planning with Skeeter Malcolm?"

He was silent for several beats. "I think I've said too much already."

"Hugh, please," I pleaded. "I know you don't want Kip to get hurt, but if they follow through with this takeover, you know people are gonna die. Kip might be one of them."

"I don't know what they're doin'. Kip won't tell me. I was pretty sure they had something planned for next week, but I think they might have moved it to tonight."

My heart skipped a beat. "Are you sure it's tonight?"

"Yeah. Positive. I heard Kip talking to Buck earlier today about some plan to get it from Malcolm. He said they'd have just cause to force a takeover either way."

I shot a worried glance to Neely Kate. We were part of that plan. Even if we showed up with the necklace, they'd assume we'd gotten it from James. We were damned either way.

I decided to take a chance. "I'm trying to figure out a way to make sure everyone's happy and no one dies," I said. "Buck seems unlikely to negotiate, but what about Kip? What does he ultimately want?"

Hugh didn't answer.

"What does he see in Buck?" Neely Kate asked. "Why did Kip get in cahoots with him?"

"Because he's ruthless. Buck's willing to burn it all down to get what he wants." He paused. "But I think what Kip likes best is that he's getting respect from people with power. He was always a minor player. Now he's aiming to be king."

And it all hinged on killing James.

I swallowed my fear. It wouldn't help me accomplish anything. "Thanks for your help, Hugh," I said. "If you think of anything else, will you give us a call?"

"Sorry. My part is done." Then he hung up.

Neely Kate and I sat in silence for several seconds. "What do we do now?" I asked, wondering if this was hopeless. Could the two of us really stop a war?

"I think we should try to talk to Leah," Neely Kate said. "What do we have to lose?"

"Does it even matter?" I asked. "Buck thinks James has it. Even if we bring it to him, he'll think James had it all along. That he was playing him."

"But at least *we'll* have it. I say we keep trying."

"Yeah," I said. "You're right."

Neely Kate's phone rang, and she grimaced when she looked at the screen. "Hey, Joe," she said, picking up the call. "Are you back in town?" She paused and listened for several seconds before she said, "Now's not a good time. Can you come over later?" She glanced at me. "Okay. Give me a call before you come." She gave me a grave look as she hung up. "Joe's back in town, and he wants to talk."

How had I forgotten about Joe?

"Did he say what he wanted to talk about?" I asked carefully, trying to hide my anxiety. I could only think of one reason why Joe would insist on talking to Neely Kate as soon as possible, and while I wanted to know what he'd discovered in New Orleans, I could only handle one crisis at a time.

She shook her head. "No, he was totally evasive, but he said we needed to stay home tonight and he'll be over later to talk to me."

I wondered if we should tell Joe what was going on. Would I prevent more bloodshed, or be the cause of it? It was more likely to stir things up even more and potentially add to the evidence that James was weak. Besides, Neely Kate couldn't handle losing Joe, and he'd definitely be in the thick of it.

No Joe.

"Let's find Leah."

Neely Kate made a few phone calls to find out where Leah was living now. I almost teased her about not knowing off the top of her head, but I was too nervous.

Several cars were parked in front of Leah's, and when we knocked on the front door, a young woman opened it. "We don't need any Avon or Mary Kay, or whatever the hell it is you're selling."

Neely Kate's brow furrowed in confusion. "What on earth makes you think we're selling makeup?"

She pointed from Neely Kate to me. "You're like before and after pics, right? You're the pretty one, and she's the one who gets the makeover."

I gasped.

"What?" Neely Kate screeched. "No! We're here to see Leah."

"Leah?"

"Leah Dyer. Is she here?"

"Hold on." Then she shut the door in our faces. Nearly a full minute passed, and I was about to knock again when Leah opened the door.

The look she gave us suggested we were as welcome as rotten eggs. "You got a hell of a lot of nerve showing up here, Neely Kate Colson. What do you want?"

"We want to ask you about the necklace."

"What necklace?"

"The one Raddy hired us to find," Neely Kate said.

She crossed her arms over her chest. "I don't know nothing about it."

"Did you see it in your mother's drawer?" Neely Kate asked.

"I never saw nothin'."

"Are you sure?" I asked.

"I'm gonna tell you the same damn thing I told my father and that guy who showed up at One Eyed Joes yesterday asking questions. I don't know where it is."

My mouth gaped open before I came to my senses and asked, "A man asked you questions at One Eyed Joes?"

Denise Grover Swank

"Yeah, right after you left, and I'm gonna tell you the same damn thing I told him—go to hell." Then she slammed the door in our faces.

Neely Kate gave me a fierce look. "I can make her tell us more."

I frowned. "You need to work on some of your people skills. No. She's not going to tell us anything. What I really want to know is who approached her, and I suspect she doesn't know. She called him 'that guy.' If she knew him, she'd have used his name, and we don't know Buck's guys well enough to recognize them by description."

"Unless it was one of Skeeter's guys."

I shot her a glare, and she gave me a half shrug.

"Now what?" she asked. "We're back to square one."

It sure felt like it. "Let's go to the office and see if we can come up with something."

It seemed unlikely at best, but I didn't have a better idea. I only hoped Jed wasn't there, although at this point, it might not matter.

We were silent the entire way there. It was close to six when I drove around the now-quiet square to make sure Jed wasn't watching before I parked in front of the office. Even if Jed drove by, he wouldn't recognize the car and put it together that we were in the office.

I put the key in the door and was surprised to find it unlocked. "We locked up this morning, didn't we?" I asked.

"Yeah," Neely Kate said. "I did. Maybe it's Marci again." But she looked as queasy as I felt.

Just to be safe, I pulled my pepper spray out of my purse as we walked into the office, which was completely undisturbed.

348

"Maybe we just thought we locked up," I said, not quite believing it.

"Or Jed came in lookin' for us," Neely Kate said. "And *he* forgot to lock up."

That seemed even less likely.

I set my purse on my desk and was so engrossed in checking the back door, I wasn't prepared for the man standing behind the screen I'd set up for Jed earlier that day. And I definitely wasn't prepared for the gun in his hand. But I shouldn't have been surprised at the face.

"Rose Gardner," Homer Dyer snarled. "You owe me a necklace."

Chapter Twenty-Eight

Well, crap. We didn't have time for this.

"Homer," I said, closing my hand around my can of pepper spray. I tried to sound nonchalant. "Hey."

He took a step toward me. "Don't hey me. I want my necklace."

Had he seen Neely Kate? Maybe she could escape. But he stepped around the screen and pointed the gun at her. He'd caught her with her hand in her purse.

"Take your hand out of the purse—*slowly.*"

She stared at me with fear in her eyes.

We really were in trouble.

Neely Kate did as he said, putting her hands in the air. "What do you want, Homer?"

"You damn well know what I want, and now I'm good and pissed that you stood me up. Hand over the necklace."

"We don't have it," Neely Kate said.

"Bullshit. You told me you were gonna give it to me."

"We thought we'd found it," I said. "But we were wrong."

He pointed the gun at me. "I don't believe you." He motioned to the chairs at the table behind the screen. "Both of you sit down."

Neely Kate looked at me, and I gave a slight nod.

Homer hadn't noticed the pepper spray in my hand. We could still get out of this.

We both sat in chairs, and he angled the screen to hide us from any passersby on the street. When he was certain we were on our chairs, he walked over to my purse and started digging around.

"Somebody's a bad girl," he said, pulling out my gun and holding it up for me to see.

Oh my word. Was he going to shoot us with my own gun?

I pushed out a breath of relief when he set it on the desk, then pulled out my Taser. "A *very* bad girl." He dumped the contents of my purse onto the table, scowling down at it. "Where's the necklace?"

We kept quiet and he moved on to Neely Kate's purse, pulling out her gun, Taser, pepper spray, handcuffs, her pink sparkly notebook, and nunchucks before dumping her bag onto the table. Several tubes of lipstick rolled off the desk and onto the floor.

Homer stomped over toward us. "Where is it?"

"We don't know," I said. "We thought we'd—"

My words were cut off when he slapped me across the face.

"Now I ain't messin' around. The last woman who lied to me ain't around to tell no tales," Homer said with an evil glint in his eyes. "So let's try this again."

"Rayna?" I choked out in shock. "*You* killed her?"

"It was an accident." His evil smile returned. "Let's hope I don't have another accident while I'm talkin' to you girls."

"We hid it," Neely Kate blurted out.

Homer turned to her with a look of satisfaction. "That's better. Where?"

"Out at Ted's Garage."

"Why's it out there?"

"It's where my husband worked," Neely Kate said. "I know the shop, but no one would think to look for it there. Take me there, and I'll show you."

Homer thought about it for a moment, then shook his head. "Nope. You tell me where it is, and I'll go look."

Neely Kate paused, then said, "In the employee lounge. In the back of the cabinet under the sink."

"You better not be lyin' to me," he warned in a low voice. He moved toward us and picked up a duffel bag I hadn't noticed before. Fear shot through my veins when he pulled out a roll of duct tape.

"I told you where the necklace is," Neely Kate said. "Now you need to let us go."

"Not until I get the necklace. Once I find it, I'll come back to set you free." He started taping Neely Kate's arms behind her back.

This was a disaster.

He soon had our legs duct-taped to the chairs, and our hands wrapped up behind our backs. Surprisingly, he left our mouths untaped. Probably because the downtown square was empty and there was little chance of anyone hearing us. Or maybe he was just too cheap to use any more than necessary.

When he finished, he took his bag and went out the front door, leaving us alone in the now semi-dark room.

"What are we gonna do, Rose? My only thought was to send him as far from the office as possible and hope we either get loose or someone finds us. When he comes back without it, he's gonna be fit to be tied."

"I know," I said. "But you bought us some time. Probably thirty to forty minutes, don't you think?"

"Yeah. But he taped us up pretty good."

"I still have the pepper spray in my hand," I said. "I tried to hide it with my other hand when he taped my wrists. Apparently it worked, but it won't do us much good in this situation."

"Maybe not . . ." she said. "Does it still have that key chain attached?"

"Yeah."

"When you first got it a couple of months ago, the ring had some sharp edges. Does it still?"

I ran my thumb over the metal can, trying to find the key chain. Sure enough, I felt its metal edge against my skin. "I know where you're goin' with this, but I'm not sure I can maneuver it around to saw through the tape, let alone use it to cut the tape on my wrists."

"Just try wiggling your hands and wrists to loosen the tape first," Neely Kate said. "We might not even need the sharp edge."

We both spent several minutes wiggling the tape, but neither of us made much progress.

"If we were standing, I could break this easy," Neely Kate said. "I learned how to escape getting tied up when I was a kid."

I stopped my efforts. "Why were you tied up as a kid?"

She ignored my question. "We need to hurry, Rose. We've already lost fifteen or twenty minutes. We can't be here when he gets back."

"We can talk while we work on it."

"No," she said, her voice tight. "I can't think about that right now. We need to focus on getting free."

What on earth had happened to my best friend when she was living with that sorry excuse of a mother? I'd had a heap of my own abuse as a child. The woman who'd raised me used to lock me in the closet whenever I had visions, and sometimes she'd beat me with a wooden spoon, but I was certain Neely Kate's experiences had been much, much worse.

Within fifteen minutes, I'd gotten my wrists loose enough that I could almost wiggle the hand without the pepper spray through the hole.

"Stop," Neely Kate whispered. "Listen."

I paused long enough to hear a car outside the office.

"He's back," she said. "Are you free yet?"

"Almost . . ." I said, straining to squeeze my hand through the opening and pull it free. It finally popped loose, and I leaned to the side to try to look around the screen, but I lost balance and my chair fell to the ground sideways.

I hit my head and my shoulder when I landed on the hardwood floor. The impact momentarily dazed me, but then I caught sight of a figure on the sidewalk. The headlights from the still-running car were on, casting the man in a backlight that made it impossible for me to identify him. But it was motivation enough for me to pull my act together and start unwrapping the tape from one of my legs.

I'd just started on the second leg—thankful that stingy Homer hadn't used much tape—when the door opened.

"I can't stomach liars," Homer said in an angry voice. "I'm gonna make you pay for wasting my time. Just like Rayna." But from his voice and his footfalls, he was still standing close to the door.

I crawled over to Neely Kate and helped free her hand from the tape, then put the can in her hand with the nozzle positioned so that she could use it. She kept her hands behind her back, pretending she was still tied up, as I crawled along the wall to the edge of the screen. Homer had left our guns and Tasers on our desks. If I could just get to one, I could try to even the playing field.

"Are you scared yet, Neely Kate?" Homer asked in a menacing voice, and I realized he was playing with us. I heard several heavy footfalls. "You should—" I heard a grunt and then a hard thud. A tube of lipstick shot across the floor, rolling toward the back door.

After several seconds of silence, I crawled around the screen. There was no sign of Homer. Had Jed shown up?

Neely Kate's desk was only eight feet away, so I got to my feet in a crouch, set my sights on Neely Kate's gun on her desk, and ran for it, shocked beyond belief when I managed to grab it. I stood, glancing around for any sight of Homer.

Then I found him—on the floor in front of Neely Kate's desk, flat on his back. His gun lay several feet from his outstretched hand.

What on earth?

"He's out cold, Neely Kate," I said as I held the gun on him and walked around to pick up his weapon.

"What happened?"

I spotted another tube of lipstick and grinned. "I think your lipstick took him out."

"*What?*"

"I think he stepped on that one tube, lost his balance, and then fell backward and hit his head."

"See?" she said with a tiny gloat. "Wearin' lipstick saved our lives. Maybe we should become spies instead of PIs."

I laughed even though I was shaking from nerves. "One thing at a time." I opened my top desk drawer and grabbed a pair of scissors. Then I pushed the screen out of the way so I could keep an eye on Homer while I cut Neely Kate's legs free.

"How much time do we have?" she asked.

I glanced over at the clock on the wall. "Less than an hour."

I cut the last piece of tape and stood. "We have to take care of Homer."

"Good idea," she said, grabbing his roll of duct tape and strutting toward him. She rolled him over with her strappy sandal and then knelt beside him and started to wrap the tape around his wrists.

He released a moan.

"He's comin' to," I said. "We have to work fast."

"No we don't." She stood and grabbed her Taser off her desk before heading back toward Homer and squatting in front of him. "Hey, you boot-lickin', no-good, *murderin'* piece of slime. This is for killing Rayna . . . and for possibly ruining my new capris with duct tape." Then she zapped him with her Taser.

He flopped around before falling limp. We had his arms bound behind his back with his duct tape, and it only took another minute for us to get his lower legs bound together. Thankfully, he was still unconscious, but we had another issue.

"We can't just leave him here bound," I said. "What if someone sees him and tries to play Good Samaritan?"

"Good point. Let's drag him behind the screen."

We both grabbed his feet and dragged him across the floor, bumping his head into the corner of Neely Kate's desk.

"Oops," she said with too much glee to sound truly apologetic.

When we got him out of sight, I moved to my desk and began putting all my belongings back inside. "We need a plan. We have to figure out a way to stop this."

"I've been thinkin'," Neely Kate said. "We didn't get a chance to finish questioning Miss Mable earlier because of that sorry excuse of a dog, but I think we were on the right track. I'm pretty doggone sure Rayna didn't keep the necklace, which means Miss Mable really *did* take it with her. The jewelry was loose in her drawer, which means she saw all the pieces. It was her momma's, so she must have realized it didn't belong."

I turned back to look at her. "Raddy said he broke in a day later and it wasn't there. And if Newton and Mable were right about when Leah went over, it was days after that." My eyes widened. "Which means Miss Mable was the last person to see it." I gestured to the back. "But what about Homer? Why's he lookin' for it?"

"Not because he saw it, but because he heard about it from everyone else," she said, getting excited. "You know how I told you that Homer kept his business away from his wife? What if she does the same with him? He's taken a nosedive off the deep end with his off-the-grid stuff, and he made Miss Mable stop goin' to church and her quilting group. What if she saw that necklace and figured it was her ticket to freedom?" Her eyes lit up. "That would explain why she got so upset when she asked if someone killed Raddy for the necklace! He couldn't find it and it got him killed!"

She was onto something. "I think you're right."

"We have to go back out to the Dyer farm," she said. "We have to get that necklace from her."

I glanced back at the clock on the wall. 7:35. All of our shenanigans had taken more time than I'd thought. "There's not enough time for us to go back out to the Dyer farm and make it to the meetin' on time." I steeled my back and tried to look forceful. "You have to get the necklace and bring it to the Trading Post. I'll stall."

"Have you gone crazy?" Neely Kate demanded. "Did that tape cut off circulation to your head? You're not going in there alone."

"No. I'm not." I grabbed my phone and placed a call. "Jed," I said when he answered. "We think we know who has the necklace, but there's not enough time for us to get it and make the meeting. I need someone to go with Neely Kate to help coerce the woman who has it into handin' it over, but I need someone else to go with to the meetin' with Buck and Kip."

"You're not goin' to that damned meeting."

"Jed!"

"No. Listen to me," he said, sounding calmer. "I have an idea. You and I both know how important appearances are in this game. Buck called you, so you call him back and tell him that if he wants the necklace, he'll meet you at nine at Putnam Industrial Park. Space 239. Tell him to bring

Wagner and two additional men of their choosing. No more, or the deal's off and he won't get the necklace. Tell him we're invoking the rules of parley."

"Parley? Isn't that for pirates?"

"We have a damn code too," he grumped.

"*Okay.*" Touchy.

"But don't call him until eight on the nose," Jed continued. "We need to buy some time, and it will give you the upper hand to flout their own rule."

"You do know that he's gonna think James had it all along. He's already pretty sure of it."

"Good. Let him. I'll swing by the office to pick up Neely Kate, and we'll get the necklace. Go home to change into something befitting the Lady in Black. Skeeter will pick you up at the farm at eight. Can you be ready?"

"I'm at the office, but I think I can make it."

"We'll meet you at the industrial park."

"Jed, there's one more thing . . . Homer Dyer's taped up in our office."

"What's he doin' in your office again?"

"He held us hostage lookin' for the necklace. Neely Kate sent him on a wild goose chase. Long story short, when he came back, we got the upper hand and he's now tied up in the back. We found out he was the one who killed Rayna."

"Did he hurt either of you?"

My cheek was still sore, but his open hand was better than a fist. "I'll let Neely Kate fill you in. Are you gonna have someone deal with Homer?"

"We'll leave him tied up in your office and deal with him after the meeting. He deserves a fittin' punishment."

"No. He murdered Rayna. When this is all done, we'll call Joe and have him arrest Homer."

"Fine, if that's the way you want to play it. Now get moving."

Jed hung up, and I filled Neely Kate in on the plan.

"Go," she said, giving me a small shove. "You need to get goin'. I'll be fine until Jed gets here. I'd love for Homer Dyer to give me a reason to shoot him."

I gave her a stern look. "Do not shoot Homer Dyer."

She rolled her eyes. "I'm just blowin' smoke. I'd be stuck cleaning up his mess. Again."

I wasn't so sure about that, but I pulled her into a quick hug. "Be careful and good luck."

"You too."

I was pretty sure we were gonna need all the luck we could get.

Chapter Twenty-Nine

James was waiting on my front porch when I pulled up. He didn't seem all that surprised to see me in Jonah's car; but then, I was sure they'd figured it out by now.

"Lady," he said in a low tone as I walked up the steps. The tension in his voice clued me in on his mood.

"I know you're probably ticked at me right now, but—"

He stood and moved closer. "This is a fool's errand, and it's puttin' you in even more danger than before."

"But if I can stop a war—"

"It's not your damn concern, Rose."

"But it is!" I said, grabbing handfuls of his shirt and pulling him closer. "You're my friend and I don't want to lose you. I *can't* lose you, James. My heart couldn't bear it. So whether we're just friends or we're more, I'm not gonna stand by and watch you get embroiled in another war if there's any way I can put a stop to it. Got it?"

He just watched me with that intent gaze of his.

"And as a citizen of this county, if I have an opportunity to keep peace and prevent more bloodshed, I'm gonna do it too." I clenched his T-shirt tighter in my hands and pulled his chest to mine. "Are there any more arguments?"

"If you go to this meeting as the Lady in Black," he said, his voice low, "you'll be stuck in this world. There will be little chance of getting out. You'll always be in danger."

"Then I'm stuck in it. My goal is to make sure no one's in danger when this meeting is done."

His hand slid behind my back, the warmth of him searing through my shirt, and suddenly he was holding me against his chest. "You know that's next to impossible?"

"I have to try. I'll always regret it if I don't."

"You're so different than me," he said, searching my face. "You're doing this for absolutely no personal gain whatsoever."

I gave him a tiny smile. "Don't be so certain of that." I released my hold on his shirt. "Jed told me to dress as Lady, so I need to get ready."

His arm dropped, and he took my keys and unlocked the door. "It's eight. You should make that call now."

I nodded, my mouth going dry. I pulled out my phone and pulled up the number Buck had called from.

"You remember the location?" James asked. "Putnam Industrial Park, space 239, at nine o'clock. Tell him the rules of parley will last an hour, starting at nine."

"What are the rules?"

"We agree to no bloodshed during that time. No weapons in the meeting. We check them at the door."

"Can you trust him to follow it?"

"I guess we'll find out. Make the call."

I swallowed and hit the call button. When it started ringing, I put it on speaker so James could hear.

"Rose Gardner," Buck said in a sneer. "You're late."

"I'm not coming." I paused to let that sink in. "But I have your necklace. If you want it, you'll come to me to get it."

"Is your boyfriend goin' to be there?"

I shot a glance at James' poker face before looking away. "Skeeter Malcolm will be there, along with his associate Jed Carlisle. They invoke parley."

"You're shittin' me."

"If you want the necklace, you'll agree to the terms."

He paused for so long I was sure he'd hung up. "Okay," he finally said with a chuckle. "Why the hell not. When and where?"

James had told me to tell him, but memories of my run-ins with J.R. Simmons came to mind. Whenever we'd given him a chance to plan ahead, he'd taken the upper hand. "For an hour, starting at nine. I'll text you the location at 8:45. It will be on the west side of town. We expect you and Kip Wagner. The both of you or no deal. You may bring two additional men."

"No way. How do I know we're not walkin' into an ambush?"

"I give you my word that you'll walk away without a scratch as long as you abide by the rules."

"*Your* word." He chuckled. "What authority do you have to give *your* word?"

James' gaze held mine. This was his warning, but it couldn't be helped. I'd known it would come to this. I'd stepped through this door last year, and there was no turning back. Maybe I could use this position for good. "As the Lady in Black."

He was silent for a moment, but he wasn't laughing when he said, "Well, I'll be damned. I was right."

"Do you agree to the terms?"

"Hell, yeah. I'll agree if I get to meet with *you*, Lady, but at the first sign of trouble, the deal's off."

"Agreed."

When I hung up, the worry in James' eyes caught me by surprise.

"What?" I asked.

"He's a little too eager to meet you. I'll have extra men set up."

"Not where we meet you won't. You get two men too. You'll follow the rules just like we expect them to. I'm gonna need about twenty minutes to get ready. Can we spare it?"

He gave a quick nod and looked away, but damned if I knew what he was thinking.

Once upstairs, I turned on the shower and stripped as the water heated up. I piled my hair on top of my head and took a quick shower. When I got out, the room was steamy, so I left the bathroom door open when I slipped into the room to grab a black lace push-up bra to give me more cleavage in my lower-cut Lady in Black dresses and a pair of black lace panties out of my dresser. I put them on in the bathroom while I waited for the mirror to defog.

I couldn't ignore the butterflies in my stomach—it was part nerves, but if I was being honest with myself, it was part excitement too. I'd missed Lady, and I wasn't sure that was such a good thing.

The mirror had defogged enough that I put my hair up in a French twist before I started on my makeup. I'd always worn the veil before, so I'd never given much attention to my eye makeup, but since I planned to wear my trademark black and it was night, I went with a darker, more dramatic look. If Buck Reynolds was eager to meet the Lady in Black, I might as well make it worth his while.

When I finished, I stepped out of the bathroom to figure out which dress to wear when I heard the door creak open.

"Lady, it's time to—" His words cut off.

I whipped around, resisting the sudden urge to cover myself. Neely Kate and I rarely closed our doors, and I hadn't expected James to come upstairs, so I'd left the door only partially closed. But now he was standing in my doorway, staring at my half-naked body, and I wasn't sure what to say. With him looking at me like that, his eyes dark with lust, I wasn't so sure I could say anything.

From his silence, neither could he.

"We need to go," he finally said.

"I was just picking out my dress. It's been a while," I said, turning back to the closet, pretending like I was used to men seeing me in my underwear.

He walked up behind me. "Do you feel too out of practice? We can call the whole thing off."

"No," I said, sliding the hangers across the rod. My Lady in Black dresses were in the back now. "I just need to figure out which one to wear. I feel like it needs to be just right since this will be the first time I've done this without a veil."

His hands found my hips, and I was achingly aware he stood mere inches behind me. "This scares the shit out of me. I can still contain this. I don't want you to risk yourself."

I glanced over my shoulder at him. "You mean kill Buck?"

He didn't respond.

"*No*. No more killing. I'm committed to seeing this through. If you know me at all, you know that once I commit to something, I don't just throw in the towel because it's suddenly inconvenient."

"This isn't some minor inconvenience, Rose. This is your *life*. It will never be the same."

I turned around to face him. "Maybe I don't want it to be. Maybe that's a good thing."

He lifted his hand and lightly cupped my cheek. "You've turned my own life completely upside down."

"Maybe that's a good thing too."

He lowered his face to mine, and I was sure he was going to kiss me. I held my breath, the anticipation making my chest tight, but instead he lowered his mouth to my ear. "We need to talk when this is finished."

"Yes. Agreed."

He reached into the closet and pulled out a dress. "This one." Then he handed it to me and walked out of the room.

Chapter Thirty

I wasn't sure what to expect at space 239 at the Putnam Industrial Park, but I hadn't planned on it being so empty. It was like a warehouse, but the only contents were two rectangular folding tables facing each other about six feet apart, with three chairs at one table and two at the other. The room itself was about thirty feet by a hundred feet, with no windows and three doors—one on the front wall and a large garage door and a smaller solid door on the back wall. The overhead industrial lights had been turned down so the lighting wasn't so harsh but bright enough to see.

"We'll sit at one table, and they'll be at the other," James said, leading me to the tables with his hand at the small of my back. I was used to him touching me, but this felt more possessive than usual. "You'll sit in the middle."

"And Neely Kate?"

"Will not be present." The tension in his voice told me that he was worried. I was worried too. The meeting was supposed to start in fifteen minutes, and neither one of us had heard a word from Jed or Neely Kate.

"We'll wait until they arrive, and then you and I will come in. Jed will greet them if he's back; if not, Merv will do it."

James had sent one of his men to check on Jed and Neely Kate, who weren't picking up their phones. "Have you heard from the guy you sent to the Dyers'?"

He shot me a look. "You've been with me every second since you walked down your stairs. When would I have heard?"

"I don't know. I'm just worried."

"Jed knows how to take care of himself. I'm more worried about him getting back with the necklace in time. You're certain Mable Dyer had it."

"Neely Kate was positive."

"I'm asking *you*."

"Ninety-five percent."

He took my hand. "Have a vision. See if Jed gets here in time with the necklace." We had reached the table, and he guided me down into a chair. Then he knelt on one knee in front of me, still holding my hand.

I almost jokingly asked him if he was about to propose, but the worry that he'd take me half seriously stopped me— not that I could imagine him *ever* doing such a thing. One more dose of reality I didn't have time to deal with.

I was lost in thought long enough for James to prod, "Go ahead."

Closing my eyes, I squeezed his hand, focusing on the meeting itself. Might as well kill two birds with one stone.

The vision was slow to come, and even then, it wasn't like a normal vision. Everything was in slow motion and deeper than usual. I sat at this table, facing Buck and Kip. Two men stood behind them. I was seeing this vision as

James, and I recognized all the men. I was categorizing their threat level as my gaze wandered. Tim Dermot stood behind Buck. He was always slow to draw and prone to thinking before he acted; threat level five out of ten.

Hugh Wagner was a surprise. He hated violence and barely tolerated fencing stolen goods at the pawn shop. It was a mystery why he'd come. I ranked him at a three.

Kip Wagner looked like he was about to shit himself from either excitement or fear, probably both. He'd waited years to be taken seriously, and after the shit he'd pulled over the last three months, he was finally getting his chance. He wouldn't screw that up. Six.

But Buck Reynolds was a different story.

The way he studied Rose told me that she was the only reason he'd accepted this parley. Possessiveness washed through me, making my gut clench. My feelings for her confused the hell out of me, or more accurately, I was confused by my inability to shut them down. I'd become adept at avoiding attachments to anyone other than Jed and Scooter, but somehow she'd wriggled in. And I was paying the price.

Reynolds had figured it out, and now he was curious, not that I was surprised, especially since he knew she'd worked with me last winter. Rose had no idea how much of a legend she'd become, and I'd tried to keep it that way. The way the Lady in Black had disappeared, along with her mysterious hat and veil, had only fanned the rumors about her. The mystery. The ambition in Reynolds' eyes as he studied her told me that he not only wanted my position— he wanted everything he thought I possessed, including the Lady in Black.

My vision turned red with rage, and my hand itched to reach for my gun. *Over my cold, dead body.*

The vision ended, and I was staring into James' face, feeling queasy and lightheaded. "Reynolds wants everything you own," I said in a rush.

James' expression didn't change. "Your fingers are like ice. What happened?"

"This vision was different."

"How so?"

I shook my head, but the movement made me dizzy and I grabbed the table.

"What happened?"

"Usually when I'm in a person's head, I can get *some* thoughts, but mostly I sense their emotions. This time I knew exactly what you were thinking."

The look on his face told me he wasn't too happy about that. "What did you see?"

"Everything was in slow motion from the beginning. You were sitting at this table."

"Were you and Jed with me?"

"You never looked to the side for me to know. I know I was there because you didn't like the way Buck was looking at me."

His face remained a blank slate, but I heard a hitch in his voice when he asked, "Did we have the necklace?"

"I don't know. You never thought of it, and I didn't see it. But you were totally focused on the men who were present. You were ranking their threat level."

"Who was there?"

"Tim Dermot was with Buck, and Hugh Wagner was with Kip."

"Anything else I need to know?"

"Why didn't you tell me that the Lady in Black legend wasn't dying down?"

He stood and looked frustrated. "Because I've been trying my damnedest to keep you as far away from this world as possible. The less you knew, the better."

"Five minutes," Brett, James' man, called out from the front door.

James reached for my hand and pulled me to my feet. "We have to go out back."

"I need to have another vision. I thought if I forced a vision of the meeting, I'd know if Jed showed up with the necklace. So now I need to have one focused on the necklace."

He started leading me to the back door. "No. I don't want to risk it. If your visions are changing, we need to be careful until we figure out what's going on."

"Who said my visions are changing?"

"You had the crossed visions at the pawn shop. Now this."

I stopped. "Why wouldn't you *really* let me have a vision of Raddy?"

Frustration filled his eyes. "What the hell are you talking about?"

"Do you know what I respect about you, James Malcolm?" I asked. "You're the only man in my life who doesn't baby me, so I'm not buying this 'I'm protecting you' bullcrap. Please give me the respect I deserve and quit lying to me. Why wouldn't you let me have a vision of Raddy Dyer?"

His gaze held mine. He looked guarded as he said, "I was worried about what you'd see if you had one."

"So you were plannin' to kill him after all?" I asked in a small voice.

"*No.*"

What else would he not want me to know about? Then it hit me. How had I been so stupid? "You wanted the necklace too."

He didn't deny it.

"So when you were questioning Raddy in the barn, you were trying to get information from him. You planned to get it for yourself."

He reached a hand toward my arm. "Rose . . ."

My anger rose up like an erupting volcano, and I batted him away. "Did you get a good laugh out of me and Neely Kate chasin' our tails?"

His face hardened. "You were never chasing your tails. And you don't know me at all if you believe that."

"But you were sure usin' the leads I was finding."

He didn't deny that either.

"Did Jed have one of your men question Leah Dyer at One Eyed Joes yesterday afternoon?"

More silence.

"And Jed is there with Neely Kate right now because he plans to take possession of that stupid necklace himself. For you. Are you even gonna give it back to Buck?"

His eyes filled with anger. "This is *my* world, Rose Gardner. You have no right to show up and make demands. I'm the king of this county. I'll do as I damn well please!"

"Then what in Sam Hill am I doin' here? Are you even interested in a truce?" Then it hit me. "You're not here for a truce at all. I'm just the bait. You want to force their surrender."

"Is that so damned wrong? *They threatened you.*"

I took two steps away from him. "You're using me."

"How is this any different than what you did for me last winter?"

"You forced me into it last winter."

"Not at the end," he said in a low voice that rumbled through his chest.

"Because we became friends. We were partners. I thought we were partners in this too." I sucked in a deep breath to regain control. "You should have told me what you had planned."

"You never would have gone through with it."

I released a short laugh. "I might have. If you'd discussed it with me."

The front door opened and Brett leaned inside. "They're pullin' up now."

"Still no sign of Jed?" James called out.

"No."

"Hold them off for a few goddamned minutes!" he shouted. When the door shut, he turned to me. His face was a blank slate, cold and impersonal. "I can force you to do this."

I held his gaze. "I dare you to freaking try."

His eyes darkened.

I could do this his way, but it didn't sit well. At all.

But I couldn't leave either. I had a reputation to maintain. I had created the Lady in Black. James Malcolm may have forced my hand and given me the name, but I'd made her into what she'd become. I could use her to avert a disaster, whether James liked it or not. And if there was one thing I knew for certain, it was that this county couldn't handle another war.

I lifted my chin and gave him a hard look. "We'll have this meeting, but *I* called it. Not you. It's *my* meeting, and I'll run it as I see fit."

He moved closer and towered over me. "*Like hell you will.*"

"How do you propose to stop me?"

The back door banged open, but I didn't dare look to see who'd entered. I was in a staring contest with the crime lord of Fenton County, and I'd be damned if I would cave first.

James cursed a blue streak as he turned to face the back door. "Where's Jed?"

"I'm sure he'll be comin' along shortly," Neely Kate called out. The tight edge in her voice caught my attention. She was a muddy mess, and her hair was drenched. She was wearing a jacket that looked like it belonged to Jed.

"What happened?" I asked in shock, taking several steps away from James.

"It's a long story," she said as she marched toward me.

"Do you have it?" he asked.

"Oh, I have it all right," Neely Kate said, then gave James a dirty look. "And no. You won't be gettin' your grimy hands on it." She turned to me. "Rose, I was right. He wants it for himself."

"Funny, James and I were just havin' that very conversation. But I don't give two figs what he wants right now." I shot him a dark glare. "I'm here as a mediator, and this parley's takin' place because you gave your damn word, *Skeeter* Malcolm!" I pointed my finger at him to prove my point.

"And I told you that my word doesn't mean shit."

"That's bullcrap if I ever heard it." I marched over to him. "Lift your arms."

He gave me a semi-amused look.

"Lift your damn arms!"

He lifted them from his side, and I ran my hands down his side and his back, finding a gun tucked in his jeans.

"If you'd wanted to feel me up, you should have told me in your bedroom," he said in a voice I wasn't used to hearing. Dirty and coarse.

I knew what he was doing, and it wasn't going to work. I knew he didn't see me the same way he saw the women he slept with. Even if his actions hadn't convinced me, that vision had. "Stop that right now," I said as I handed the gun to Neely Kate. I crouched and felt his legs, finding another gun in one of his boots and a knife in the other.

"I can't protect you if you take all my weapons." The edge in his voice told me there was some truth in his words. The vision backed it up. But we weren't doing this his way. We were doing it mine.

I stood and lifted my chin, holding his gaze. "Then we better hope your men do a much better job of searching Buck's men than they did with you."

His anger was back, but the front door opened, and Brett stuck his head in. "They won't wait any longer."

"Send them in, Brett," I said as I turned to James, giving him a defiant look. "We're ready to begin."

Chapter Thirty-One

I walked over and grabbed the back of one of the chairs on his side and positioned it between the two tables.

James looked like he wanted to wring my neck.

Let him try.

The door opened, and Buck burst through, with Kip following behind. The glare on Kip's face told me he was furious. There was already turmoil between the partners. I could use that to my advantage. Hugh and the other man from my vision trailed them.

"I don't like to be kept waiting, Malcolm," Buck said as he strutted toward the table, looking like he wanted to wrestle a bear.

"It was me who kept you waiting," I said, standing at the end of the table.

A lusty grin spread across Buck's face. "Darlin', you clean up nice. If you needed a few extra minutes to slip into that dress, I'll be more than happy to give them to you if you'd let me help you out of it."

The dress James had chosen had a deep, plunging neckline, and the lacy push-up bra was doing its job. Maybe a little too well.

Neely Kate marched right over to him and grabbed his crotch. "Apologize to Lady."

His eyes bulged and he reached for her neck, but I lifted the hem of my dress and pulled my gun out of the leg holster Jed had given me last winter. I aimed it right at his head. "I think it's the perfect time to set a few ground rules."

Neely Kate released her hold and stepped back as Buck bent over coughing and groaning.

Kip turned to James and demanded, "Why does *she* get a gun?"

"This is her damn meeting," James grumbled. "Her rules."

"If she's your woman, then she'll do as you say."

"Let's get this perfectly straight," I said, walking between the tables. "I am *no one's* woman. I am *no one's* property or possession. I am my own person, and I don't follow *anyone's* orders, including Skeeter Malcolm's." I stared Kip in the eye. "Have I made myself clear?"

"But Malcolm—"

"Is here because I insisted. I assure you, he's just as unhappy about this as you are."

The back door opened, and Kip and Buck jumped.

A quick glance over my shoulder confirmed my suspicion. "Glad you could join us, Jed," I said. "Neely Kate's going to check you for weapons."

"What the hell?" he muttered.

"Do it," James barked, and when he looked at me, the pride in his eyes made my heart skip a beat.

You are not affected by that man. He was going to use you.

Too bad my heart wasn't listening.

Lordy, I really was a fool.

Neely Kate patted him down and removed two guns and two knives, setting them on the chair I'd dragged over.

"Gentlemen, take a seat."

They all sat, although there were some grumblings, especially from Buck, but I wondered if some of his grumbles were a lingering effect of Neely Kate's punishing grip.

"Okay," I said, lowering the gun to my side. "Now that we're all here, let's set the rules. Rule number one: You will treat me with respect. You will get one warning, and then if there's another instance, you will be removed from the meeting. Rule number two: in this room, tonight, you will treat each other with respect. You will not shout over each other. You will listen to what the other side has to say. You will be offered the chance for rebuttal."

"What the hell is this? A damned presidential debate?" Buck demanded, finally able to speak. "I'm here for my damned necklace."

"And you'll get it when we're done."

"How do I know you even have it?"

"Neely Kate?"

She reached into her jacket pocket and pulled out the gaudiest necklace I'd ever seen. "This proof enough?" she asked.

Buck reached for it. "Give me that."

I pointed the gun at him again as she tucked it back into her pocket. "Like I said, you'll get it when we're done."

The look in James' eyes told me there was gonna be a skirmish over it. Had I been foolish to try this? Maybe so, but I had to give it a shot.

"I thought this was a damn parley," Buck muttered. "What the hell are you doin' with a gun?" He'd probably been chewing on that since Neely Kate had quieted him.

"How many weapons did Skeeter's man pull off you when you came in?" When he didn't answer, I lifted my eyebrows. "Well, there you go. I have a gun because I'm the mediator and it's my job to make sure none of you kill each other. We'll stay here as long as it takes to come to a resolution that keeps peace in this county."

"I only agreed to an hour."

"Well, then maybe you should start first," I said, "because, as I said, *no one's* leaving until you reach a resolution." I decided to start with the lesser of the evils. "Kip. What's your beef with Skeeter Malcolm?"

He started gabbing about how he wanted to expand his business to include prostitution, and while I had to bite my tongue—and reprimand James several times for interrupting—I let the man have his say.

I swiveled to face James. "Your turn."

James told Kip he'd put a ban on prostitution after the deaths of two prostitutes in March. While they'd died of drug overdoses, he suspected their pimp was the one who'd provided them with lethal doses.

I'd been oblivious to it all. He hadn't shared a word of it with me during our weekly meetings, and while I was fit to be tied, he'd been dishonest with me, my respect for his rule over the county increased.

"Any time the law's looking into an illegal venture," James said, "it puts anyone associated with the person being investigated at risk. But more importantly, most pimps are selfish pricks who treat women as property. I won't tolerate that kind of behavior in this county."

"How's it any different than you havin' the Bunny Ranch?" Buck asked with a sneer. "I see. It's a case of do as I say, not as I do."

"The Bunny Ranch is a strip club, which is watched over by the sheriff's department. I treat my dancers better than most places. They get guaranteed wages, and I offer health benefits. I'm pretty much the only place in the state to offer that."

"They're still sleepin' with customers for money," Kip said. "Prostitution."

"What they do when they leave the club is their own damn business. We recommend that they don't for their own safety, but we don't stop them either. And we sure as hell don't take a cut." James' eyes turned hard. "So no, Wagner. It's not do as I say. I don't condone prostitution, and I won't allow anyone to run a prostitution network in this county."

"Then how the hell am I supposed to make money?"

"I have several opportunities for men who've proved themselves loyal to me. I'd be more than happy to take a meeting, Wagner, but you have to prove I can trust you. After this stunt, you're back at square one. But I'm willing to revisit this again if you choose to prove yourself."

Kip looked genuinely shocked.

"Any more questions, Mr. Wagner?" I asked. "Anything else you'd like to discuss?"

"No," he snapped, but he seemed less angry than when he'd first walked in.

"You're not falling for his bullshit, are you, Wagner?" Buck asked in disgust.

"Mr. Reynolds, what Mr. Wagner and Mr. Malcolm discuss is between them. If you would like to bring your own matter to the table, feel free."

"Fine. I want my damn necklace."

I crossed over and stood in front of him, staring down into his arrogant face. "I told you that you would get it when we're done."

He lifted his eyes to mine. "What's to stop me from takin' it right now and walkin' out?"

Neely Kate picked up one of Jed's guns from the chair and aimed it at Buck. "How about this big ol' gun?" She cocked her head to the side. "I don't miss; ask anyone in this room who's seen me shoot. And unlike Lady, I have no problem takin' care of the trash when it needs to be taken out."

Buck's face turned red, but he didn't budge from his chair.

"Mr. Reynolds," I said. "How many men are supporting your takeover? Five? Ten?"

He glared at me.

"I know all about your coup attempt—storm the pool hall and eliminate Skeeter and Jed—but it's a fool's plan."

He jerked upright, his mouth dropping open before he managed to shake off his surprise. "How the hell would you know that?"

"Are you serious? First off, it's going to be so obvious who's responsible that even the Henryetta Police Department could figure it out. Sure, you might be king, but for how long? A few days? Since it's the Henryetta PD, your reign might take a week or two, but it hardly seems worth a lifetime in prison. It would be hard to rule there, and even harder to enjoy the fruits of your labor."

"I've got a plan," he said with a smirk. "And I've got an inside man at the sheriff's office."

I laughed. "I have several. And, I assure you, mine are higher placed than yours."

He pointed his finger at me. "I told you that you're Malcolm's bitch."

My gaze turned cold. "I warned you."

He grinned, comfortable in his conviction that I didn't have the power to follow through on my threat.

"Neely Kate," I said. "Give me the necklace."

She gave it to me, and I held the gaudy necklace up, pretending to examine it. "What did Raddy say these stones were? White sapphires?"

"That's right." Buck sounded more amused than angry.

I cocked my head. "I don't know much about white sapphires. Are they as hard as diamonds?" I asked, surveying the room for a reaction. "Anyone know? How easy is it to smash a sapphire?" I shot a glance at James. "Do any of your men happen to have a sledgehammer?"

"You wouldn't dare," Buck growled.

I turned my cold gaze to his. "Try me." I set the necklace on the table behind me. "You broke rule number one, Mr. Reynolds, and if you do it again, I will crush every stone in this necklace and have you removed from the premises. And I suspect you won't get far because you won't get your weapons back."

The fury in his eyes told me he didn't like his options, but he kept his mouth shut.

"I don't know how you came to the belief that women are beneath you, Mr. Reynolds, but you are sadly mistaken. I saw Trixie's face. You are a lowlife piece of scum."

"That's no concern of yours." His hands, resting on the table, were clenched into fists.

I was close enough that he could lunge across the table and grab me. My ability to keep a cool façade rested in the certainty that the two men behind me would rip Buck Reynolds apart if he so much as laid a hand on me.

"I'm *making* it my concern, Mr. Reynolds," I said, leaning over the table as I looked into his heartless eyes. "The well-being of the people in this county is my utmost concern, and *you* have proven that you have little regard for human life." I stood up straighter and took a step back. "Yes, I worked *with* Skeeter Malcolm last winter, but I joined forces with him to eliminate an evil threat. We had a common purpose—to take down J.R. Simmons. I won't think twice about joining forces with him again to present a united force against you. And I assure you that we *will* win."

"Who the hell are you?" he asked. "What kind of power do you think you have?"

"She's like Harry freaking Potter," Neely Kate said. "Daniel Crocker tried to kill her twice, and both times she took him out and became stronger than before. Then she took out J.R. Simmons when no one else could. Trust me. You don't want to test her patience." Neely Kate curled her upper lip in disgust. "You, Buck Reynolds, are no Daniel Crocker."

Buck looked like he was beginning to have second thoughts, but it was equally obvious he didn't want to let on that he'd been thwarted by a woman.

I decided it was time to finish this thing. "I'm weary of the constant upheaval in this county. You may not like Skeeter Malcolm, but frankly, I don't care. I'm not too fond of him myself right now. But he's the best ruler this county has had in years. I don't condone criminal activities, but I'm not naive enough to think they're going away anytime soon. So I'd rather have a levelheaded man with a business mentality overlooking the county than a hothead who beats women and thinks Fenton County is his own personal Wild West. But I assure you, should Skeeter Malcolm abuse his power, I'll take up arms against him too." I grabbed the necklace and let it dangle in front of him. "You will slink back to the hole you crawled from, and you will end all attempts to take over this county. If I hear you've renewed your attempts, we will be enemies, Mr. Reynolds." I leaned forward. "And that is something you do not want."

I took it as a good sign when he remained silent.

I held his gaze. "I need you to agree to my terms."

His eyes bugged out and his head jutted forward. "You want what?"

"You will neither interfere with Mr. Malcolm's rule, nor will you provide support to anyone who intends to overthrow him."

He snorted. "You've got to be kidding me."

I walked over to the chair and picked up James' biggest handgun, before I set the necklace on the table in front of James and Jed and turned on the safety. The two men watched me with expressionless faces, but I saw a twinkle in James' eyes as I lifted his gun over my head, ready to smash the butt of the handle against the center stone.

"All right!" Buck shouted. "I agree!"

Picking up the necklace, I turned around to face him. "I want to hear you say the words."

"Fine. I won't make a run for Malcolm's throne, and I won't help anyone who is."

I hid my relief and remained aloof. "And you won't use this necklace to aid in any takeover attempts."

"I won't."

I paused. "And you won't hit Trixie."

He hesitated, then said, "Fine. I won't hit her."

I dropped the necklace on the table, then put my hand on his shoulder and forced a vision of whether he would attack James. The vision quickly filled my head.

I saw Kip sitting across the table from me—Buck—in One Eyed Joes.

"You really gonna let it go?" Kip asked. "They weren't lyin' about her killin' Daniel Crocker, and rumor has it she pulled the trigger on the gun that killed J.R. Simmons. His son just took the credit. I'm not sure it's smart to mess with her."

"We'll let it go for now. Lady freakin' scares me, but her friend scares me even more. I won't be able to screw Trixie for a week. It feels like my balls are about to fall off."

The vision lasted a second or two, but when I opened my eyes and said, "You're not gonna screw Trixie for a week or your balls will fall off," the look in his eyes told me I'd just scared him even more.

He cast a glance over to Neely Kate, then said in a panicked tone, "Fine! I won't touch her!"

Turning toward James, I tried to control my expression. *They* were scared of *me*? "Do you have anything you'd like to address, Mr. Malcolm?"

His face remained impassive, but the slight twitch at the corner of his mouth told me he was fighting a grin. "No. I think you've covered it all."

I pivoted back to the troublemakers on the other side. "We're done here. Don't make me call you back. I won't be so lenient next time."

Buck snatched up the necklace, and the men beat a hasty retreat to the door. Before they left, Hugh glanced back at me and winked.

When the door closed behind them, I let myself relax slightly, even though I was far from finished. It was time to deal with James.

I shifted and took a few steps so I was standing in front of James, the table between us, my heels echoing in the empty space. "No argument about handing the necklace over to Buck Reynolds?"

"I'm not happy about it, but you handled it well. The look on his face when he thought you were going to smash it would have been enough to make it worthwhile." He held my gaze. "You forced a vision."

"I had to be sure he'd honor the agreement."

"And will he?"

"For the time being. He's scared of me and Neely Kate."

"It was pretty effective when you told him you didn't work for Skeeter," Jed said with a grin. "That you'd only joined forces with him."

"I meant every word."

Jed's grin faded.

I turned back to James. "You were going to make me look like a fool, James Malcolm."

He stood. "I never would have let that happen."

"You deceived me."

The emotion in his eyes shuttered closed.

I pressed on. "You've come to me with information about your world for months now, and I never once thought of using it for my own personal gain behind your back. I never strung you along trying to get information."

He clenched his fists at his sides. "Rose, goddamnit, that's not how it was."

I put a hand on my hip. "Then how was it? Because here's how it looks to me—you found out that I was looking for the necklace, and once you realized how much it might be worth, you decided you wanted it for yourself. And when you found out it belonged to Buck Reynolds . . . well, that's quite the trophy, isn't it? Tell me if I've gotten any of this wrong."

He remained silent.

"So you let me and Neely Kate do all the grunt work, but you sent Jed to follow us around in case we actually happened to find it."

His jaw set with anger. "That's not true. He was there to protect you."

"Well, then he was there for dual purposes. Lucky you. You got a twofer."

"He was never going to take it from you."

"But he wasn't going to let me turn it over to Raddy either, was he?"

Silence.

Dammit. He wasn't even trying to lie to deny it.

"I understand why you wanted it. If you'd told me your reasoning, I probably would have agreed with you. But what I can't stomach is that you played along with this meeting after I called it. You decided to play me the fool and use it to your advantage."

"That's not true."

"You practically admitted that you were going to call them to task for their misdeeds. You were going to use this meeting to mete out punishment!"

He pointed his finger at me, shouting, "I run this goddamned county! Do you know what would happen if a man like Buck Reynolds was in charge? And we both know what he planned to do with that necklace once it was back in his possession. I can't let men get away with undermining me, or this aggression will *never* end."

"Seems to me that I brokered a truce."

He shook his head. "It won't last. It's temporary at best."

"At least I tried." I took a step toward him. "James, I know your job's not easy. I know you have to maintain this tough exterior or you're a sitting duck. I get it. But I thought I proved to you last winter that I could negotiate deals for you. That we were partners."

"We are."

I shook my head, close to tears. "Not tonight. You used me to get them here."

"I had to do it this way. You never would have approved."

"We could have reached an agreement *together*."

He must have seen the pain on my face. "You said you didn't use the information you got from me for personal gain," he said, his temper running hot. "When we both know good and well that you were using it to help that damn traitor prosecutor who ran off and abandoned you as soon as he was in the clear."

Tears stung my eyes. "The difference, Skeeter Malcolm, is that you knew from day one why I was helping you. I never once hid that fact from you. You used me, and I have never been so disappointed by you."

His eyes turned hard. "I don't know why you're so surprised. You know I'm a lowlife criminal, only slightly higher on the scumbag rung than Reynolds. You *knew* I couldn't be trusted."

"And that's the saddest part of all." My voice broke. "You've proven yourself trustworthy so many times, James. I trusted you with my life. I trusted you in nearly every conceivable way . . . and you betrayed that."

A war waged in his eyes. "What do you want from me?" he finally said. "You want me to apologize? Don't hold your breath. You knew who I was going into this. You knew, yet you were fool enough to trust me. So don't go blaming me for your own poor judgment, Rose. The only person to blame here is yourself."

My mouth dropped open. "You truly believe that?"

His war of emotions continued in earnest, but then his eyes turned cold. "I can't believe you don't."

He was lying. I knew that. And I knew I was ripping his heart out, but he'd hurt me too. I wasn't going to stand there and let him hurt me more. "I think we're done here."

"I guess we are."

When I stomped off to the back door, I could hear Neely Kate's footfalls behind me. I turned around one last time and saw James still standing behind the table, still wearing that damn impassive face.

Chapter Thirty-One

After Neely Kate and I went home, I took a long hot shower and had a good cry. Then I changed into my pajamas and found Neely Kate downstairs, already cleaned up.

"I made us both a cup of tea," she said from the couch. She was curled up in front of two mugs. "But maybe you'd rather go to bed."

"No. I'm too keyed up," I said, joining her. "Did you hear anything more from Joe?" She'd called him after we left the industrial park and told him to pick up Homer at our office.

"He was overseeing Homer's interrogation. He's already confessed to killing Rayna *and* holding us hostage. Joe was furious we didn't tell him sooner. He's coming over as soon as he finishes some preliminary stuff with Homer."

Great.

"What happened with Miss Mable?" I asked. "How did you get all muddy and wet?"

"It's a long story, but the bottom line is that she finally confessed she'd hidden it in a bag in the pigsty. But she wouldn't tell us where, so we had to search high and low. Jed was the one who finally found it."

"Then how'd *you* get it?"

"He gave me his coat, and his phone was in his jacket pocket. It dinged, so I pulled it out to give it to him, but then I saw Skeeter's text. It said you'd set up the meeting and you still believed you were giving the necklace to Reynolds. Jed had already given me the necklace, so I dropped his phone in the pigs' water trough, got in his car, and left him there in the mud."

"How'd you know where to go?"

"Jed had set up the location. He'd already told me."

"And Jed?"

She shrugged. "I figured he'd call one of his boys somehow."

"You know he's gonna come get his car back at some point."

"I'm not stopping him. It's parked out front with the keys in the ignition," she said with a shrug, then grinned. "You were awesome tonight."

"I was pissed."

"Well, it worked in your favor."

I laughed. "I can't believe you compared me to Harry Potter."

"If the analogy fits . . ." She grinned. "But I want to be Hermione. Not Ron."

"*Of course.*"

We leaned back against the sofa in silence for several moments before she said, "I'm sorry about Skeeter."

My throat burned, but I swallowed the lump. "Don't be. I should have expected it, right?"

"I don't know, Rose. He's changed. Anyone can see that, and I know it's because of you." She gave me a leery look. "You said there was nothing between you, but lately you two have had major chemistry."

I closed my eyes, deciding to confess. "We kissed . . . the night after I met Raddy at the fertilizer plant, but James pulled away. He told me he'd never be the man I need. A guy with a steady job, a house, and kids. I told him he had no idea what I needed, but he was probably right. Maybe he did this to drive me away from him. For my own good."

Neely Kate shook her head. "I think you're giving him far too much credit. Sure, he cares about you, but he cares about himself a whole lot more. It's what makes him a ruthless criminal."

"I suppose." But I didn't believe that. Sure, he was ruthless, but he cared about other people. My vision had proved how much he cared about *me*. He just didn't want to admit it.

A knock on the door scared us both enough to jump. We grinned at each other, and I got up. "I'll get it in case it's Jed."

But Joe was waiting on the other side of the door. I'd expected wrath; the resignation on his face scared me. "Sounds like you two have had a busy night."

"Hey, Joe. Come in."

Neely Kate had gotten up, and she ran to him and threw her arms around his neck. "I've missed you." It made my heart twist to see the two of them together.

"I missed you too."

Neely Kate fixed him a cup of tea, and he took our statements about our run-ins with Homer. He looked grim the entire time, but he kept his questions professional.

When we finished, he said, "You should have called me. What was so pressing you couldn't call immediately after you tied him up?"

Neither of us answered, but we exchanged a look.

Joe leaned back in his chair, pinning me with a glare. "I heard some crazy rumors tonight."

"Is that so?" I asked.

"I heard that the Lady in Black is back and she took a meeting tonight."

"What?" I asked, trying to sound like it was the craziest thing I'd ever heard. "That's impossible."

"That's what I thought too. Because I can't think of a single good reason she would make an appearance now that my father's no longer a threat." He continued to watch me. When I didn't break, he turned to Neely Kate. "You told me you were talkin' to Rayna on Raddy Dyer's behalf, but it sounds like you two were actually lookin' for this necklace. Even after it got the two of them killed."

Neely Kate lifted her shoulders in a shrug. "Like I told you. We were just helpin' out a friend."

His mouth pressed into a frown, and he looked dubious. "It's a good thing that that's all it was, because I know you wouldn't be going around calling yourselves private investigators. You need to have a license to do work as a PI; otherwise, it's a felony offense."

I tried to hide my shock, but Neely Kate didn't look all that surprised. "Well, it's a doggone good thing we were just helpin' a friend then, isn't it?" Then, presumably in an effort to change the subject, she said, "So tell us about your trip. What kept you in El Dorado for three days?"

Joe shot me a worried glance, then shifted his gaze to his sister. Leaning his elbows on his knees, he said, "I wasn't in El Dorado, Neely Kate. Not the entire time."

"Where were you?"

"New Orleans."

"What kind of family business took you to New Orleans?"

Joe waited a beat before diving right in. "I got a tip that Ronnie was down there, so I went to check it out."

I expected her to be angry, but she just looked confused and anxious. "Oh. It was a false alarm, right? No one else has found anything."

Joe remained silent for several seconds, then said, "Neely Kate, I think I found him."

The color left her face, and I thought she was going to pass out. "What?"

He leaned forward and grabbed her hand. "It took me two days. I needed to head back home for my shift tonight, but I followed one last lead to the bus station and saw him. I'd intended to make him sign your divorce papers, but he got on a bus headed to Memphis. It took off before I could reach him."

"*Memphis?*" She shook her head. "*No.* You must have seen someone else."

He grabbed his phone from his pocket and pulled up his photos. "You tell me. Is this him? There are several photos on there, but . . ."

"But what?"

"You might not like what you see."

She snatched the phone from him. The photo was of a couple standing next to a bus in a tight embrace. They were kissing, and the next several photos portrayed them in escalating stages of groping. Then there was a photo of the man looking down at the blonde woman. I had to admit that his profile looked a lot like Ronnie's. But when Neely Kate swiped to the next photo, I gasped.

Ronnie was facing the camera full-on, his arm wrapped around the small blonde woman. But the biggest shocker was the ring on his left ring finger. He was wearing a wedding ring, and it wasn't the one Neely Kate had given him less than a year ago.

Ronnie Colson had married someone else, and he wasn't even divorced yet.

***

Trailer Trash: Neely Kate
Rose Gardner Exposed Novella
April 18, 2017

For the Birds
Rose Gardner Investigations #2
July 11, 2017

Acknowledgments

Authors will tell you that writing is a solitary venture, but that's not entirely true, at least not for me. I have a team who support and encourage me throughout the process.

First, I couldn't do this without Angela Polidoro, my developmental editor and friend. I count on her for advice and support when I feel like I've hit a wall. She reminds me that the story will come, and often gives me a nudge to get me going again. She plays a significant role not only by editing my books, but helping to plan my future books and career. I'm grateful to have her in my corner.

Shannon Page is often the second person to read my book after I incorporate Angela's suggestions. While Shannon's job is to copy edit my story, she also gives me much needed reassurance that my readers are going to love the book.

Carolina Valdez-Schneider gives my book a thorough read-through, looking for proofreading errors. She's a true professional, but also a friend. I'm thrilled she's part of my team.

Next, I'd like to thank my children, especially Jenna, Ryan, and Emma. I often work long hours. They take it in stride and hang out in my office so we can all work together. The moments when I'm working at my desk while they tackle homework on the sofa and my office floor are some of my sweetest memories.

And finally, I'd like to thank you, dear reader. Your enthusiasm gives me the spark I need to keep up this crazy pace. There are over three million books available for you to read, and yet you chose mine. That is *never* lost on me. Thank you.

Get a peek at

Center Stage

(Magnolia Steele Mystery #1)

Available now

Chapter One

I stepped onto my mother's front porch for the first time in ten years. Typical of my mother, not much had changed. Same red brick with white trim. Same black, steel-reinforced front door. Same silver knocker, the word STEELE etched into it in bold capital letters.

"Get it?" my dad used to ask when I was a little girl. "The door is made of steel, and our last name is Steele."

I worshiped my father, so I always laughed even though I *didn't* get it. I would have done anything to please him.

My mother put a lot of stock into the safety of that front door. When I was younger, she would tell me it kept the boogeyman away. A month after my father left—when I was fourteen—I heard my mother whispering with her best friend Tilly as they lay sprawled out on the patio chairs on the deck, drinking their third—or was it fourth?—white wine sangria.

"If only he'd been home that night," my mother drawled with a slur. She may have spent most of her adult life in

Franklin, Tennessee, but you couldn't remove her Sweet Briar, Alabama roots.

"Lila," Tilly groaned. "Not that again. The Good Lord has his mysterious ways."

My mother had bolted upright and pointed her finger at her best friend, swaying in her seat. "The Good Lord had nothin' to do with it, Tilly Bartok. It was that good for nothin'—"

She looked up at me and her face went blank. "Magnolia. How long have you been standin' there?"

"Not long. I just finished my homework."

"Then go on upstairs and tell your brother to wash up for dinner." She gestured toward the house.

I turned around to do as I was told, wondering if the Good Lord wasn't to blame for my father's absence, who actually *was*? But I knew better than to ask. Besides, I'd heard the whispered rumors.

"Magnolia!" she called after me. "Did you lock the front door?"

"Yes, Momma."

"Good. You can never be too careful."

A lesson learned too late. Perhaps if I'd been more careful after my high school graduation, the big bad thing wouldn't have happened.

But now I stood before her front door again, prepared to eat a heaping slice of humble pie, wearing the wrinkled clothes I'd worn to the theatre yesterday afternoon. Maybe the disheveled look would make my groveling more convincing.

While I had grown accustomed to the anxiety that slammed into me whenever I thought about coming home, I wasn't prepared for the wave of fear that almost brought me to my knees. I was nervous about my mother's reaction, yes, but this was pure terror.

I started to turn around, but the door swung open before my fist made contact with the wood. My mother stood in the threshold, looking noticeably older. I counted backward to the last time we'd seen each other. Had three years really passed since that Christmas in New York City?

She gaped at me in shock, her face turning pale. She looked like she was staring at a ghost. I hadn't haunted her house in ten years, so I could hardly blame her. It wasn't as if I'd issued a warning.

The sight of her quieted my fear. "Hello, Momma."

"Magnolia." She blinked, taking in the sight of my two large suitcases. "You've come for a visit?"

I shifted my weight, fighting every instinct to flee. "I've come home to stay."

"For how long?"

"Maybe for a while." Although I sure as hell hoped I was wrong about that.

"But . . . what . . ."

My mother was speechless, but I was too nervous to truly bask in the moment. Maybe hell was freezing over.

She finally regained her senses, wrapping her arms across her chest and squeezing tight. "I thought you were making your big Broadway debut this week."

I grimaced. "I did." Last night, actually.

"Then what are you doing here?"

Rather than answer her, I glanced over her shoulder into the entryway. Like the exterior of the house, it appeared as unchanged as if it had emerged from a time capsule. But one thing was different: me. I was no longer the sheltered naïve girl my mother had raised. I was cynical and jaded, and it had nothing to do with the ten years I'd spent in the Big Apple, even if all the scraping by and trying to make a living in the theatre world had sharpened my edges.

"Oh," she finally said. "I see." She took a breath, still blocking the entrance, a true sign that I had thrown her off her game. She would never dream of keeping a guest standing on the front porch. Even me. "Do you have a job?"

"What?" I asked, surprised by her question. "No." Two days ago I'd been the lead in *Fireflies at Dawn*, the hottest new musical to hit New York in several years. Now I was jobless, penniless, and homeless.

Oh, how the mighty had fallen.

That seemed to jar her out of her stupor. "Then you can help me out tonight." She stepped through the doorway, grabbed one of my suitcases, and rolled it over the threshold. "I know you're into theatre music, but have you heard of Luke Powell?"

"Luke Powell?" I asked in disbelief. You had to be living off the grid—and for the past five years at that—to have never heard of the hottest country music star. "Yeah, I've heard of him."

"We're catering a big event at Luke Powell's to celebrate the release of his new album. It starts in two hours, and I'm short one member of the wait staff. It has to go over

402

perfectly. I only have inexperienced fools to take her spot, so you can fill in."

"*What?*" My mother's catering business must have exploded if she was working the hottest country music star's album release. But she wanted me to work as a waitress? Had she lost her mind?

She sensed my reluctance. "You used to wait tables up until three years ago, right?"

Two, not that I was about to admit it. "Well, yeah. I have food service experience, but I was on Broadway, Momma. I can't be wait staff."

"If you're so high and mighty on Broadway—" she said the name as though it were a curse word, "—then what are you doing here?"

I couldn't tell her. At least not yet.

She pursed her lips. "That's what I thought. If you're moving back home, you'll need to pay rent. And since you're unemployed, you'll need work. I can apply your salary to your balance."

"Rent?"

She put a hand on her hip. "It wouldn't be fair to your brother if you didn't. Roy lived here for two years after he graduated from the University of Tennessee, and he paid rent the entire time."

I pushed out a sigh. "I'm not living here forever, Momma. Just until I figure some things out."

She put her hand on her hip, looking down her nose at me even though we both stood five foot seven. "And Roy didn't live here forever either. But if you plan on doing nothing but fussin' and thinkin', you've got plenty of time to fill in for Patty at this party. She's going to be off for another two weeks with a sprained ankle."

"Momma, I just got here. I've had the worst two days of my life, and I just want to hide out in my room."

Fire filled her eyes. "Magnolia Steele, I raised you better than that. We don't hide from our problems. We take 'em *head on.*" She curled her hands into fists and shook them.

I'd done the exact opposite after my high school graduation. I'd run as fast and as far as I could. But of course my mother didn't understand why I'd packed a single suitcase and left town without warning. No one understood.

Not even me.

Hazy dreams had haunted my sleep for those first two years in New York City. Each night, I would cry myself to sleep from fright and loneliness, trying not to wake my cranky roommate. But the very thought of going home was enough to give me a panic attack, so I never did. No matter how much it hurt my mother.

Something had happened the night of my high school graduation party. Something I couldn't entirely remember. The nightmares had faded over time—terrifying dreams I couldn't remember when I woke—but the horror was still a part of me. But I was sure I knew someone who did know what happened. . . or was maybe even responsible.

Of course Momma didn't know any of that either. Sometimes my acting skills had a practical purpose. "You're made of steel, Magnolia Mae, so no whining. Now carry your suitcases up to your room, and I'll bring you a uniform to change into."

I stayed on the porch for a moment, trying to decide if it was worth crossing the threshold. If I walked over that line, it would mean going back into her world, her rules. I would be reopening the very Pandora's box that I'd shut the moment I stepped onto that plane on a warm May afternoon ten years ago. But if I stayed on this side, I had nowhere else to go. I'd burned too many bridges.

I took a deep breath, and walked inside.

If I'd known then what I know now, I would have turned around and run.

I wasn't just crossing the threshold to my mother's house. I was walking through the gate to hell.

CPSIA information can be obtained
at www.ICGtesting.com
Printed in the USA
LVOW05s1749070817
544127LV00015B/1623/P